REVEREND
RANDOLLPH
AND THE
AVENGING
ANGEL

Charles Merrill Smith

REVEREND RANDOLLPH AND THE AVENGING ANGEL

G.P. PUTNAM'S SONS

NEW YORK

SBN 399-11859-4

Library of Congress Cataloging in Publication Data

Smith, Charles Merrill.
  Reverend Randollph and the avenging angel.

  I. Title.
PZ4.S6433Rd   [PS3569.M5156]   813'.5'4   77-6617
PRINTED IN THE UNITED STATES OF AMERICA

*This is for Harriet, Belinda, Julia, Gina,
Mary, Tami, and Veronica,
who have brought so much happiness
into our lives.*

REVEREND RANDOLLPH AND THE AVENGING ANGEL

One

Murder, the prospective killer reflected, was a tricky business. Especially when you had a tight timetable. Fortunately, a wedding reception, this wedding reception anyway, would degenerate into a drunken bash. Nobody would notice much of anything. It was the hotel staff you had to fool, and you had to avoid, as far as possible, that little mistake at the wrong moment which could betray you. The prospective killer was philosophical about it. The decision was made, the plan carefully laid out. Every foreseeable contingency anticipated. You had to take your chances on the unforeseeable.

The killer thought: I could decide not to do it. I do not need to spend the rest of my life carrying the guilt for this crime I will soon commit. But a hatred as inexplicable as the dark side of the soul replied: You do have to do it. To recoil from this brutal act, to retreat now from your bloody plan, would mean that your life would never again be worth the living. You have to kill.

Two

C. P. Randollph listened with growing exasperation to the man sitting next to him prattle about the Bible. His resolution not to get into an altercation over the nature of Holy Writ was visibly weakening when Samantha Stack interrupted the monologue.

"We'll take a moment for a message of interest," she said into the camera, leaving the source of Randollph's irritation gulping back a chunk of pious rhetoric. "We'll be right back." She smiled sweetly at the frustrated speaker as if to say, You get another crack at it, buster.

The monitor ran a tape touting the profits and joys accruing to those who joined the United States Army. Sam Stack leaned toward Randollph and said, "I've got a friend who's coming in to see you about getting married. She's a member of your church, sort of."

"We have any number of members who are members, sort of," Randollph said.

"I'll bet you do." Sam surveyed her guests to see if they

were ready to hare after more theological irrelevancies as soon as the cameras picked them up again. Satisfied, she turned again to Randollph. "But Lisa hasn't lived in Chicago for ages, though her family's still here."

"Lisa who?" Randollph asked. The army band banged out a noble climax to some martial air.

"Tell you later," Sam whispered. "We're back," she said to the camera. "Now, Pastor Wakefield, you were saying before we cut away . . ."

Pastor Wakefield needed to diet, Randollph noticed. The sisters of his off-brand congregation must stuff him with potatoes and gravy several times a week. He had two chins, going on three.

"I was saying that you either believe the Bible's God's inerrant word, the whole Bible, every bit of it"—he slapped his palm on a black Fabrikoid-covered book on his knee— "or you don't believe any of it. Who needs a 'holey Bible?' That's spelled h-o-l-e-y." He leaned back and shot the cameras a triumphant look. Pastor Wakefield, clearly, had been on television talk shows before.

Randollph, reminding himself that Christian charity is to be extended even to fools and ignoramuses, pitched in.

"I would point out to the pastor that he has stated a faith position which it is anyone's privilege to embrace. It is not his privilege, however, to make it the test of my faith. That is sanctified ignorance masquerading as authority—"

"Now, just a minute," Pastor Wakefield sputtered.

"And I further remind the pastor that the Bible is not a book, but a collection of books," Randollph went on, ignoring the pastor's frantic attempt to regain control of the conversation, "and that it includes many different types of literature—history, short stories, love poetry, letters, murder, sex, incest, almost anything you can think of. In fact, if you translated some of the steamier Old Testament stories into the vernacular of our day, they'd be classified as pornography. The pastor surely does not expect me to believe in a psalm the same way I believe in a gospel."

The rabbi, who looked like a banker, smiled and nodded in agreement. The priest was grave and thoughtful, reflecting the composure of an institution which knew that these theological dust-ups are transitory but the church is eternal.

"Now that's a—" Pastor Wakefield wound up to burn another high hard one across the doctrinal plate, but Sam Stack called time. She turned toward one of the cameras and said, "We've been discussing the topic 'Does the Bible Have Relevance for Life Today?' with Rabbi Harvey Korfman, Father James Denton, the Reverend Mr. Jack Wakefield, and the Reverend Dr. C. P. Randollph. Thank you, reverend gentlemen." Then, to the future audience which would be blessed and enlightened when the program was shown, "And be with us next week when we present another interesting and timely discussion with leaders of our community." The panel of reverend gentlemen shook hands and departed to serve whatever god commanded their various allegiances. Randollph remained because he wanted to hear the rest of Sam Stack's story about the wedding he presumably was to conduct.

"Somebody has to do these dumb public-service programs." Sam sounded like an archbishop caught carrying out the garbage. "We take turns, and I got stuck with this bummer—which explains why, reverend doctor, you get a little free TV exposure. Because we've been keeping company—how's that for a nice old-fashioned way of saying it?— I rope you in for any kind of show that needs a theologian. Is that nepotism? Every preacher in Chicago pesters us to get on the tube, you know. Whatever happened to Christian humility like they taught me in Presbyterian Sunday school?"

"I'm humbly grateful for your invitation to be on this program," Randollph said, "though I doubt it will convert many heathens to godly ways. What about this wedding?"

Sam gathered up her script. "I'll tell you about it on the way."

"On the way where?"

"Didn't I tell you? I've made an appointment for you with an employment agency?"

Randollph was startled. "No, you didn't tell me."

"Must have slipped my mind."

Samantha looked smug, Randollph thought.

"But whatever for?" he asked her. "I'm already employed."

"I know that, silly. This is to find someone to cook for you and look after you in that ... that ..."

"Try 'sumptuous,' " Randollph said.

"Thanks, that sumptuous penthouse your filthy-rich church calls a parsonage."

"You sound like a socialist, Samantha."

"No, just envious. I'm going with you to the agency. You wouldn't know how to pick a domestic if your life depended on it."

"But I only need someone to fix my breakfast, and maybe dinner two or three times a week," Randollph protested. "Surely a grown man can—"

"Don't argue," Sam said, taking his arm. "Let's go."

The weary-looking man behind the desk sized up his visitors in little more than a glance. He wasn't much interested in them, but years at the job had taught him that if he could get a quick psychological reading on new clients, it was easier to manipulate them. His professional eye rapidly gathered the information he needed. Man, fortyish (hints of gray in the dark hair); successful (self-assured, and fit-looking, suggesting membership in an expensive athletic club); not a banker or a lawyer (dressed with a little too much flair and color, hair a mite too long). Probably in advertising. Made a lot of money. Lived in Winnetka or Lake Forest in a house with three mortgages. Two children in private schools. Up to his belly button in debt. Maybe five years away from his first heart attack.

The wife, now. Probably a second or even a third wife (a real dish, flaming red hair, great legs, six or seven years younger than the guy). Nagging the poor sap to hire a live-in maid. Live-in maids were status symbols. She looked vaguely familiar.

"I'll bet you're here to find a maid." The weary-looking man remembered to arrange his face in professional friendliness.

"No, I wish to employ a cook," Randollph said.

The man struggled to retain his smile. "I got plenty of maids, I can give you a chauffeur in any size or color, but cooks, they're hard to come by." He gave the impression that the shortage of cooks was the result of a conspiracy against him. "But I got a few." He pulled a file card from a tray on his desk and picked up a ball-point pen. "Your name?"

"C. P. Randollph. Randollph is spelled with two *l*'s."

"Oh?" the man said, writing it down. "Don't see it spelled that way often."

"That is why I added an *l*," Randollph said.

He's got to be in advertising, the man told himself. They're all a little strange. "Your occupation?"

"Clergyman."

The man brought his head up with a jerk and stared at Randollph.

"You're kidding me!"

"He's a minister, I'll guarantee it." Sam flashed a sympathetic smile at the man. The man shook his head as if it were a personal affront when people didn't fit his stereotypes. "You don't look like any preacher's wife I ever saw," he said.

"Oh, we're not married."

The man was completely bewildered.

Sam laughed. "You think we're living in sin. It might be fun, but the dear dignified Christians at the Church of the Good Shepherd wouldn't stand for their pastor installing a mistress in the parsonage."

"Ah, about the cook ..." Randollph asked.

The weary-looking man gave up. He was out of his depth and knew it. He reached into his drawer and brought out a small packet of cards.

"This is what I got in cooks," he said. Then, gearing up to make the sale, he pulled a card from the pack. "Now, here's one you might like. Know her personally. Good plain cook. Sixty, and very religious lady.

"Sounds fine to me," Sam said.

"Excessive piety at breakfast is bad for the digestion," Randollph said.

"Here's a younger lady. Thirty-eight. Recently divorced. Misses cooking for a man, she says. Very nice-looking girl."

"She won't do." Sam spoke with conviction.

"Why not?" Randollph asked. "She wants to cook for a man. She sounds like she has possibilities."

"That's why she won't do, dear doctor," Sam said, smiling sweetly. "Don't you have any men cooks?"

St. Paul, Randollph reminded himself, suffered shipwreck, persecution, prison, and, probably, innumerable bad meals for the faith. Yet here he was, successor to apostles, saints and martyrs, trying to hire a cook to fix his breakfast.

"There's Clarence Higbee," the man said. "He's kind of strange. Britisher. Been a butler, ship's cook, hotel chef. I bet I've found him a dozen jobs. He quits when his employer doesn't measure up to his standards."

Randollph was dubious about a domestic to whose exacting canon he would have to conform. But Sam brightened immediately.

"He sounds ideal," she said.

Randollph abandoned protest. "Will you arrange for me to meet with Mr. Higbee?"

"Right away, Reverend Randollph," the man assured him. "Anytime you—"

Randollph interrupted him. "Among my idiosyncrasies is a profound distaste for being addressed as 'reverend.'"

The man was surprised. "I call my pastor 'reverend,' everybody does, and he likes it." He reflected for a moment, then tacked on an explanatory footnote. "I'm a Baptist."

"That's nothing to be ashamed of," Randollph said. "But since 'reverend' is an adjective, not a title, I prefer to dispense with it."

"Yeah," the man said.

"You'll send Mr. Higbee around to see me, then?" Randollph asked as he and Sam rose to go.

"I'll do that, Reverend Randollph," the man said. "Count on it."

Back on Michigan Avenue, the city was dressing itself for spring. Girls in bright cotton blouses clustered below the fierce stone lions in front of the art institute. An occasional convertible with top down punctuated the traffic like a period between overlong sentences. Two portly pigeons planed down on a pedestrian island and went to work on a squashed banana.

"About that wedding," Randollph said.

"She's a sorority sister. Just about my best friend in college. I'm the maid of honor, or is it matron of honor for a divorced lady like me?"

"I'll look it up. Small private wedding?"

"No, the works. She wants it in a church, heaven knows

why, she probably hasn't been inside a church for years."

"You know," Randollph said thoughtfully, "I've never conducted a big formal wedding. The penalty or blessing, I don't know which, of never having been a pastor until this temporary job. My only experience with weddings is the few I've done for my students in the seminary chapel."

"Time you learned. This one will get you a lot of publicity. The bride's a pretty well-known movie and television actress. Lisa Julian."

"Ah," Randollph said.

"Now, what does that mean?"

Sam looked at him suspiciously, but decided to let it pass. "I'm very fond of her. She's a swinger, not that it's against her, but she's—let's see how I can phrase this so as not to offend the clergy—she's freer with her favors than I'd want to be, and that's an understatement. If she wears white for the wedding, it will be a misrepresentation of the facts."

The film of Randollph's memory was unreeling some scenes from his past he was grateful that Samantha couldn't see.

"I, ah, have met Miss Julian," he confessed.

Sam stopped abruptly, forcing a man hurrying along behind her to shift directions quickly, muttering, "Dumb broad."

"You what?"

Randollph managed to look grave. "It was years ago. In my former profession I had frequent opportunities to associate with ladies in the films."

"I'll just bet you did!" Sam said. "I don't want to hear about it. How close was your so-called association with Lisa?"

"I thought you didn't want to hear about it."

"I don't. But tell me."

"Our acquaintance was quite casual." Randollph was

grateful that the Almighty is always ready to forgive our sins, including lying a little for a good purpose.

"Hah!" Sam said. "With Lisa that could mean a dozen trips to the hay."

Randollph decided it was time to guide the conversation into other channels.

"Tell me about some of the swinging times you had in college, and after," he said.

Sam stopped abruptly again. "You're just trying to change the subject. But, my dear Reverend Doctor Cesare Paul Randollph, even though I know you are a pastor qualified to hear guilt-ridden ladies confess their indiscretions, if you think I'm going to tell you about my past, lurid or not, think again, pal!"

"Just thought I'd ask, Samantha." Randollph smiled genially at her. "Just thought I'd ask. Come on, I'll buy lunch."

The Kon Tiki Room of the Chicago Sheraton advertised all sorts of exotic rum concoctions reportedly originating in remote Pacific islands. Samantha Stack said, "I'll have Wild Turkey on the rocks, please." Randollph specified a martini with Bombay.

Sam pushed an ice cube around her glass with a swizzle stick. "The Julians all belong to Good Shepherd, or so Lisa said in her letter, but never attend. Oh, maybe on Easter. Lisa said she was glad the family church at least had a handsome nave that lent itself to a fancy wedding."

"Good of her to speak well of the architecture," Randollph said.

"Don't be cynical, C.P. Anyway, in case you're interested, it's a family of doctors, except for Lisa, of course. And she's marrying one."

"The Julian Clinic," Randollph said. "I seem to recall

that the bishop goes there when he has a pain in the episcopal belly."

"Could be. It caters to the society trade. Lisa's twin brother is a doctor in the clinic. So is her half-brother, who is a couple of years younger. Tell me more about your so-called association with Lisa."

"Ah, here's the food," Randollph exclaimed heartily. He quickly popped a hot shrimp into his mouth to preclude further conversation. Sam gave him a disgusted look and dug into baby spare ribs.

"Tell me more about the Julian family."

Sam wiped her fingers on a napkin, leaving a red-orange smear of barbecue sauce. "Ask Lisa."

"I'll do that when she comes round to book the wedding. With that barbecue sauce on your upper lip, you look like a cannibal who has just disposed of a portion of succulent missionary. It's quite becoming."

Three

The Church of the Good Shepherd is old, as Chicago institutions go. Though New England would look on it as a recent addition to the sacred scene, it predated the founding of the city by a number of years, beginning in a log hut as a mission to the Indians, who, according to all well-informed Christians of the time, would be benefited beyond measure by accepting baptism and selling their land cheap to the Christians. As the city grew, the leaders of the church perceived that the real mission to which God was calling them was not the Indians but the hog butchers and freight handlers (executive level), who were the nearest thing the raw young community had to a burgher class. Thus, when enough generations had passed to make possible a distinction between new Chicago money and old Chicago money, the Church of the Good Shepherd was graced with old-money families, not to mention healthy endowments. This gave it high status, supposedly in the eyes of God, and certainly in the social structure of the city.

But in this transitory world, all things change. Good Shepherd's faithful no longer debarked from chauffeured Packards and Pierce Arrows to hear the word of the Lord in their gloomy old brick Romanesque building, which looked something like a penitentiary. The trustees, wanting only to make an extra buck for Jehovah, tore down the old church and replaced it with a hotel and office building. A church, complete with commodious nave, offices, classrooms, and a gymnasium occupied the first three floors. On top, like one of God's afterthoughts, was an enormous pseudo-Gothic tower, into which—as it otherwise would have been wasted space—the trustees had crammed a large and spectacular penthouse as the residence for the pastor. In between the church and the penthouse were thirty-some stories of gratifyingly productive offices, hotel rooms, bars, and banquet halls.

The old moneyed families didn't come to church much anymore, because they all now lived in North Shore suburbs many miles from the Loop. But they kept their memberships with Good Shepherd. The people who now made up the Sunday congregation were tourists and businessmen (and their wives, if they had seen fit to bring them along) attending the hundreds of conventions which meet annually in Chicago and who nested in the dozens of hotels within walking distance of the church.

Pastors of Good Shepherd had lengthy incumbencies. There were many reasons why they stayed on, among them the extravagant salary (for a clergyman); the sumptuous penthouse parsonage (free to the pastor, and legally exempt from his taxable income); the constantly changing congregation (which made it possible for the pastor to use jokes and sermons over and over like a professional after-dinner speaker); and the large income from the church's endowments and rentals, freeing the pastor from that most onerous of clerical tasks, beating the drums for money.

When the Reverend Dr. Arthur Hartshorne, Good Shepherd's senior pastor for more than a quarter century,
reached the mandatory retirement age and reluctantly
moved out of the penthouse, the number of pastors who
felt called to serve God in Good Shepherd's pulpit was large
enough to be, if not an army of the Lord, at least a
respectable brigade. Competition for the job got so nasty
that the bishop decided to cool it by naming an interim
pastor who had no ambitions for permanent status.

Randollph was discovering facts about the pastoral office
that, unless you have been one, you don't ever know. One
fact was that the head minister of a large, long-established
congregation does not spend his days being a cure of souls.
Not many of them, anyway. Mostly, he is an administrator.
He sees people. He meets with committees. He calms the
squabbles that develop within the organization. He makes
decisions that have little to do with preaching the word and
duly administering the sacraments. He supplies a shot of
unction on public occasions with an invocation or a benediction. He is a front man for God and the congregation.

He had learned another fact. An old, established congregation is likely to have an old, established church secretary who, though a menial by job description, gathers power
through long tenure and firmly fixed connections with the
powerful members of the congregation. Miss Adelaide
Windfall had grown heavy with authority, partly through
lengthy service, and partly because the Reverend Dr. Arthur
Hartshorne had spent most of his time between Sundays
addressing Rotary clubs in the wilds of Ohio and Michigan,
leaving a power vacuum which Miss Windfall, by inclination as well as necessity, filled. Miss Windfall pretty much
ran the ranch.

Randollph was glumly staring at a blank sheet of paper
when the office intercom buzzed. Miss Windfall, who was
very strict about disrupting routine, would not have broken

into his study time without a compelling reason. But it
came as a relief. Though Trinity Sunday was weeks away, he
was trying to get a head start on a sermon explaining the
triune God to a modern congregation which vaguely believed in a deity combining the qualities of Uncle Sam,
Santa Claus, and a hanging judge. So far, he hadn't even got
off the mark.

"Yes, Miss Windfall?"

"Miss Lisa Julian is here to see you," Miss Windfall
informed him. Miss Windfall would have forced the mayor
to make an appointment and sent minor ecclesiastics pack-
ing, Randollph knew. But the Julians were socially established members of Good Shepherd, a legitimate royalty
privileged to push pastors around if they chose. Miss
Windfall was ordering Randollph to see the lady.

"I'll come out to greet her," he said.

Lisa Julian was as stunning as he had remembered. She
was tall, a good five-nine; her crimson pantsuit contrasted
agreeably with her long dark hair. She wasn't wearing much
makeup that Randollph could see, although she had probably done something subtle to soften a face a trifle long and
a nose too prominent for real beauty.

"Miss Julian, this is Dr. Randollph." A mere pastor was
presented to a Julian by Miss Windfall's lights, not the
other way around.

"I'm pleased—" Lisa Julian said; then her eyes widened.
"My God, it's Con Randollph!" She threw herself onto him.
"I can't believe it! It is you, isn't it? Your nose isn't crooked
anymore, but it is you, isn't it?" She was kissing him
between babblings, and Randollph noted with satisfaction
that Evelyn, the receptionist, was taking it all in with
amazement. Miss Windfall, mouth open, looked stupefied.
Jarred the old girl out of her pretentious superiority, he
thought. Give her insight into a new dimension of her boss's
character.

Lisa Julian finally disengaged herself from Randollph.

"Whatever are you doing pretending to be a preacher?" she asked.

"I'm not pretending."

She followed him into his study, shaking her head.

Randollph, uncomfortable talking to people across the barrier of the broad mahogany desk that Dr. Hartshorne had deemed appropriate for a pastor of his eminence, had installed a conversation center around a coffee table. Seating Lisa in the most comfortable chair, he took a place at the end of the scruffy brown leather sofa.

"I can't get over it," she said. "You a preacher! And my pastor, insofar as I can lay claim to one."

Randollph shifted uncomfortably in his seat. "I'm not actually a preacher by trade," he said.

"Then what are you doing here?"

"Oh, I'm ordained. But my real profession is teaching. Church history. In a seminary in California. I'm just confusing you, aren't I?' It's so good to see you again, Lisa."

"It's good to see you, too, love, although I should be very angry with you yet. But I repeat, what are you doing here?"

"It's just temporary, Lisa. The bishop, who was one of my teachers at the seminary, persuaded me to take a sabbatical and spend it as interim pastor while the church looks for a permanent pastor."

"Ah, so. And you'll officiate—that's the right word, isn't it?—at my wedding. The man I wanted to marry will marry me to a man that . . ." She let her voice trail off. Randollph fidgeted in the silence. Lisa giggled. "Don't worry, Con dear, I'm over you. Years ago. Maybe it was just the glamour of going around with Con Randollph, the great Rams quarterback, that melted my heart. My God! From pro football to the pulpit! From the Rams to religion! Did you have your nose straightened?"

"A little cosmetic surgery."

Lisa cocked her head. "I think I liked it better the way it was. You've lost that lovely brutal look." She straightened up. "But I didn't come to talk over the past. I'm going to live in Chicago now, or most of the time."

"You're giving up your career?"

"Not really. I'll do a picture every year or so. It doesn't take long to fly to California. But I am going to settle down, be a married woman. Maybe I'll come to church. Sometime I want to hear about how you got hooked on religion. Are you very pious?"

"Not at all."

"Don't you have to be if you are a preacher?"

"Not if you are only an interim pastor. It helps, I suppose, if you are making a career of it. Tell me about the man you are marrying."

She settled back in her chair. "Carl Brandt. Dr. Brandt. He's with my father and brothers in the clinic. You know about the clinic?"

"A bit. You're finally in love?"

"I've been in love a hundred times. Maybe more. I'm tired of love. No. There aren't any rockets going off. The earth isn't moving. He's a good man. Decent. Kind. A little stodgy. Very conscientious about his work—he's a surgeon, like my twin brother, Kermit. He's very much like Kermit. No imagination, but dependable. Maybe I'm marrying him because he's like Kermit. Dad was always so busy he didn't pay much attention to me. Kermit was like ... well, a father, though he wasn't my father."

"Surrogate," Randollph said.

"Yes, that's the word. He was fiercely protective. Maybe I'm just looking for someone to protect me."

Randollph made noncommittal sounds.

"Oh, you think that isn't enough for a marriage?" Lisa was defensive. "Well, let me tell you, Con Randollph, doctor of divinity though you may be—"

"Doctor of philosophy," Randollph corrected her.

"Whatever. I've had all the bright and shining glamour boys I need."

She sighed and calmed down. "What am I yelling at you for? It's just that . . . oh, well, I suppose you could call it a spiritual change. I haven't gotten religion or anything like that. I'm tired of my life as it is. I want some stability. I want roots. I even want children. Is that so strange?"

"No, not at all," Randollph told her. "Those are very normal feelings. And, I would imagine—though contrary to the romantic mythology purveyed by Hollywood—not a bad basis for a sound marriage. Not bad at all."

Lisa brightened. "Thanks, Con, for understanding. Hardly anybody does. Oh, Daddy's happy I'm settling down. And my brother Kermit feels the same way. They've never quite approved of me. But my younger brother—my half-brother, actually—thinks I'm crazy. All my friends think so, too. They say I'll be bored with Carl and with being a housewife. But I'm ready for it. I just can't convince them of that."

"You don't have to convince them. Only yourself."

"I know," she said, sounding almost positive. "Well. Let's talk about the wedding."

Randollph soon realized he was in over his head. He knew enough to arrange for Lisa to meet with Tony Agostino, Good Shepherd's choirmaster-organist, and that a rehearsal would be necessary. But as to the logistics of a formal wedding he was benignly ignorant. He supposed that the bishop could chock him full of instructions on how to perform this routine pastoral function before rehearsal day.

"I am acquainted with your matron of honor," he said, watching Lisa crossing off items on what appeared to be an endless list.

She looked up quickly. "You are? How does a dignified pastor get acquainted with Chicago's most popular television personality? She a member of your church?"

"No. I was a guest on her show shortly after I came here."

"Does she know anything about us?"

"She *is* aware that we were friends some years ago."

"Did you tell her how good friends?"

Randollph squirmed around on the sofa. "I believe she is under the impression that our relationship was quite casual."

"So you lied to her, eh, Con?" Lisa laughed. "You must like the girl. Well, old casual friend, I won't tell if you won't."

Randollph was ashamed of himself for feeling relieved.

Lisa stood up to go. "I'm over you, Con, thank God. It took a long time. Longer than for anyone else I ever thought I was in love with. But we'll be seeing a lot of each other for a while, and there's no reason we can't be good friends. There's only one thing bothering me."

"Oh? What is that?"

"When I come down that aisle and see you waiting in your clerical getup, I might be remembering things a bride shouldn't be thinking about." She planted a kiss on his forehead and left.

Four

When Randollph got back to his office after lunch, Miss Windfall said, "The bishop is waiting to see you. And," she added, "there is a backlog of correspondence to be taken care of." Miss Windfall recognized the importance of bishops, but did not think they should be allowed to interfere with the efficient production of paperwork.

Randollph found the bishop sitting in one of the scruffy brown leather chairs reading a paperback book.

"Sorry to keep you waiting, Freddie," Randollph said.

The bishop dog-eared a page and closed the book. "I wasn't in any hurry for you to get here. C.P. Not that I didn't want to see you, but actually I'm hiding out."

"From whom?" The bishop looked more than ever like a plump cherub, Randollph thought.

"From one of my brother bishops. I happen to know he's in town, and I suspect he's going to call on me and persuade me to find a parish for one of his problem pastors. In addition to that, he's a fool and a bore. So I pretended it was my episcopal duty to call on you and see how you're getting on with Good Shepherd. Convenient to have an office in your building. My real purpose was to sit here and read this trashy cowboy novel."

"Though your motives are perhaps ignoble, Freddie, you're welcome. And I am always in need of professional advice, it seems." Randollph pulled up a chair and sat down. "I've just booked a formal church wedding, and I haven't the foggiest notion of how to run one."

"Formal weddings," the bishop mused. "How I loved them when I was a pastor. They're one of the things I missed most when I was dean of the seminary. A wedding is joy, hope, anticipation, a creation of something new." He sighed, as if for a past happiness that would not come his way again. "I'm glad you're having one. Formal weddings aren't as popular now as they once were. You could spend your entire year at Good Shepherd and go back to your teaching without conducting a church wedding. Who's getting married?"

"Lisa Julian."

"Oh, that's Rex Julian's daughter, isn't it? He's my personal physician."

"A good one, I hope."

The bishop got up and walked over to the window. "Who knows if a doctor is capable or a charlatan? They thump you and poke you and listen to your heart, solemnly nodding their heads as if privy to some esoteric message unintelligible to mere laymen. Then they give you some pills and send you a bill. The girl's an actress, isn't she?"

"Yes."

"Then you may have some extra problems." The bishop resumed his seat. "The greatest hazard to a well-run formal wedding is the bride's mother, who shows up at the rehearsal with a copy of Amy Vanderbilt under her arm. She means to run the show. You have to be firm with her. And with the wedding consultant. They are a nuisance."

"You'd best give me all the bad news, Freddie," he said.

"Well, there's the bridegroom who is hung over from his bachelor dinner." The bishop ticked them off on his fingers. "Or the best man who's partaken of too much liquid courage and can't find the ring. And in this case you'll have reporters and TV cameras to cope with. They'll hang over your shoulder and pop flashbulbs in the bride's face when she says 'I will'—if you let them." The bishop rose. "I think it's safe now to go back to my office. I'll lend you a book that lays out the procedures for a formal wedding."

"Thanks, Freddie, I'll appreciate that."

The bishop paused at the door. "C.P., I know that one reason you accepted my invitation to spend your sabbatical as interim pastor of Good Shepherd was to find out what it is like to be in the trenches, so to speak."

"There's that," Randollph admitted, "among other reasons."

"You. must remember, though, that Good Shepherd is not a typical church. I have mixed feelings about a church in the belly of a high-rise hotel and office building, which it owns. And I wonder about a church as heavily endowed as this one. The symbolism's all wrong. It's too close a coupling of God and mammon."

"Tell you what, Freddie, would it make you feel better if Good Shepherd withheld its contributions to your office?" Randollph grinned at his old friend.

"Heavens no, C.P.," the bishop answered cheerfully. "I have these twinges of conscience from time to time, but good administrators never let conscience interfere with the operation of the institution. I just tell myself that the generous sums Good Shepherd contributes are for the greater good of the church at large. Then my conscience is soothed, and I get on with the job." He slipped his cowboy novel into the pocket of his jacket and left.

Five

The nave of the Church of the Good Shepherd is a mixture of architectural styles and tastes, both good and bad. Very large as churches go, it affects a Byzantine motif touched up with a little Romanesque and a bit of Gothic. Processions of structurally unnecessary columns caked with blue-and-gold tile mosaics appear to support a pitched roof. Solemn Gothic windows, on whose casemented saints sunbeams never danced, shine with the bland light of concealed neon tubing. Gold-leafed medieval Christians on an ancient triptych (probably stolen a century ago from some fifteenth-century Italian church) gravely inspect a sixteenth-century altar. Randollph, though recognizing the nave's architectural incongruities and occasional vulgarity, rather liked it. It probably reflected accurately the fragmented and unsettled character of the congregation, he thought.

People had been spilling in from the narthex for several minutes now, clotting into a group at the rear of the nave like displaced persons waiting for the next train in some gigantic station. Randollph was uncertain what to do next, but Dan Gantry said, "Let's get 'em down in front, boss, and count noses. O.K.," he shouted in a voice that needed no electronic amplification to carry it to ears anywhere in the nave, "everybody front and center. Let's get on with it." Randollph was startled, but Dan said to him, "You've got to act like a drill sergeant to get 'em moving."

The clot dissolved into a string of people. They came tentatively, as if testing unfamiliar territory. Dan rounded up the stragglers, herding them into the front pews.

"All right, let's get acquainted." Dan stood in front of the group, hands on hips, jaw aggressive, voice authoritative. He's running a wedding rehearsal like the sports director at a kids' camp, Randollph thought. "Where's the bride?"

"Be here in a minute," a slim blond girl in a minimum skirt said. "She and Sam Stack had some errands to run."

"O.K. Sam Stack's a good friend of mine, but I've never met the bride. I'm Dan Gantry, one of the pastors of Good Shepherd. This is Dr. C. P. Randollph." Dan nodded in Randollph's direction. "He's conducting the wedding. Since this will be his first wedding in this church, he's asked me to help with the rehearsal, kind of block it out for you. And this"—he pointed to a dark-haired, smiling man in a blue denim walking suit—"is Tony Agostino—Mr. Anthony Agostino—who is Good Shepherd's organist. Tony's the best organist in Chicago, but keep an eye on your girlfriends. He's hell on wheels with the ladies." This got a nervous laugh from the group.

Randollph wondered if Dan's breezy approach to this pastoral duty was typical. When he'd asked Dan to help, Dan had said, "Sure, boss. I don't get many chances to handle a big wedding, but I always did the rehearsals for old Arty Hartshorne. He hit the road on Monday morning and usually didn't get back till Saturday night. So somebody had to rehearse 'em. I know the ropes."

One of the ropes, apparently, was introducing oneself to the individual members of the wedding party. Dr. Rex Julian looked to be about sixty-five, Randollph thought, a stolid, powerful man with strong, heavy features and a lot of gray-white hair. Dr. Kermit Julian was a younger replica of his father, but with conventionally cut thick black hair.

Randollph inspected the bridegroom with interest. Dr. Carl Brandt didn't look much like Dr. Kermit, for whom, Lisa had suggested, he may have been a surrogate. His features were more finely drawn, just escaping a feminine quality. Blue eyes, light brown hair. He had an expression, though, that suggested he and Dr. Kermit looked at life through similar eyes. What had Lisa said? Stodgy. No imagination. Randollph could believe it.

Dr. Valorous Julian, the half-brother, didn't appear to belong to the same family. Modishly cut straw-colored hair hung around a slightly plump face and lively blue eyes. He wore a yellow zephyr-weight wool polo shirt set off by a brown-and-yellow ascot and a camel-tan cashmere jacket. About seven hundred dollars on the hoof, Randollph estimated. Dr. Valorous Julian, to all evidences, did not have a stodgy outlook on life.

Dan said, "This is Dr. Valorous Julian. Shall we, Val?"

"Why not?" Dr. Val Julian said. "Bride's not here yet. Can't start the party till she gets here." He stepped to the front and joined Dan.

"One, two, three," Dan said. Then the two men broke into "Yessir, That's My Baby," accompanying it with an exaggerated Charleston. Randollph, amazed, wondered if whatever long-gone deacons of Good Shepherd whose spirits might be hanging around the church would report this in heaven as a desecration of a holy place or as dancing before the Lord.

The dance came to an end. The group cheered and whistled. Dan and Val slapped palms.

"Excuse us," Dan said, slightly winded. "Val and I are buddies in the downtown amateur Theater Troupe. That's a little number we did together in the last production." Val solemnly inspected Dan's wide-flare patch-pattern slacks, open-neck suede shirt, and silver medal hanging from a leather thong. "Hippie clothes and dancing in church," he said. "Clergy's gone to hell."

Mrs. Rex Julian was obviously Val's mother. About ten years younger than her husband, Randollph calculated. She and Val had the same straw-colored hair, baby face, and tendency to roundness. She had no copy of Amy Vanderbilt under her arm, but she had some ideas.

"I believe that it would be best to remove the altar and that picture on it—"

"Triptych," Randollph said.

". . . whatever you call it, and get rid of the pulpit, and that thing with the Bible on it—"

"Lectern," Randollph said.

". . . then we could use a blow-up of a scene from one of Lisa's pictures as a backdrop, and Mr. What's-his-name there could play the theme from one of her pictures—from *Love's Return*, I like that one—for the processional." She spoke as if ordering salesclerks at Bonwit's to trot out some more dresses. "That would give a nice theme to the wedding."

Tony Agostino, Randollph could see, was speechless. Dan Gantry's face was red. He started to speak, but Randollph put a silencing hand on his arm.

"I'm afraid that wouldn't be possible, Mrs. Julian." Randollph said it quietly.

"I don't see why not." Mrs. Julian had the air of a countess about to take her patronage elsewhere. "It's our wedding. We can have any theme we want. We can do as we please."

Randollph replied patiently. "A wedding in a church already has a theme, Mrs. Julian. Its theme is the invocation of God's blessing on this union in the presence of the community. The church prescribes how this is to be done. If Lisa wishes to have a secular wedding, she may hire a public hall and a justice of the peace and plan any kind of occasion that is to her taste. But if her wedding is to be in this church, it will be conducted according to the ritual for the solemnization of matrimony. And since I represent the church, it is my responsibility to decide what is and is not appropriate."

"I still don't see—"

Val interrupted her. "He's telling you, Mother dear, in the nicest way possible, that he's in charge here, and that it doesn't make a damn bit of difference what you want. So why don't you knock it off and we can get on with it." He turned to Randollph. "Con, if I may use your professional nickname, when you were quarterbacking the Rams, did you ever get arguments in the huddle about your play selections?"

Randollph smiled. "Occasionally," he said, "but never more than once from the same man." Randollph was certain that he could get to like Dr. Valorous Julian.

Mercifully the tension was broken by the breathless arrival of the bride and matron of honor.

"Sorry, everybody." Lisa kissed Randollph on the cheek. "Hello, Con dear." Sam Stack also kissed him on the cheek and murmured, "Hello, Con dear."

"Ahem," Randollph said. "Shall we proceed with the introductions?"

The ushers' corps, he discovered, would be under the charge of Dr. Val, and would be bolstered by several much-publicized actors. There was Amos Oregon, who was always cast in laconic, fast-gun parts, formerly for grade-A westerns, but, with the decline of that art form, now reduced to an occasional television role. He looked at Lisa as if he hoped to bed her before the night was over. There was Jaime DeSilva, faintly Latin, a superb dancer and passable singer who had co-starred with Lisa in a number of musicals. There was Harmon Ballantine, a handsome sinister-looking man who had beaten, blackmailed, embezzled, and murdered his way to fortune if not fame as the heavy in scores of television movies.

The bridesmaids were also representatives from the films. There was Annette Paris, blond and well-curved, who had been promoted as a new Ann-Margret but had never quite made it. He recalled that Annette and Lisa had shared an apartment for a time. He was introduced to Marty McCall, who looked remarkably like a young Doris Day, and Willa Ames, tiny and exquisite, a serious actress who started on Broadway and now had two Academy Award nominations to her credit.

This was no ordinary wedding, Randollph reflected. The swarm of reporters and photographers was likely to resemble the invasion of the seven-year locust. But more extraordinary was the tangle of human relationships. What had been Lisa's relationship with Oregon and DeSilva? How did Lisa get on with her father; her stepmother; her twin brother; did the Julian brothers like each other, and how did they feel about Dr. Brandt coming into the family? Randollph was uncomfortably aware of the unusual relationship between the officiating clergyman and the bride. How many threads of affection and jealousy, passion and dislike, love and hate tethered all these people to one another? He was glad he didn't know.

"All right, now we know each other, let's have the bride and groom, best man, matron of honor, father of the bride, bridesmaids, ushers here at the chancel rail. I'll run you through what you do when you're all here and the processional is over and the ceremony begins." Dan had resumed the role of drill sergeant.

"Don't you need me?" Mrs. Rexford Julian was bloody but unbowed.

"Nope," Dan said. "I'll tell you when I need you. You just sit there and look pretty for now."

Mrs. Julian was not having a good day, but Randollph was unable to scrape up any Christian sympathy for her.

With Randollph at his side, Dan quickly arranged the wedding party and led them through the ritual. "Now we'll do the processional," he announced. "Everybody but the groom and best man beat it to the narthex. Double-time." Dan might affect the appearance of a flower child, Randollph knew, but he had the managerial instincts of an admiral or a bishop.

Randollph, ritual in hand, waited at the chancel with Dr. Brandt and Dr. Kermit Julian. Dan, in the narthex, lined up the party to his satisfaction, then yelled, "O.K., Tony, let 'er go." Tony Agostino unleashed the great organ, trembling the fake roof beams with blasts of Purcell. The ushers marched down the aisle, two by two, apparently to Dan's approval. But when Willa Ames, the lead-off bridesmaid, entered the nave with a stylized hesitation step, he yelled, "No, dammit, no! Cut it, Tony." Then, to the flustered actress, "No drag step. It looks like hell. A dignified walk." Big-name actresses evidently were expected to do as they were told, just like anyone else, when Dan was running the rehearsal. Randollph was grateful that Dan was in charge of the troops.

After three run-throughs they all finally got the hang of it, Randollph included. Dan carefully rehearsed the groom kissing the bride, a part of the ceremony an embarrassed Dr. Brandt performed as if undertaking a mournful duty. "Kiss her good," Dan ordered. "She won't break." Lisa giggled.

"You might want to practice that kissing on your own time," Dan admonished the bride and groom. "O.K., ushers, be here an hour early. There'll be a lot of gate-crashers, so we'll have some security people to help, if you have any trouble. No cameras in the church. Never usher a lone man to a seat. Just indicate where he may sit. Any questions? Then rehearsal's over. Try to show up sober tomorrow."

The party began to straggle out. Randollph noted that Jaime DeSilva and Harmon Ballantine were leaving with a couple of pretty bridesmaids whose names he couldn't remember. But a scowling Amos Oregon hurried out alone.

"Rescue me from a lousy day, C.P.," Sam Stack said. "Take me home. Comfort me with apples. Now, where did I pick up a goofy line like that?"

"It's the title of a novel. Of course I'll take you home. My lack of gallantry in failing to ask you earlier can be attributed to preoccupation with my first wedding rehearsal. Forgive me?"

"Don't take me for granted, C.P. I'm half gone on you, but don't take me for granted."

"That I'll never do. Among your attractions, too abundant to enumerate, is that you cannot be taken for granted."

Sam Stack brightened. "Now, that's more like it. Feel free to enumerate some of my *other* attractions, too, C.P."

"A pleasure. But for the ones I had in mind, a bit more privacy is required."

She took his hand. "Then why are we hanging around here?"

Outside, a thin warm rain was lightly washing the city's streets and sidewalks, reflecting in the lights of passing traffic the illusion of cleanliness. A street preacher under a theater marquee was haranguing three bored listeners with the certainties of some antic theology. Two black hookers in miniskirts and krinkly white boots hung around the edge of the crowd in front of Church of the Good Shepherd's hotel, estimating with emotionless professionalism the potential business in this group. The doorman ushered hotel guests, in town on a toot, into waiting cabs, collecting his quarter, and sending them rocketing off into the night, aimed for whatever cultural activity or variety of sin they fancied.

As they waited their turn for a cab, Sam Stack said, "I've been depressed all day."

"Why?" Randollph asked her.

"Because weddings excite me and make me feel romantic—"

"How very nice."

"Quiet, lad. But not this wedding."

"My experience with formal weddings has been, heretofore, solely as a guest. But they always seemed pretty much alike to me. How does this one differ from any other?"

Sam thought for a minute. "Partly because I don't like some of the people involved in it."

"Such as?"

"Annette Paris, for one."

"What's wrong with her? I failed to detect any glaring flaws."

"You wouldn't!" Sam looked at him with the expression of a mother superior about to tell a novitiate that every sister isn't as filled with holiness as she might be. "You're a man. And besides, I don't know exactly why I don't like her."

"Who else in the party fails to enlist your affection?"

"Amos Oregon. He's surly. Jaime DeSilva."

"Why him?"

"He managed to slip up behind me and got a hand on one of my boobs. He asked if I'd like to show him a good time tonight."

Randollph took an instant dislike to Jaime DeSilva.

"I've got lots of experience handling guys like that, of course," she said.

"Tell me how you handled him."

"I batted his hand away and told him I was too mature for little boys with such crude techniques. Then I gave him the address of a good whorehouse and said he should ask them to teach him about women."

Randollph chuckled.

"But mostly it's the family that has me depressed," Sam continued. "Lisa's dad hasn't any emotion, good or bad, that I can see. I detest Lisa's stepmother. And who's steamed up about this wedding? Lisa? You saw her tonight. She'd have been more nervous if it had been a movie part. Carl Brandt? Dan could hardly get him to kiss the bride. Kermit? I know he adores his little twin sister, but you'd think he didn't care whether the wedding took place or not. Val's the only one of the family that's getting any fun out of it, but then, Val enjoys everything." She shivered and pressed closer to Randollph. "It just doesn't have the right feel to it."

"Cab, sir?"

Randollph helped her into the cab. "Sometimes," he said, "the Rams would have a rotten week of practice, but on Sunday we'd have a great game. Let's hope that's the way it will be with this wedding." He settled back as the doorman gave the driver the address of Sam Stack's apartment and shut them in.

Six

The Drake is in the class of Chicago's large old hotels. Situated where North Michigan Boulevard joins the Lakeshore Drive, its gray hulk, like a ritzy fort, placidly guards the city center against invaders by sea. It has no glass elevators chasing each other up and down poles like frisky transparent bugs, and the lobby is old-fashioned. But a large and loyal clientele uses it for every occasion requiring a service best performed by a hotel. It handles a lot of wedding receptions.

Randollph arrived late. It would have been appropriate for him to appear at the reception in clerical garb, he knew. But he had just bought a pale-blue raw silk summer dinner jacket and an even paler blue ruffled shirt and he was itching to wear them. Besides, the stiff clerical collar scratched his neck. So he had taken the time to change. Dan Gantry, a wedding guest by virtue of his association with Dr. Val, had volunteered to wait for him and drive him to the hotel. Dan, Randollph was glad to see, had abandoned his usual bizarre haberdashery for a decent-looking white formal jacket.

Dan tooled the plain green Ford that the Church of the Good Shepherd leased for the use of its pastoral staff through the confusion of late-afternoon Loop traffic.

"Went fine," he said, cutting off a belligerent taxi and sliding through an intersection on yellow. "Thanks to my expert direction of the rehearsal, and getting the processional started right in the narthex."

"I didn't know you were back there," Randollph said.

"Yep. Always have somebody in the narthex to get 'em started in order, space 'em right. Usually have trouble with the wedding consultant, too. They foul up the processional."

"Oh? How?"

"Fuss and fuss with the bride's train. Tony booms up the organ for the bride and her father and the damn consultant keeps fooling with the bride's dress."

"What do you do?"

"Tell her to get the hell away and let the bride go. You speak nice to her and she doesn't pay any attention."

Randollph recalled the bishop's warning about wedding consultants, but doubted that Freddie would wholly approve of Dan's methods.

"You should have been at the bachelor dinner." Dan went on.

Randollph was glad he hadn't been. "Was it fun?"

"If you can call a bunch of drunken bums telling dirty jokes fun," Dan said. "Oh, it wasn't bad. Even Kermit and Carl loosened up. Some guys, even serious types like them, you get them lubricated and they come on real genial. Val, well, he's made for this kind of a brawl. He was master of ceremonies. He got Carl and Kermit to do a duet of bawdy songs. He did a medical speech about a birth-control pill for men. It was a riot. Do you know what the name of the pill is?"

Randollph didn't know.

"Sulpha-denial," Dan said, squeezing by a pokey Mark IV. "And then Val put on a wig and did a surprisingly good impression of Lisa singing a love song in one of her musicals. Then I gave a pastoral-counseling speech to the groom. I guess it was pretty good. Everybody laughed a lot. They were all so pickled, though, that they'd have laughed at 'Mary Had a Little Lamb.' Some of those actors were pretty good, too. Except that Oregon guy. Big, strong, silent type he's supposed to be. He was drunk when the party began, and he just kept drinking and crying. Finally conked out. Jaime DeSilva and Harmon Ballantine, though, they were the life of the party. All the clinic doctors were there, but mostly they just drank." Dan threaded the Ford through the slim opening left by double-parked cars and turned it over to the hotel doorman.

Inside, Randollph asked a clerk for directions to the reception.

"Which one, sir? We have several receptions in progress at the moment."

Randollph told the clerk that he was looking for the Brandt-Julian reception.

"That would be ballroom C," the clerk said, with professional detachment, and gave crisp directions.

The reception had already progressed to the dancing stage. Samantha Stack, Randollph saw, was in the arms of Harmon Ballantine and looking enchanted. He snatched a glass from the tray of a passing waiter, and though he was not fond of champagne, he gulped it down.

"Something troublin' you, doctor?" It was Val, a glass in each hand, looking at Randollph with an amused smile.

"Oh, hello." Randollph summoned up a cheerful look.

"If you're just thirsty, I have the solution to that," Val said. "Now, in this glass"—he held one hand high—"is champagne. Tasty stuff. Damn good year. But no wallop. Now, this glass?" He held up the other hand. "Contains a modicum—'ja get that, a modicum—of very fine brandy. I stole a bottle from my revered poppa's private cellar, and I have it se— secreted, thas th' word, se-cre-ted, in a shpesh . . . shpecial place nearby."

It occurred to Randollph that Val's speech had become markedly slurred rather rapidly. Maybe he was having a little fun with the clergy. Or maybe brandy and champagne in combination created a synergy vastly accelerating the action of the alcohol. Or maybe Val had just worked harder on the brandy than the champagne.

"Brandy's jus' constren—conshentrated champagne, anyway," Val said. "Why d'they call you Con?"

"Because the sportswriters said that he wasn't an outstanding passer, and not a very good runner, but that he had great hands for deceptive ball handling, and the soul of a confidence man in calling plays," Dan Gantry said. "What am I doing talking to you guys with all these beautiful women and me a carefree bachelor? I think I'll find Marty McCall. I've already got a little something going there."

"A remarkable young man," Val said, as Dan worked his way through the dancers. "Beneath that, ah, unorthodox ecshterur beats a heart passhntly committed to his faith." He drained his champagne glass. "Speakin' of faith, why'd you eccs-eccshange th' role of football hero for a turnaround collar? Get converted all of a sudden? Thas' how it's done, ishn't it?" He looked at his empty glass. "Need a refill."

"No, nothing that dramatic," Randollph told him. "I just decided I'd spent enough of my life playing a boy's game, no matter how pleasant."

"Got banged around a lot, didnja?"

"True. But the life was exciting, and quite lucrative."

"I'm getting drunk," Val said. "Prob'ly won't 'member anything y' tell me. Don't drink much, 'shept on big happy occasions like this. Doctor shouldn't drink."

"The surgeon needs a steady hand," Randollph said, thinking it an inane remark.

Val looked at him scornfully. "Who's a surgeon? Surgeon's jus' a mechanic. Fine for dull chaps like my dear brother, an' my dear newly aqu ... my new brother-in-law. I'm an internist. Takes 'magination, keen mind, 'venturous spirit. Well, better find a refill." He wandered off.

Randollph wasn't sure what the officiating clergyman was supposed to do at the wedding reception. He tried to recall the many weddings he had attended as a guest and capture some memory of anonymous reverend gentlemen and their postceremony conduct. One clear picture emerged—a dumpy divine in a tight black suit refusing the punch because it was spiked, and giving a little temperance lecture, to the discomfiture of the other guests. This, he was sure, was not an ideal model for pastoral conduct. At the wedding at Cana, Jesus, when the wine ran out, had simply performed the miracle of turning some water into enough wine to keep the party going—turned it into vintage stuff, too. It was one of Randollph's favorite Bible stories. But no divine replenishment was likely to be needed here, as the waiters kept the punchbowls filled. He supposed he ought to mingle with the guests, greet, at least, the principals. What he wanted to do was find Samantha and cut in on whoever was dancing with her, but he subordinated this desire to the duty, however vague, that was a concomitant of his office. An interim pastor could ignore many of the stereotypical restrictions which jacketed the pastoral personality, but he could not ignore them all.

He made his way to the long table which held the punchbowls, bottles of champagne in silver buckets, and the large tiered wedding cake. The wedding cake, the little bride and groom figurines tottering precariously on the still-virgin top tier, had a gaping section hacked out of it. The remains resembled a temple from some forgotten culture, wounded by centuries and neglect. Randollph accepted a slice from the server, though he did not intend to eat it. Wedding cakes, he knew, were designed to be admired, not consumed.

Dr. Rexford Julian was standing by the table, a mutant penguin in a white dinner jacket. He greeted Randollph solemnly.

"Lovely ceremony, Dr. Randollph."

"Thank you. I'm sure it will be a joy to you to have Lisa back home."

If it was a joy to Dr. Julian, no look of pleasure crossed the craggy old face. "She's married a good man, a good doctor," the old physician said. "I only wish her mother could have been here today. She died when the twins were born, you know." He seemed lost in memories of what had been. Randollph wondered what this said about the present Mrs. Julian.

"I believe my bishop is one of your patients," Randollph said, for lack of anything else to say.

"What?" The doctor came out of his reverie. "Oh, yes, fine man. Favorite of mine. Entertaining conversationalist. Well thought of in the city. Bishop doesn't have an easy job. Not that I know much about it. Don't get to church much anymore myself. Hard for a doctor to keep regular hours."

It was a half apology for not having heard Randollph preach. Randollph had listened to the same sort of speech from several Good Shepherd members, and supposed it was the kind of annoyance to which all pastors learn to resign themselves. His inclination was to reply, "It is a matter of supreme indifference to me whether you attend church or not." But he knew this would not reflect a proper pastoral attitude. Perhaps the half apology came from some residual feeling or leftover habit that said one ought to be in the house of the Lord on the Lord's day, and absence required a justification. Anyway, for the rest of the year he was Dr. Rexford Julian's official pastor, whether Dr. Julian availed himself of his pastoral services or not.

"Hello there, Padre." It was a flushed Dr. Brandt, who had danced up to the table with Annette Paris. "Haven't had a chance to compliment you on the splendid ceremony." A champagne-induced euphoria was making the groom uncharacteristically loquacious. He got a cup of punch for Annette and a glass of champagne for himself. "Isn't my bride lovely?" He gestured at Lisa, dancing with a scowling Amos Oregon. Annette, Randollph noted, looked pouty at the mention of the bride.

"Where are you going on your honeymoon?" Randollph asked.

"Ireland," Dr. Brandt answered. "My mother was from west County Cork—Bantry. Beautiful, beautiful country." He refilled his glass. "Lisa's never been there. So it's a double sentimental journey. I'm taking my bride to see the country of my ancestors. We'll drink Guinness in the pubs, and Paddy's whiskey in the bars, and sing 'Galway Bay' and 'The Rising of the Moon,' and go up to Cork City and kiss the Blarney Stone." He gulped the rest of his champagne. "I think I'll find my lovely bride and cut in on whoever is squiring her around." He disappeared into the pack of couples squirming more or less in time to the sedate music of Homer Levin and His Society Orchestra. Dr. Carl Brandt was not really a barrel of fun, Randollph mused, but when happy and slightly squiffed, he was at least human.

"Dance with me?" Annette Paris, abandoned, was a maiden in distress.

"I was about to ask," Randollph lied with what he hoped sounded like sincere gallantry. "You look extraordinarily lovely."

"Thank you. So do you," she said, her derriere knocking a hole in the crowd for Randollph to dance them through. "I haven't been around a minister since I was a little girl in Sunday school, but I thought they just wore baggy black things and had bad breath."

"I'm betting that your acquaintance with the clergy was quite limited." Randollph smiled down at her.

"Maybe so. But one doesn't expect to find that the best-dressed man at the reception is the marryin' parson. That's one of the handsomest dinner jackets I've ever seen."

He felt a flush of unchristian pride. He considered replying with, "Clothes are one of my numerous weaknesses," or, "I rather liked it when I saw it in the store window," or "It's rented." Instead, he groped for another category of small talk. He noticed Lisa dancing with her new husband and said, "Have you known Dr. Brandt for long?"

He felt Annette stiffen in his arms, and though her head was on his shoulder, he was certain that she had resumed the pouty look he had noticed earlier.

"I can't imagine why she married that dope!" Annette spit the word out like a foul-tasting morsel of food. "No good will come of this. I'm psychic, you know. And I see a dark, ugly cloud hanging over them. I told Lisa something bad would happen, and it will. I feel it. I feel it intensely. And when I feel something this strongly, I'm always right." Annette had stopped dancing and was talking to Randollph like a true believer declaiming to a potential convert. "She shouldn't have married that dumb Carl Brandt. She shouldn't have married anybody. It's not in her stars to marry!" Randollph was afraid she'd be drenching him with tears, but Harmon Ballantine, looking like a top-level gunsel in a continental-style rose jacket, said, "May I, Doctor?" and swept her away. Randollph sighed and decided he'd have to review his conviction that the Almighty does not intervene in the petty affairs of mere mortals.

Stranded in the midst of the crowd, Randollph looked for Samantha Stack with the intention of cutting in, but couldn't spot her. He did see Lisa dancing with her husband, and pushed his way to them.

"Will medicine give way to divinity?" he asked. "I haven't danced with the bride yet."

"Be my guest," Carl Brandt said, handing Lisa over. "I could use another glass. Dancing's dry work."

"Happy?" Randollph asked as Lisa nestled her head on his shoulder.

" 'Satisfied' is a better word to describe me," she answered.

"Dr. Brandt seems very, ah—"

Lisa laughed. " 'Satisfied' is the word for him, too. And why shouldn't he be satisfied? In addition to me, he gets a full partnership in the clinic—that's Daddy's wedding present. And he gets a quarter-million life-insurance policy on me—and I get one on him—though little good it will do him. I come from a family that lives practically forever. But he wanted us to do it for each other."

"Sounds very practical," Randollph murmured in her ear.

"Oh, it is. We're two mature people who like each other and have good sound reasons for marrying each other. Ecstasy is for kids. I don't get goose pimples when he touches me, but I'm comfortable with him. This marriage is going to work because I'm going to make it work. I know what I want."

"Annette Paris doesn't think it will work," Randollph said.

"She been talking to you? Poor Annette. I shouldn't have had her as a bridesmaid, but she might have killed herself if

I hadn't." Lisa laughed gaily as Randollph maneuvered her around a ponderous man he vaguely remembered as a movie producer, who was dancing with Willa Ames. "Amos Oregon is threatening to kill himself because I didn't marry him. Harmon Ballantine, who can be just as mean as he looks, talks darkly of eliminating Carl, who, he says, stole me away from him. Ha! And Jaime DeSilva babbles away about how I'll be sorry. He's been after me to marry him for years. They're all dear boys in their way, but there isn't any husband material in the lot. They can't get it through their heads that I don't want their kind of life. Not one of them will ever grow up. They all think life is just like playing a part in a film. Well, so did I, but I've grown up."

Randollph saw Samantha Stack. Looking over the shoulder of some anonymous partner, she waved to him. Randollph couldn't see the man's face, but he was certain the blackguard was staring down into Samantha's ill-concealed bosom with a lascivious smirk. Probably had a sweaty palm on her fanny, too. He'd like to rescue her, but one didn't abandon the bride in the middle of the floor.

"You'd like to dance with Sam, wouldn't you?" Lisa said.

Startled, Randollph could only make weak noises of protest.

"Dance me over to the table," Lisa directed. "I'm thirsty. Anyway, it's about time the bride and groom retired to the bridal chamber. We leave early tomorrow, you know."

"Dr. Brandt told me."

"Then you can go find your Sam. Why don't you marry her, Con?"

"I think she's a little gun-shy, Lisa. She is, as she puts it, a one-time loser. And I'm sure she would be reluctant to abandon her career and live the quiet life of a seminary professor. That's what I'll be when my year here is over."

"Give her time. She'll change." They were at the table. "Thanks, Con. It's lovely to have you as my good friend.

When the honeymoon's over, we'll have a talk. Now, run along and find Sam."

The brass section of Homer Levin's Society Orchestra stood up and blared out a chorus of *Lohengrin*. Dr. Brandt, with Lisa on his arm, proceeded out the ballroom door to a bank of elevators, trailed by a line of guests. A bellboy guarded an open elevator. Lisa turned and tossed her bridal bouquet among the bridesmaids, and Annette Paris caught it. Sam, Randollph noticed, had her hands behind her back. Dr. Valorous Julian, swaying slightly, lifted one of his two glasses in salute to the pair. Dr. Kermit Julian waved to them as the elevator door closed. Dr. Rexford Julian was nowhere to be seen.

Seven

"Carl," Lisa said, "carry me across the threshold, and don't complain about your sacroiliac. I'm not that fat."

"Gladly, my dear." He handed the sullen bellboy a dollar bill. "Upsy-daisy."

Inside, Lisa said, "Put me down now. The ceremony has been observed. Ow! My poor feet." She kicked off her white satin pumps and stretched out on the sofa that sat at a right angle to a fireplace. "Too bad it's summer, or we could light a fire and sit around imagining we're growing old together."

The phone rang.

"Dammit to hell!" Dr. Brandt said. "Some of our dear friends probably think it's funny to pester us—"

"Answer it, Carl," Lisa said calmly. "After all, it's not like we're a couple of panting virgins."

Dr. Brandt snatched the phone out of the cradle. "Hello! What the hell do you want? Oh. Yes. Yes. I understand." He mumbled swift instructions into the mouthpiece. "I'll be there in ten minutes." Putting down the phone, he said,

"I'm truly sorry, Lisa. One of my patients seems to be having a relapse."

"Carl," she said, "a bride ought to raise hell when her husband leaves her on their wedding day. I could scream about you loving your work more than you love me. I could throw a tantrum and yell at you that you are overconscientious. But that's one of the reasons I married you. I admire a man who refuses to shirk his duty."

"Thanks for understanding, Lisa. I'll be back in half an hour."

Lisa giggled. "It's just like *High Noon*."

"What?"

"Never mind. Trot along."

Alone, Lisa stretched out again on the sofa. She should get out of her wedding dress, she thought, but her feet hurt, and she was tired. She was drifting off into a half-sleep when there was a knock on the door.

"Go away," she said.

The knocking persisted.

Lisa roused herself. "What do you want?"

"I'm the floor maid, ma'am. I have to deliver extra towels."

"You don't sound like a maid. Go away."

"I've got to deliver these towels. Housekeeper will give me a terrible time if I don't."

Drowsily Lisa said, "Oh, all right. Just a minute." She swung her feet off the sofa, yawned, and went to the door. Not fully alert, she fumbled with the safety latch. "Damn!" She finally got the door open. "Make it quick, pl . . . You're not the maid. What the hell do you want?"

The blond figure in a floor-length skirt and white knit blouse snugged over prominent breasts replied pleasantly, "No, Mrs. Brandt, I'm not the maid. Notice that I have in my hand a small but quite efficient automatic. Now, back into the room, and don't make any noise."

Lisa felt she must be dreaming all this. She was actually still asleep on the sofa, and this was one of those weird hallucinations that sometimes come in that state between wakefulness and slumber. It couldn't be real.

"Where is your money and your jewelry?" the intruder asked.

Lisa was relieved. Just a burglary. One of those slick gangs that specialize in robbing guests in expensive hotels. Well, they wouldn't get a lot. Just what she was wearing and a few things packed for the trip. "In the bedroom," she said.

"You first."

"What's a nice girl like you doing in a racket like this?" Lisa asked.

"On the bed. Facedown. Turn over, and I'll shoot you in the ass. Ruin your honeymoon."

Lisa obeyed. The thief carefully undid the clasp that held the diamond pendant necklace Lisa was wearing and slipped it from her throat, which was pressed into the ivory-and-blue coverlet on the king-size bed. "Where's your jewel box?"

"In the blue suitcase."

"Ah, yes, here it is. And what's this? The doctor's passport case? Well, well, look at all these traveler's checks. And cash. Reminds me, dear. I must go through your purse. And did I forget that lovely diamond watch you're wearing? Keep your face down! Now, I must run out to the other room for a sec, but don't move. I'd shoot you before you got to the window."

Lisa wasn't terribly frightened. She had heard that intelligent thieves abhorred violence, and this one was intelligent. It would make a good story for the papers, and something to tell her grandchildren. "Did you know that on her wedding day Grandma was robbed by a well-dressed lady with an automatic pistol? ..." The thief looked vaguely familiar, but then, robust blond women all looked more or less alike. She hadn't really taken a good look at this one—just noticed the rather conventional shoulder-length hair, a sort of Veronica Lake style obscuring half the face. Long eyelashes; she'd noticed that. Fakes. Careful, graceful walk, as if she'd been afraid of tripping over her long skirt. What color were the eyes? And the shape of the nose? Lisa caught her breath, Oh, no! It couldn't be! A hot terror grew in her like a mounting fever. She jerked herself upright, only to see the thief standing over her.

"So you know, you bitch," the blond intruder said, raising a fireplace poker.

Lisa screamed, and tried to shield herself with both hands.

"You bitch," the thief hissed at her, "I hate you! I hate you! I hate you! I hate your ..."

The poker crashed through Lisa's skull, severing her life from her body. The thief continued the savage battering for more than a minute; then, dropping the poker on the bed, quickly slipped out the door and left.

Eight

Randollph was having a good time. He had, at last, detached Samantha from her numberless dancing partners—actors, television actors, directors, producers, screenwriters, young doctors, business managers, investment specialists, vendors of malpractice insurance, disc jockeys, and every other profession likely to be found on the guest list of a physician-actress wedding. Now he held her with an authority that said, "Don't cut in." The departure of the bride and groom an hour or so ago hadn't dampened the celebration of their union. If anything, the party was more boisterous than ever.

"Con, dear boy, you've been neglecting me all afternoon," Sam Stack said.

"Nonsense, Sam, I couldn't get near you."

"I must be fair. You're right. I've had quite a day. I've had thirteen propositions—eleven from men, and two from girls. Three producers want to make me a movie star. One famous photographer would like to snap me in the nude.

Quite a day." She sighed happily. "Why don't you make it fourteen propositions? Thirteen's an unlucky number."

"O.K. When this soiree expires, may I escort you to dinner?"

"That's a proposition?"

Randollph guided her through a momentary opening so as to avoid a lone male who looked about to tap him on the shoulder. "Have you considered the price of a meal in a good restaurant?"

"I'll bet there was a time in your life, Con dear, when you were more explicit about it."

Randollph couldn't think of an appropriate reply.

"So," she went on, "you must have changed. Were you converted? Did you have an experience like St. Paul on the Damascus road, with a light from heaven knocking you down and the voice of Jesus telling you to shape up? I remember that from the pictures in the Sunday-school lessons. I was a Presbyterian before I became an agnostic."

"No."

"No, what?"

"No, I didn't have a Damascus-road experience."

"Then you didn't have a change of nature, like St. Paul? Like you are supposed to have if you want to be a true-blue Christian? What the hell am I talking about? This started out to be a conversation about propositions, and now we're discussing religious conversion."

"People don't change their natures, Sam, even though they sometimes imagine that they do. They change their values. And you started this line of conversation, I didn't." He saw Harmon Ballantine alone in the middle of the floor, looking more like a man wanting to be noticed than a dancer in search of a partner. Randollph steered Sammy the other way, though, just in case.

She snuggled closer. "Randollph, you are one complex guy, and I don't begin to understand you. Most of the guys

I go out with talk about TV business, or how their stocks are doing, or the big deal they just pulled off. Then they say, 'Hey, let's find a bed.' Here we are dancing, and you explain religious conversion to me, and I love it! And me, an agnostic."

Randollph chuckled. "It occurs to me, Samantha, that perhaps I've invented a new style of courtship. If it catches on, it will be known as the Randollph Approach, and I'll go down in history." He felt as good as he could remember feeling. He also felt a tap on his shoulder. "Go away," he said to the unseen intruder into his happiness. "I won't relinquish her."

"It's Sergeant Garboski, Con dear. You remember him? Mike Casey's crude minion. ... Hey, I'm beginning to talk like you . ... I don't think Garboski is asking to dance with me."

Randollph stopped dancing.

"The loot ... Lieutenant Casey'd like to talk to you," Garboski said. It came out as a hostile growl. If you weren't a policeman or Polish, Garboski looked on you as an enemy. Lieutenant Michael Casey, along with Garboski, had once investigated murder on the premises of the Church of the Good Shepherd. Randollph became friendly with Casey, but wondered if even God had trouble mustering affection for the sergeant. The last time he had seen Garboski, Randollph remembered, the weather had been cold and the sergeant had been wearing a purplish-brown suit without cut or contour, and a gray felt hat with sweat stains soaked above the band. Today he wore a gray seersucker suit, also without shape, and his light tan summer straw was already stained. Garboski's one virtue, he reflected, was that he helped keep alive the movie sterotype of the tough, crude cop.

"Where is the lieutenant?" Randollph asked.

"Upstairs. I'il show you."

"May Mrs. Stack accompany us?"

"I got no orders about that."

"Come along, Samantha," Randollph instructed. "If Lieutenant Casey wishes to see me alone, you can come back here."

"Now, just a minute," Garboski protested, "I got my—"

"Let's go, sergeant."

The sergeant went.

They took an elevator to the tenth floor. Once on the floor, it was apparent that something was happening. At the end of the hall a uniformed policeman was standing by a door. A man with a professional-looking camera was walking toward the elevator, along with another man carrying a doctor's bag. Randollph had an undefined sense of alarm, such as one has when keeping a dental appointment—he didn't know what was about to happen but was pretty certain that it would be unpleasant.

"In here." Garboski motioned to the door guarded by a policeman. "It's O.K., Dennis," he said to the young cop, "the loot sent for him." The cop looked questioningly at Sam but made no protest when she went in too.

Lieutenant Michael Casey did not look like a movie stereotype of a homicide cop. He looked, as always, more like a hot-shot junior executive headed for the top, Randollph thought. He wore a tan summer cord suit with a deep tan shirt and a maize-and-brown figured tie. Randollph would have laid a tidy bet that Casey's brown loafers encased the feet of brown over-the-calf hose.

"Dr. Randollph." Casey nodded. "Mrs. Stack, glad to see you again. I'm afraid I have some shocking news. That is, if you confirm what I think is the case, it'll be shocking to you. Dr. Randollph, I'd like you to make positive identification of a body."

"Oh!" Sam gasped. "Who?"

"There is very little doubt that it is Lisa Julian—Lisa Brandt."

"Oh, my God!" Sam crumpled into a chair. "Not Lisa. It couldn't be!"

"I'm afraid it is," Casey said gently. "But we haven't had positive identification."

Randollph was unable to sort out his feelings. Shock, to be sure. Confusion. A grinding awareness of incongruity—the day of joy turning into this day of sorrow. The celebration of life transformed into a ritual of death. But where was his feeling of grief? He felt nothing. It was as if his emotions had been temporarily deadened by a fast-acting drug. Never mind. Grief and sorrow would come when they would come, and they would be heavy and powerful. Of this he was certain.

"I assume your presence means that she was murdered," he said to Casey.

"That's right. Would you care to step into the bedroom and make the identification now?"

"Should I come too?" Sam asked in a small voice.

"I wouldn't forbid it, of course, but it isn't a pretty sight. It might be best if you remembered her as she was." Lieutenant Casey knew how to handle people too prominent to be shoved around—which was one of the reasons he was a lieutenant way ahead of normal seniority advancement, Randollph suspected. If you were rich or prominent and somebody shot your mother-in-law or strangled your maid, odds were that Michael Casey would turn up in charge of things. The Sergeant Garboskis could handle the scut work. They were good enough to deal with pimps, hookers, knife artists, heisters of gas stations, and the variegated assortment of cheap crooks who were always getting themselves knocked off. No tact or charm was required for processing the lower classes, because nobody cared if they were offended. But special provision has to be made for people with clout. An unsubtle word, an inept question, and the structure might be shaken all the way from the mayor down to detective third grade. A Michael Casey can eliminate many, many unpleasant moments from a police commissioner's life, contribute to the felicity of his marriage, and keep his ulcers from kicking up. That is why the Michael Caseys get to be lieutenants well ahead of their peers.

Casey led Randollph into the bedroom. Randollph looked at the girl in a wedding dress on the blood-spattered bed. He didn't want to look at her face, but he knew he had to. It was horribly mutilated. The nose was mush. Dark hair matted on top, as if saturated by mucilage. Crimson stains all over the dress. All the facial bones must have been fractured in many places. Casey had been right. It wasn't a pretty sight.

"That's Lisa. Lisa Julian," Randollph said, and turned away.

Nine

"I called on you because Dr. Brandt was incoherent,"
Lieutenant Casey explained to Randollph. "We had to
send him to a hospital."

They were back in the sitting room of the bridal suite.
Samantha Stack was huddled in a chair, crying quietly.

"How did you know I was on the premises?" Randollph
asked.

"Oh, we keep up with what is going on around town."
Casey smiled slightly. "This wedding has not been a well-
kept secret, you know. And anyway, Liz—my wife—was
talking about it at breakfast. 'That sexy-looking ex-jock
preacher friend of yours is going to officiate at Lisa Julian's
wedding,' she told me. 'Do you suppose he could slip me in
as a guest?' Liz is a big movie buff," he added, as if to
explain his wife's ridiculous request.

"I'd have been glad to slip her into a seat somewhere,"
Randollph said. What were they doing, he wondered,
chatting casually about Casey's wife, with Lisa battered and

dead? Perhaps in the midst of tragedy it was necessary to make small talk in order to hang on to a sense of reality. "Do you have any idea what happened, who did it?"

"Looks like robbery. Dr. Brandt was able to tell us, confused as he was, that he got a call from the Julian Clinic about a patient of his who'd taken a turn for the worse. But the call was a phony. The patient was O.K. When he got back—less than an hour it took him—his wife was on the bed in there as you saw her. All her jewelry is gone, and his money and traveler's checks."

"Do thieves usually go to the trouble of making a phone call to lure someone away from a room before burglarizing it? And do they murder anyone they find in the room?"

Casey, for all his urbanity, could not quite conceal the patronizing air of a theologian explaining a point of doctrine to a lay audience, Randollph noted. "Dr. Brandt was certain the phone call was arranged by one of his good friends having a little joke. It came through about three minutes after he and his wife arrived in their room, so I expect he's right. As I reconstruct it, the thief picked the lock, slipped into the room, and found Lisa Julian Brandt asleep on the bed. He picked up the poker to threaten her in case she woke up. While he was going through her suitcase, or taking the jewelry she may have been wearing, she woke up and started to scream. He panicked, and hit her with the poker."

"So many times? So brutally?"

Casey frowned. "I admit that's unusual. These hotel thieves, the real pros, are seldom violent. This could have been an amateur. Maybe a hotel employee. It doesn't quite fit the usual pattern, but I've seen about every possible combination of criminal behavior. If I had to make a guess, I'd say that we'll turn up a junkie busboy or kitchen worker who had to get money for a supply. He'd be pretty nervous, and would look for the nearest thing he could steal. It was just Lisa Julian's tough luck that he tried her room."

Samantha snuffled, then blew her nose. "Why'd it have to be Lisa?"

Casey half-smiled again. "My pastor at St. Aloysius would say that it was God's will," he said. "Or perhaps a punishment for sin."

"Your pastor is an old poop!" Samantha was coming out of her abject misery. "What sin?"

Casey looked a little taken aback. "Oh, he'd say that if there wasn't any obvious sin, then it was some secret, hidden sin."

Randollph thought it wise to interrupt a budding controversy between Roman Catholic and agnostic theology. Sam, he suspected, was near hysteria, and just might seize on any excuse to boil over. "That, if I remember correctly, was exactly the argument Bildad the Shuhite used on his friend Job," he said. "Job insisted that he hadn't sinned, and Bildad said, 'Oh yes you have, or you wouldn't be plagued by all these calamities.' " It suddenly occurred to Randollph that shortly he would be conducting the funeral service for Lisa Julian—just days after he had read her marriage ceremony. What was he going to say? He didn't know. But he knew what he wasn't going to say. He wasn't going to say it was God's will. He'd heard too many funeral sermons which proclaimed this simplistic theology. It was a cheap and easy way to justify tragedy, to answer the always-asked question, "Why me?" or "Why my husband or wife or child or father or mother?" Sometimes—often—the preacher attempted to comfort by adding, like an extra tranquilizer, the thought that the deceased had been translated to a better world, a happier existence. Randollph considered this blasphemous and a cruel hoax. He admitted that he had no final answers for the problem of evil. But he knew that this was not a world in which the virtuous prosper without fail and the guilty always suffer. Nor was a putative celestial bliss an adequate solution to the nagging questions of injustice and tragedy and defeat, the manifest unfairness in which our earthly portion is sliced and dished out. God didn't run things like a Sunday-school-attendance contest with gold stars for the winners. Being extra pious didn't buy you a free ride, or an exemption from the slings and arrows of outrageous fortune. Nor did blatant and persistent sinners necessarily get blasted by a divine zap. True, evil usually produced evil. If Casey's reconstruction of Lisa's murder was correct, then the evil began with the evil men who purveyed drugs for profit, and continued in the drug-sodden personality of the anonymous junkie who cared nothing about inflicting suffering on others, so long as his craving could be quieted. Lisa, then, was the fortuitous victim of an unselective evil. To call it God's will was to call God a dirty name.

"I think," he suggested to Casey, "that you might advise your pastor to read the Book of Job again."

Casey seemed genuinely shocked. "A mere layman does not criticize, even indirectly, his priest's theological views—at least, not my priest at St. Aloysius. He's a crusty old Irishman who thinks the church should stick to preaching about mass duty, condemning birth control, and promoting bingo, and lay off all that theological stuff, which only confuses a good Catholic's mind. Liz, my wife, agrees with you, Mrs. Stack, that he's an old poop." Casey, Randollph could see, was tactfully trying to divert Sam's mind from Lisa's murder.

"Then why do you put up with him?" She was continuing conversation in which she could have little interest, because it kept her from thinking of the horror in the next room.

There was a knock on the door; then a man in white pushed it open. Separating him like a hyphen from another man in white was a sheet-covered cart. "Ready for us, Mike?" the first man asked.

"It's all yours. In there." Casey motioned toward the bedroom. Randollph glanced at his watch and was surprised at how little time had passed since he and Samantha had arrived.

"I'd better be seeing the family," he said, rising.

"Has the family been notified?"

Casey got up also. "Dr. Rex Julian has been told. He was at home. Dr. Kermit and his wife left the hotel before we could get to him, and no one knows where they are. But we have been unable to locate Dr. Valorous."

"From his condition the last time I saw him, he's probably asleep under a table somewhere," Randollph said.

"We'll look around," Casey said.

Downstairs again, Randollph told Sam that he'd just taken a look to see if Dr. Val had wandered back to the reception.

"I'll wait here," she said. "I couldn't bear to go back to that party."

The reception was shrinking, he saw. People had left for early dinner engagements. Assignations had no doubt been arranged and were being kept. The pace of the party had abated somewhat, presaging an imminent breakup of festivities. Randollph was a neophyte at conducting weddings, but a veteran at assessing the state of a social gathering. This one would peter out in about half an hour, he estimated. There were going to be some shocked guests when they discovered that they had been dancing in honor of a bride already dead. He returned to the lobby.

"He's not there," he reported to Sam. "Neither is Dan. I'll need to see Carl Brandt and Dr. Rex Julian. I'll take you home."

Outside, the tides of life were flowing, untouched by the recently interrupted life in the hotel. Cars pulled up and emptied into the hotel, early diners headed for their choice of the Drake's restaurants. The bride and groom from another wedding reception were hurrying to a much-festooned white Ford LTD, the bride clutching her bouquet in one hand and her long skirt in the other, and both ducking the gentle buckshot of tossed rice. Randollph guessed that an experienced staff and a discreet Lieutenant Casey had handled the details of the Lisa Brandt murder so unobtrusively that almost no one noticed anything unusual going on. But what difference would it make, he asked himself, if he should step over to the white LTD, gaudy with paper streamers, and say, "I think you should know that another bride was brutally murdered this afternoon right here in the bridal suite"? Would they be shocked and saddened? Or would the bride say, "Well, thank God it wasn't me"? What if he announced the murder to the people swarming toward the restaurants? Would they pause to weep for the passing of a lovely young woman, a fellow human being? More likely they would say, "That's tough, buddy, but I'm hungry," and hurry on.

"Taxi, sir?" The doorman's polite question brought Randollph out of his maudlin reverie.

"Please. I'll drop you at your apartment, Samantha, then go and make my calls."

Inside the cab, Sam said, "Hold me. Just hold me."

Randollph held her.

She pressed her face into Randollph's shoulder and sobbed. As the taxi neared her apartment, her sobs tapered off to snuffles. She sat up and swiped at her eyes with a lacy handkerchief.

"I'm afraid I've soaked your beautiful jacket, C.P.," she said.

"A small price for the privilege of your head on my shoulder."

"Now that was sweet, real sweet." Sam again put her head on his shoulder. "Now, here's my program for the evening. First, I'm not going to sit alone with my thoughts in that apartment."

"Maybe you could go to work," Randollph suggested.

"On Saturday? Have you ever been around a studio on Saturday night? It's like a morgue. Oh!" She clapped her hand over her mouth. "Why did I say that?"

"You could come with me," Randollph said hastily. "Or you could wait here while I make my calls."

"Thanks, doc," Sammy replied, "but too much waiting around with my thoughts. I think I'm going to get drunk."

"Oh?"

"Don't be shocked. I haven't been drunk in ages. And I don't much like the feeling. But I just can't handle this . . . this . . . thing tonight. There's a nice little bar just across the corner from my place. Studio people and neighborhood people I know hang out there. That's where I'm going right now. When you get done with your calls, you come for me there. I'll probably be pretty well swacked by that time. Then you walk me or carry me home, as the situation requires." She blew her nose, then opened the door of the cab. "And that's an order."

"Yes, ma'am," Randollph said. He kissed her gently and helped her out of the cab.

Randollph decided he'd better change clothes before he sought out Dr. Brandt and Dr. Julian. Back in the penthouse parsonage, he paused for a moment to look out of the enormous glass sides of the living room, which was half of the octagon-shaped lower floor. Normally the stunning view of the city and the inland sea which bounded it escalated his spirits and soothed the abrasions of the day. But not this afternoon. The juxtaposition of man's cleverness and nature's awesome accomplishment, ordinarily so pleasing to sight and imagination, offered no solace. It was as if God had temporarily absented himself from his creation, taking with Him the sense of unity and glory Randollph always felt when he looked upon it. The world was out of round today.

He climbed the corkscrew stairway with open treads to the bedroom level, suddenly realizing how weary he was. The master bedroom, which Dan Gantry said looked "like a high-class whorehouse," was carpeted in expensive soft gold and contained an oversized bed, a moss-green sofa and coffee table, two easy chairs upholstered in white with a design worked in gold thread, and plenty of empty space. Randollph pushed a sliding door and fingered through his suits to find something appropriate. He'd thought of going in what he was wearing, but decided that it would be too reminiscent of the brief happiness before the tragedy. He selected a plain black lightweight worsted with just a touch of jauntiness in the cut. With a gray shirt and a dark gray tie with a subdued design of white and red, the black suit would be sober but not funereal. This would be the third costume of his working day, each one symbolic of his roles. Clericals for the priest at the wedding. Dinner jacket for the guest at the reception. Tasteful mufti for the pastor-comforter. Clerical garb would have been in order for the pastor-comforter, he knew. But, until coming to Good Shepherd he hardly ever wore it, and wasn't quite at ease in it. Clericals made him feel so official.

The green phone on the table beside the bed uttered a soft buzzing summons. Randollph thought of ignoring it, but habit or a sense of duty insisted that he answer it.

"C.P., I just heard about it on the news." The bishop's

voice struck a note of troubled sympathy. "What a terrible, terrible thing."

"So it was, Freddie. I probably haven't fully assimilated it yet."

"Can I help?"

Randollph thought a moment, then said, "You might tell me how to make a pastoral call on Dr. Brandt and Dr. Rex Julian. I've never done anything like this before, you know."

"C.P., would you think it an intrusion if I accompanied you to Rex Julian's? He's an old friend, I should see him. It might make it a little easier for you."

Randollph believed in shouldering his own responsibilities, but the relief he felt at the bishop's offer told him how much he had been dreading the call on Lisa's father. "Freddie, I consider your suggestion as inspired by a beneficent providence. Give me time for a quick shower, and I'll meet you in the lobby—say, fifteen minutes."

The Julian Clinic-Hospital was a few blocks north of the Loop, not far from the lake. The area bristled with hospitals, a medical school, and office buildings which, Randollph guessed, housed an extraordinary number of medical doctors.

"I don't know Dr. Brandt," the bishop said, "so you'll have to go it alone here. I'll come in and wait in the lobby. I brought along a report to read. Rather unpleasant reading, I'm afraid. The executive secretary of one of our national denominational boards, it seems, has been investing board funds in a land-development scheme."

"Is that illegal?"

"Not so far as I know. Unwise and unsavory, though. Seems the chap is a major stockholder in the land company."

"What can you do about it?" Randollph paid the cab-driver. He wasn't much interested in the sleazy business practices of a fellow clergyman whom he didn't even know, but realized that the bishop was indulging in shop talk to take his mind off the gloomy nature of the impending call.

"The fellow's quite pious about it. Claims he was just trying to make a little extra money for the Lord. We'll probably find him a good church to pastor. He won't like that one bit, but he'll just have to lump it. Slow down, C.P., my legs aren't as long as yours."

"Why won't he like it, Freddie? You keep telling me that being a pastor is the most rewarding of jobs."

"So it is. But these church bureaucrats get so they like the freedom from regular preaching, and from the annoyance of dealing with parishioners—not to mention their good salaries and expense accounts. They all protest that they'd really like to be back in the pastorate, it's kind of a ritual. But when they have to go, they scream bloody murder—oh, I'm·sorry, that was an unfortunate choice of words."

Randollph opened the glass door for the bishop. "Freddie, I think you're a bit of a fraud. How long has it been since you were a pastor?"

The bishop looked around the hospital lobby, then made for a comfortable-looking chair. "Let me see," he said. "I began teaching at the seminary, hmm, I taught for seven years, then was dean for ten years, and I've been a bishop for six years. Oh, my, that's twenty-three years, isn't it?" He sat down and unzipped a blue vinyl paper carrier. "You may be right. I keep talking about how happy I'd be if I could go back to the pastorate, but I wonder if I really would want to." He unsheathed a pair of half-moon reading glasses from a soft leather case. "Run along, now, and make your call."

"Dr. Brandt? That would be the hospital wing. This is

the clinic. If you'll go down those steps there and turn right, you'll come out at the hospital information desk." The pretty receptionist gave Randollph a smile which said "So glad I could help you." He supposed it was important for a profit-making medical institution to do everything it could to make the customers happy.

The hospital receptionist was also friendly. "Room 431," she said, "although he's not supposed to have visitors."

"I'm his pastor," Randollph told her. It was stretching a point. For all he knew, Carl Brandt was a Seventh-Day Adventist or a disciple of Guru Maharaj-ji.

"Oh, that's different." She turned on a smile. "Check with the desk on four."

The Julian Clinic-Hospital was larger than Randollph had expected it to be. The hospital had seven floors, and the clinic wing matched it. He hadn't counted the posted list of doctors, but had estimated it to be forty or so. A full partnership in what was obviously a going business must produce a most respectable annual income, he guessed, not including all the tax dodges available to a medical doctor. He wondered if Dr. Rex Julian would withdraw the wedding present of a full partnership in the clinic, now that Dr. Brandt was a widower, the marriage presumably unconsummated. Probably not. Dr. Julian had told Randollph he approved of the marriage and his son-in-law. Probably, too, the partnership had been legalized before the wedding, and Dr. Brandt—grief-stricken though he was—would not let his tears blind him to his own best interests.

Leaving the elevator at the fourth floor, Randollph thought the hospital unnaturally quiet. A woman who must have been six feet tall and two hundred and fifty pounds pushed a stainless-steel hot cart along the hall, stopped, and carried a covered tray into a room. Three nurses, apparently going off duty, waited to get on the elevator, talking in a subdued twitter. They showed no interest in Randollph.

The nurse at the desk was not so public-relations oriented as the receptionists downstairs.

"You from the police?" It was more of an accusation than a question. "I told whoever called that Dr. Brandt's under sedation and can't talk to anyone tonight." Her makeup and skin texture put her down as fifty trying to look forty.

He tried a smile on her. "I'm not a policeman. I'm Dr. Brandt's pastor." He had noticed, in his short time as temporary helmsman of the Church of the Good Shepherd, that when people discovered he was a pastor there was usually a perceptible shift in their attitude toward him. Not to deference. More like a wary respect. At the least, it bought a little extra consideration.

But not with this nurse.

"I don't care if you're the pope," she snapped, "you can't see him tonight."

"I wasn't insisting." Randollph spoke gently. "I just want him to know that I'm concerned. Will you see that he gets this?" He handed her his card. "And tell him I'll see him as soon as he is ready to receive visitors."

The nurse, expecting to defend her ultimatum, perhaps needing to do battle in order to work off the tensions of a demanding day, was flustered. "Oh. Ah. Yes. Yes, I'll tell him, reverend." She turned to file the card. Randollph was reminded of a maxim he'd picked up in seminary: Be kind to those that despitefully use you, because it will drive them nuts. He was also chagrined at the relief he felt to have escaped, however briefly, a pastoral duty he dreaded.

"There's no way to instruct anyone on being a pastor to a family victimized by a senseless tragedy." The bishop shifted his plump bottom into the corner of the taxi. "It's hard enough when a child has been killed, or a young wife has died of cancer. Most people in such situations are stunned by what has happened to them. They wonder why it had to happen to them."

"Yes, I know," Randollph said. "Lieutenant Casey and I were discussing it this afternoon."

"How is the lieutenant? Dapper and well-spoken as ever? He's a bright lad. I look for him to be the youngest police commissioner in the history of Chicago."

"We're pretty good friends. He drops by the office now and then. He likes to practice his Roman Catholic theology on me."

"Oh? Maritain, or the like, I presume. Or maybe even Hans Kung?"

"He doesn't let me forget that he's a college man, not just a dumb cop," Randollph answered.

The taxi picked its way around a couple of double-parked cars, then shot off for North Michigan Avenue. The bishop picked up the threads of his lecture. "As I was saying, in the case of untimely death, the family is stunned and grief-stricken, but they know these things happen. For them, it has always happened to the other fellow till now. However difficult it is for them, they have some basis for making an adjustment. But in this case, I don't know. There's the violence, the brutality, the utter pointlessness of it—except to the murderer, of course. I heard on the radio that the police believe the murder was incidental to a burglary."

"That's Lieutenant Casey's guess. He doesn't commit himself, of course. Casey believes that crimes are solved by patient collection of facts which, when assembled, construct a hypothesis that leads to the right answer."

"The inductive method," the bishop said. "I don't know why Conan Doyle called it deduction. Sherlock Holmes was too keen to make a mistake like that."

"Casey thinks he's likely to turn up a drug addict who for some reason chose Lisa's room to rob."

"No matter," said the bishop. "It was brutal and sense-

less, and apparently just bad luck that Lisa was the victim.
That's hard for the family to adjust to, if I may end a
sentence with a preposition."

"Then what do we say to them?"

"As little as possible. The mistake most pastors make at a
time like this is to talk too much. They get started with a
few words of sympathy, then feel something more is needed,
so they branch off into the theology of evil, or make inane
remarks about how things could be worse. Better they
should have stayed at home."

"My situation is somewhat unique," Randollph said.
"Did you know that during my football days Lisa and I
were good friends?"

The bishop eyed him speculatively. "No, I didn't know
that. How good friends were you? No, I withdraw the
question. It's none of my business. Did it make the wedding
a little awkward for you?"

"A little." Randollph squirmed uncomfortably against the
cracked plastic seat. "She was more attached to me than I
was to her, although I did write her some letters which, if
my memory is accurate, were, ah, quite affectionate. I hope
she had the good sense to destroy them."

The bishop sighed and rubbed his eyes. "I wouldn't count
on it. Women have a way of tucking away things that are
precious to them. Just be grateful that your past indiscretions are forgiven and can't be held against you."

"I know that, Freddie. But they can embarrass me.
However, that's a problem of no consequence. I hadn't seen
Lisa for years. And she assured me that she had fully
recovered from whatever feelings of attachment she had had
for me."

The bishop chuckled. "I don't mean to make light of
your discomfort, C.P., but an errant thought just came to
me."

"Oh?"

"I was a very proper Christian as a young man, full of rectitude and moral probity. On reflection, I must have been a bit of a prig. I am afraid that other parents pointed me out to their fractious offspring and said, 'Why can't you be like young Fred?' I was the kind of boy who surprises no one when he chooses the cloth. But it just occurred to me that someone like you, with a history of a misspent youth, is really better equipped than I am to deal with the messes people get themselves into. It is unlikely that you would ever be censorious. It is likely that you would naturally have empathy for a sinner, where it would not be natural for me. I wonder what would happen if I suggested this idea the next time I address a group of seminarians? Would the papers come out with headlines: 'BISHOP ADVISES SEMINARIANS TO SOW A FEW WILD OATS'?" He chuckled again. "Of course, I won't do any such thing. Now, when we get to the Julians . . ."

The sun, like a tired swimmer about to give up, was sinking into the lake. The night, held at bay by daylight saving time, would soon blot up what was left of the natural light. Residents of the Gold Coast's luxury apartments who had been sunbathing or enjoying strolling along the beach were scuttling like rabbits to their expensive hutches, aware that with the dark would come their natural enemies, the muggers and the rapists.

The taxi abandoned Lakeshore Drive for a street that admitted it to the driveway of one of the newer apartment buildings, a slab of concrete and glass. An unctuous doorman ushered Randollph and the bishop out of the cab and into the foyer, which, Randollph noted, was decorated in a kind of chintzy elegance. After a brief phone call, the doorman put them on an elevator, his duties performed.

A young black maid in uniform let them into the Rexford Julian apartment. It was elegant without any chintziness

whatever. Randollph didn't know much about rugs, but
he'd have been willing to bet that the red-and-blue Chinese
in the large foyer was worth the bishop's not ungenerous
annual salary. His quick appraisal of the ballroom-dimen-
sioned living room included more orientals carpeting a
shining parquet floor, and what he took to be replicas of
French period furniture—maybe Louis XVI. The glass wall
framed the lake, which was listlessly flicking a few red-
orange splotches from the dying sun at the oncoming
darkness.

Dr. Rex Julian sat in a chair large as a throne. To his left
were Mrs. Rex Julian, Dr. Kermit Julian and his wife, then
Dr. Valorous Julian, who was leaning his chin on one hand
and nursing a cup of coffee with the other. To Dr. Rex
Julian's right, sitting on a spindly-looking sofa, was a thick-
set man of about fifty, wearing a bold plaid suit. With that
hefty build he ought to lay off plaids, Randollph thought.
Beside him was an overdressed blond woman perhaps ten
years younger. Randollph had never seen either of them. He
was surprised to see, sitting opposite Dr. Rex, Lieutenant
Michael Casey.

The bishop went immediately to Dr. Rexford Julian,
grasped his hand, but said nothing. Either a powerful will or
much experience restrained him from speaking, from even
muttering the pious banalities which clerics keep on tap for
comforting the bereaved. Silence, Randollph realized, is
awesome in a situation like this. Since it is a clergyman's
business to say something appropriate to the occasion, it is
difficult for him to shut up.

But Freddie's prolonged handshake was all that was
necessary, Randollph saw. After a moment the old doctor
spoke.

"It is good of you to come, bishop." Then, turning to
Randollph, who had thought it best to follow and emulate
the bishop, "and you, too, Dr. Randollph." The old man's

face was grim, but then, Randollph thought, it always was.

"You know my wife." Dr. Rex was introducing the bishop to the others. "My son Kermit and his wife. My son Valorous. Mr. and Mrs. Edelman, our neighbors. And Lieutenant Casey of the police."

"I know Lieutenant Casey," the bishop said.

Silence.

The quiet grew gradually more painful, like an old-fashioned dentist's drill working its way carefully toward the nerve. What was there to say? Randollph wondered. How do you speak of the unspeakable?

Suddenly the Edelmans, perhaps unable to bear the quiet any longer, stood up and began talking.

"We'd better be going," they said in unison. Then Mrs. Edelman minced over to Mrs. Rex Julian and chattered at her in an inaudible whisper.

"Got a dinner date, you know," Mr. Edelman announced with the false cheerfulness of a child submitting a dubious excuse to the school principal. Randollph thought the fellow might as well have announced that he was anxious to get out of this morgue and back to the land of bourbon on the rocks and sixteen-ounce sirloins.

"What awful people," Mrs. Rex Julian said when the door closed. "Lieutenant Casey, could you take up your business with us now and get it over with? We'd like to be alone as a family."

"Now, Mother, don't be rude." Dr. Valorous Julian put his coffeecup on a fragile-looking end table. "The lieutenant was good enough to find me and bring me home—'help me home' is more accurate. He found me passed out under a table at another wedding reception." He grinned weakly. "I'm probably still drunk. A shocked, wide-awake drunk." He leaned back and shut his eyes. Randollph thought he looked like death itself.

"I'm glad to be of help," Casey said, a diplomatic rebuke

to Mrs. Rex Julian's rudeness. "I thought that while I was here anyway, I would report to you that we expect it will turn out Lisa was the victim of a robber, probably a drug addict. All money and jewelry in the room were taken. We have arrested a hotel employee, an addict with a record of this kind of burglary."

"If the police would pay more attention to putting these vicious criminals in jail and quit . . ." Mrs. Julian searched for some nefarious or at least superfluous activity favored by the police, and failed. "Goodness knows we pay enough taxes to protect us against hooligans."

"Yes, I know. It's a persistent problem." Casey smoothly defused her irritation. "We don't know, of course, that this is what happened. We have to cover all possibilities. Might I ask if, to your knowledge, Lisa had any enemies? Anyone angry enough to do this thing?" Randollph noticed that, like a mortician, Casey employed euphemisms for "murder' and "death."

"Look among her ex-boyfriends," Mrs. Rex Julian snapped. "She had plenty of 'em."

"Mother!" Val spoke sharply. "The family knows you weren't too crazy about Lisa. But you don't need to announce it to the world."

Casey again smoothed over a contentious situation. "We always evaluate that kind of information when the situation warrants it." He stood up. "I'm sorry to intrude on your bereavement. I want to express my sympathy to you." Casey, Randollph decided, would have made a good pastor. He, too, knew when not to talk too much.

"Thanks, lieutenant, thanks for getting me home in one piece. Although, the way I feel now, I wish I'd never wakened." Val rose wearily and walked to the door with Casey.

As soon as Val returned to his seat the bishop said, "Would you permit me to say a prayer?"

"Please do," Dr. Rex Julian said.

The bishop pulled a thin black book from a side pocket of his jacket and opened it to a page marked by a purple ribbon.

"Let us pray," he said. "Almighty God, who art eternal and knowest not death, hear now our prayer for these thy servants who are bowed down with sorrow. We give thanks for the life of their loved one, now departed. We are glad for the years that were hers, for her accomplishments, and for the joys life bestowed on her. Preserve the precious memories. In the midst of our sadness, give us the strength to return to the duties of life with earnest purpose. And make us to know that the eternal God is our refuge and strength, an ever-present help in this and all other tribulations in this transient life. Through Jesus Christ our Lord. Amen."

Ten

It promised to be a difficult Sunday.

"You'd best post extra ushers tomorrow," the bishop suggested on their way back from the Julians'. "There'll be hordes of tourists swarming round the church after they read the stories in the morning papers. Better instruct the ushers to prohibit cameras in the church, or you'll think you're being attacked by a plague of lightning bugs."

Randollph called the bar where Sam Stack said she'd be waiting and had her paged.

"I'll be there in an hour or so," he told her.

"You should hurry, Randollph," Sam replied in a slightly thickened speech. "Another hour, and all my defenses'll be so relaxed, one of these barstool cowboys might take advantage of me."

"I'll hurry," he said.

He tracked down the head usher and gave him instructions. Then he went through his sermon manuscript and excised all humorous passages. Tomorrow would be no time for levity. Finally, he called Tony Agostino and asked him to change the listed anthem, a lighthearted, joyful number, to something more stately.

"I'll pull out an old one, something we can get ready with a couple of run-throughs tomorrow morning," Tony assured him.

Sunday was worse than the bishop had predicted.

Though the augmented crew of ushers strove valiantly, a number of camera-toting tourists managed to get in. Randollph could see from the chancel that the congregation was speckled with bright sport shirts and vividly colored casual summer dresses. Not that he cared how people dressed for church. But these people were here to gawk rather than to pray, a conviction strengthened by the incessant winking of flashbulbs.

After the service he was besieged by petitioners for his picture.

"Stand right there, reverend, will ya? This'll only take a minute."

"Would ja pose with my little girl, so when she grows up she can say I got my picture took with the preacher that married the actress dame that got beat to death."

"Go stand in front of that whatchamacallit, the altar, just like you did when you married the dead lady, reverend, so's I can get a picture."

Randollph, whose success as a professional quarterback he attributed partly to his ability to remain calm under provocation, was furious. He wanted to slug these miserable excuses for human beings. He wanted to draw blood. When one extremely fat man in a Hawaiian shirt and straw hat yelled, "Hey, reverint, papers say you saw her right after she was kilt, was she a real bloody mess?" he almost took after the fellow. But between polite refusals to be photographed ("I don't think that would be appropriate") he kept saying to himself, "God loves these people" ... "Christ died for that fat idiot." It helped.

On Monday Randollph was reminded of the bishop's prayer: "In the midst of our sadness, give us the strength to return to the duties of life with earnest purpose." Many parish clergymen, he knew, took Monday as their day off—probably on the theory that the postpartum depression occasioned by delivering the word of the Lord on Sunday incapacitated them temporarily for creative pastoring. But he wanted to sink himself in work, as if it would somehow banish Saturday's demons. He would be glad for mountains of trivial tasks. he would even welcome the normally loathed paperwork Miss Windfall usually heaped upon him.

The one thing he didn't want to do was work on a sermon.

During his first few weeks at Good Shepherd he had been almost dismayed at the rapidity with which Sunday came round and, whether ready or not, he had to stand up before a thousand or so people and be edifying and inspiring. He was accustomed to the less-structured ambience of the classroom, in which he lectured on material with which he was thoroughly conversant. He hardly needed notes.

But sermons were different. Granted, most of his congregation was new every Sunday. That was one of the peculiarities of Good Shepherd's unique situation. People came because it was a famous church; because it was convenient to their hotels and was advertised in the hotel lobbies; because it had a noted organist and an excellent choir made up of professional voices; because back home, in Great Bend, or Bucyrus, or Evansville, they customarily went to church on Sunday morning, and they came out of habit; or because they wanted to cram every waking minute of their trip to Chicago with a new experience.

Hardly anyone came especially to hear a sermon. They

might hope that it would be a good sermon. They might even assume that a large and fancy church would refuse to hire a pastor who was not an outstanding preacher, unaware as they were that persuasive and prophetic preaching had little to do with advancement in the clerical profession. But, unlike the parishioners in a normal congregation, they didn't come to hear a good sermon and would not be distressed if they heard a bad one. They would take their worship bulletins to their home pastors and say, "See, we went to the Church of the Good Shepherd last Sunday."

The bishop had explained all this when he had asked Randollph to come to Good Shepherd as interim pastor and was seeking to make him comfortable with the idea of preaching every Sunday. But, perhaps because of his years with the Rams, Randollph had a professional concept of his job. To a professional, it didn't make any difference if the crowd appreciated the way he did his job or not. What mattered was that he was satisfied that he did the best that it was in him to do.

So he attacked the job of preaching with professional techniques. He laid out a preaching program for the entire year of his incumbency, organizing it around the Christian calendar. That way, he knew what was coming up and he could store up ideas and illustrations for future sermons. Then, each Monday, he would write an outline for next Sunday's sermon. After that, each day of the week he filled in the outline until he had what he hoped was twenty minutes of exposition worth hearing.

He was grateful when Miss Windfall buzzed him on the intercom. She no doubt had some tedious, boring task to lay on him. Normally he would search for excuses to postpone it, thus earning Miss Windfall's chilly disapproval. But today, any ennui-producing drudgery would be welcome.

"There is a person here who claims you wish to see him," Miss Windfall informed him in her expressionless office voice. "He says his name is Higbee, Clarence Higbee."

Randollph had learned to translate what Miss Windfall said into what she meant. She was actually saying, "A man who does not present the appearance of an upper-middle-class citizen, who is definitely not from the level of society which we find acceptable at the Church of the Good Shepherd, is pestering me to see the pastor. Since dubious characters of one kind and another frequently intrude on the pastor's time, I will be glad to shoo him out if the pastor wishes. In fact, I recommend it."

But who was Clarence Higbee? Randollph searched his memory for a moment before it came to him.

"Yes, Miss Windfall, I wish to see Mr. Higbee. Please send him in." It pleased him to picture Miss Windfall's vexation over having her judgment rejected.

Clarance Higbee was like nothing Randollph had ever seen.

He was small. Five-three at most, Randollph estimated. His black suit of ancient British cut had a greenish cast. But he was neat. His white shirt was freshly laundered. The old suit was pressed. His black high-vamp shoes of a style Randollph remembered as similar to that favored by his grandfather, sparkled in the light of the study chandelier.

Clarence Higbee was completely bald. His skin, burned by countless suns and lashed by wind and rain off the world's various seas, had the appearance of old mellow leather. He could easily pass as an Asian, Randollph thought, except for the bright blue eyes.

Clarence Higbee, in a stiff, respectful way, appeared quite at ease. "The employment agency informed me that you are in need of a cook, sir." It was a clipped, correct accent, not quite Oxbridge, but with none of the nuances peculiar to what the British referred to as the serving classes, although the "sir" came through to Randollph's ear as "sor."

"Indeed I am!" Randollph, startled by the sum total of

Clarence Higbee, managed to reply with what he hoped was sufficient enthusiasm. He noticed that Higbee's feet, even though he sat on the edge of the big lounge chair, barely touched the floor.

"I'm a very good cook, sir." Higbee spoke with the quiet pride of the artisan. "I've been a chef on ships of many nations, so I have mastered numerous cuisines. I've been in the kitchen of Mirabelle in London and the Ritz in Paris, not to mention the gentry I've served as butler and major-domo. I know wines—"

Randollph held up his hand to halt this culinary biography. "I have no doubt that you are more than qualified, Mr. Higbee. The question is, would you be satisfied to cook for a single man who probably hasn't the palate to appreciate your art?"

Higbee, for the first time, smiled slightly. "If the situation is congenial, sir. And palates can be educated."

Randollph was anxious to end what he considered the hardship of going out for breakfast, and the necessity of eating every meal in a restaurant or relying on his own sketchy endeavors with the skillet. "If you're willing to give it a try, Mr. Higbee, I'd be pleased if you'd accept the position. Your compensation, as indicated by the employment agency, is satisfactory to me. And you'll like the living accommodations, I'm sure."

"Oh, yes, sir. I've never served in a penthouse. That's one of the attractions of the position. I welcome new experiences." But, Randollph noticed, he fidgeted, as if something was bothering him.

"Are there questions you have about the position?" he asked the little man.

Higbee seemed relieved. "There's a question I feel I must ask."

"Ask it."

"Perhaps I should explain that I was an orphan," Higbee

said. "I was born a cockney, within the sound of Bow Bells, so to speak. At an early age I was put in a C-of-E orphanage—that's Church of England."

"I know."

"Of course, you would, sir. You being a gentleman of the cloth. The orphanage was strict, but the fathers were kind. They gave me an education. When I expressed an interest in becoming a chef, they saw to it that I received the basic training. They taught us the manners and accent of the upper classes. Accent is very important in England. You can see, sir, that I owe my chance in life to the Church of England. My loyalty to it is most intense."

Randollph was puzzled. "I find that attitude most commendable. But how does it create a problem?"

Clarence Higbee squirmed around in the oversize chair as if no position quite suited him. "It's this, sir. Never having been in the employment of a gentleman of the cloth, I'm wondering if I'd be expected to attend services at your church?"

Randollph almost laughed, then saw that the leathery little man was serious. "No, of course not, Mr. Higbee. Compelling employees of the church to support the church would constitute an abridgment of the freedom of religion. As a matter of fact, our organist-choirmaster is a Roman Catholic. I wish to employ you for your skills, not your theology."

Higbee appeared greatly relieved. "I'm a churchgoing man, sir, make no mistake about that. And it's not just my gratitude for all the C of E did for me." He rose to go. "Of course, here I have to make do with the Protestant Episcopal. It's the nearest thing, if you avoid the parishes with a rector who goes in for folk masses and guitar players. I regard the Church of England as the one true church, sir. But I wish you to know that I hold no prejudices against those who do not adhere to it."

Like an answered prayer, Randollph's day was so full of
the office traffic normal to the life of a city pastor that he
had no opportunity to brood about Lisa Julian.

Clarence Higbee was followed by a Mr. Edgar Otis,
whom Miss Windfall identified as a member of Good
Shepherd, but in a tone of voice which said that while Otis
was perfectly respectable, he did not belong to the class of
people who, in Miss Windfall's view, actually owned the
church.

Otis, who was probably about forty-five years old, Randollph decided, looked to be in his fifties. He had brown
hair, thinning on top, and blinked at Randollph from
behind extra-thick lenses set in conventional half-plastic,
half-metal frames. A dark brown suit of above-average
quality conveyed an impression of conservative prosperity.
But he shouldn't wear a white shirt, Randollph thought.
White made him look pasty.

Randollph got him seated on the sofa and took a chair
for himself. "I'm happy to meet one of our members," he
said, to put the man at ease. "I'm afraid that the peculiar
nature of this church makes it difficult to get acquainted
with very many members of our congregation."

"I know that, Dr. Randollph." Otis was trying to be
hearty, but underneath, Randollph sensed an anxious spirit.
"My wife and I have heard every sermon you've preached
since you've been here. We live in Glenview, but we think
it's worth the trip in, just to hear you. Of course, we were
both raised in this church." He said it half-apologetically, as
if it took away from the value of faithful attendance on
Randollph's sermons.

"I appreciate your favorable opinion of my sermons."
What did the man want? Randollph wondered. A problem
with his wife? Unlikely. It was wives who came to talk
about marital difficulties, Randollph had discovered. Husbands were too proud to admit that they couldn't handle

their emotional problems. Perhaps someday a man would come in and say, "My marriage is falling apart, help me." But it hadn't happened to him yet. Maybe there was trouble with a child, a son or daughter on drugs, or a generation gap through which communication was blurred and uncertain. But in that case it would have been normal for the wife to come, too. He gave up guessing and asked, "What is your work, Mr. Otis?"

Otis relaxed immediately. "That's what I've come to talk to you about." Then it all came out, like a tapped gusher. "I'm an electrical engineer, a good one, and until six months ago I was head engineer for an appliance-manufacturing company. We were bought by a German firm, and in the consolidation a lot of us lost our jobs. I can't find another job. They want younger men, and I'm at the end of my resources, I'm desperate!" Edgar Otis put his face in his hands and broke into great snorting sobs.

Randollph was embarrassed, and ashamed of his embarrassment. There was no reason why a man shouldn't cry. It just took some getting used to. He supposed that veteran pastors learned how to deal with it.

When Edgar Otis' heaving sobs trailed off to hiccuping whimpers, Randollph went to his desk drawer, where he kept a box of tissues. Freddie had told him never to be without Kleenex handy, and Freddie had been right.

Edgar Otis took a tissue, blew his nose, and said, "I'm sorry. I've been carrying this around so long, I guess I just had to let it out."

"Good that you were able to." Randollph tried to sound reassuring.

"It's just that I've never had to deal with anything like this. I got ahead rapidly in the company. I'm not boasting, but I'm very good at my job."

"I'm sure that you are," Randollph murmured.

"Well, these Germans"—Otis said "Germans" almost ven-

omously—"they put their own people in as department
heads."

"Unfortunate."

"What I don't understand, I'm a good Christian. My wife
and I, we live a Christian life. We go to church. I don't
cheat on her, never have. We pay to the church. Not tithe,
exactly . . ." He paused, perhaps considering if this was the
chink in his armor of righteousness, the overlooked vul-
nerability through which the Lord had smitten him. "But I
don't do anything bad. So why does God let this happen to
me?" He settled back in the sofa, confident that he had
scored an uncontestable point, waiting for his pastor to
explain God's failure to take note of the pious merit points
Edgar Otis had piled up in heaven.

"Why not?" Randollph asked.

"What?"

"God doesn't work that way, Mr. Otis."

"He does so." Otis was petulant. "I learned in Sunday
school, right here in this church, that you have to be good if
you expect God to be good to you."

Randollph sighed. "Mr. Otis, I apologize for the bad
theology you picked up in Sunday school. There is no
promise that God will protect you from the vicissitudes of
life. There is only the promise of grace sufficient to bear
them. Why can't you get a job?"

"Oh, I can get a job, that's not it."

"I thought it was."

"No. I guess I didn't make myself clear. I can't get a job
at anything near my former level. I was department head,
making fifty thousand a year. Best I've been offered is
twenty-two thousand as an assistant designer. I can't live on
that. Besides the loss of prestige. Even with my wife's
thirteen thousand from her teaching job, we couldn't make
it."

Randollph decided he'd been living out of the real world

too long. He was completely unable to comprehend how a family able to command a thirty-five-thousand-dollar income could be menaced by poverty.

Mr. Otis explained. "House payments are seven hundred a month. It's a nice house, not a mansion, but nice. Lease on the Mercedes is four hundred. Payments on the Buick are two-thirty. And two hundred on Edgar Jr.'s Porsche—we got it at a steal, secondhand. Then, the country club runs three or four hundred a month, usually. Then, there's dental bills—you wouldn't believe my dental bills. And I'm heavily insured. And Edgar Jr.'s at Northwestern, and Emily's going to Vassar next year, and entertaining—well, it takes a lot of money to live these days."

Randollph, who was seldom inclined to advise anyone as to how they should conduct their lives, fought back an impulse to give Edgar Otis a tongue-lashing for his stupidity. Yet, he supposed that the country, and maybe even his own congregation, was filled with Edgar Otises, who, in spite of ducal incomes, were sinking slowly under the waves of expensive living and consumer debt.

"Have you thought of accepting a lesser job, Mr. Otis, and reducing your standard of living?"

"Well ..." Otis hesitated. "We did think of resigning from the country club. But we both enjoy golf, and all our friends belong. How do you explain it to your friends?"

"And do you need a Mercedes and a Buick, and does Edgar Jr. need a Porsche? Perhaps you could get along with cheaper transportation."

Edgar frowned unhappily. "Well, you know, it would look bad."

Randollph gave up. It would take months of patient counseling to uproot Edgar's culturally acquired notions that only losers go without suburban villas, prestigious foreign automobiles, and skiing vacations at Aspen. He would be in bankruptcy court long before that happened.

"Mr. Otis," he said in a voice which he hoped approximated that of the prophet Amos when he called the silly society women of Israel "you cows of Bashan," "have you thought that God is punishing you for your pride and your greed? Has it occurred to you that God is displeased with your ultraluxurious living, and has chosen to humble you? Consider that the loss of your job is God's way of cleansing your spirit, and that he wants you to live and work, for a while anyway, at a more modest level."

Edgar Otis' mouth dropped open in amazement as Randollph spoke, but comprehension and something akin to a look of having been absolved of his sins gathered behind his eyes. Randollph suspected that Edgar's strict Protestant training had left him with a sense of guilt, sternly repressed, over his lush life-style. It was this guilt he was trying to exploit.

"Do you ... do you suppose that's it?" Otis' look of relief was growing. "I'll bet that's it. I worried about things even before I lost my job. Why couldn't I see it?" He straightened up and squared his shoulders. "I don't want to go against God. We'll make some changes at our house. I came in here to ask you to help me find a big job. But now I'll take one that's been offered me. I thank you so much for helping me to see the truth, Dr. Randollph. I'll be all right now. See you Sunday."

Randollph knew he should feel good over helping a beaten man get on top of his life, but he felt terrible. It was a cheap trick, falling back on a fallacious theology in order to obtain immediate results. Does the end justify the means? He believed that, within reasonable limits, it probably does. Given the gloomy premise that people, on the whole, were more powerfully motivated by a superstitious belief in a spooky supernatural explanation than in a clearheaded, reasoned analysis of a problem, he had no doubt been right in providing Edgar Otis with a scary divine judgment that he'd better face reality, and fast. But there was no law of pastoral counseling which said that, after employing tacky means to a commendable end, the counselor had to feel good about it.

After Edgar Otis, Randollph had to dispose of the state secretary for the Association for Total Temperance (Saying "no" to liquor is where it's ATT), who wanted (1) to take over the pulpit of the Church of the Good Shepherd for a Sunday, present the cause of ATT, and take an offering to support the organization; or (2) the church could just send a generous donation without turning over the pulpit to ATT. Randollph, still irritated with himself, told the secretary that you couldn't modify the word "temperance" with "total," that if they meant "abstinence" they ought to say so, and that he would consult with the officials of the church about supporting ATT. He neglected to add that he would strongly recommend against supporting ATT.

A woman whose husband was an alcoholic wanted Randollph to seek the man out and reason with him. Recalling Freddie's advice never to counsel anyone unless they come to you, he refused as gently as he could.

The local manager of the hotel, which the church leased to a national hotel chain, phoned to ask how Randollph would feel about leasing the church's gymnasium to the hotel for conversion to meeting rooms for conventions. "That's where the profit is, convention business," the manager said. "We'd pay a good price. We're awfully short on large meeting rooms. You don't use the gym much, anyway." Randollph said that Mr. Gantry had some kind of recreational program going, but he'd check it out. A young couple came in to book a small wedding in Good Shepherd's chapel. The undertaker phoned about arrangements for Lisa Julian Brandt's funeral tomorrow (private service). The representative of a fund-raising company got past Miss Windfall's guard (Randollph wondered what subterfuge he had used, and decided it was probably charm) and offered the services of his company, for a "reasonable fee," to raise Good Shepherd's budget, building program, addition to the endowment, anything. Told that the church had no problems with its budget, had no building program, and had a large endowment, the man lost much of his charm.

Randollph decided he'd had enough, and was about ready to leave when Miss Windfall buzzed him again.

"Lieutenant Michael Casey of the police department is here to see you," she announced.

Eleven

Lieutenant Michael Casey had spent most of the day at the Drake Hotel. By the time he parked the black unmarked police Pontiac in a restricted zone, the freshness was gone from the morning. The somnolent blue surface of the lake quivered here and there, stroked by a lazy breeze. Traffic on North Michigan and Lakeshore Drive heated the warm air with the dumpings from thousands of exhausts. The sun promised to work hard all day.

Casey was glad for the air-conditioned island of the Drake. His blue short-sleeve shirt was already sticky, and his beige tropical jacket felt heavy as an overcoat. He identified himself at the reception desk and was immediately conducted to the office of the hotel director.

Martin Hamlin, unblemished in a gray silk vested suit and maroon tie, greeted Casey with the manner of polite superiority affected by trained hotel employees. Yes, he wanted to be of every possible help to the police, although the publicity over this "unfortunate incident" had been damaging to the hotel's reputation. He gave Casey the impression that in Martin Hamlin's scale of values a violent death was far less deplorable than inconvenience to his hostelry.

Casey didn't expect to get much of anything out of the director. He asked if any employees had quit since Saturday, or if any had not returned to their jobs. Hamlin made a brief phone call and reported that there were none. He asked if there had been any incidents of an unusual nature Saturday or Sunday, anything out of the ordinary.

"What do you mean, 'out of the ordinary,' lieutenant?" There was nothing impolite in the director's voice, but he sounded like a man performing an onerous duty.

Casey managed to keep down his irritation. "If I knew exactly, Mr. Hamlin, I would be specific. Someone got into Lisa Brandt's room, killed her, then got out. I know it is easy to move around in a large hotel without attracting attention, but we have to inquire. We've already talked to the maids on duty near the Brandts' room at the time. Nothing from them. I'm asking on the off-chance that some employee noticed something that might help us, and reported it. You do get reports on that sort of thing, don't you?"

Wearily the director extracted a manila file from a desk drawer, pulled out a sheaf of papers, and began flipping through them.

"Two drunks were ejected from the bar Saturday night, both threatened to sue, but of course they won't," he said. "One of our security officers picked up a known pickpocket in the lobby and persuaded him to leave." He flipped a page. "One guest who was supposed to have checked out yesterday unaccounted for. Several couples suspected to have registered under false names, but we don't make an issue of that as long as they pay their bills." He put the papers back in the folder. "Nothing unusual there."

"Who is the guest unaccounted for?" Casey asked.

Martin Hamlin reluctantly opened the folder again. "Ms. Laura Justus. Made reservation two weeks ago by phone. Checked in at one-ten P.M. Friday. Reservation was for Friday and Saturday."

"Why do you say she is unaccounted for?"

"Because, when she didn't check out yesterday as scheduled, and didn't answer the maid's knock, the maid let herself in with the passkey. That's what we always do. People do die of heart attacks or . . ." He was about to say something else, but didn't. "She wasn't in the room, but her luggage was still there. It still is this morning."

"Had the bed been slept in?"

Hamlin consulted the paper again. "No."

"From your knowledge and experience, what do you make of it?" Casey did his best to inject a note of flattery into his voice.

The director spread his hands in a who-knows gesture. "She might be a wife using the hotel as a cover while meeting a gentleman friend elsewhere."

"Then why didn't she get back and check out on time?"

"Maybe she was having a good time and didn't want to come back when she'd planned."

"Then wouldn't she have phoned to extend her reservation?"

"That would have been normal, yes."

"Then her behavior doesn't fit a usual pattern?"

Martin Hamlin assumed the air of a man who has seen everything. "No, it doesn't. But in this profession one learns that there is no normal behavior. Hotel guests do things that make no sense to anyone but themselves."

Casey said, "I'll be wanting to talk to the clerk who registered her in, and the bellboy who took her to her room. Then I'll take a look at her room. Please see that it isn't disturbed till I can get to it."

"Oh, now, see here, lieutenant, is this necessary? Our guests are entitled to their privacy. We've no reason to think that Ms. Justus doesn't intend to come back. After all, her luggage is still in her room."

Martin Hamlin's self-importance and Casey's mild manner led the director to believe he could intimidate this young cop.

"Mr. Hamlin, I'm glad Sergeant Garboski, who often works with me, isn't here instead of me. Sergeant Garboski is crude. He wouldn't ask for your cooperation. He'd describe to you all the problems the city can create for a hotel if it wishes. There'd be restaurant inspectors, and fire marshals, and elevator inspectors who might need to stop all elevators for several hours. Now, I don't believe in doing things that way. I believe that most people want to cooperate with the police when asked politely. Don't you agree?"

Hamlin, his face red with embarrassment and fury, picked up the phone and said, "Send Vanderwater to my office."

George Vanderwater, in a summer blue suit that Casey admired, was a cheerful young man who had not yet acquired the professional hotel man's air of bored civility. He seemed delighted that Casey had asked for his help.

"Yes, I checked her in," he told Casey.

"Do you remember her well enough to describe her?" Casey supposed that a busy hotel clerk barely looked at the guests he registered, but it didn't hurt to ask.

"Of course. I remember all the guests I register. We're taught to be observant. But, anyway, I have a very good memory. I'm interested in people. I like to guess what they do, why they are here. So I notice."

"Can you describe Ms. Justus?"

"Sure. Tall, for a girl. Five-nine, maybe. Blond hair, long, she wore it to cover half her face, like that old-time movie actress. Lots of girls wear their hair partly over their face, but this was extreme. Blue eyes, one blue eye anyway, I didn't see the other one. Rather heavily made up. Dressed in an expensive pastel green pantsuit, and a matching lightweight jersey blouse. She wore her jacket like a cape, loose on the shoulders. She had big bazooms."

"Vanderwater." Hamlin's voice was a reprimand.

"Sorry, director, I'll rephrase that. She was of buxom build, with a fully developed chest." Vanderwater didn't appear to be disturbed by the director's intervention. He's probably very good at his job and knows it, Casey thought.

"How old would you say?" Casey asked.

"Around thirty, give or a take a little."

"Did she say anything to you?"

"She asked for a room on a lower floor. I gave her 334."

Casey thought a moment, then asked, "Since you like to guess about the people you register, what did you decide about Ms. Justus?"

George Vanderwater's face broke into a boyish grin. He looked at the director, then said, "I put her down for an expensive hooker."

"Vanderwater, you know we don't cater to that sort of trade!" Hamlin's voice was another rebuke.

"I know we don't, sir." Vanderwater was unperturbed. "But they don't come in wearing signs saying "I'm a five-hundred-dollar whore.""

"Why did you guess that she was a hooker?" Casey asked.

"The heavy makeup. Not vulgar or, or ...."

"Obvious?"

"Yes. Not overly obvious. Not like you'd find on the girls in cheap North Side bars. She knew how to use it. But she obviously wasn't a young matron from Milwaukee. And I think her hair was a wig. If it was, it was a good one. You can nearly always tell a wig, but I couldn't be sure."

"Voice?"

"Normal girl's voice. Nothing unusual about it."

"What address did Ms. Justus give when she registered?" Casey directed the question to Martin Hamlin, who reached for the folder again.

"Twelve-twenty-one Copper Beach Lane, Indianapolis." Vanderwater supplied the information before the director could find the right paper. Casey wondered if George Vanderwater would consider joining the police force. He wished that Sergeant Garboski and some of the other officers he worked with had Vanderwater's orderly, retentive mind.

Casey said, "May I use your phone, Mr. Hamlin?" He was punching buttons by the time Hamlin completed a grudging nod. He spoke briefly, waited, then spoke again and hung up.

"Now, may I see the bellboy who took Ms. Justus to her room? And would you show me the room, Mr. Vanderwater? I'd like you to identify the luggage." He thanked the director for his help.

The bellboy, located quickly, because George Vanderwater remembered which one had taken Ms. Justus to her room, was named Ernest. He looked neat enough in his uniform, but the indifferently trimmed thin gray hair and the worn shoes proclaimed to the observant that "here is one of life's losers." Yes, he recalled taking the lady to her room. No, he hadn't paid much attention to her. What he remembered most was that she'd tipped him a couple of bucks, which was better than ladies usually tipped. That Ms. Justus was generous with her gratuities stirred something in Casey's mind, but it was too vague to grasp.

"If Ms. Justus was a high-priced hooker," he asked George Vanderwater, "would it be in character for her to be a big tipper?"

The young hotel man pursed his lips, then said, "No. Most hookers don't give anything away. They think in terms of selling."

George Vanderwater, Casey guessed, would go far in the hotel business or in any other profession which put a premium on the ability to understand people. He mentally filed the information that Ms. Justus was free with a buck, and that hookers, as a rule, aren't.

Room 334 had the appearance of a room that was ready to live in, but hadn't been lived in. A suitcase of good quality but sold by the thousands under a nationally advertised brand, was opened on a folding stool provided by the hotel for that purpose. Casey quickly inventoried its contents. Stockings, freshly laundered lingerie; all very wispy and expensive-looking, but of a widely sold make. Set out on a dressing table was a collection of makeup jars along with the instruments for application. In the bathroom Casey found mouthwash, toothpaste and brush, aspirin, a bottle of half-used nonprescription sleeping pills, an iron supplement touted as essential to the health of women past thirty, and a nearly empty bottle of birth-control tablets with the name of the drugstore and physician scratched off.

The closet contained two dresses, both apparently of excellent quality, but, to Casey's eye, not quite to be classed as designer originals. One was a simple sleeveless electric-blue shantung silk cocktail dress, the other a red-on-white polka-dot summer street dress. There was a pair of white patent pumps. Casey looked for the store labels in the dresses. They had been snipped out.

"Maid's cleaned up the room," George Vanderwater said after a quick appraisal. "That's why it's so neat."

"Could you find the maids for me?" Casey asked. "I'll be needing to talk to them."

"No problem."

"I want to make a call. This phone O.K.?"

"Just dial nine, then your number. The hotel will be glad to pick up the charge." George Vanderwater grinned cheerfully at the detective.

Casey's call didn't take long. When he hung up he said, "There is no Copper Beach Lane in Indianapolis, and no record of a Laura Justus living in the city. I'll want this room sealed until our laboratory men can examine it. If Ms. Justus should return, please notify me immediately."

He did not think that Ms. Justus would be returning.

Casey talked to Annette Paris, Amos Oregon, and Jaime DeSilva, all staying at the Drake, all remaining for Lisa Julian Brandt's funeral.

Annette Paris was very feminine in white lounging pajamas with very little material above the waist. Casey couldn't help but think of George Vanderwater's ingenuous description of Laura Justus—"She had big bazooms." Annette Paris invited Casey into her suite with the air of welcoming a clandestine lover. Arranging herself in a corner of a jumbo sofa, she invited him to sit with her.

"You can imagine how shattered I am, lieutenant, and I've got to face up to the funeral yet. I don't know how I'm going to stand it." She sniffed into a pretty lace handkerchief. "My best friend murdered. Murdered! My God! I never knew anybody that was murdered. Murder is something that happens in mystery stories and sensational newspapers. It happens to other people. I played in a murder mystery—on the stage, that is—when I was just getting started in the theater. It was fun. It was a game. It wasn't real life. Nice people don't go around murdering people in real life." Annette Paris was babbling, and Casey wondered why.

"I'm interested in your statement that nice people don't go around murdering people," Casey said to her, stopping her monologue. "The prevailing theory is that Lisa Julian was killed by a burglar. That's what the papers have said. Do you have information we don't have?"

Annette Paris looked shocked, then confused. "I ... I didn't mean anything by that."

Casey knew that it would not be as easy to enlist Annette's cooperation as it had been to convince Martin Hamlin that his best interests were served by doing all he could to help the police. A nationally known movie star couldn't be badgered, even had he been inclined to badger her. He had nothing with which to threaten her, even subtly. He could haul her down to the station and question her, but her lawyer would be there in minutes, the studio would create a fuss, the mayor would raise hell with the commissioner, who'd dress down the division commander, who'd give Casey's captain a tongue-lashing, who'd then take it out on Casey. In this world it surely paid to be rich and prominent, Casey reflected. They did not have to suffer the rudeness, the indignities, and the inconveniences visited upon those citizens who, unfortunately for them, were in no position to do anything about it. No, his best method was to be the friendly, warmhearted cop who needed her help in clearing up the murder of her friend. Encourage her to talk. She liked to talk.

"I just need all the help I can get in finding who killed Lisa Julian," he said gently.

"Well ..." Annette Paris was visibly torn between clamming up and spilling the beans. "Well, I just mean ... I suppose, I guess I was thinking that there might be, I mean there are people who were plenty upset about Lisa's marriage." Annette looked like she was about to cry, Casey noted.

"There were?"

"Oh, yes!" The pretty blond actress, like an alcoholic who finally takes the forbidden drink and knows there is no stopping now, rushed on with her revelations. "Amos Oregon, he's in a mean mood. He's been drinking all

weekend and muttering about how nobody jilts him. Not
that Lisa jilted him. He's just one of many ex-boyfriends.
But men are such egotists!" She said it venomously. "They
all think if a girl gives them a little attention that she must
be passionately in love with them. Jaime DeSilva's the same
way, though he's more civilized about it than Amos, I'll give
him that. But he's been after Lisa to marry him for years.
He thought sooner or later she'd get tired of playing the
field and come to him. Silly ass! She got tired of playing the
field, all right, but she didn't come to him. She came to
Carl Brandt. Now, how do you figure that? What'd he have
that got to Lisa?" She wasn't asking him, Casey knew. The
question was rhetorical.

Annette didn't slow down. "That's what bugged Jaime, I
think. He'd have been brokenhearted anyway. But to pick
somebody like Carl Brandt—that infuriated him. Probably
bruised his precious little ego, he couldn't win over a Carl
Brandt. He probably would have accepted it if she'd settled
on Con Randollph. That, Jaime could have understood.
But a clod like Brandt? Never!"

Casey was genuinely surprised. "You mean the Reverend
Dr. C. P. Randollph?"

It was Annette's turn to look surprised. "Yes, of course. I
can only think of him as Con, because when I knew him he
was playing with the Rams. Lisa said she almost had a
stroke when he came out of that church office and here the
pastor was her old boyfriend, Con Randollph. You mean
nobody told you? They had a heavy romance going for a
year or so. Then it broke up. Con quit playing football and
just disappeared. He broke it off with Lisa. She was gone on
him. Carried a torch for a long time. I thought you knew."

"No, nobody told me," Casey said. He was thinking
especially that the Reverend Dr. C. P. Randollph hadn't
told him. He liked Randollph. He even admired him for
giving up his blossoming pro-football career and taking up

the Christian ministry. Casey didn't know why he admired this in Randollph, because, Casey reasoned, only a damn fool chucks the money and the glory that are the rewards of the successful professional athlete, trades them for a low-pay, low-profile life-style in the church. It didn't make sense to the ambitious young detective. But, he supposed, being a good Catholic lad, or at least having been raised to be one, he'd probably absorbed some of the church's teaching about selfless service being a better way than self-aggrandizement. He probably had it soaked into his bones, also, that to become a priest was to hear the highest of earthly callings. Still, though, Randollph wasn't exactly a priest, not in the one true church. But he was near enough to tap Casey's Catholic reservoir of respect for the clergy.

But Randollph hadn't mentioned his prior relationship with Lisa Julian. Casey speculated a moment on the unusual situation which Randollph faced when Lisa came in to book her wedding. Still, Randollph hadn't told him. Casey didn't see how the Lisa-Randollph thing could have any bearing on the murder. But he'd make Randollph squirm a little.

Annette was talking again. "I didn't mean Amos or Jaime killed her, you understand. They didn't. They couldn't have. Or any of Lisa's other boyfriends, and there were plenty. It's just that, well, she excited strong feelings, strong attachment in her men friends."

"What about women?" Casey spoke very quietly.

Annette Paris abruptly sat up straight, her face red. "What do you mean by that?" Her voice was angry.

"Perhaps there are women who lost a gentleman friend or even a husband to Lisa Julian," Casey said soothingly.

"Oh, that." Annette relaxed a little. "Yes, I suppose so. There probably are plenty of those. I don't think of anyone special at the moment. You'd better look into it, though."

"We will," Casey promised. "And, to your knowledge,

did Lisa ever have any ...   " Casey struggled to phrase the question. "What I'm wanting to know is, did Lisa ever have any romantic interest in another woman?"

Annette's face got red again. "You bastard! You've been listening to rumors, haven't you? You've been leading up to this!" She pounded a sofa pillow with her fist. "Well, let me tell you something, Mr. God Almighty, uptight, square detective. Whatever Lisa and I had was very beautiful! She loved me, I know she did, and given time, she'd have realized that this was true love. She didn't love Carl Brandt. She even said so to me. I'm psychic. I see the future. I told her that I saw tragedy ahead if she married Brandt, but she just laughed and called it a self-serving prophecy. Well, she knows now, wherever she is, that I was right. Oh, why couldn't she have listened to me! Why couldn't she have listened!" Annette Paris threw herself full-length on the sofa and pounded it with both fists, like a child having a tantrum. "Get out, you tricky bastard!" she screamed at him. "Get out! Get out! Get out!"

"You the lawman?" Come on in." Amos Oregon had been drinking. He shut the door and went immediately to a small bar to pour himself a drink, letting the detective find a chair.

"Ain't nothin' I can tell you, can't figure why you want to see me," Oregon said. He lifted the lid of a silver ice bucket and, ignoring the silver tongs, scooped a handful of ice cubes into a generously filled tumbler of whiskey.

"We're just checking with everyone who knew Lisa Julian, Mr. Oregon. Someone may be able to give us a lead. I understand that you were quite close to her."

To Casey's surprise, Amos Oregon set down his glass, covered his face with his hands, and shook with dry sobs.

"Loved that gal! Really loved her!" Oregon said when he regained control of himself. "Seemed like my life was over when she said 'I will' to that pipsqueak sawbones."

Casey was baffled by this star of a dozen or more western movies. Was he putting on an act now, just playing his familiar role of a laconic, untamed son of the old West, a character that entranced millions of arrested adolescents and, reportedly, appealed strongly to women? Casey was unsure about what it was in Amos Oregon that appealed to women. He didn't really understand women—or so his wife, Liz, had told him.

"A man who has a way with words gets to a woman, Mike," Liz had explained. "If he knows how to say the right things with sincerity—or at least convince her that he is sincere—he can melt her heart. I'll bet that priest friend of yours, that Randollph, knows how to do it."

"He isn't a priest, he's a Protestant clergyman," Casey had corrected her.

"Priest, clergyman, whatever," Liz had rattled on, "times I've seen him on television, he talks awfully well."

"He talks like a professor," Casey had replied, a little miffed.

"Now, Mike, don't be jealous. You talk awfully well too. That's one of the things I love about you." She gave him a quick kiss. "But there are men who don't have to talk. They just have a, well, I guess you'd call it an animal magnetism. They're primitives. Any woman senses it. It says, 'I want you.' It makes a woman tingle with excitement."

Oregon, Casey supposed, fell into the latter category. He had a kind of rugged good looks. Perhaps his churlish manner was what Liz had meant by primitive. He'd have to ask Liz. What he couldn't figure out was if the Amos Oregon he was talking to was the real person or the screen personality. It was possible, of course, that the two had merged in such a way that even Amos Oregon didn't know where one left off and the other began.

"Just for the record, Mr. Oregon, could you give me a rundown on what you did, where you were, after the bride and groom left the reception?"

Oregon stopped his glass halfway to his mouth. "You sayin' I'm a suspect?" There was menace in his voice.

"No, of course not." Casey tried to be diplomatic. "We have to do this with everyone."

Oregon took a long swallow from the tumbler of whiskey. "Don't see why. I surely didn't have nothin' to do with killin' her. I loved her. Now, I might have killed that sawbones. There's some men left don't take kindly to havin' their women stole. I admit I thought about killin' him. But not her. I loved her."

"You've been reported as having said that no woman can jilt you and get away with it," Casey told him.

Oregon slapped his glass down on the bar, where he had been about to freshen his drink. "Now, who told you that?" he said angrily. Then, calmer, "If I did, it was just drunk talk."

"About your whereabouts after Lisa and Dr. Brandt left the reception," Casey reminded the actor.

"How would I know?" Oregon was sullen. "I don't even know when they left. I was drunk. Stinkin' drunk. Don't remember hardly nothin' about the reception. Just stinkin' drunk."

Too drunk, Casey wondered, to slip up to the bridal suite and beat Lisa Julian Brandt into a bloody pulp?

Jaime DeSilva was a pleasant contrast to Amos Oregon, but no more helpful.

"Yes, lieutenant, I've been in love with Lisa for years," he said with an attitude of complete frankness in answer to Casey's question about his relationship to the dead girl. "I probably always will be in love with her." He gazed sadly into the distance, his large dark eyes mirroring pain and despair. Desolate though he may have been, he'd managed to dress himself meticulously, Casey noted. White linen slacks and a brillant red polo shirt emphasized his dark

Latin looks. He wore soft white suede loafers, but no socks. Casey's quick eye noticed a lipstick-stained cigarette in a large crystal ashtray. Perhaps he'd always love Lisa Julian, but it had not taken DeSilva long to avail himself of the solace and comfort to be offered by feminine companionship. Casey guessed the girl was probably waiting discreetly in the bedroom of DeSilva's suite.

"Tell me, Mr. DeSilva, can you recall your whereabouts after Dr. and Mrs. Brandt left the reception?"

"Am I a suspect?" DeSilva smiled without humor, a smile that said this is but one more burden my broken heart must bear.

"Police routine," Casey answered blandly.

"Of course. I want to help all I can. You see, lieutenant, I'd asked Lisa to marry me. Many times. Over many years. She always refused. 'I love you, Jaime,' she'd say to me, 'but you aren't husband material.' I don't mind telling you that we carried on a romance, off and on, for several years. We were very good friends. We worked together in many pictures. It was a relationship like, well, like one of these open marriages they talk about so much these days. We were attached to each other by a semishared life of work, by affection, but with no strings tied to each other. I wanted more. I am Spanish. I have pronounced ideas about marriage and family. But she didn't want more."

"Then her marriage came as a shock to you?"

"Yes. A surprise and a shock." Jaime DeSilva lit a long brown cigarette with a thin gold lighter. "I could endure her refusal to marry me. But to marry someone else, a dull man like Carl Brandt, yes, that was a shock."

Mostly to your Latin ego, Casey thought. "About the reception?" he asked.

"Yes, of course." DeSilva blew copious smoke at the ceiling. "After the bride and groom left, there was a finality about it for me. I went back to the dance floor and danced with someone; I don't know who, but I'll probably remember. But I couldn't get it out of my mind. I kept thinking, are they consummating the marriage now? I was so upset I just left and took a long walk. I'm not even sure where I went, except I remember I didn't get far from the lake. Came back to the hotel a couple of hours later."

Casey sighed and closed his notebook. Amos Oregon, son of the old West, was true to his ersatz tradition when he said he wouldn't have killed Lisa, he'd have killed the man. But Latins were more likely to take it out on the woman they thought had wronged them. DeSilva was polite and charming, but he was what he was. Casey decided to do a thorough check on Jaime DeSilva.

Twelve

Captain John Manahan didn't much like Lieutenant Casey. The captain, a short, beefy Irishman with a round baby face and thick curly gray hair, had risen from foot patrolman to executive through a couple of lucky breaks, but mostly by being a shrewd player of Irish Catholic police politics. Like most hard-nosed, self-made men, he was contemptuous of the new breed of college-educated policemen, the contempt partly a mask for fear and awe. Manahan was bright enough to know that they were the wave of the future. He joined with his buddies in calling them sissies, and agreed that the best cop was the cop who fought his way up from the ranks. But Manahan didn't believe it. He disliked Casey because he suspected that Casey looked down on him. Manahan had the man of action's antagonism toward intellectuals. By "intellectuals" Manahan meant people who read books.

But Manahan knew that Casey was a very able detective. He knew that because of Casey his command got all the

high-class murders. Casey's ability to handle important
people was a pearl without price to Manahan, because it
eventually reflected to the credit of the captain. So he
tolerated Casey, and even made occasional efforts to be
friendly with him.

"How you doin' on the Julian thing, Mike?" Manahan
leaned back from a cluttered gray steel desk, spilling cigar
ash on his white shirt. Casey thought Manahan a slob, but
was always careful to conceal his distaste. Casey knew
something about Irish Catholic police politics, too.

"I'm nowhere," Casey admitted. "Of course, it's early."

"We're gettin' pressure to handle it fast," Manahan said.
"How about that junkie we got? He do it, maybe?"

"No, captain, he didn't. We're holding him on a drug
charge. But he's in the clear on the murder."

"Too bad," Manahan said. "We could have nailed it
down. Everybody likes a hophead for a killer. Makes 'em
say, 'Tut-tut, ain't it awful what the scum does to us decent
folk?' Well, we can tell the press that we're still questioning
the kid. Don't need to tell 'em it's about drugs, not murder.
What about motive?"

"Motives I've got, captain. Oregon, the cowboy actor, and
DeSilva, who'd been in a lot of pictures with Lisa, were
both apparently in love with her and have muttered dark
but vague threats. The Paris woman was in love with her,
too."

"What!"

"I don't know if it's significant or not. They have some
pretty unconventional sexual arrangements in Hollywood."

The captain licked tobacco shreds from his lips and spit
them into an ashtray. "That'd make a juicy story—a real
juicy story. Well, well!"

"And who knows how many other ex-boyfriends, or
women whose boyfriends Lisa stole. It'd take an army to
check it out."

"Ain't got an army. What about the doc?"

"There's no reason he couldn't have done it. You heard about the insurance policy Lisa and Brandt took out on each other?"

"Yeah. But why'd a high-price doctor need money that bad?"

"I don't know."

"Assumin' he did it. You guess maybe he got himself a hired gun, in a manner of speakin', faked that phone call somehow, and was conveniently absent long enough for the dirty work to get done?"

"Could have been that way. Doesn't make much sense with what we've got now. But then, things often don't make much sense until you know the reasons for them."

Captain Manahan grunted and relit his cigar. "So maybe he did it himself. We have only his word about that phone call, don't we?"

"Yes," Casey said. "The switchboard operator doesn't remember. She had lots of calls. Could have been one or more to the Brandts, could have been none."

Captain Manahan enjoyed spinning these scenarios, Casey knew, and waited patiently for more to come.

The captain gazed at the ceiling as if expecting information from above.

"Lessee, then—assuming he did it himself—how he'd go about it. He says to her, soon as they get to the room, 'Why don't you stretch out on the bed, dearie, you must be pooped.' Soon as she closes her eyes, he gets the poker an' whacks her. Then he goes to the clinic. When he comes back, he goes into shock, just barely havin' the strength to call for help."

"Or," Casey said, "he goes to the clinic, knowing that Lisa will most likely grab a nap. He comes back, she's asleep on the bed—then he kills her."

"Can't haul him in," the captain said regretfully. "Some

punk, we could. He's Gold Coast. Couldn't keep him in if we did."

"I'll have a talk with him," Casey said. "But if you're getting pressure from the commissioner to wrap this up, I'll need men—"

"They got the pressure on, all right," Manahan complained. "But they want me to do it shorthanded, no extra help. What do you need, Mike?"

"Two men to check out everybody that could possibly have made that phone call Brandt claims he got, and I mean everbody. Get a street guy to ask around if anyone's heard of a doctor hiring a hood to knock off his wife. Check the fences to see if any of the loot's been offered. That'll be a waste of time probably, but we've got to do it."

"Jesus, Mike, you don't want much," Manahan groused. "We got other crimes, you know."

Casey smiled genially at his superior officer. "Can you think of an easier way, captain? You said the pressure's on to wrap it up. Even with all that, I've still got to work with the insurance company. They'll be investigating as soon as Brandt files a claim. And I've got to deal with Brandt himself."

The captain sighed. "I'll try, Mike, I'll try."

"You're most welcome here, as always, lieutenant," Randollph said, ushering the dapper detective to the large brown leather sofa that was the base of his conversation center. "However, I suppose that you didn't drop in just to discuss Roman Catholic theology."

"I'd like to," Casey admitted. "My pastor at St. Aloysius thinks Father O'Brian's devotional booklet *Sixteen Reasons Why We Say the Rosary* is a dogmatic work far more useful than the *Summa Theologica,* and our communion-breakfast speaker is usually some good Catholic running back from the NFL who tells us why going to Mass faithfully helps him blast through the line."

Randollph, tired and dispirited as he was, laughed. "You have described the way things are with us separated brethren. Only, the pamphlet would be the Reverend Somebody-or-other's *Sixteen Ways to Walk with Jesus*, and the running back would be a Protestant. Why don't you change parishes?"

"Roman Catholics don't change parishes," Casey explained. "Your parish is determined by where you live. Of course, I could attend another parish. But it's not worth the trouble. For a Catholic, life in a parish church is a total thing. Your friends. The church organizations you belong to. Your relationship with the pastor."

Randollph had no trouble translating this to mean, "An ambitious young policeman needs the backing of his pastor if he wants to get ahead in the mayor's police department and the pastor of St. Aloysius has plenty of political wallop."

"But," Casey continued, "we'll defer theology till another time. Dr. Randollph, why didn't you tell me that you were an intimate friend of Lisa Julian?" It was as if Casey had transformed himself instantly from friendly acquaintance to hard, impersonal police detective. Randollph was angered, especially by Casey's slight emphasis on the word "intimate." He wanted to say, "Because it was none of your business," but restrained himself.

He said, "Because I have had no opportunity to tell you, lieutenant. And because it did not occur to me that it was relevant to your investigation."

"Everything's relevant in a homicide. You could have told me at the hotel, when you identified her."

"Described, in front of Mrs. Stack, my former relationship with Lisa Julian? Come now, lieutenant."

Michael Casey thought of how Liz would react to hearing him tell someone the intimate details of one of his earlier loves, and decided that Randollph was a sensible man. He smiled and said, "Sorry, doctor, I just thought I'd jar you a little. I guess I was intrigued by the coincidence of your close friendship with Lisa Julian."

"Formerly close friendship," Randollph corrected him. "I hadn't seen her in years." Randollph stretched his legs and relaxed in his chair. "Does this mean you've abandoned the theory that robbery was the reason for the murder?"

"No. It's still the most logical explanation of what happened."

"But you see other possibilities?"

Casey's smile was just short of patronizing. "There are always other possibilities. People kill because of jealousy or money or anger. People that wouldn't kill when they're sober will kill when they're drunk and their inhibitions are down. There were several people in the wedding party who had motives for murder. We also have a hotel guest unaccounted for." Casey told him about it.

Randollph was skeptical. "Motives for childish tantrums, perhaps. But murder? These actors are spoiled brats, as actors often are. But I have difficulty envisioning one of them wielding that poker."

"I'm afraid you're a little naive about that, Dr. Randollph. You're used to dealing with nice upper-middle-class people, and nice people don't ordinarily knock each other off. But they do. Believe me, they do."

Casey got up to go. "However, most homicides aren't committed with clever advance planning to conceal the murderer and the motive. That's for detective stories. We always look for the simple, obvious answer, and in this case it's robbery."

"Let's hope you're right," Randollph said, "though I'm

perishing to know more about that disappearing lady at the hotel."

"Laura Justus? So am I."

"But that's just my vulgar curiosity."

"I'll let you know when we find her," Casey said, moving to the door. "And please excuse my bluntness in asking you about Miss Julian. That, I'm afraid, was caused by *my* vulgar curiosity."

About the time Casey was leaving the Church of the Good Shepherd, Dr. Carl Brandt was leaving his apartment. He'd gone to the clinic hospital that morning to check on a few postoperative cases, but then he'd gone home. It didn't look good, he figured, for the bereaved bridegroom to be doing hysterectomies and taking out gall bladders the day before his late wife was to be buried. That was one nice thing about being a full partner in the clinic. If he'd been in private practice, he'd have been fretting over the two thousand dollars or so he'd lost by not operating this morning. God knew he needed the money. But as a full partner the money came rolling in whether he missed a day or not.

He pushed the button for the elevator and pushed the thought of money from his mind at the same time. He was in a mess, but it looked as if he was going to get out of it. He resolved never to gamble again.

"Hello, Dr. Brandt, your car's ready." The doorman, caparisoned like a general in a banana republic, spoke with obsequious familiarity.

"Afternoon, Ernest—or is it evening? Got anything good for tomorrow?"

"Have I got something good!" Ernest let his voice sink to a conspiratorial whisper. "I've got Arthur's Hope at eighteen-to-one in the sixth at—"

"Put a hundred on him."

"Yes, sir." Ernest almost saluted. He held the door of a bright blue Mercedes sport coupé on the driver's side, forcing a cruising taxi driver to slam on his brakes. "I've got the air-conditioning going, so it's nice and cool inside."

"Thanks, Ernest." Carl Brandt slid into the car, almost subconsciously responding to the soft tawny leather upholstery and thick blue carpeting. Carl Brandt liked elegance. It was a door shutting out the memory of his impoverished boyhood. He whipped the Mercedes into the tide of late-afternoon traffic. He did not notice a gray Chevy Vega leave the curb a half-block back and blend into the line of cars behind him.

Brandt worked his way out to Lakeshore Drive and turned north. Traffic was heavy, but it moved. The Drive was a path with the glittering lake on one side and luxury apartment buildings, stretching like a fenestrated wall, on the other. Carl Brandt liked to drive in heavy traffic. His car was more powerful and more agile than the clumsy Cadillacs and Buicks, the slow-footed Dodges and Mercurys and Pontiacs which almost swamped him. It was great fun, the doctor thought, to work your way forward through the pack, switching the little Mercedes from lane to lane, darting for a momentary opening, jockeying into a space barely large enough for the short coupé. If another driver cursed at him, he took it as a token of victory. There was something mightily exhilarating in taking a risk and winning.

It was a little slower going on Sheridan Road, no chance at all to beat the other guy. In Evanston he turned west and drove through Skokie and Morton Grove. Then, by a series of back roads, he got around to the north edge of Arlington Heights. A half-mile down a narrow macadam lane he came to a low redwood building with an enormous parking area. Neon tubes traced ANGELO's in hot letters against the still-bright sky. The parking lot was already a third full.

Carl Brandt nosed the Mercedes through the parked cars to the back of the building. This also was a parking area, but not so large as out front. There was a row of automobiles snugged up to the building, probably belonging to the help. A brown Plymouth sedan sat under a tree at the extreme back edge of the lot. Brandt pulled up next to it, locked his car, and got into the front passenger seat of the Plymouth. He spent a brief moment looking at the blond woman in a white sleeveless dress, then grabbed her almost roughly.

"God, I've missed you, Kitty!" He kissed her on the mouth, then the neck, running his hand up and down her thigh. The woman held him, then pushed him away.

"Time enough for this later. We've got some talking to do, Carl."

"I know, Kitty." He got out and went around to open the door for her. "You're beautiful," he said.

Inside, Angelo's was dark and noisy. To the left was the cocktail lounge. The long bar was crowded. A jukebox was sobbing about a heart left in San Francisco; a hostess in a long dress stood by a small lectern which guarded the entrance to the restaurant.

"Dr. Carl Jones, I have a reservation for the Roma Room."

"Certainly, Dr. Jones." The hostess made a check mark on the sheet in front of her. "Right this way." She picked up two large red-and-gold menus and led them through a series of rooms partially filled with early diners. The Roma Room was the farthest from the door, lit very dimly, and consisted entirely of spacious booths done in red velvet.

"Linda will be here in a moment for your orders from the bar. Have a nice evening." The hostess swished away.

Linda, costumed like a Playboy bunny without the cottontail, said demurely, "May I bring you something from the bar?"

"A daiquiri for the lady, and a double scotch on the rocks for me. Make it single-malt if you have it." Carl Brandt much preferred Kentucky sour mash, but he was trying to like scotch because he had been told that bourbon was middle-class. He'd learned the other day that single-malt scotch was chic.

When Linda left, the blond woman said, "All right, Carl, talk."

Dr. Brandt opened his menu. "Maybe we ought to decide what we want to eat first." He wasn't sure how he wanted to go about this conversation. He'd hoped that his coming on strong with love and passion out in the car would soften her up, make explanations unnecessary. But that hadn't worked.

"No, now."

"Well, Kitty, I got to admit that I've been, uh, kind of a bastard, the way I treated you." That was it. Be hangdog ashamed. Arouse her sympathy.

"That doesn't even begin to describe it, Carl." Kitty's voice was hard. "How long have you been sharing my bed? How many times have you laid me in that third-floor laundry closet? Oh, I liked it. I like you. I loved you. I still do. But I'm not a slut, Carl, not one of those cute little nurses who go in for a quick bang whenever a great god doctor crooks a finger at them. You gave me every reason to think that you wanted to marry me, would marry me. Then, all of a sudden, it comes out in the papers that you're going to marry the boss's daughter. No explanation to me. Just 'Good morning, Miss Darrow, how's that bowel resection in room 55?' "

"Your drinks, sir. Glenlivet all right?"

Carl didn't have the faintest idea what Glenlivet might be, but he was extravagantly grateful for Linda's unwitting punctuation to Kitty's bitter speech. He took a sip of the whiskey, shuddered at its pungent flavor. "Ah," he said, "great! Just great, honey."

Kitty paid no attention to her drink. "So?" she said.

"O.K. O.K., I did you wrong. I should have told you about it, told you why, only I was afraid you wouldn't understand, do something drastic."

"Understand what?" She laughed derisively.

Carl Brandt leaned forward, turning intent and sincere. "O.K., Kitty, what I'm trying to say is that I had a good reason for doing what I did, and I was going to tell you at the right moment." The blond woman started to speak, but Brandt stopped her. "Hear me out. I had to have that full partnership in the clinic. Do you realize what that's worth? A quarter of a million per year, maybe more. I've had some financial reverses—"

"Been gambling again, Carl?"

He ignored her remark. "Do you know what I've been making? A lousy seventy, eighty thousand, just working there. Now I've got the partnership, all nice and legal. Old King David can't take it away. I'd planned, soon as things settled down, to get together with you again."

"In the laundry closet, Carl? A little something on the side when you got bored with Lisa?"

"Cut it out, Kitty. That was a marriage of convenience. For Lisa. For me. It'd probably have broken up in a year or two. But I'd still have the partnership."

"You really are a bastard. Did you kill her, Carl?"

He sat up with a jerk, as if she'd thrown her untouched daiquiri in his face. "Now, that's a hell of a thing to say!" He was angry. "What about you? It's crossed my mind that you could have done it. You had the motive. Did you kill her?"

Kitty put on what Dr. Brandt would have described as an inscrutable smile, had he been familiar with the word.

"Don't you wish you knew, Carl?" She swirled the green puddle in her glass with a clear plastic straw. "Don't you wish you knew?"

Neither one had noticed the approach of a tallish blond girl in white slacks and a long green jacket. She slid into the booth beside Kitty, unslung her large white shoulder bag, and set it on the table.

"Good evening, Dr. Brandt, you son of a bitch . . . good evening, dearie."

After a stunned moment, Carl Brandt said, "Who the hell are you? I don't know you. Anyway, who could tell with all that hair over your face. Why don't you just buzz off?"

"You don't like my hairdo? How rude of you to say so." Brandt put his hands on the table and started to rise. "Sit down, doctor," the intruder said in a cold feminine voice. "What you see in my hand is a small but efficient automatic. No one will notice that I'm pointing it at you, because my hand is shielded by my bag—which is why I set it on the table just so." The girl turned to Kitty, keeping an eye on Brandt. "And you, dearie, don't you try anything. I could put five shots into the good doctor's head before you could get a hand on me. And I'm a big healthy girl who knows how to take care of herself, so I could handle you without any trouble. And by the way, this little gun doesn't make much noise. They wouldn't hear it in the next room."

"Wh-what do you want?" Brandt was beginning to be frightened.

"To shoot you. I'm here to shoot you, doctor. You deserve it, you know. Your late wife not even buried yet, and here you are, out with another bird."

"You, you don't understand—"

"Oh, I understand, doctor. I saw you pawing her in the car before you came in. Not that I care about your morals. You might say I'm here to avenge the death of Lisa Julian. I think you killed your wife, doctor. Or was it your little

cupcake here? Maybe I'll have to shoot you both. Won't
that make a fine story for the papers?"

"You're crazy!" Brandt spoke with difficulty.

"No, not crazy, doctor. But curious. If you and/or your
bird didn't do it, who did?"

"How in hell would I know?" Humor the dame, talk to
her, maybe she'll ease off. Anyway, Brandt figured, the only
possible way out of this is to talk my way out.

"Remember, doctor, that I'm the avenging angel—"

"Why? Why are you doing this?" Get her to talk. Talk
about herself. Maybe she'll put that damn gun away,
Brandt thought.

"Never mind why. Let's just say I have my reasons. And
as I was saying before you so rudely interrupted me, doctor,
avenging angels aren't too particular about who they punish.
Maybe you did it, maybe it was your little pal here, or
maybe you did it together—I shoot you both, and I get the
killer. If one of you is innocent, so what? If you're both
innocent, well, that's tough."

"Jesus, you're cold-blooded!"

"Avenging angels usually are, doctor. Now, tell me if you
have any idea who killed her. If you come up with a likely
suspect, I might just let you two lovebirds live."

Carl Brandt fought down panic. Think of someone.
Come up with a theory she'll buy. *Think fast!*

"If it wasn't a robber," he said, his voice shaky, "it was
some jealous guy. I've been thinking it was probably that
Amos Oregon. Lisa told me he had it for her bad." Yes,
that's a good theory, Brandt thought. Touch it up for this
crazy dame. Pour it on strong. "Lisa was afraid of him,"
Carl improvised. "He'd threatened to kill her if she married
anyone else. He was mean. And Lisa said that when he
drank a lot he just lost control of himself. If it wasn't a
robber, he's the one."

"You should be writing movie scripts, doctor. You're

making that up." The intruder flicked the safety catch of
her little automatic on and then off. "Amos Oregon
couldn't find the men's room when he's drunk, let alone
track Lisa to the bridal suite and kill her. Try to remember
if Lisa ever told you anything about her past, any special or
out-of-the-way—shall we say—'relationship' which might be a
clue to the killer."

All the starch went out of Brandt. He couldn't think of
anything else to tell this madwoman.

"Uh, well, no. Lisa never talked much about her past.
'Let bygones be bygones,' she said."

The intruder pointed her gun at Brandt's head. "Too
bad, doctor. Now, since I'm tenderhearted, I've decided to
let your bird live. But I'm going to have to shoot you." She
pulled the trigger.

Nothing happened.

"Goddamn automatic. Half the time they jam. Oh, well,
I can get you later." She dropped the gun in her handbag.

Brandt lunged to get out, but the intruder had anticipated him. She shoved the table against him, pinning him
in the booth.

"Your problem is that you're stupid, doctor. What would
you do if you caught me? Who'd believe your story of what
happened? Or would you beat me up? Tomorrow's newspapers would have a story: Lisa Julian's widower, accompanied by lady friend, assaults woman in suburban
restaurant.' It would be published on the day of Lisa's
funeral. Is that what you want, doctor? Also, I could sue
you for malpractice or something. If you're not a murderer,
you're a fool, doctor. Well, I must be going. Have a lovely
evening."

She strolled casually out of the room.

Thirteen

Carl Brandt lit a cigarette with a trembling hand. It was Kitty who recovered first.

"We've got to go to the police," she said.

Carl snapped his lighter shut and pocketed it. He drew heavily on the cigarette, as if from a lungful of smoke he could derive both solace and wisdom.

"What, are you crazy? Admit to the cops we were out together? Tell them we've been chummy for years? Now, how is that going to look? Do you have a good hard alibi for when Lisa was killed?"

Kitty admitted that she didn't.

"You know I don't have one. I could have done it a couple ways. There's that damn phony phone call that got me to the clinic. I think it was one of my dear friends thinking he was playing a big joke. But no one admits it. So what would you think if you were a cop?"

Kitty didn't know what she would think.

"I'll tell you what they think," Carl informed her. "They

think I made up that story about the phone call. They think I either killed her and then went to the clinic, or that I went to the clinic and then went back and killed her. They'd have pulled me in by now if they had any evidence at all. Now, you want us to walk in and hand them a ready-made, handy-dandy motive."

"But that doesn't make any sense, Carl. Why would you kill her on your wedding day?"

Brandt dawdled over lighting another cigarette. "Oh, the partnership in the clinic."

"Oh, nuts. You already had that."

"Well, they might think that I had the hots for you and—"

"And couldn't wait?" Kitty laughed bitterly. "I wish you had that kind of feeling for me. But it wouldn't take the police long to find out that you don't. Come on, Carl, you're hiding something."

Dr. Brandt told her about the insurance policy.

"That looks bad," Kitty admitted. Then she brightened. "But only a real dumbo would kill his wife on their wedding day for the insurance," she said. "You would have been smart enough to wait awhile."

Carl Brandt avoided her eyes. "It isn't quite that simple, Kitty."

"You'd better tell me everything."

Carl told her.

"Oh, my God!" Kitty was near tears. "Carl, how could you get yourself in such a mess?" She found a tissue in her handbag and blew her nose. "But that's all the more reason to go to the police. They'll find out about the insurance and all the rest, if they haven't already. But if you act like you want to cooperate with them, you'll look more like you're innocent than if you try to cover up."

"Yeah?" The doctor was sarcastic. "How do we explain our little rendezvous this evening?"

Kitty matched his sarcasm. "Have you ever thought of trying the truth, Carl? Just tell them that you dumped me without explanation, and you decided to tell me why."

"They'll just think I was trying to get laid—with my wife not even buried yet. Cops have dirty minds."

"Wasn't that what you had in mind, Carl?" The contempt in her voice withered him. "Well, I can assure them that nothing like that was on the evening's program. If you have no sense of decency, I have." She gathered up her handbag. "Let's go."

"I'm not going to the police, and that's that." Brandt's hangdog expression changed to rigid resistance.

Kitty knew he meant it. Exasperated, emotionally exhausted, she searched her mind for some way to save this man from himself. Finally she said, "All right, Carl. If you won't go to the police, you've got to go to someone. You've got to find someone who's objective about it and let them advise you."

"You thinking of a lawyer? I hate lawyers. Besides, it looks bad if I hire a lawyer before I've been charged with anything. It'd get out. People would take it as an admission of guilt."

"All right, a priest, then."

"I'm not a Catholic," he said sharply, then added, "anymore."

"You don't have to be a Catholic to go to a priest," Kitty explained patiently. "You need advice. You need to get your thinking straightened out."

"No." Brandt was stubborn again.

"Very well, Carl, if you won't save yourself, I'll just have to let you sink, and save myself."

"Now, what do you mean by that, Kitty?"

"I mean I have information that might be . . . that bears on a crime, a murder. It is a crime to withhold it from the police. I'm not going to jail." She got up.

"Wait a minute, sit down, Kitty," the doctor pleaded with her.

"Only if you have something to suggest," she said frostily, but she sat down.

"Tell you what I'll do. We'll go talk to that preacher that married us—Lisa and me. Randollph. I like him. He'd have to treat anything I said like it was said in the confessional, wouldn't he? Even if he isn't a priest?"

"I'm sure he would, Carl." Kitty was uncertain about the legal protection covering disclosures to a non-Roman divine, but she was too anxious to get Carl to someone who could convince him that he was being a damn fool to raise the point.

"Then let's go find him," Brandt said.

Randollph inspected the six smallish shrimp arranged on a tired lettuce leaf under the little bowl of cocktail sauce. He knew the shrimp would be rubbery and flavorless. He knew this, just as he knew the veal parmigiana to follow would be stringy. He tried to avoid eating in Good Shepherd's hotel coffee shop, but it had two virtues: it was handy, and the service was fast. On days that kept him late in his study, and required an early evening appearance at some church function, the coffee shop was almost his only alternative to starvation. All that would change tomorrow, when Clarence Higbee was to begin his duties. The thought cheered him.

His thoughts turned to the meeting scheduled for that evening.

Tonight he was to meet with the committee on Missions, which would address itself to allocating the not inconsiderable amount of money Good Shepherd, each year, spent on snaring the souls of various kinds and colors of heathen from their revolting idol worship and turning them into good Christian natives. Randollph was quite aware that modern Christian mission work wasn't like that at all. But a lot of laymen still pictured it that way. As a qualified expert in the history of the Christian faith he was all for missions. He knew that when the church lost its zeal to carry the gospel to faraway places with strange-sounding names, then it was already dead. He wanted to help Good Shepherd's committee on missions. But not tonight. He wasn't really needed tonight. The Reverend Mr. O. Bertram Smelser would be there with all the facts and figures. He was quite competent to run the meeting. But Smelser wasn't the chief. An appearance by the pastor-in-charge, however symbolic, was a necessary part of his job, Randollph had discovered. It underlined the importance of whatever variety of the Lord's business was being conducted. He wondered how many hasty dinners and damaged pastoral digestive systems could be laid to this fact of clerical life.

He disposed of the edible parts of the veal, paid his check, and headed for the church offices. Mr. Smelser had left him a formidable pile of mimeographed reports, which supposedly would prepare him for the evening's labors. He'd better glance through them, anyway. Smelser might ask if he'd read them, and to say no would be a rebuke to the little gray business-manager/pastor.

When Randollph unlocked the door to the church office, the phone was ringing. Hastily switching on the lights, he went to Miss Windfall's desk, punched the button that was glaring at him, and answered, "Church of the Good Shepherd. May I help you?"

"May I see . . . , that is, may I speak to the pastor?" The voice was female, young, troubled, uncertain.

"This is the pastor."

"Reverend Randollph?"

Randollph winced. "Yes."

"You don't know me. My name is Kitty, Katherine Darrow. I'm a nurse at the Julian Hospital. I'm—"—she sounded as if she were struggling to get it out—"I'm a friend of Dr. Carl Brandt. We, Dr. Brandt and I, well, we'd like to see you."

"Surely," Randollph said. "Tomorrow's a busy day for me—"

Kitty Darrow interrupted him, sounding desperate. "We'd like to see you now, this evening, reverend. We've got to see you."

"I have a meeting scheduled for this evening." Randollph tried to suppress the ignoble hope that the lady would persist in her efforts to see him, thus providing him with a respectable reason for absenting himself from the committee meeting. He was framing apologies and explanations to Bertie Smelser when she said, "Please, it's got to be right now, as soon as we can get there. It's . . . it's life and death."

Randollph seated Carl Brandt and Kitty Darrow in front of his desk rather than at his informal conversation center. He wasn't sure how this conversation would proceed, but sensed that he represented to this couple some kind of authority figure. Just as well, then, for him to play the role they had selected for him.

Carl Brandt shifted nervously in his chair, gulped, then said, "I . . . that is, we, Miss Darrow and I were, uh, well, you see, I needed to talk to her, that is, there was something I needed to clear up . . ." His voice quavered and gave up.

Randollph, in his brief time at Good Shepherd, had already listened to a lot of tremulous confessions. His recently practiced ear informed him that Brandt, like a guilty schoolboy, was nerving himself to blurt out something to his own discredit, and was putting off the painful disclosure as long as possible. Had he come to confess the murder of his wife? Not likely. If he'd made up his mind to do that, he wouldn't hum and haw about it. He'd have an attitude mixed of despair and relief, not this air of having been caught stealing chickens from his neighbor's coop. Randollph let him continue.

"Well, see, reverend, Miss Darrow and I just happened to run into each other at this restaurant, and—"

"You'd better let me tell it, Carl." Kitty Darrow spoke with a kind of weary authority. Brandt, Randollph noticed, once his male prerogative to speak first had been observed, seemed relieved to have her take command.

"We didn't run into each other at the restaurant. We arranged to meet there. We thought it was far enough out that nobody would recognize us. Carl even made the reservation under a false name. We've been lovers for years . . ." She paused, expecting some moral reprimand, but Randollph said nothing.

"I read in the papers that Carl was going to marry Lisa, and that's the first I heard about it. He never explained."

"Isn't that unusual behavior?" He kept his voice neutral.

"Not for Carl. He's a coward when it comes to facing up to situations which he's created." She said it without hostility or scorn.

Randollph decided it was time to get to the point. "How can I be of help?"

"Carl's got himself in a mess." Kitty Darrow looked at the doctor with what Randollph interpreted as affection. Dr. Brandt looked into the distance as if contemplating existence on some distant and inaccessible island.

"I insisted he had to talk to someone, and he won't go to the police or a lawyer. He said he liked you and would talk to you, provided whatever he says is, you know, like when Catholics confess—the police can't get it out of you. Is that right?"

Randollph nodded.

"Carl's afraid there's a lot of evidence that he killed his wife," Kitty said.

Randollph covered a startled reaction by resettling himself in the big comfortable executive chair that had for so many years accommodated the ample posterior of the Reverend Dr. Arthur Hartshorne. "Tell me about it." He addressed the remark directly to Kitty Darrow, figuring that Dr. Brandt would only hem and haw and splutter. Kitty Darrow impressed him as a sensible young woman somewhat unhinged by her inexplicable passion for Dr. Brandt. "Why would the doctor want to kill his wife?"

"Money," Kitty said. "He needed money badly. He owed a lot of money to banks."

"May I ask why?"

"Carl's a gambler. He gambles all the time, on everything. You name it, he bets on it—the stock market, horses, games of any kind. And he loses."

"That hardly seems a compelling motive for murdering his wife," Randollph said. "At least, not so soon. I assume you are afraid that the police will connect the doctor's need for money with the insurance policy he took out on his wife just a few days ago, especially since it was his idea."

Brandt, who had been slumping miserably in his chair, sat up. "How did you know that?"

"Lisa told me. But banks are usually quite lenient with doctors. They have large earning power, and in Dr. Brandt's case, he had just become a full partner in the clinic. His financial prospects would look excellent to a banker."

Kitty looked at the doctor. "Maybe you should tell him, Carl."

"I'm in hock to a loan shark." Brandt's voice was tinctured with despair. "He's threatening to break up my hands unless I pay up. Where would I be if I couldn't use my hands? The police, they find this out, they'll think I killed Lisa because it was the only way I could get a lot of money quick."

"Did you?" Randollph was impersonal.

"No, no, no. I swear to God! I'm a gambler. Can't seem to quit. I married Lisa for, ah, well, to help my career. People do that all the time. What's so bad about that?" Randollph, in his short time as interim pastor of the Church of the Good Shepherd, had become wearily accustomed to people trying to paint the dull gray of dishonorable behavior in the brighter colors of conventional conduct. He let it pass.

"But murder, no. Like Kitty says, I'm a coward about some things. Even if I'd thought about it, which I swear to God I never did, I wouldn't have had the guts."

"Carl's a great surgeon. He's the star of the hospital staff." Kitty, Randollph supposed, felt the need to enter some positive item in Dr. Brandt's dossier.

"Now, Kitty," Brandt countered with a weak protest, "Kermit's an awfully good surgeon."

"Nobody said he wasn't." Kitty was almost testy. "But just ask any of the surgical nurses. They'll tell you that Carl is a brilliant general surgeon. The best."

"What about Dr. Valorous Julian?" Randollph asked. "What do the nurses think of him?" He could guess what the nurses thought of Val, but he'd heard all he wanted to hear about the sterling qualities of Dr. Brandt.

For the first time since Randollph had ushered her to her seat, Kitty smiled. "Val? He's not like a doctor at all. At least, not like any doctor I've ever met."

"A clown," Brandt muttered. "Doesn't take medicine seriously."

"That's not fair, Carl." Kitty was defensive. "He's as brilliant an internist as you are a surgeon."

"How is he different from other doctors?" This did interest Randollph.

Kitty tried to think how she, a professional, could explain it to a layman. "I don't know if I can make this clear or not."

"Try," Randollph encouraged her.

"Well, medicine is supposed to have a ... I guess you would call it a great tradition."

"Solemn and exalted," Randollph suggested.

"Yes, that's it. Doctors like to think of themselves as ... as unselfish healers bringing health to suffering people. It's ... well, it's like they are some way special ..." Her voice trailed off as she searched for a way to explain herself.

"Like they've been ordained?" Randollph suggested.

Kitty brightened. "Yes, and it gets to them, most of them. Dr. Rex talks about the sacred art of medicine. Dr. Kermit is pompous about it. Carl is pompous about it."

Dr. Brandt roused from his lethargy. "Oh, now, look here, Kitty—"

"You are, Carl. But Val isn't. I don't mean he isn't serious about his work. But he laughs about what he calls the solemn pretensions of medicine."

"People who've been ordained are often pompous about it," Randollph said. "It apparently goes along with the laying on of hands."

"What?" Kitty asked.

"It isn't important."

"I don't think Val cares a lot about money," Kitty continued.

"Everybody cares about money," Carl Brandt said.

Kitty ignored him. "When Dr. Rex talks about the sacred art of medicine, Val starts talking about the sacred art of extracting a big fee."

"And the other doctors don't like that?"

"They hate to be reminded that they're a greedy lot," Kitty answered. "But the nurses love him."

"Why?" Randollph was certain that Lieutenant Casey wouldn't be asking apparently aimless questions, flushing out a raft of pointless information. Casey would be incisive and get to the heart of the matter, such as, Did Carl Brandt and/or Kitty Darrow kill Lisa Julian? But Casey was a detective. Randollph was a pastor, and a pastor was interested in human qualities and relationships.'

"Do you know anything about doctors and nurses?" Kitty asked.

"Not much."

"Well, a nurse is completely . . . I don't know what word I want, but a nurse has to do exactly what a doctor says. She can quit her job, of course, but otherwise she has to take any kind of cussing or nastiness the doctor wants to . . . to . . ." She groped for a way to explain it to a layman.

"You mean the doctor can shout at her, or be rude or demanding if he wants to, and she has to put up with it?" Randollph tried to be helpful.

"Yes, that's it. They're not all mean, but some of them are. Carl isn't mean. Or Dr. Kermit, or Dr. Rex. More impersonal. They'd say, 'Nurse, attend to this,' or 'Nurse, go get this or that,' but not Dr. Val. He knows all the nurses' names, calls them by their names, joshes with them. A lot of them just call him Val when other doctors aren't around. You couldn't do that with any other doctor."

"I see," Randollph said. "Tell me about the Julian women."

Kitty was glad to oblige. "Nell—Mrs. Kermit—she's just society. Isn't interested in the clinic except that the money keeps her in Cadillacs and servants and clothes. We hardly ever see her."

"And Mrs. Rex Julian?"

Kitty's face hardened. "A pain in the . . ." She stopped and amended her spontaneous vulgarism. "An unpleasant woman. Bossy. Determined to have her own way."

"And what is her own way?"

"Anything to push Dr. Val. He's her only chick and child. She was a young nurse when Dr. Rex married her, so she thinks she's an expert and tries to tell all of us how to do our jobs. She lectures us all the time, but she always gets in something about how Dr. Val is the greatest doctor who ever lived."

"I'd think that would make the nurses dislike him."

"It would, except, like I told you, he's so friendly with the nurses, they overlook it."

"And Dr. Val? How does he feel about his mother? He must know how she acts around the clinic."

Kitty Darrow tapped her teeth with a forefinger, as if to dislodge the right answer. "I'd say he's exasperated by it but can't do anything. He's affectionate toward her, but he's always trying to tone her down."

"And how did she get along with Lisa? Perhaps I'd better ask you, Dr. Brandt?"

Brandt roused himself from whatever gloomy thoughts had made him look like a man who'd just heard that his house had burned the day after his insurance had lasped. "Huh? Oh, Lisa didn't have anything against her. Didn't see her very often. She—"

Kitty interrupted. "But she wasn't terribly fond of Lisa."

"Why wasn't she fond of Lisa?"

"I don't know," Kitty said.

"Make a guess."

"Well, as a guess, I'd say that she resented it that Val and Lisa were very close. They're, ah, they were a lot alike."

"How so?"

"Oh, they both think, thought ..." Kitty was having trouble straightening out her tenses, talking about the live brother and his dead half-sister. "They looked at life as just a bowl of cherries, they didn't take it seriously. 'Fun-loving' would describe it."

"And Mrs. Julian didn't want competition for Val's affection?"

"That's my guess." Kitty sounded quite positive about it.

"Val's the only thing in this world she really cares about."

"Is that the reason he's a bachelor?"

"No, I don't think so. Maybe. Who knows? He's got plenty of girlfriends. He's no monk. When he finds the right girl, he'll marry her. Whether Mama likes it or not. Val does as he pleases."

There was a pause in the conversation. Kitty Darrow, after the easy business of recounting the ins and outs of the Julian relationships, was nerving herself to say something that wasn't easy for her. Finally she said, "Reverend Randollph, I've got to tell you about a strange thing that happened at the restaurant tonight."

"Yes. What was it?" Randollph had learned that sometimes you had to prod a reluctant confessor to spill the beans.

Kitty told him about the blond gunwoman. Randollph made the connection immediately.

"Does the name Laura Justus mean anything to either of you?"

It didn't.

Randollph spoke gravely. "You come to me as a pastor, presumably seeking counsel. What you have told me may be evidence in a homicide investigation. I feel certain that it is. My counsel to you is to go at once to Lieutenant Michael Casey and tell him what you have told me."

"No," Dr. Brandt said.

"Carl, I told you—" Kitty began.

"No."

Randollph recognized the childish stubbornness of the weak personality and knew he would not be persuaded. "I will not betray your confidence, Dr. Brandt. As a pastor, I may even withhold evidence of a crime which I have heard in a confessional situation. But how long do you think it will be before the police come into possession of these facts? Not long. If, for whatever reasons, you won't go to the police, may I report to Lieutenant Casey what you have told me?"

The doctor thought about it. "O.K.," he said. "To Casey. He seems a decent fellow. To Casey, but no one else. I know I look bad in all this. But I didn't kill my wife. I'll be glad to talk to Lieutenant Casey if he comes to me. I don't want to go to the police station."

Randollph rose. "I'm glad you came in to talk to me. Call me if you need me."

As soon as Brandt and Kitty Darrow were out the door, he called Casey's station. The lieutenant wasn't on duty. He called the Casey home number. No answer.

Randollph looked at his watch. The mission-committee meeting was probably in full swing. Duty, which William Wordsworth once infelicitously called the stern daughter of the Voice of God, insisted that he catch the remainder of the meeting. "The hell with it," he said, and summoned the elevator to his penthouse parsonage.

Fourteen

Randollph pulled on thin black over-the-calf hose, stepped into the trousers of his black tropical worsted suit, and used a shoehorn to pry on black patent-leather loafers with small gold bars across the front. The shoes were a trifle frivolous for clerical garb, he supposed, but they were the plainest he owned. He decided not to put on the black shirt and clerical collar now, although the bishop would be wearing his clericals, because he thought it would make him feel too somber and formal at breakfast.

He pulled a scarlet polo shirt over his head. Maybe it would be a good idea to force the clergy to wear the garb of office at all times. It would certainly eliminate the pride in appearance, which he supposed contributed to the false and overweening spiritual pride about which the Scriptures warn, not to mention saving the uncounted hours spent in shopping for clothes. On the other hand, did the constant wearing of a uniform, even a uniform to proclaim the wearer God's special agent, encourage pride in the office?

Wasn't it easy for the collared clergy to walk down the street exulting through their garb, "Look at me! I am not as other men." Deciding it was six of one and a half dozen of the other, he selected a bamboo-shade linen jacket.

Clarence Higbee had moved into one of the guest rooms the day before, then presented himself for instructions. Randollph was hesitant about asking him to prepare breakfast for three guests on his first day as chef and majordomo, but Clarence was not at all perturbed.

"It will be my pleasure, sir," he'd said. "But I must confer with you as to provisioning the larder."

Randollph had looked at him blankly.

"The purchase of comestibles is one of my responsibilities, sir." Clarence was trying to be enlightening. "But I must know if you wish to select menus in advance."

"Why don't you just surprise me?" Randollph told him, sensing that this would be his preference.

"Very well, sir. I will need to know, that is, er ... He hesitated.

"A problem?" Randolph thought he knew what Higbee was trying to ask.

"You see, sir, I must know what pecuniary limitations you wish me to observe." The little man was almost embarrassed. "Never having served a man of the cloth, and, ah, that is ..."

Randollph laughed. "Don't be embarrassed, Mr. Higbee. You are thinking that perhaps I must of necessity be parsimonious with the food budget. While I do not wish you to indulge in unchristian extravagance, we surely do not need to compromise with quality."

Visibly relieved Clarence said, "I'm not certain how you would define unchristian extravagance, sir. Being a Christian man, I do not approve of waste. But I look on food as a gift of God, and see it as a Christian duty to prepare it palatably and serve it attractively."

Randollph wasn't certain about the dividing line between the appropriate treatment of God's gifts and luxurious indulgence, but was glad to leave that to Clarence Higbee's Christian conscience.

"I agree with that," he said.

"Thank you, sir. And now, may I ask, who is your wine merchant?"

"My what?"

"I'm able to find only two bottles of California claret and one of a domestic white table wine with which I am not familiar. I'm sure you will wish me to replenish your supply." He was, Randollph judged, being rebuked for his negligence.

"I am not knowledgeable about wines," he confessed, hoping that Clarence wouldn't think ill of him. "I'm sure you know a good, er, wine merchant. Why don't I leave the selection to you, Mr. Higbee?"

"Thank you, sir. And may I request, sir, that you address me as Clarence?"

Randollph was startled. "Whatever for?" he asked.

"It is appropriate for the masters to address those who serve them by their Christian names, sir. I am most comfortable in a situation where these distinctions are observed. I am convinced that the world was much happier when everyone knew the station to which he had been born and aspired to be only the best he could at what life had assigned to him."

Randollph could hardly believe what he had heard. "You talk as if you are a monarchist, Clarence," he said.

"I am a monarchist, sir. And now, if there is nothing else, I'll be about my duties."

When Randollph came down the penthouse's winding open-tread stairway, it was only 7:30. His guests weren't due till 8:30. He wanted time to take the elevator down to the lobby of the hotel, pick up a morning paper and his mail, and enjoy a few moments of leisure before beginning what would be a long and exausting day. He looked into the dining room to see if Clarence was there. He wasn't, but there was a copy of the Chicago *Tribune* in a small rack on the table and a neat pile of letters on a silver tray. Clarence, it appeared, had already been down to the lobby.

The glass wall of the dining room framed a slice of sky that was dark with rain. Sudden lightning ripped the clouds, which emptied on the penthouse, streaking the window with a thousand tiny rivers tracing their courses down the glass to some unseen estuary. Gloomy weather for a gloomy task, Randollph thought.

He opened the *Tribune*, slipping the sports section from its casing of thefts, homicides, rape, and rumors of war. The Cubs had lost a doubleheader. The Sox had won. There was a story about the upcoming All-Star football game, claiming as usual that this was the best crop of college players ever, and that Oakland had better take them seriously. Randollph doubted that Ken Stabler was worried. Some atavism from which he thought he had escaped forever made him wish, however fleeting the feeling, that he was gearing up to go to training camp, getting ready for the coming season. He hastily put the thought aside with the sports section.

Among the accounts of atrocities and outrages committed recently in Chicago Randollph found, at the bottom of page one, a story captioned "Police Report No Progress in Julian Murder." It briefly recapped the details of the killing. The last paragraph noted that private services for Lisa Julian would be held today at the Bockmeister-Riordan Funeral Home, with the Reverend Dr. Cesare Paul Randollph, pastor of the Church the Good Shepherd, officiating. It also named the bishop, "a longtime friend of the family," as a participant in the services.

Randollph, intent on the paper, had not heard Clarence come in.

"Good morning, sir," Clarence said. He put down a tray on the sideboard, deftly spread a napkin across Randollph's knees, and placed a silver bowl of crushed ice in front of him. Randollph could see, just peeking out of the ice, a small glass of pale yellow liquid.

"I thought you might like some refreshment while you open your mail," Clarence said. "There's a small pot of coffee here on the sideboard when you wish it. I failed to ascertain if you took cream and sugar, sir, but I felt sure that you wouldn't."

"You guessed correctly," Randollph said, sipping the orange juice. Fresh squeezed. He might have known.

"May I assume that your guests will be prompt?" Clarence asked.

"Yes, they'll be prompt."

"Then I shall be ready to serve shortly after eight-thirty, sir." As Clarence left, Randollph noticed that he was wearing a black double-breasted jacket over gray striped trousers, white shirt with batwing collar, and a gray tie.

Randollph sifted the letters. He quickly put all the machine- or sticker-addressed envelopes in one pile and pushed it aside. They would all contain pleas for him to buy something, or promote some cause, dubious or worthy, in and through his church, or to send his personal contribution to some cause, dubious or worthy, as promptly as he could write out a check.

There was only one letter left. The envelope bore the crest of the seminary in California where, had not Bishop Freddie persuaded him to come to Good Shepherd as interim pastor, he would be telling budding successors to Savonarola and Henry Ward Beecher why Ignatius Loyola preferred to evangelize the upper classes, or what Erasmus said about Dr. Luther's reformation. He slit the envelope with a table knife, thinking that Clarence would probably disapprove.

DEAR C.P. [he read]:

Why do you not write? All your friends here in this obscure corner of academia are anxious to hear what life is like in the real world. Are you saving any souls? Are you leading any intellectual revolutions? Are you manning the barricades for the victims of a greedy and materialistic society? Just what the hell are you doing?

As you know, nothing ever happens here. The department of systematic theology is insisting that it must have an additional professor, even though everyone knows there is no such thing as systematic theology anymore. And anyway, who'd want to study systematic theology? The wife of the new professor of Christian Ethics was caught shoplifting, but the dean had enough clout to hush it up.

I wish the students would organize a protest against something, anything. It would liven things up. But no. All they want to do, this present breed of student, is to get their credentials and grab off the best job they can lay their hand on.

I hope your life is more exciting than mine. What ever possessed me to take up the teaching of the sociology of religion? I surely serve the Lord in quietness and obscurity. I envy you. Write and tell me what life is like in the trenches.

Dominus Vobiscum,

JED

Randollph chuckled and drained the glass of orange juice. He thought of finding pen and paper and dashing off an answer right there at the dining-room table. But Clarence would be coming in, and Clarence would consider such behavior gauche. He poured himself a cup of coffee and took it with Jed's letter across to his study.

Dear Jed [he wrote]:

I had planned to render you a report on "life in the real world," as you put it, as soon as I had collected enough data to provide a reasonable basis for authentic conclusions. Surely you, as a sociologist, suspect as your branch of that science or art may be, can appreciate that. But since you are so eager to hear of my adventures among the philistines, I shall submit a preliminary account.

As you know, Freddie persuaded me to take on this task so that I might learn what it is like to be a parish pastor. He was lyrical about the blessings of being a pastor, and how the experience would broaden my outlook and add substance to my teaching. He said it would be good for my soul.

I came to this task a virgin (so far as pastoral experience is concerned). I've learned that Sundays come around rapidly, and that you have to fight for time to prepare a sermon. I've learned that the senior pastor of a church this size devotes more time to administration than to being a cure of souls. Bishop Freddie, who operates about as he did when he was our Dean Freddie, tells me that it is no longer the star preacher but the hotshot clerical administrator who gets the best jobs in the church. This depresses me, and I think we should keep it a secret from our students. They'll learn it soon enough anyway. I think Freddie regrets all this, but, as he often says, he has an institution to run. The church, he says (always with a sad look), can tolerate bad theology much easier than it can tolerate bad management.

As to the blessings Freddie mentioned, there are some. I have large crowds to preach to. The church is heavily endowed, so money is no problem (I gather that it is a

problem in most churches). I live in splendor in the parsonage penthouse. My salary is so generous that I shall not
mention the figure lest you be tempted to unchristian envy.
I have numerous staff and employees under me and am thus
like the Centurion in the Gospel of Matthew who, when he
told people to come, they came, and when he told them to
go, they went. I am a person of importance in the city by
virtue of holding this job. Politicians seek my approval.
Community leaders are deferential. All these things, I suppose, can be counted as blessings. I am not sure, however,
that they are good for my soul.

I am enclosing a newspaper clipping about a murder in
which I am somewhat involved. You no doubt know of Lisa
Julian, but you probably are not aware that ten years or so
ago she and I were very close friends. It has been a
harrowing experience for me, and it isn't over yet.

The newspaper clipping does not explain, of course, that
the Samantha Stack, who was the matron of honor and is
something of a local celebrity because of her popular television show, is also a very close friend of mine, and has been,
almost from the time I arrived (I was a guest on her show). I
could rhapsodize about her beauty and charm, but I'll just
say she's a good-looking redheaded divorcée with a keen
mind and a sharp wit. And I think that's all you need to
know about this relationship, or at least it's all I'm going to
tell you—except that she finds my company acceptable
despite her conviction that preachers are supposed to belong
to a third sex.

As I continue in the life of a parish pastor, I'll do my
utmost to fight the temptations of loving the power of my
position, and of being seduced from the simple values by the
luxury in which I am kept. Perhaps you should ask all my
friends on the faculty to pray for me—that is, if prayer isn't
considered intellectually disreputable out there.

I'll keep you posted. My regards to everyone out there who merits it.

> *Pax,*
> C.P.

He was sealing the letter when he heard the door chimes. Almost immediately, voices sifted into his study, informing him that Freddie, Samantha, and Dan Gantry had taken the penthouse elevator together, and that they were making themselves known to Clarence. He hurried out.

"Good morning, C.P.," the bishop said. He handed the oversize vinyl garment bag which contained his pulpit robe to Clarence, and shook hands.

"Morning, boss. You aren't going to a funeral in that getup, are you?" Dan Gantry said.

Sam gave him a quick kiss.

"Breakfast is served when you wish it, sir," Clarence announced.

Randollph was amazed at the transformation in the dining room. The white tablecloth emphasized the elegance of the place settings, the silver, the napery, the crystal water goblets. An opaque crystal bowl, like a frail but lovely boat on a white sea, carried a sheaf of buttery yellow roses. At each place was a silver bowl holding half a melon snugged down in crushed ice. Randollph wondered where Clarence had found all the linens and dishes, but supposed that they had been buried somewhere in the capacious kitchen when the Reverend Dr. and Mrs. Arthur Hartshorne had reluctantly abandoned the parsonage to their unnamed successors.

The melon was of a ripeness and flavor seldom found outside the dining rooms of very expensive hotels. By the time they had finished, Clarence was back with a serving cart carrying chafing dishes, silver pots, plates, cups, and saucers. With the unhurried speed and economy of motion managed by people who have mastered their craft, he transferred the cart load to the sideboard and lighted the burners under chafing dishes.

"I've placed everything here, sir," he said to Randollph, "thinking you might want to proceed as your schedule allows." He began the removal of the melon dishes, placing them on the cart.

The bishop took a plate and removed the cover from one of the dishes. "My word! What have we here? Kippers? I haven't had a kipper since I was at Oxford."

"Yes, m'lord, kippers," Clarence said. "I'm pleased that you fancy them. You will also find eggs Benedict, omelet, and sausage, which I obtain from a farmer who grinds it daily. I recommend it highly. The sticky buns I bake myself. I hope you'll pardon me mentioning it, but I'm quite proud of them."

"A veritable feast," the bishop said.

"Thank you, m'lord."

"Ah, Clarence," the bishop said, "I know that Church of England bishops hold the status of lords, but we are more democratic here. I am not a lord, so there is no need to address me by the title."

"Begging your pardon, m'lord, but I'm accustomed to addressing bishops as 'your lordship.' It is my conviction that all bishops, even those of a nonconformist persuasion, deserve the honor. With your permission, I shall continue to address you as such. I'm more comfortable in a situation where these distinctions are clearly observed, m'lord." He turned to Randollph. "If you need anything, you've only to ring," he said, and pushed the cart toward the kitchen.

"God, this is good!" Dan Gantry said, working diligently on a plate of eggs Benedict. "I'm going to have some of everything but the kippers."

"You'll get fat as a pig, Randollph, with this kind of cooking every day," Sam said.

"You are responsible, then," he told her. "It was your idea that I employ him. I favored the nice-looking divorcée who missed cooking for a man, if you will remember."

"I know you did, dear boy. That's why I insisted on Clarence."

"What is the profit, then, Sam, in protecting me from temptation to illicit carnal connection only to deliver me to the sin of gluttony?" Randollph found himself enjoying this banter with Sam, enjoying his guests' pleasure in the food, all so inappropriate, given the nature of the day. Were these light moments barriers they erected against the reality they would all be facing at the funeral home? Were these normalities their unconscious affirmation that though in the midst of life we are in death, so also in the midst of death we are in life, the world goes on, the gift of laughter is still given, food is consumed, human relationships continue? It occurred to him that "The Appropriateness of the Inappropriate" might make a good subject for a sermon, but he supposed that someone had already done it.

Sam was about to answer Randollph when Dan Gantry said, "Damn fine sausage! And, oh, those sticky buns! I think I'll go back for thirds." He stood up.

Sam thumped him in the stomach. "Better lay off the starch, Danny Boy, or you'll be growing a pot on that youthful frame."

"I burn it off, beautiful, I burn it off," Danny said, heaping his plate.

The bishop said, "C.P., I hope you aren't offended that Rex Julian asked me to have a part in the service today." The mood changed immediately, as if the teacher had announced that recess was over.

"You know I'm not, Freddie. Why would I be?" He'd have to be careful not to call the bishop Freddie in front of

Clarence Higbee, Randollph reminded himself. That wouldn't do at all.

"Some pastors are very touchy about it. Dan, could I trouble you to pour me a drop of coffee? Thank you. As I was saying, some pastors, particularly senior pastors of our large churches, feel threatened if anyone else, even associate pastors, has anything to do with their funerals or weddings."

"Old Arty Hartshorne wouldn't let anyone horn in on one of his weddings or funerals," Dan said. "Not even me, unless the old boy was sick or out of town. I think he just hated to let anyone else cadge a fee. He was a greedy old ..." Dan thought better of what he was going to say and let his voice trail off.

"Some pastors are greedy," the bishop said, "just as some are envious, and some are prideful, and some are lustful."

"You've destroyed my illusions, bishop," Sam said. "I grew up believing that pastors never did a bad deed or ever had an evil thought. Lustful! They never had enough juice in them to be lustful. Of course," she added, "I was raised a Presbyterian."

"I'm afraid, my dear, that your pastors pretended to be above the sins with which we can reproach most of the human race." The bishop unbuttoned his black suit jacket and clasped his hands over his plump belly. "You see, laymen like to think their pastors are mild and inoffensive, so pastors oblige them by acting as if they were. It is not good for the pastors, and it is not good for the laymen. Happily, though, the younger men, many of them, are refusing to make the pretense."

Clarence appeared in the doorway and addressed Randollph. "I beg pardon for the intrusion, sir, but a Miss Windfall from your office wishes to speak to you. She says that it is urgent. If you wish, I will tell her that you are engaged."

Randollph was tempted to let Clarence do battle with Adelaide Windfall just for the fun of seeing which one would win, but decided that confrontation was bound to come about sooner or later anyway.

"Bring the phone in here, if you will, Clarence. There's a jack there by the door."

"I know, sir. I'd already located it."

"I'm sorry to disturb you, Dr. Randollph." Miss Windfall did not sound sorry. "There's a woman who insists she must speak to you right now. I have her on hold."

"Who is she?"

"She won't give me her name." Miss Windfall's voice tone said that anonymous callers were not worthy of her notice, and Randollph wondered why she was bothering him.

"However," she continued, "she claims to be a member of the church, in desperate need of pastoral counsel." That explained it. A member of Good Shepherd, even an anonymous member whose claim might be spurious, deserved checking out, so far as Adelaide Windfall was concerned.

"Put her on," Randollph instructed, considering if there were too many barriers between him and people who wanted to talk to him. One would have to be persistent to get past both his secretary and his majordomo. Probably he ought to make himself more accessible. On the other hand, he would then spend all his time answering the phone, and his office would be invaded by religious eccentrics, penny-stock salesmen, and a variety of long-winded visitors who just wanted someone to talk to.

"Dr. Randollph," a feminine voice of no particular character said into his ear, "you don't know me, and I'm not going to tell you my name, I don't want your secretary to write it on your appointment pad, I don't want to come to your office, I might be recognized." She stopped for breath, and Randollph was about to make a vague encouraging noise when she continued. "I'm in desperate trouble. I need advice. Will you see me? Today?"

"Today is very crowded," he said, "but if we can find a mutually agreeable time—"

"Five o'clock. Will five o'clock be all right? In the chapel. I often go there to pray at five o'clock. There's hardly anyone there at that time. If there's anyone else there, you can pretend to pray—oh, I don't mean that, you wouldn't pretend, would you? Just wait until they've gone. No one ever stays long. Five o'clock in the chapel." She hung up without giving him a chance to say no.

When he had cradled the phone the bishop said, "I assume you wish me to give the eulogy today?"

"I'd appreciate it," Randollph said. "I think I might have a hard time doing it. I'll be all right reading the service."

"The dependable refuge of the ritual," the bishop said. "It speaks for us when we can't speak for ourselves, and it says what we feel, so much better than we can say it. Does anyone mind if I smoke a cigar?"

"The limousine from the funeral home won't be here for an hour," Randollph said. "But, Freddie, I don't recall ever seeing you smoke."

The bishop reached into the inside pocket of his jacket, took out a beautifully finished gold cigar case, and extracted from it a long dark cigar. "I seldom do. But one of our laymen for whom I was able to do a little favor recently—just blessed the food at his corporation's annual employee dinner, actually—came in yesterday with a whole box of these"—he sniffed the cigar appreciatively—"and this lovely case. They're Montecristos, which means he smuggles them in from Cuba or Canada, I suppose. May I offer them to anyone?"

"Everyone to his own taste," Dan said, lighting a cigarette.

"I'll take one," Sam said, holding out her hand. "It isn't every day a girl gets a chance to smoke a Montecristo."

"Freddie, you're breaking the law, you know," Randollph told him. "Possession of Cuban cigars is illegal in this country. And you a Christian bishop! Doesn't your conscience hurt you?" Randollph tried his best to sound stern.

"Not at all, C.P." The bishop held a match just beyond the end of the cigar, warming it. "I don't know these cigars are smuggled in. I suspect they are Havanas, but no one has certified them as such to me. What my conscience doesn't know for a fact can't hurt it."

"That's sophistry, Freddie, and you know it." Randollph grinned at the bishop.

"Of course it's sophistry, C.P. How else could I justify what I already intend to do? However, if it will help *your* conscience, let me state in my episcopal authority and wisdom that it is a Christian duty to break silly laws which have been constructed for doubtful political ends. Like the one prohibiting possession of Havana cigars."

"Then you are an antinomian," Randollph stated. It was always fun to needle Freddie, though you never could nail him.

"Not an antinomian, C.P. But not a petty legalist, either. We Christians, if nothing else, are supposed to know the difference between a moral demand on us and a stupid restriction. Anyway," the bishop said, blowing an umbrella of blue smoke, "committing a small, harmless sin now and then keeps us in good moral trim. Saves us from the whopping sin of self-righteousness."

Fifteen

An extravagantly long Mercedes 600 with a discreet steel plaque inside the back window reading "Bockmeister-Riordan" was parked in front of the hotel entrace. It was an arrogant car, Randollph thought. With the name of the funeral home displayed, however tastefully, it said to the world "We bury the best people." He wondered if, even in death, it was necessary to maintain the deceased's status by the selection of the right undertaker. He'd have to ask Freddie about that.

A man in a neat black double-breasted suit which looked like an understated uniform stepped up to them, said, "Right this way, bishop, Dr. Randollph," and held the door for them. Sam, Randollph, and the bishop sat on the rich gray brocade bench seat, Dan Gantry taking a commodious jump seat. The driver, Randollph noticed, was insulated from the passengers by a thick plate-glass window, releasing him from the burden of listening to inane chatter and answering stupid questions.

   With the big car cruising silently toward the north side
Randollph, hoping to break the quiet which had settled
over them, told about the woman who wanted to meet him
in the chapel for counseling.

   "Counseling, huh!" Sam spluttered. "Whatever she wants
—and I'd be willing to guess what she wants—it isn't
counseling."

   "In the chapel?" Dan was incredulous. "I admit that this
dame could have the hots"—he looked at Freddie and
amended—"she could be on the prowl for the boss. But in
the chapel? Be reasonable, Sam old girl."

   The bishop cleared his throat. "Stranger things have
happened," he said. "I remember one case ... But no, I
won't go into that. Suffice to say, female parishioners do
occasionally become enamored of the pastor. I wish I could
state that this only happens when the pastor is an uncommonly attractive personality. But that wouldn't be true. It
has been my experience that some ladies fall in love with
pastors whose romantic appeal entirely escapes the objective
eye. My objective eye, at least."

   "What you're going to find out, boss, when you've been
in this racket awhile, is that plenty of women have clods for
husbands, guys that all they think about is making a buck or
getting a promotion. They don't have any time for their
wives. They think if they're good providers that's all they
need to be. Romance they don't understand. They aren't
even much interested in sex, some of them, hard as that is
to understand. So these women get to looking around. Can
you blame them? And here's the pastor, real handy. He's at
least educated, has a few manners, he's nice to the ladies. So
the first thing you know, she's got fantasies about him. And
if she's aggressive, she goes after him. Ten to one that's it
with this babe that wants to pray with you in the chapel."

   "Do you speak from experience, Danny Boy?" Sam asked.

"I'll take the Fifth on that, beautiful. Can I help it if I'm a handsome, charming bachelor?"

Randollph looked at the bishop across Sam. "What's your counsel, Freddie? I could just fail to appear, although that would be a bit irresponsible of me."

"Wear your track shoes and run at the first sign the girl would like to know you better," Sam said.

The bishop laughed. "That might be wise counsel, C.P. But let's not jump to conclusions. The lady claims to be suffering with some unspecified emotional problem. She says she comes to the chapel often to pray, so the problem is not new. Probably, then, it has come to a head and she doesn't know what to do. Why not take her at her word? If she wants her pastor to pray with her, why, then, do it. It is a pastor's responsibility to pray for his flock, especially when one of them requests it. Be cautious, to be sure. She may be emotionally unstable. But a pastor cannot afford to be skittish about his parishioners, even lady parishioners. Even attractive lady parishioners."

"I couldn't have put it better myself," Dan said.

"I just thought it was a rather strange request," Randollph said.

"It won't be the last strange request made of you," the bishop said.

"I'm a little shaky on counseling procedures, having had little training and no real pastoral experience." Randollph leaned back into the soft, luxurious upholstery of the limousine. "But I expect I can handle it."

"Are you bragging, reverend?" Sam asked.

"I hate to be addressed as 'reverend.'"

"I know," Sam said with a sweet smile.

The limousine drove up to the rear entrance of the

funeral home, a sprawling red-brick building behind the facade of an antebellum Southern mansion.

"Look at all those Jags and Caddies! There's even a Bentley. Now, that's class," Dan said.

"Doctors' cars, I expect," the bishop said. "Doctors are the most affluent members of our society among those who work for a living."

"I think I'll circle around and go in the front way," Dan said, "and see if I can have a word with Val before the service. He's the only reason I'm here. Want to come with me, beautiful?" He offered Sam his arm.

"Might as well," she answered, marching off with him.

The chauffeur, carrying their robe cases, conducted Randollph and the bishop into a small hallway with rooms opening on either side. A tall man with slicked-down thin gray hair and whose garb was quite similar to Clarence Higbee's costume this morning, except for the batwing collar, Randollph noted, hurried up to them.

"Bishop," he said, "Dr. Randollph," extending his hand first to Freddie and then to Randollph, "I'm Albert Bockmeister III."

How did he know which of us was which? Randollph wondered, then remembered that Freddie was wearing a rabat of episcopal purple. This old boy certainly would know everything a high-toned funeral director would need to know about spotting distinguished clergy.

"So glad both of you could be here to comfort the Julian family in their hour of sorrow. They will always be grateful, I know," Albert Bockmeister III murmured with the spurious sincerity of those who cultivate you because there's something in it for them. "If you'll follow me, I'll conduct you to the clergy room." He motioned with a gray-gloved hand. "We are the only memorial home in the metropolitan area which maintains a room exclusively for the clergy."

Bockmeister led them to a small room with a full-length mirror, two straight-backed chairs, and a rack with several coat hangers. "That door is to the lavatory," Bockmeister said. "Exclusively for the clergy. I'll be back to conduct you to our Chapel of Memories shortly before time for the service."

"They specialize in euphemisms here, don't they? Memorial home, Chapel of Memories." Randollph shucked off his jacket.

"Ah, yes, and they've plenty more. The funeral industry invented the euphemism," the bishop said, slitting the belly of his garment bag by peeling down the full-length zipper, exposing its entrails of rich black silk. "The undertaker chaps have a right to make a living; we do need them. But I do wish they'd abandon their pretense that no one ever dies. Both Judaism and Christianity are sturdy religions which face the fact of death squarely. Then we have to conduct the final ritual in this atmosphere of unreality, where people aren't spoken of as dead, but as departed, or resting, or a beautiful memory." He shrugged into his clerical gown.

"My, my, Freddie, you do feel strongly about it, don't you?"

"I do, indeed, C.P.," the bishop, calmed a little, replied. "It is good for me to feel strongly about some things. I hold an office the essence of which is compromise and accommodation. I need some convictions on which I will not yield. Let's have a prayer before that glorified floorwalker comes to get us."

The Chapel of Memories, Randollph saw, was severely colonial in decor. White pews and chancel furniture were edged in dark walnut. Heavy white drapes shot with gold thread hung where windows might have been. On the altar, two burning candles kept vigil beside a plain gold cross, the only religious symbol in the chapel. If Freddie was right about funeral-parlor theology's being a neo-paganism, then colonial, with its roots in the style of Athens and Rome, was the correct architecture. He could also see its versatility. By substituting a crucifix for the cross, the chapel became Roman Catholic. Or a menorah would convert it to a synagogue, all at no cost and little effort for Albert Bockmeister III.

The thin whispers of an unseen electronic organ damped down and gave signs of dying. A small red light on the lectern, for his eyes only, came on and stared at him, warning that it was time to begin.

Through an act of will, Randollph erased from his mind that this was the funeral service for Lisa. He knew that he had to do this or he would never get through it. He had to be professional, take refuge in the ritual.

When he was finished and it was time for Freddie to deliver the eulogy he looked around for the first time. There were flowers, acres of flowers, mountains of flowers— small baskets, large baskets, huge intricate floral pieces, flowers everywhere. He now saw that the chapel had been designed to accommodate and display flowers, but not this many. The bronze casket, mercifully closed, was almost hidden by blankets of roses.

Randollph, listening to Freddie with one ear, picked Annette Paris out of the crowd. Her black dress showed her freshly coiffed blond hair to advantage. She was sobbing quietly. Behind her was Amos Oregon, scowling. He was flanked and surrounded by other Hollywood people whom Randollph had met at the wedding reception but could not now name. In the last pew he could see a sorrowful-looking Jaime DeSilva.

In an alcove to the left of the colonial-style raised pulpit was a room open to the chapel but affording semiprivacy for the family. Dr. Rex Julian's face was set and emotionless—but then, it always was. Mrs. Rex Julian ostentatiously kept dabbing at her eyes, but she looked petulant. Carl Brandt, newly widowed, slumped in what appeared to be utter dejection. Beside him, Dr. Kermit Julian's face imitated his father's, while Mrs. Kermit was covertly surveying the crowd. Only Dr. Valorous Julian showed strain and real sorrow. Randollph guessed that he was holding back tears only with a powerful effort.

He wondered if Lieutenant Michael Casey might be about somewhere, then remembered he hadn't been able to reach Casey to tell him about Dr. Brandt and Kitty Darrow. He'd have to find time today to try again. He wasn't in the congregation, apparently. No. Casey wouldn't work that way. He was still going on the assumption that Lisa was the victim of a burglar. But he was also checking out every other possibility. Did he still have his eye on some of Lisa's Hollywood friends, her ex-lovers? Probably. Was he breathing down the neck of Dr. Carl Brandt? Casey always liked the surviving spouse as a suspect. Could any of these more or less decent, prosperous, upper-middle-class people out there listening to Freddie have done Lisa in? Preposterous! But if so, would they have the gall to come to her funeral? It seemed unlikely.

His listening ear told him that Freddie was about to close. Randollph flipped the black morocco-bound ritual to where a thin slice of purple ribbon marked the closing prayers and benediction. His task was nearly finished.

It had been a long ride to the cemetery, and when he got back to the church, it was nearly two o'clock. He'd like to have gone up to the parsonage and change out of his clericals, but he knew that there was a basketful of responsibilities, some fixed, others collecting in his absence, which must be attended to before his five-o'clock appointment in the chapel. It would be a race to get through all them. So he went directly to the office.

Miss Windfall, who combined a respect for the office of pastor for the Church of the Good Shepherd with an unshakable conviction that he would never get anything done without her firm prodding, was waiting for Randollph with her usual list.

"We must have the copy for Sunday's worship bulletin in time for Evelyn to type it and take it to the printer, along with your editorial for *The Spire*." Miss Windfall's tone implied that he was planning to procrastinate but that she would not tolerate it.

"I know," Randollph said.

"Mr. Agostino will be here at three, as usual. Mr. Smelser would like a word with you at three-forty-five. Mr. Thurman from the hotel says he must see you today. I put him down for four-thirty."

"Mr. who?"

"Mr. Wilfred Thurman, the manager of the hotel."

"Oh," Randollph said. "Yes, I expect I know what he wants." He remembered that he hadn't checked with Dan Gantry about the current use of the church gymnasium. "When we're done here, get hold of Mr. Gantry and ask him to drop by for a minute, will you? Is there anything else?"

"Here's a list of patients at the Julian Hospital."

"Can't Mr. Sloane cover it?" Randollph was momentarily irritated. The Reverend Mr. Henry Sloane was a retired minister who, during a lengthy career in middling churches, had built a reputation as an uncommonly dull preacher but exceedingly effective pastor. Good Shepherd maintained him on the staff with the sole responsibility of calling on the shut-in and the sick. Then Randollph remembered that he'd taken this job to learn what it was like to be a pastor, and put aside his irritation.

"Mr. Sloane is covering the other hospitals. But Mrs. Victoria Clarke Hoffman is at Julian. I was sure you would want to see her yourself."

Randollph knew that, on Miss Windfall's scale of values, Mrs. Hoffman deserved attention from the top clerical dog at Good Shepherd, not because of some peculiar and acute spiritual need, but because she represented the weight of money and social standing, maybe both.

"The Clarkes were among the founders of this church, and Mrs. Hoffman has inherited fortunes both from her parents and from her husband. We understand this visit to the hospital is terminal. Dr. Hartshorne believed that she intended to leave a generous bequest to Good Shepherd, but she has never confirmed this."

"Yes, I should see her," Randollph said. Perhaps it was to be regretted that the rich sick got special care even from their chaplains. Perhaps it was undemocratic of him to trot out to see Mrs. Victoria Clarke Hoffman while dispatching Mr. Sloan, the low man on the totem pole of Good Shepherd's hierarchy, to dispense pastoral unction to members of the flock unwashed by money or social credentials. But Miss Windfall was right. He'd better call on her. Good or bad, this was the way things were. Oh, well, he comforted himself, she deserved his attention on the grounds of her family's lengthy record of faithfulness to Good Shepherd. He'd call on her gladly for that reason alone. But he'd be damned if he'd ask her about the rumored bequest.

Miss Windfall, judging that she'd ladled enough on Randollph's plate for the moment, sailed back to her office, probably, Randollph thought, to cook up more piddling chores for him.

The preparation of the worship bulletin and his column

for the weekly church paper (which arrived at the homes of members on Friday as a reminder that one of their options for the weekend was attendance at divine worship) were fixed points in the pastor's week. He did not look on them as piddling chores, and had discovered that he enjoyed doing both. But, like the weekly sermon, time did not wait for the pastor's inclination. You did these things whether illumined by the pellucid rays of divine inspiration or with a brain befogged by too much on it, because they had to be done to keep the holy show going.

He took a copy of last week's worship bulletin, striking out "June 6," then "Pentecost or Whitsunday." He penciled in "June 13" and "Trinity Sunday." He'd write in the hymns after consultation with Tony Agostino. He'd planned to write an affirmation of faith and a prayer of confession, but decided he didn't have time. So he made a note for Evelyn to type up the Apostles' Creed, knowing that she kept a copy of it handy. It was so familiar that it probably slid right across the minds of the worshippers without making a dent. It was appropriate anytime, and especially for Trinity Sunday. He fished a prayerbook out of a desk drawer and rummaged around in it till he found a confession that wasn't too long and didn't go in too heavily for grievous sins or for bewailing our manifold wickedness. He wrote another note to Evelyn on the margin, giving her the page number in the prayerbook and the first line of the confession. He drew a line through last Sunday's sermon topic and wrote over it "God's Other Names," then put the bulletin aside.

Now for the weekly editorial. He found a sheet of paper and stared at it. The paper stared back. It taunted him. It said to him, "You have nothing to say, but you have to say something. Why don't you just string some words together? Just drop in an occasional piety word like 'faith,' and 'prayer,' and 'dedication.' You know the lingo, all preachers do. It's easy, it'll save you the time you need so badly. It won't mean anything, of course, but everyone will think it a lovely message."

Randollph was tempted. But he'd learned as a football player and as a teacher that if you lowered the standard of your craft once, it was easy to do it twice. Then, before long, you'd lost the fine edge of competence. The least a pro could do was to perform consistently up to his capabilities.

Across the top of the paper, he doodled a church spire with lightning striking it. Then a long car. Then a thicket of tombstones. Suddenly he reached for a fresh sheet of paper and wrote across the top, "Last Week I Lost a Friend." Then, without identifying Lisa, or even saying that the lost friend was male or female, he described his feelings—numbness brought on by shock. The following sorrow and sense of loss. A resentment that the universe would permit a young and buoyant personality to be snuffed out to no apparent end. Then, how he tried to fit the problem of this tragic death—which was an example of the problem of evil—into the framework of faith.

He finished the column and rang for Evelyn. He hoped that by sharing his own experience, his words would be of help to others who either had endured a similar experience or, sooner or later, would face it.

He felt better for the writing. For the first time he was able to reflect on Lisa's death. Someone had seen a benefit worth killing for in her death. But what benefit? A thief picking her room at random, or even a thief privy to the hotel guest list and calculating that bride and groom would be carrying a fair haul of valuables, would have benefited only had Lisa surprised him and had a good look at him. But why the excessive brutality?

Her husband? Carl Brandt did not strike Randollph as an especially prepossessing character—but scarcely murderous, however great his need for immediate cash.

Someone from her life in show business? A former lover? A jealous woman? Possibly. Who was this Laura Justus? He'd known not a few actresses who were mean enough to murder if provoked to it. He'd never heard of a Laura Justus, but then, that probably wasn't her name anyway. He wondered if Casey had succeeded in tracing her, and remembered that he had to call the detective anyway. He buzzed Miss Windfall and asked her to see if Casey was in.

He was. He was polite, but brief, which meant that he was busy.

"What can I do for you, doctor?"

Randollph told him about Dr. Brandt and Kitty Darrow, and Brandt's gambling, and a loan shark named Manny Friedman.

"I'll see them tonight," Casey said crisply. "Best see them at the hospital, I suppose." Randollph wondered if it took an effort of will on Casey's part to suppress the policeman's natural instinct to haul them both down to the police station, or if Casey's gift for handling the upper classes allowed him to go to them without irritation.

"I'm going out to the hospital this evening, too," Randollph said. "Maybe we'll run into each other."

"They've got a coffee shop there. Why don't you buy me a cup of coffee—say, after visiting hours?" Casey had dropped his brusque executive tone.

"Public servants should not accept gifts from taxpayers, lieutenant," Randollph said. "Avoid the appearance of evil, you know."

"Then I'll buy." Casey chuckled and hung up.

Miss Windfall announced Mr. Agostino, and added that

Mr. Gantry was also waiting impatiently to see him. Miss Windfall's standards of rectitude and conventional clerical behavior for the pastors of Good Shepherd inexplicably did not apply to Dan Gantry. For some reason that Randollph could not divine, she was not put off by Dan's brash manners or frequently outrageous costumes. Anyone else waiting impatiently would be told icily to wait his turn.

"Send them both in," he told her. He'd barely hung up the phone when Dan, flinging a "thanks, Addie" over his shoulder, was at Randollph's desk.

"Boss," he said, placing both hands on the desk and leaning forward, "do you know what that son of a bitch Wilfred Thurman is doing?"

"I've no idea," Randollph said. "But since you're going to tell me, sit down and calm down. And apologize to Tony for butting in on his time."

"Yeah, yeah, I better do all that. Sorry, Tony, I'll make it up to you," he said to the choirmaster, who'd followed him in and sat down. "Maybe I could give you the names of a couple of girls I haven't got time to look after."

"No need, Dan," Tony said amiably. "I can't keep up with my own list."

Dan slumped in a chair and found a cigarette. "Boss, that Thurman wants to take over our gym and make it into meeting rooms for conventions. Don Miller on the trustees tipped me off that the bastard has talked with every trustee, giving them a line about how the hotel's going to pay us a fortune and that we don't need the gym anyway. He's got most of 'em persuaded it's the thing to do."

"He shouldn't have done that," Randollph said. "But do we use the gym, Dan?"

"We sure do!" Dan struck a match three times before he got it to burn. "Three nights a week we got programs—two basketball leagues, and a girls' volley-ball association. These

are all kids from crummy areas you can almost walk to from
here. And they need us. Where else are they going to go? I
don't run it, they've got their own leaders, and some of the
men social workers come in and ride herd. It's the only
thing this church does for the poor in this neighborhood.
They spend plenty on foreign missions, but do next to
nothing for the people that live in the shadow of their own
spire. Call a meeting of the trustees, boss, and let me at
'em." Dan was pleading now. "I'll give 'em theological
reasons why we got to keep this gym program going. I'll
even give 'em a lot of pious talk, God help me, if that's
what they want."

"I admire any man's passion for doing what he sees as the
right thing." Randollph grinned at his wrought-up assistant.
"But sometimes, excessive enthusiasm obfuscates the logical
solution to the problem. I learned that as a quarterback,"
he added.

"Yeah? What you getting at?" Dan ground out his
cigarette in an ashtray Randollph had hastily excavated
from a bottom drawer of his desk.

"I mean, let's do it the easy way." Randollph was patient.
"If we have a trustees' meeting, we'll have people taking
sides, and pretty soon the church will be polarized, with half
the members thinking we ought to lease the gym and half
thinking we ought to keep your program. Wars have been
started over less."

"I don't see any alternative."

"If Mr. Thurman withdrew his offer, it would solve the
problem."

"That greedy bastard? He won't do it."

"Oh, yes, he will," Randollph said. "I'm going to explain
to him why your programs in the gym are a Christian
witness which the church considers vital to its ministry in
the city."

Dan laughed sarcastically. "That's the kind of talk I was going to give the trustees, boss. Thurman's a pirate. He wouldn't know what you're talking about."

Randollph glanced at his watch, a thin eighteen-karat-gold Rolex which had cost him a bundle, even though he'd bought it in Geneva. The afternoon was slipping away, and still much to do.

"Believe me, Dan, he'll see the light. Trust me, and beat it. Tony and I have to look for hymns, and the printer won't wait."

Dan got up. "O.K., boss." He didn't look entirely convinced. "Sure you don't want the names of those girls, Tony?"

"If you're giving them away, they're probably dogs," Tony said. "I do my own hunting."

When Dan had gone, Tony Agostino said, "I can see that you're pressed for time, doctor, so I have some hymns for Sunday already picked out. For your approval, of course." Tony's Roman Catholic training with its respect for anyone in a clerical collar made him careful of overstepping ecclesiastical authority. "For Trinity Sunday it's easy."

Randollph reached to the corner of his desk for the red book which contained the praises and laments that the denominational music experts had approved for use in divine worship. Selecting hymns, he had discovered, was often an exasperating endeavor. When you found one whose text fitted the season and the sermon theme, it turned out that the tune was unsingable, or the poetic images were weak and sentimental, or that it expressed reprehensible theologies.

" 'Holy, Holy, Holy' is a good processional hymn," Tony said.

"Fine."

"Then, how about 'We Believe in One True God' and

'Come, Thou Almighty King'? Good tunes. Trinitarian theology. You're preaching about the Trinity?"

I am if I find any time this week to write a sermon, Randollph wanted to say. He remembered that he had started early on this sermon, that Lisa Julian had come in to arrange for her wedding, interrupting its preparation, and he'd never got back to it.

"Yes, of course," he said. He took a quick look at the two hymns. There was a passage in "We Believe in One True God" which irritated the theologian in him. And he was dubious about expressing Christian zeal in terms of monarchies and swords, as did the text of "Come Thou Almighty King." But then, he supposed, you couldn't make much of a hymn out of "Come, Thou Almighty President" or "Gird Up Thy Mighty Briefcase." People who didn't flinch at "The Man Upstairs" probably wouldn't recognize a distasteful theological concept or be offended by the Christianity of battlefield and buckler.

"They'll do," he told Tony. "And thanks for looking them up in advance. I *am* pressed today."

The Reverend Mr. O. Bertram Smelser had been on the pastoral staff of the Church of the Good Shepherd for more than twenty years. His assignment, almost from the beginning, was to look after the business affairs of the church. Unblessed with powers of oratory or the interest in other people which is a prerequisite for a good pastor, he seldom was called on to preach or visit. But he did tend diligently to the collecting, recording, spending, and investing of the money which flowed—if not in rivers, at least in full and lively streams—into the sacred bank accounts of the Church of the Good Shepherd.

The trouble was, from Randollph's point of view, the Reverend Mr. Smelser felt compelled by duty, or pride in his work, or a craving to talk about his function in the scheme of things, to come in once a month and present, like an *Apologia Pro Vita Sua*, a lengthy and exceedingly dry account, amply documented, of the church's business.

Randollph tried to curb his impatience compounded by irritation. The visible kingdom of God on earth probably required a custodian of the tithes and offerings to record and allocate the Lord's funds and see that they were not wasted, subverted, or pilfered. But was it also required that he, Cesare Paul Randollph, a soldier of the cross posted only temporarily as commander-in-chief of this battalion, should be bored stupid by the incomprehensible dronings of this gray little man? He sighed. He supposed that it was required.

The Reverend Mr. O. Bertram Smelser took off his gold-rimmed glasses and stabbed them at a figure on the paper he was holding.

"So you can see, what with the rentals from the hotel—"

"Mr. Smelser," Randollph interrupted, "when does the present lessee's lease on the hotel run out?"

"One year from the thirtieth of last month. We've already had some preliminary talks about a new lease with the company."

"Is the hotel profitable for the lessee?"

"Very. I have many inquiries from other hotel companies about its availability."

"Thank you, that's all I need to know."

Smelser went on with his figures, pleased that Randollph was beginning to show a real interest in the business operation, the heart and soul of the church.

He had half an hour to dispose of Wilfred Thurman, but he was not inclined to spend that much time with the rather handsome young-middle-aged man with sparse brown hair and a paunch he tried to conceal with good tailoring.

Randollph motioned the hotel manager to a seat and remained behind his formidable desk which had protected the Reverend Dr. Arthur Hartshorne from pesty parishioners, garrulous visiting clergy, and supplicants for bizarre mission enterprises.

"I expect you've come about leasing our gymnasium," Randollph said in what he hoped was a crisp executive voice. "I'm sorry, but I've checked with Mr. Gantry, and he feels the recreational programs he's carrying on there are a significant contribution to the community. We'll be needing the gym."

Thurman tried to suppress what Randollph thought of as a crafty smile.

"I am given to understand that the trustees of the church would look favorably on our proposition."

"You shouldn't have gone behind my back to suborn the trustees, Mr. Thurman. That was dirty pool."

"Just business." Thurman inspected his manicured nails.

"Meaning that it was legal, however unethical?"

"Business is business. We need that space. The trustees of the church control it. It made sense for me to talk to them about it."

"Not this time, Mr. Thurman. Had you done your homework, you would have discovered the constitution of this church stipulates that any action of the trustees may be vetoed by the pastor and the bishop, if, in their opinion, it is detrimental to the welfare of the congregation."

Thurman tried to hide his surprise with bluster.

"I'll go to the bishop! He's a businessman, he'll see the sense of my proposition."

"If you wish, and have nothing better to do with your time. I can assure you that the bishop will follow my recommendation."

"Look, reverend, you're just a preacher, you don't understand these things." Thurman decided a threat might help his cause. "My company might not renew its lease if it doesn't get that space."

"Inform your company that several hotel associations are anxious to bid on the lease, and if it isn't interested in renewing, it should tell us so. And I dislike being addressed as 'reverend.'"

"Huh?"

Randollph tipped his chair back and clasped his hands behind his head. "Mr. Thurman, you're stymied. You tried an underhanded trick, and it failed. And then you rationalized your shabby behavior by claiming that this is the way business is conducted. That is reason enough to dismiss your petition to lease our gym. But do you know what I find particularly offensive about your conduct?"

"Huh?"

"I am particularly resentful of your assumption that a clergyman is bound to be a fool and an easy mark who allows smart, hardheaded businessmen to push him around."

"Now, look here—"

"No, you look here. You will inform the trustees of the church that you are withdrawing the offer at this time. You will inform your superior, who, I'm sure, has the pressure on you to acquire this space, that it is not available. And you will advise him not to pester us about it anymore."

"You can't make me do that." Thurman, knowing it was time to retreat, tried to salvage some honor from the lost battle.

"Oh, yes I can. If you do not do so—and with copies of both letters to me—I shall inform your company that the church will not negotiate with it for renewal of the lease because of what we consider the unethical interference of the manager in the affairs of the church. The company will immediately remove you, but I can't imagine that it will be to a promotion. I can be hardheaded, too, Mr. Thurman. Shall we say day after tomorrow for those letters to be on my desk?"

Thurman would have liked to pound the desk and threaten, but he was out of threats. He decided the best thing he could do was to get the hell out.

Randollph was thinking that administration did have its compensatory moments. He decided that for the sake of his Christian conscience he would cast Wilfred Thurman in the role of the devil's envoy. This would permit him to enjoy the routing of the stupid, greedy hotel manager without qualms about his own less-than-the-minimum Christian concern for the other chap's feelings. Wilfred Thurman was not a very menacing example of evil and his posturings of power had been easily challenged. Maybe this was a cameo of slippery ethical conduct and morally ambiguous ends in conflict with eleemosynary enterprises. Maybe the bad guys would take to their heels more often than they did if the other side would stand up to them.

Randollph knew these musings were an oversimplification of the whole affair, but they gave him pleasure. It was about time to meet Ms. X. in the chapel, and he wasn't looking forward to that. But the vanquishing of Wilfred Thurman in the name of righteousness had provided a bright spot in a long and busy day that was even now only over by little more than half.

The hotel manager was about to open the door and skulk out when Randollph said, "Oh, by the way, Mr. Thurman."

"Yes." It was a surly answer.

"I would like to remind you that avarice is one of the seven deadly sins. Good day, Mr. Thurman."

Sixteen

Captain Manahan said, "Mike, the commissioner keeps calling the chief about when are we going to make an arrest in the Julian homicide, and you know what that means."

"Sure I know, captain," Lieutenant Casey said with a humorless smile. "The commissioner chews you out, and you have to keep the fire hot under me."

"Now, Mike, you know I got confidence you're doin' all you can." The captain was busily trying to untangle a paper clip and make it into a straight wire. "It's just that this's whatcha might call a real sensitive situation. Can't bury this one on the back pages. We don't come up with an arrest pretty soon, the department's gonna look bad. Then the commissioner, he'll be unhappy, which means that the chief's gonna hear a lot about it, which means—"

"That you'll hear a lot about it, and then it gets down to me. I know, captain."

"Got anything at all?"

Casey admitted to himself that he had quite a bit that

added up to practically nothing at all. He was almost ready
to abandon the robbery scenario. The stolen jewelry hadn't
turned up in any of the usual outlets for hot merchandise.
They hadn't heard a whisper among street informers about
the job. He wasn't dismissing the possibility of a former
lover having done her in. Or the wife of a former lover. Or
the girlfriend. The brutality of the killing gave it the look of
a crime of passion. It wouldn't be the first murder he'd seen
done out of rage or jealousy, rigged to look like it was done
for money. He was going to have another go at Amos
Oregon and Jaime DeSilva and Annette Paris.

But he liked Dr. Carl Brandt best for the part of the
killer. Everything fit—means, motive, opportunity. More
than that, to Casey's mind, was that Brandt fit the familiar
pattern, almost banal, of the husband killing the wife for
money—or the other way around. Casey always felt better
when a homicide fell into a familiar pattern.

"I haven't got anything I can use to make an arrest,
captain," he said. "I'm going to work on Dr. Brandt and
Kitty Darrow again tonight."

"You think they did it?"

"If I had to place a bet right now, I'd bet on the doctor.
I don't know about her. But that's only a hunch. I've no
hard evidence."

"You can't throw a man like Brandt into the pokey unless
you've got it tied up tight," the captain said. "Too much
prominence, too many connections. Make us look bad.
Maybe get sued for false arrest."

"I know," Casey said. "But Brandt had to have a lot of
money, and fast." He explained about Dr. Brandt's gambling debts.

"Who's the shark he's into?" Manahan asked.

"Manny Friedman."

"The worst," the captain said. "Brandt tell you?"

"No. We picked it up." Casey did not think it necessary to explain that he had picked it up from a preacher who had volunteered the information. Let the captain assume it was clever police work.

"Manny threatenin' the doc?"

"Yes."

"Love to hang this murder on Manny. Any chance?"

"Probably not. But we'll check it out."

"Shake him down. Shake him down hard. Send Markowitz. He's good at that kind of work."

Lieutenant Phil Markowitz was a big man, at least six-four, and, at forty-two, beginning to run to fat. He'd gone into police work because he liked to knock people around. He was accomplished in jujitsu, karate and more arcane forms of whacking people so that it hurt or, if necessary, killed.

He sat slumped in one of Lieutenant Casey's chairs, legs crossed, cleaning his nails.

"What you got for me, Mike?" He rather liked Casey. He was entirely unaware that Casey thought him an animal.

"I'd like you to shake up Manny Friedman."

"A pleasure. What's he done?"

Casey told him about Dr. Brandt's involvement with the loan shark.

"So what do you want me to find out?" Markowitz asked.

"I'm going to see Brandt tonight. I want to know for sure if Manny had anything to do with killing Lisa Julian ... Lisa Brandt."

"To scare the doc into paying up? That's not Manny's usual *modus operandi*. Break the doc's kneecaps—that's more like Manny."

"I know," Casey said. "But look at it this way: he injures Dr. Brandt, the doctor can't work, which means he can't

earn the money to pay his loan, or the vig on the loan. He
sends a couple of his boys to see Lisa, first making a phone
call to the doctor to get him out of the room. They're just
supposed to rough her up a little, maybe break an arm or
knock out a few teeth. They get too enthusiastic. First thing
they know, she's dead."

Markowitz looked thoughtful. "I don't care much for it,
but it could be."

"I don't care much for it, either, Phil. But I have to be
sure before I see Brandt. Shake it out of Manny, did he or
didn't he have anything to do with it. I expect you know
how to engage Manny in conversation, you knowing him so
long and all." Casey smiled.

"That I do, Mike." Markowitz got up. "I'll just go down
there right now and renew acquaintance with my old friend
Manny."

"Take Garboski with you," Casey said. "Let him have a
little fun too. And, Phil . . ."

"Yeah, Mike?"

"I don't mind if you lean on him heavy. Only if you have
to, of course. But I need that information."

Manny Friedman kept a pawn shop northwest of the
Loop, several blocks past the point where respectable neighborhood stores began to fade in favor of cheap girlie bars
and ratty porno establishments. The dirty iron-barred window offered two guitars, an accordion, seven watches of no
great value, and a shelf of assorted transistor radios.

When Markowitz and Garboski opened the door, an
overhead bell tinkled. Behind the counter, a very fat man
with hair like millions of fine gray wires spliced into his
scalp looked past his customer with a smile of welcome
which froze and then dissolved when he saw the two
policemen. The customer, a young Mexican or Puerto

Rican, quickly put his hand in his pocket and sidled away from the counter.

"Good afternoon, Manny," Markowitz said pleasantly. "You remember my friend Mr. Garboski, don't you? Mr. Garboski and I, we didn't have much to do, so we said, why don't we go visit our old friend Manny Friedman, whom it has been a long time since we've seen." The customer was edging past the detective when Markowitz, without taking his eyes off Friedman, shot out a meaty hand and clamped the young fellow's arm. "Don't be in a hurry, lad," he said. "Garboski and me, we wouldn't want to drive any of Manny's trade away. Let's see what you're offerin' for sale."

The boy kept his hand in his pocket. "You got no right—" he began.

Markowitz suddenly dug his fingers into the boy's shoulder. The boy screamed.

"Let's see it, or I'll break your goddamned arm," the lieutenant said in a soft, friendly voice. "Well, how about this? A diamond ring—big dude, too. And a lady's gold cigarette lighter. Now, I'll just bet you found a lady's handbag somewhere, and after a long and exhaustin' search to find the true owner, you gave up and decided you might as well dispose of the contents."

"They're my mother's, man." The boy looked at the floor.

Markowitz slapped him viciously across the face, sending him reeling into Sergeant Garboski.

"On the other hand, could be you got a rap sheet as long as your whore mother's list of customers. Take him out and handcuff him to the steering wheel, sergeant, and if he tries to run, shoot his balls off. Meanwhile, Manny 'n' I'll be chatting over old times."

The pawnbroker stepped back as Markowitz approached the counter. It was a fear reflex, and the detective knew it.

Friedman's chins, lapping over the collar of his clean white shirt, trembled with anxiety. But the little gray pig eyes, too small for his massive head, were flecked with hate.

"Actually, Manny, this isn't a purely social visit," Markowitz said. "Your friend Mike Casey—Lieutenant Casey of homicide, that is—well, he asked me to come over and have a little conversation with you about Dr. Carl Brandt."

"I don't know any Dr. Brandt."

Markowitz leaned across the counter and quickly slapped Friedman's fat cheeks, one side of his face with the back of his hand, the other with his palm, snapping his head first one way, then the other. The pawnbroker grabbed his face with both hands. Involuntary tears of pain glazed the animal eyes.

"Did that hurt, Manny? For a guy who's always havin' people beat up, breakin' their legs and kneecaps, you're awfully sensitive to a little slappin' around. I always figured you ought to have your kneecaps busted, Manny, just so you'd know what it feels like. I might just do it myself. I know how. Help you understand how your customers feel."

Friedman backed toward a desk and reached for the phone. "I want my lawyer."

Markowitz was around the counter so fast that the fat man had no chance to move. He brought the side of his hand down across the French-cuffed wrist on the desk. Friedman screamed.

"Now, why would you want your lawyer, Manny? This here's just a chat between friends. See, Lieutenant Casey thinks you sent a couple of your gorillas to rough up Mrs. Brandt as a sort of warning to the doctor, and they overdid it and killed her. You must have read about it in the papers. See, there's a lot of heat on for us to make an arrest in this case, and Casey figures we could pin it on you, everybody'd be happy. Seein' as how you are a no-good loan shark that'd steal the fillings out of your mother's teeth. The public would be happy to have a menace to society like you in the slammer. And when the public's happy, the commissioner's happy. And that makes the chief happy. And when the chief smiles, our Captain Manahan, why, he's just tickled pink. And Lieutenant Casey's a man that's pleased when he's got a case wrapped up. So everybody's happy, except you, of course. Get the picture, Manny?"

Manny got the picture.

"You got no proof," he whimpered. "I didn't have nothing to do with that murder. I don't do nothing to women. You couldn't have no proof."

"You'd break your grandmother's neck there's a couple bucks in it for you," Markowitz said. "I know you got a good lawyer. We put you in—material witness or somethin', it don't matter—he's got you out in no time."

Manny Friedman looked like he was feeling better.

"So we don't put you in, Manny. What we do, we get some of our guys to follow your collectors all the time. Soon as they catch one acceptin' more than legal interest, we put him in. You know about usury laws, don't you, Manny? Also, we keep a cop in here durin' business hours. How much business you going to do with a cop in here? And how much you got out on the street? A million? Even if it's only half a million, the vig's forty, fifty a week. You in a position to see all that dry up, Manny?" He paused to let the figures sink in. "Now, you want to chat about Dr. Brandt?"

Manny Friedman loosened the perfect knot of his blue-on-blue Dior tie and unbuttoned the collar of his shirt. Nodules of sweat specked his face and neck.

"Dr. Brandt's got a loan with me."

"How much?"

"Fifty."

"He been keepin' up the interest?"

Manny hesitated. "No. He's behind."

"And?"

"And what?"

"And what? Come on, Manny, quit actin' like a god-damned virgin in a whorehouse." Markowitz took two steps toward the pawnbroker. "Do I have to knock it out of you?"

Friedman retreated. "No. No, I'll tell you. Just don't hit me. We've been pushing the doc a little to keep up with the vig."

"Rough stuff?"

"No."

"Threats?"

Again Friedman hesitated. "I sent a man to talk with him."

"Who?"

"A Mr. Luigi Trentino."

"Luigi the Louse? That stupid hood. What did he say to the doc?"

"I wasn't there."

"What did he say, Manny?"

"He ... he—"

"Come on, Manny." Markowitz stepped closer.

"All right, all right. He said the doc'd better come up with some money, or—"

"Or what?"

"Or we'd have to take measures."

"What measures? Did you threaten him or his wife? His wife-to-be, that is? That's the kind of crum-bum thing you'd think of doin', threatening his woman."

"Him. I swear it. If Luigi threatened the woman, he did it on his own."

The bell over the door tinkled. Sergeant Garboski said, "Look who I met coming in to see Manny, lieutenant."

One of the men was in his forties. Fading red hair showed beneath his brown felt hat. He wore a cheap plaid sports jacket and unpressed brown slacks. The other man was about thirty, his thick barrel of a body magnified by bright-green-and-white-checked slacks and a white jacket. His thick black hair glistened with an abundant pomade.

"Why, it's Mr. Donovan and Mr. Trentino, I do believe," Phil Markowitz said. "So nice to see you. Come right in, gentlemen. Manny and I, we were just talking about you, Mr. Trentino."

"So?" Trentino was insolent.

Markowitz kicked him in the crotch. Trentino fell to the floor, clutching his injured parts, rolling and moaning.

"I don't like I-talians," Markowitz said. "They all got big smart mouths. I especially don't like stupid I-talian hoods like you, Trentino." He leaned down, grabbed a handful of Trentino's shirt front, and jerked him to his feet. "Upsy-daisy, Mr. Trentino. You'll get your pretty white coat dirty rollin' around on the floor like that. Now, tell me what you said to Dr. Carl Brandt when you told him to pay up or else."

Trentino tried to twist away from Markowitz's grip. "You can't shove me around, you—"

The detective spun him around and sent him crashing into the window display amid the watches and ·radios and guitars.

"Pick him up, Garboski, and bring him back." Markowitz felt in the side pocket of his jacket and brought out what looked like four metal rings fused together. "Now, Mr. Trentino, you know what these are. You probably use them now and then in your work. They're called brass knuckles. I slip them on my hand like so. Now, I can knock those beautiful white teeth down your throat. That hurts. The stumps of the teeth, they hurt like hell till you get them pulled. Also, I can break your nose easy. In several places if I want to. Ever try breathing through a nose that's busted up to a pulp, Mr. Trentino? Oh, I see by the look on your face that you've busted a few noses yourself. You know how the victim suffers. Good. Now, I'm softhearted. If you tell me everything you said to Dr. Brandt, and everything he said to you, I'm not going to hurt you."

"O.K., O.K., you don't have to be so goddamn rough. I told him he'd have to come through or we might crack his fingers and he couldn't be no big-shot surgeon no more. That's all I told him."

"You tell him you might rough up his wife. They weren't quite married by then, but you'd have read about it in the papers—that is, if you can read. Manny knew about it. He can read."

Trentino swallowed at the insult, but didn't respond to it. "No. I don't rough up no dames in line of business. For fun, sometimes, but not for business."

"You're a charming man, Mr. Trentino. Now, Lieutenant Casey, he's going to have a real personal talk with the doc tonight, and he's going to ask about this conversation you had about the doc's debt, and if it turns out you lied to me, I'll be back with the brass knuckles."

"I'm telling you the truth."

"Let's hope so." Markowitz took off the knuckles and toyed with them. "Was the doc scared?"

"Plenty. He begged."

"For what?"

"For more time. Said he'd be comin' into a big hunk of money soon, then he'd pay."

"Did he, now?" Markowitz's eyes lit up. "Mike Casey'll be interested in that. Well, Garboski, I guess that's about all."

Friedman and the two hoods were visibly relieved.

"Oh, by the way," Markowitz said. "Manny, lay off the doc. He'll pay you sooner or later, unless he gets tagged for a murder rap, in which case you're out of luck. Takes a long time to make fifty G's manufacturin' license plates. When he gets around to payin', assumin' he does, I'll be in with him to see that he gets a receipt paid in full for fifty thousand. No interest. I don't care about the doc, don't even know him. That's your punishment for your sins. Doesn't near cover them."

Markowitz took time to light a cigarette, then turned to Trentino. "Now, Luigi, you got any stupid Sicilian idea of revenge on me, you better forget it. I'll inform them at the station, anything happens to me, its your fault. So then they'll be on Manny's tail here, practically shuttin' down his business, all on account of you. Then you'd become an embarrassment to Manny, and Manny, he don't like to be embarrassed, specially if it costs him money. And Manny's got connections. Manny might think it best to rub you, and you know what? The boys at the station might just be lookin' the other way. Well, sergeant, we better be going. We thank you all for a pleasant afternoon."

"Markowitz," Trentino said.

" 'Lieutenant Markowitz, sir' to you," the detective said.

"Lieutenant Markowitz, sir, there's plenty of people hate you, one of them might get you, and then I get rubbed for it."

"It's an unjust world, Mr. Trentino," Markowitz said. "I was you, I'd go to Mass every day and pray for my safety. Have a nice day, gentlemen."

The Church of the Good Shepherd's chapel is a transept off the nave. In contrast to the eclectic architecture of the nave, it is pure Gothic, an appendage like a whimsical afterthought. It was added to the nave several years after the original construction through the generosity of Jeremiah D. Pembroke, in memory of his devout and mousy wife, Lydia. Mr. Pembroke, who had made it big in pork-belly futures, had two spurs prodding him to his magnificent gesture. He wished to expunge the guilt or social censure accrued by marrying a lady from the chorus of a current musical hit before his beloved Lydia had time to cool in her coffin. And he had once been to Chartres and had fallen in love with Gothic architecture.

So an architect who specialized in fake Gothic was called in to cram a petite Notre-Dame into space hacked out of offices and storerooms. It was, if spurious, impressive, and much sought after for weddings with guests too few to fill the nave. It could be entered from two directions. There was a door from an outside hall that ran the length of the nave and brought one in next to the altar rail. It could also be entered from the nave itself. On weekdays a screen partially separated the chapel from the nave, affording privacy to those who came to the chapel to pray. On Sundays the screen was removed. Then, by an ingenious patented construction, the backs of the pews were reversed, adding a hundred or so seats to the church—a nifty twentieth-century idea that would have astonished the Abbot Suger of St. Denis. The chapel was officially designated the Lydia Pembroke Memorial Chapel. It was usually referred to around Good Shepherd as "Lydia Pinkham."

At five o'clock Randollph slipped inside the screen at the back of the chapel, hesitating a moment to let his eyes accustom themselves to the dimly lit room. Around the perimeter of the floor concealed tubes sprayed enough light to keep a worshipper from stumbling on the rough stones. A theater spot fixed to the vaulting over the choir glared unwaveringly at a crossless altar. (Mr. Jeremiah Pembroke, innocent of theology but with the sentimentalized ecumenical inclinations often found in those who don't give a damn for any religion, specified that the chapel was to be for all faiths, thus free of sectarian symbols.) A flickerless perpetual altar lamp (electric) gleamed in a ruby bowl suspended by a chain, symbolizing not the presence of the reserved host, but, like an abstract painting, whatever anyone thought it meant.

Randollph, once his vision had cleared, could make out three people in the chapel. There were two women, seated quite apart from each other, in the pews. One had her head resting on her hands, which were folded on the back of the pew in front of her. The other was sitting quietly, he supposed with her eyes closed. A third woman, long blond hair trailing over the jacket of a pantsuit, was kneeling at the end of the altar rail nearest the door, where the outer edges of the spotlight revealed her presence without illuminating the details of her appearance.

Randollph slipped into a back pew. He didn't know which lady was Ms. X, so he'd have to wait until two of them eliminated themselves.

One did almost immediately. The upright figure stood up decisively and walked past the woman kneeling at the altar, letting herself out. Had she been here to offer thanks for some recent blessing in her life? Was she praying for a sick husband, relative, or friend? Was she facing a dangerous operation, or was her life in chaos because of some insoluble personal problem? Had her sojourn in this spooky ersatz mini-cathedral brought her peace and courage? Randollph hoped that it had.

A few minutes later the other woman in the pews raised her head. She found a tissue in her bag, wiped her eyes, then blew her nose. She, too, went out the door by the altar.

"Come and kneel beside me, Dr. Randollph." The

woman at the altar did not turn around as she spoke, and her voice, distorted by the rain-barrel acoustics of a Gothic room, was feminine but without any character except a faint huskiness.

Randollph wasn't sure this was a good idea. If Ms. X wanted him to hear a confession, nothing more, perhaps kneeling at an altar with a penitent could be considered a nonconformist equivalent to the confession booth. But Ms. X had intimated that she was in need of pastoral counsel. How effectively this could be dispensed, or dialogue carried on, with counselor and counselee leaning over an altar rail, staring at a stone floor, Randollph did not know. He felt certain the hotshot clerical psychologists who taught counseling in the seminaries had a prefabricated answer for situations like this. All he could think to do was comply with the lady's request.

"Thank you for keeping the appointment, Dr. Randollph." Ms. X kept her head bowed, face covered by her hands as she talked.

"I want to be helpful," Randollph said. He was sure he sounded pious and patronizing.

"You were once very close to Lisa Julian, were you not?"

Randollph thought for a moment he had misunderstood her. "That can have nothing to do with your, er, problem," he said.

"Oh, but it does. You say you want to help. You can help me by answering some questions about Lisa."

"If you had wanted to talk about Lisa Julian, you could have come to my office." Randollph started to rise.

"Please remain kneeling, Dr. Randollph. What you feel jabbing you in the side is an automatic pistol, small but effective. It might not kill you, but three or four bullets would be most painful, and would lay you up for months. Now, shall we continue our conversation? If anyone should come in, pretend that you are praying."

Randollph, to his own surprise, was interested in his reactions to this grotesque situation. His first thought was of Thomas à Becket, bravely submitting to the loutish minions of Henry II as they beat him to death with their broadswords near the altar at Canterbury. Among the Christian martyrs whose unpleasant modes of dying he recounted every year to postadolescent divines who were determined not to suffer in a parish whose parsonage had less than two bathrooms, Becket was his favorite. He discovered now that, admire him as he did, he had no wish to imitate the sturdy Thomas. Also, Randollph couldn't think of anything in his past or present life that remotely qualified him for the role of Christian martyr. He'd just be an unfortunate clergyman plugged by a dizzy dame.

"Now, let's get down to business," Ms. X said, still keeping her face hidden. "To answer a question which you are about to ask, I'm doing my own investigation of Lisa's death. Think of me as an avenging angel."

"You surely don't think I killed her," Randollph said, more alarmed now.

"I don't think anything. No, I'm sure you didn't. But you may have information, some clue as to who did kill her. That's what I want."

"I don't—"

"I have your letters to her, doctor. She saved them, you know. They're very good, very, shall we say, specific."

Randollph wondered if he was blushing, and decided that he probably was.

"My point is, doctor, that at one time in your life you knew her very, very well. I want you to think, think hard, if she ever told you about any incident in her past, any unusually intense relationship, something out of the ordinary that might have led someone to brood or simmer for years until they felt compelled to kill her."

Randollph thought hard.

"If I had a clue, I would not hesitate to reveal it to you," he said. "Not only are you prodding me with that pistol, which would eliminate any reluctance I might have about telling you, but I am as anxious as you are to find out who killed her. Our interests would seem to be the same."

"Go on."

"Lisa never told me about her past, which, at that time, couldn't have been very extensive. She was a girl who lived for the moment, and I, well, I was young and my life was as yet unfocused. I got the impression that there had been one rather serious attachment in her life, but that she was over it. She never told me who it was, and I didn't think it important enough to ask."

"Too bad; I'd like to have had that name." Ms. X sighed, supposedly in resignation, but Randollph thought it sounded like a sigh of relief.

"I believe you, doctor," she said. "I believe you because I think you would be a poor liar. Now, remain kneeling. I'm sorry to inconvenience you, but I'm going to have to tie you up so that I can get away without you chasing after me. You're curious. You want to know what I look like, who I am. And while I'm a healthy girl, you're a big guy, an ex-quarterback who keeps in shape. The only way I could handle you would be to shoot you. So I'll have to tie you up." She got up from the altar rail, still with face averted. "Now, put one hand under the rail, and one above it," she instructed. Randollph could see her gloved hands with a section of thin nylon cord in them, and thought of seizing her while she had momentarily abandoned her gun, but before he had a chance to move, Ms. X had deftly lashed his wrists together, then hitched them around a post in the altar rail. She has fast hands, he thought, even in gloves.

"Is your name Laura Justus?" he asked.

"My name is legion," she said. "Now, doctor, I've left the knot loose, and you should be able to free yourself in ten or fifteen minutes. I'll be long gone by then. Thank you for your help." She slipped out the door.

Dan Gantry came into the chapel from the nave. At first he didn't see anyone. "Hey, boss, you here?" he said. Then, walking down the aisle, he saw Randollph's kneeling figure. "Oh, I'm sorry, boss, I didn't know you were praying."

"I'm not praying, I'm tied up," Randollph shot back over his shoulder, hoping he didn't sound as vicious as he felt. "Come here and untie me."

"My God, boss, you hurt?" Dan knelt in front of Randollph and began unlacing Ms. X's knot.

"The only thing that's hurt is my dignity," Randollph said. "And that will heal itself in no time."

Dan chuckled. "You look like maybe you joined a new order of flagellants that tie you to the altar befor putting the whip to you. What happened?"

Randollph told him.

Seventeen

When Randollph had first come to the Church of the Good Shepherd, he'd had a conference with the bishop about his new duties.

"I know that preaching a sermon every Sunday is a pastor's first duty," he'd said.

"Perhaps here at Good Shepherd, where your congregation is new every Sunday, it is, though I doubt it," the bishop said. "Good preaching, I'm sad to tell you, is no longer a requirement in most congregations."

"Then why, Freddie, have I always been told that it was?"

"Because it is an inspiring myth that the profession tries to perpetuate. Good preaching, thoughtful, responsible preaching, takes time. The smart lad ambitious of preferment doesn't waste time on preaching. He soon learns that making holy noises in an agreeable manner is quite enough, and then he has all that time left over for administrative duties."

Randollph grinned at his old friend. "Freddie, I hope you still have enough conscience left to weep for the demise of prophecy in the modern pulpit. But I know how to go about my preaching responsibilities; and it won't be by making holy noises. What I don't know how to do is to make a pastoral call on the sick and afflicted. That is a pastoral duty, is it not?"

"As old as the injunction in the New Testament that we visit the distressed in body as well as spirit." The bishop obviously liked talking about the work of the parish pastor, as—Randollph was to learn—do all pastors who have escaped the parish into one of the church's executive slots. Talking about the parish persuades them that those were their happiest days, though most of them pull every political string within reach to keep from going back.

The bishop leaned over and untied his shoes. "I hope you don't mind, C.P., my feet hurt, and good friends are people with whom you can converse in your socks."

"Don't mind me, Freddie. But instruct me in the art of hospital calling."

The bishop leaned back in his swivel chair and put his stubby black-hosed feet on his desk. "It is an art, C.P., which means it cannot be taught as easily as a craft. You have to develop a feel for it, a sense of what to do and what to avoid." He gazed out over the heart of the Loop, where big deals were being made, large schemes cooked up, and enterprises of every sort planned and assessed, all to the end that money would be moved from one account to another.

"Going to the hospital to visit the sick, comfort them, perhaps pray for them, was the duty I reserved for the late afternoon, the tag end of the day, when one's spirits are low anyway."

"Why, Freddie?"

"Because by that time my mind would be too muzzy to do good sermonizing, and I'd disposed of my appointments and administrative duties, at least for the daylight hours. I usually had a committee meeting in the evening, so I couldn't go then. If the evening was free, I liked to linger over dessert or read a novel."

"I hope you read good novels."

"Dickens, Sinclair Lewis, Kenneth Roberts, Willa Cather. Trash, too. Everyone should read a little trash. Good for the soul. But you didn't come here for a literary lecture. As I was saying, I used to have to whip myself to go to the hospital those late afternoons ..." The bishop's voice trailed off as he relived what he thought were simpler, happier days—Randollph guessed—then picked up again. "But I was always glad I'd gone. I invariably came away from the hospital exhilarated—emotionally drained sometimes, of course; sad, often; but always exhilarated."

Randollph hadn't thought of visiting the sick as potentially exhilarating. The bishop elaborated.

"I keep forgetting that you've never performed some of these basic pastoral tasks, C.P. It is a symptom of our pride that we think everyone understands what we understand. That's what leads otherwise sane pastors to preach sermons on process theology or the Johannine problem."

"I'll remember to refrain from preaching on Augustine's affection for Platonic philosophy or what Erasmus thought of the Occamists," Randollph said.

"I would, if I were you," the bishop answered. "But back to visiting the sick. These days, due to the medical profession's disinclination to make house calls, the sick are nearly always in the hospital. On any given day you call at the hospital, some of your flock will be there just for tests, or the repair of a hernia, or other minor inconveniences. But there will be, usually, one or two who are in serious pain or who are pretty sure that they won't be going home again. You wonder what in the world you can do to minister to them, what word you can say, what prayer you can pray that will help them. But it turns out, more often than not, that you needn't have worried. Instead of you ministering to them, they minister to you."

Randollph looked blank.

"Let me put it this way, C.P.," the bishop went on. "You discover the amazing fortitude which plain, ordinary people can muster in the face of death. You will also be embarrassed at their gratitude for a simple little thing like a pastoral visit. It lifts you up ..." Again his voice trailed off, as memories too moving to explicate fluttered back across the years. Then, pulling himself back to the present, he said, "By the way, what did Erasmus think of the Occamists?"

"He thought that, like all the Schoolman sects, the Occamists got so bogged down in debating irrelevant theological questions, they lost the gospel of Christ. He also said that their literary style was horrendous."

The bishop shook his head. "Both are sins to be avoided."

Randollph was mulling over the bishop's counsel on the art of comforting the afflicted as he approached Julian Hospital's information desk. He couldn't decide if he was looking forward to the visit or not. On the one hand, there was the opportunity to experience another dimension of the pastoral profession. But he felt unprepared. The seminary where he had taught, as did all other seminaries now, had courses in pastoral care of the sick. You could even take a major in it, which led to a resident chaplain's job in a large hospital. Apparently looking after the members of your flock who had fallen afoul of the numerous ailments that human flesh is heir to was now not just a matter of a cheery word and a prayer but a highly complex business which required several credit hours of instruction to perform satisfactorily. Also he was nervous about the limits of his

Christian patience when trying to administer God's comfort to a rich old bat, probably senile, who would no doubt think he ought to beg her to leave the Church of the Good Shepherd a wad of dough—and then be smarmy grateful for whatever crumbs she tossed to it.

The middle-aged woman with carefully coiffed hair looked up from the cards she was sorting. Her face jumped into the smile greeters reserve for those officially due grade-one treatment.

"Can I help you, father?" ("Wear your clerical collar to the hospital." Randollph remembered now that this was part of Freddie's instruction. "Nobody challenges the clergy-man's right to wander around a hospital." Randollph hadn't remembered to put on a collar. He just hadn't had time to take it off.)

Randollph told the lady that he was here to call on parishioners and needed their room numbers.

"Oh, you must be new here," the matron chirped. "We have a clergy room, at the end of the hall next to the chapel. There are several duplicate files there, patients listed by denomination, then under each denomination by congregation. We also like you to sign in and out. You'll see the book."

The clergy room was a windowless cave painted institutional tan. There was a coatrack, which, come the season of stinging snows and malign winds, would be burdened, but was now empty. A cluster of fat fluorescent bulbs in the ceiling rained a harsh perpetual light on the sparse and ugly furniture. A brown plastic table in the corner held a telephone, three card files, and a ledger-type book. A few plain chairs and several standing ashtrays looking like chrome toadstools invited visiting parsons to sit, have a smoke, and shoot the breeze with a clerical buddy. In the corner, three men in collars were engaged in lively conversation. All three were marked with the thinning hair and early worry lines which bespeak tired disillusionment. Seminary buddies, Randollph guessed. They had the look of Lutherans about them. Maybe they were discussing the Augsburg Confession, but more likely they were chewing over the latest synodical scuttlebutt. There were several other men in the room, some in clerical garb and some not, servants of Christ about to take off on their appointed rounds carrying the unguent of the gospel to their sheep felled by infirmity or a physician's penchant for extensive and expensive laboratory tests. They all nodded to Randollph, but none of them intioduced themselves. These big-city pastors, like their parishioners, had learned to avoid casual and profitless personal involvement, even with a brother in the sacred fraternity.

All the card files were in use, and Randolph had to wait his turn. When one became available, he quickly found Good Shepherd's patients and noted their room numbers on the cards Miss Windfall had given him. He almost forgot to sign the logbook. When he looked at it, he found that he was expected to write his name, his church, the time he had checked in, and the time of his departure. What possible use this information would serve, he couldn't imagine. Like most institutional procedures, it probably had no discernible purpose.

As he left the clergy room, he thought he might as well take a quick look at the chapel. No Jeremiah Pembroke had lavished excess profits on this place of prayer, he saw immediately. It was a smallish plain room with a few pews. Like Good Shepherd's Lydia Pinkham, the altar was free of sectarian symbols, although half-covered with flowers. The cover lighting was medium dim, but it was easy to make out who was in the chapel. At this moment there was only one person, a dark-haired young man, face in hands, sobbing quietly. Although Randollph couldn't see his face, he was certain that this was Dr. Kermit Julian. He supposed Dr.

Julian was weeping for his dead sister. Though it did seem out of character for the young Dr. Julian, who, like his father, normally kept his emotions behind an impassive exterior, to be sobbing in the semipublic hospital chapel. Randollph quickly withdrew and left the doctor to his grief.

Although he had had a professional football career remarkably free of cracked bones, torn ligaments, and the various abrasions and contusions which were the normal concomitants of participation in that ultraviolent game, he had been bedded a few times. These were usually for X-rays after particularly vicious sackings, ordered not out of the club's concern for his welfare, but to make certain he could perform the next Sunday without undue risk to the owner's investment in a valuable property. He'd also been in hospitals plenty of times to cheer teammates with ripped-up knees, mangled ankles, and mashed noses.

But this was different. Now the antiseptic smell and hospital whites, and a sheeted figure on a bed cart being silently wheeled to an appointment with anesthetic and a knife, carried a message of final things, solemn rites, termination.

But mainly, it was different because of his collar. As a professor, his ordination scarcely differentiated him from colleagues on whose heads episcopal hands had never been laid. He preached now and then, but laymen could do that. About the only time he exercised a right reserved to the clergy was to perform the marriage of one of his students in the seminary chapel.

But now he walked these antiseptic halls wearing the badge of his office. His role was defined. Because he was identifiable, he might be summoned at any moment to baptize a stillborn infant, or even asked if he could administer the last rites to a suddenly expiring Roman Catholic. His garb proclaimed that he was officially qualified to offer appropriate prayer.

He'd asked the bishop if it was mandatory to offer a prayer for each patient, and had been cheered when told that it wasn't.

"There is a school of pastoral theology which holds that any kind of pastoral visit is incomplete without a prayer," Freddie had said, "but I have never subscribed to it."

"I heartily agree with you," Randolph said, "though my attitude is based only on the marshy ground of my personal aversion to informal public piety. I'd be comforted by something theologically sturdier to lean on."

"I think your aversion is sturdy enough, C.P.," the bishop replied. "Those who feel compelled to offer prayer on any pretext whatever are cheapening the whole concept of prayer."

"How do I know when to pray for a patient?"

"The rule is: when in doubt, omit it," the bishop answered. "Some people will ask you to pray. Others would like you to pray but won't ask. You have to learn to sense when to ask if they'd like a prayer. Most patients, though, just want a visit. They appreciate it when their pastor, whom they think of as a very busy man, takes the trouble to call on them. Do you have a prayerbook for the sick?"

"I didn't know there was such a thing, Freddie."

The bishop leaned over and opened the bottom drawer of his old rolltop desk and rummaged around in it. "Ah, here it is," he said, extracting a thin black Fabrikoid-covered book with a couple of maroon silk place-markers curling out of it like delicate colorful worms. He read the bright gold script on the cover aloud: *"The Pastor's Companion for Hospital and Sickroom—Inspiring Thoughts and Prayers of Comfort for Those Who Suffer.* Despite the deplorable title, this is a most helpful little book, C.P. I'd avoid use of the inspiring thoughts—they're mostly in the form of treacly poetry—but the prayers are good." He riffled through the pages. "They've selected the prayers from good sources.

Here's one by Sören Kierkegaard. You wouldn't think that gloomy old Dane would have a prayer for the sick, would you? But he did. He may have had a lugubrious outlook on life, but he writes a clean, precise prose." He handed the book to Randollph. "I do wish they'd had the sense to bind it in bright red. The black's too reminiscent of a funeral manual. Take it along. You'll find it useful."

Randollph's first patient, he saw by the neat card Miss Windfall had typed for him, was a man named Alfonse DeWindle, age thirty-eight, multiple fractures, businessman. Alfonse DeWindle in the flesh was a big man being fast overtaken by middle age and overweight. He had a generous double chin thickly spiked with a day's supply of black whiskers, and a round head being shaved by time more or less down the middle. One leg, monstrous in its plaster cast, pointed toward the ceiling as if it had just delivered a swift kick.

Randollph identified himself.

"Oh, yeah, my wife's church," DeWindle grunted after a perfunctory handshake. "Don't go, myself. Live a good life, follow the golden rule, that's my religion. Man doesn't have to go to church to be a good man, I always say, don't you agree, reverend?"

Randollph made noncommittal sounds. Freddie had neglected to warn him about amateur theologians.

"Busted this goddamn thing playing touch football," DeWindle went on. "Ought to known better than be playing a fool game practically invented by the Kennedys and the goddamn Democrats. I've got a nice little company—I'm in the stationery and office-supply game—well, you can hardly make a buck anymore. The tax laws—"

Randollph managed to arrest this familiar lament with an inquiry as to the circumstances of the injury.

"I was back to pass, see." DeWindle apparently enjoyed detailing the minutes of his misfortune as much as pro-

nouncing maledictions on the Democrats. "Well, if you
expect to get off a pass just right, you have to wait until the
last possible second before your blocking breaks down, just
like the pro quarterbacks do. You being a reverend, you
wouldn't know about that, but believe me, that's what
separates the men from the boys in a quarterback. Well,
see, Charlie Sipes was holding out Hank Dorf, and Hank,
who's a big bastard, maybe two-twenty, two-thirty, puts on
the pressure, and Charlie slips, the grass was kinda wet, and
both of them fall into me just as I let the ball go, and
knocked me ass-over-tincup, and both of them fell on me
and broke my leg in three places."

Randollph summoned up sympathetic noises and left. He
judged that DeWindle wasn't aching for a prayer. It was
not an encouraging beginning to his pastoral care of the sick
and busted up. But then, he supposed, one should have
some sympathy for a man who has to go through life
burdened with the Christian name Alfonse.

Out in the hall again, he was part of the variegated traffic
that gives a hospital its special ambience. Since it was the
hours for public visitations, the hurrying nurses, orderlies,
and interns were well mixed with civilians. There were
family groups bearing flowers or candy or something from
the gift shop. There were people who looked happy, and
people with solemn faces, and occasionally someone sup-
pressing tears. There were men in clericals, who nodded to
Randollph in recognition of a common profession and a
common duty. He realized that he was beginning to acquire
a sense of his unique function in this little world of many
unique functions, a feeling of being special among specialists. His dog collar certified his function just as the nurses'
whites or the interns' stethoscopes told at a glance what
they were doing here.

A visit to Alma Rivers (forty-five, single, public-school
teacher, gall bladder removed) was a distinct improvement

over the session with Alfonse DeWindle. Miss Rivers was getting along nicely, and discussed with approval a Randollph sermon she had heard shortly before entering the hospital. A Mr. Earl Havens, Jr. (fifty-six, married, automobile dealer, prostate operation), was a genial salesman who, though in some discomfort, joked about his tube and bottle.

He had one more card, Mrs. Victoria Clarke Hoffman, the rich old lady who, soon to shuffle off this mortal coil, maybe would remember the Church of the Good Shepherd in her will. Miss Windfall had noted Mrs. Hoffman's vital statistics as "elderly, widow, kidney complications, probably terminal." Miss Windfall had also added her own commentary: "wealthy, old-line Good Shepherd family, considered eccentric, bequest to church anticipated."

Suddenly Randollph was weary and extraordinarily hungry. He remembered that he hadn't eaten since breakfast. Clarence's calorie-packed menu had supported him till now. He reasoned that the wise thing to do was rush to down to the hotel coffee shop and refuel. It wouldn't be long, anyway, before he was supposed to meet Lieutenant Casey, and he wouldn't want to miss the lieutenant because he was staying overlong at his pastoral visits. He could come and call on Mrs. Victoria Clarke Hoffman tomorrow, maybe.

He thought of several other reasons to postpone the visit before he realized he was dogging it. What if Mrs. Hoffman's fragile kidneys collapsed tonight? What if she somehow discovered he had been here and neglected to visit her? What kind of chicken-livered pastor was he, anyway, shrinking from a clear duty because he thought it might be unpleasant? He took the elevator to Mrs. Hoffman's floor.

Mrs. Hoffman had a suite of rooms. The room Randollph entered resembled a well-appointed parlor in an upper-middle-class home. Mrs. Hoffman, dressed in an oriental robe of green and gold and delicate reds, was sitting in a large chair reading what Randollph judged from the dust jacket was a mystery novel. She was a wisp of a woman, with thin white hair and the translucent skin often seen in the aged ill.

"So you are the famous Dr. Cesare Paul Randollph," she said, after he had identified himself. "I was hoping you'd get around to paying me a call." She absently inserted a marker and let her book rest in her lap. "Did Addie Windfall type that card?" She held out her hand. "Let me see what she put on it."

Randollph handed it over. Mrs. Hoffman did not seem to him the type who took no for an answer. Also, he was rather looking forward to her reaction to Miss Windfall's appraisals.

"Hah!" the old lady snorted. "Elderly! Why didn't she just say eighty-nine and be done with it? She's got the record. I was baptized in that church. Not the present building, of course, the old prairie Romanesque building that was gloomy as a jail. I must say it matched the theology of the time. My paternal grandfather was one of the founders of Good Shepherd. The pious old pirate made a fortune trading cheap whiskey to the Indians for furs. I'm glad Addie put down that I'm considered eccentric. Do you have any idea why?"

Randollph admitted that he hadn't.

"Because I made a habit of speaking my mind on politics and business, things only men were supposed to know about, back when nice women were expected to be interested only in their homes and the social season. I was for Wilson, and I said publicly that Cal Coolidge was silent because he couldn't think of anything to say. I was also for Franklin Roosevelt." She chuckled, a dry, raspy sound. "That almost broke up my second marriage."

Randollph was wishing he'd known Victoria Hoffman before her worn-out flesh had brought her next door to eternity.

Mrs. Hoffman looked at the card again. "Yes, I've got kidney complications. They're just about worn out. And it is terminal. Well, why not? Eighty-nine years is all one has a right to expect from a pair of kidneys. I've had a pleasant, interesting, and sometimes even an exciting life. I should be ready to go."

Randollph didn't quite know how to reply to this, but quickly discovered another rule of pastoral visitation on the sick: When you can't think of a sensible comment, shut up. Mrs. Hoffman went right on talking.

"Do you know Edgar Lee Masters' poetry?"

"*The Spoon River Anthology?* I've read it. I can't say that I know it."

"Eddie Masters was a Chicago attorney. I knew him well. He has a poem in the anthology I'm fond of. It's called 'Lucinda Matlock.' Lucinda talks about her full life, then says, 'at ninety-six I had lived enough, that is all, and passed to a sweet repose.' Well, Dr. Randollph, that's the way I want it to be with me."

Randollph was about to murmur something banal about this, but Victoria Hoffman went on.

"But do you know something? I'm not yet able to feel that I've lived quite enough. Measured by any reasonable standard, I have. I've had three husbands, and I've enjoyed them all, not to mention lord knows how many gentlemen before, between, and after the husbands. I've always had so much money I never even thought about it."

She paused reflectively, then took this inviting conversational detour.

"Do you have money, Dr. Randollph?"

"A little. I had sense enough to save and invest some in the days when I was being rather extravagantly paid for my work."

"Oh, yes, the Los Angeles Rams. I'm a fan of most sports. I've seen you play. But I'll wager you aren't motivated by money. You're like me. I was always glad to have it, but I think I'd have been just as happy poor. I've always enjoyed life, and I'd have enjoyed it with or without money."

Randollph said this pretty much stated his own thoughts on the subject, but ventured that it might be easier to be happy if you could pay your bills.

"Yes. Hang on to some of that money, Dr. Randollph," she admonished him. "When you come to die, you begin to appreciate the value of money. Instead of living out my days in the stink and indignity of some miserable nursing home, I am able to die in comfort in these pleasant rooms, attended by private nurses. I can afford that awful machine that washes out my kidneys and keeps them going a little longer." She seemed suddenly tired, and Randollph rose to go.

"You know what I'd like, Dr. Randollph?" she asked. "I don't have any particular qualms about the state of my soul. But I'd like to hear a prayer from *The Book of Common Prayer*. I don't suppose you modern clergymen carry a prayerbook, do you?"

Randollph chuckled, then quickly apologized. "Your remark called to my mind an occasion when the Earl of Sandwich had twelve Church of England clergymen as dinner guests. He bet them that every one of them had a corkscrew in his pocket, but that there wasn't a prayerbook among them."

Mrs. Hoffman's eyes sparkled. "Did he win?"

"He won."

She was delighted. "I'd like to have known those fellows. They'd be more fun than most of the preachers I've met in a long lifetime. Art Hartshorne, your predecessor at Good Shepherd, is an old gasbag. Bertie Smelser is a bookkeeper. I do like your young Dan Gantry, though. He's visited me several times. He's got spirit! You'll conduct my funeral, of course. In the church. I'd hate to be laid away from a commercial funeral home. Might as well have the service at

Marshall Field's. But I want Dan Gantry to assist."

Randollph promised her that her wishes would be followed, then said, "Unlike the Earl of Sandwich's guests, I have no corkscrew in my pocket, but I do have a prayerbook on me. It isn't *The Book of Common Prayer*, but I expect it has a prayer taken from it." He leafed quickly through the pages. "Yes, here's one." He glanced at Mrs. Hoffman and saw that she had bowed her head.

"Let us pray," he said; then, from the book: " 'Almighty God, our heavenly father, who of thy great mercy hast promised forgiveness of sins to all them that with hearty repentance and true faith turn unto thee; have mercy upon us, pardon and deliver us from all our sins; confirm and strengthen us in all goodness; and bring us to everlasting life; through Jesus Christ our Lord. Amen.' "

"Amen," Mrs. Hoffman said. "Those words have such a marvelous ring to them, you can't help being moved by them." Randollph noticed a tear in the corner of one of her eyes. "I do hope you'll be able to come again, Dr. Randollph. I shan't expire for a few months yet, they tell me, and you've no idea how much your visit has helped me."

What was it Freddie had said? "They minister to you." He turned to go.

"Tell Addie Windfall not to worry about the bequest to Good Shepherd. I kept Art Hartshorne dangling about it. He was too eager, and I liked to see him sweat. I put it in the will, though. And it's a large one. Lord knows why. But I've got a lot to give away, and Good Shepherd's no worse than most who are getting a share of my money, and better than some."

Visiting hours were over when Randollph left Victoria Hoffman's room. The halls were quiet. Nurses, many of them wearing white slack suits, were silently bearing trays of medicine from room to room, most of it sleeping potions or pellets to defend against pain. Angels in pants, Randollph thought. The hospital was buttoning up for the night.

When he got off the elevator at the ground floor, he almost bumped into Samantha Stack, who was leading a procession of men carrying a portable television camera, cases of lights, and coils of black cable.

"Well, Pastor Randollph, hello." She looked at the prayerbook, which he had forgotten to put back in his pocket. "Making your rounds?"

"That I am. And what brings you here?"

"Doing a news bit on the latest medical wonder machine. Seems it's in use all day, so we had to film it in its off-hours."

"You're all done?"

"Yep."

"Then perhaps you'd be open to an invitation for a bite to eat. I haven't had a morsel since breakfast."

"Come to think of it, neither have I," Sam said. "Fellows, you go ahead," she added, dismissing the camera crew.

They found a disconsolate-looking Lieutenant Casey nursing a Coke in the hospital coffee shop.

"Are we all hungry?" Randollph asked.

"Starved," Sam said.

"I haven't had dinner," Casey said.

"Do either of you fancy a stale chicken-salad sandwich or a greasy hamburger, which is about what's available here?"

"No," Casey said.

"Ugh!" Sam said.

"Then excuse me a moment, and I'll try to make arrangements for something better."

"Where?" Sam asked.

"Trust me," Randollph told her, and disappeared. He was back in five minutes. "Let's go. Lieutenant, you have a car?"

The lieutenant had a car. Samantha and Randolph slid into the front seat with Casey.

"Where to?"

"My place," Randolph answered.

"You going to cook us something?"

"Hardly. You aren't aware that I have a resident chef and majordomo, lieutenant. Name of Clarence Higbee. I called to see if he could fix us a simple supper. He said it was no trouble at all."

"Randollph, I had breakfast with you in your place, now I'm having supper with you in your place. We might as well be living together," Sam said.

Suddenly Randollph knew that he wanted to marry this girl. He had thought of it before. They had talked about it at a half-jocular level, both wary, neither ready to commit themselves. He knew that Sam didn't fit into his life. He tried to envision her as a seminary faculty wife and saw that she would be restless and bored in that placid setting. He tried to think of some way he could adjust his life to accommodate the needs of her career, her independence, her identity as a television personality. But that would be no good, either, if he had to give up too much of himself. And he knew that she wouldn't allow him to. Nor was he sure why he felt this way about her. She was bright, and great-looking. But then, so were lots of girls. She was sexually exciting to him, but this was not a new experience. She had an interesting mind, but there was nothing unique about that. You could add up all the reasons why he might want to marry her, and the total would be no different from what he'd seen in a dozen or so ladies he had known. All he knew was that beyond any rational decision and beyond any doubt, he wanted to spend the rest of his life with this girl.

Eighteen

The plump little man clapped his hands for silence.

"All right, same time tomorrow night. And please be on time. You know I'm simply devastated when you string in here at all hours. Mary Ann, dear, please try to learn your lines tomorrow." His voice gentled. "And Dr. Val, I do appreciate your coming tonight. We all know, ah, that is, well, what an effort it must have been."

"The show must go on," Val Julian said, a tiny bitter edge to his voice. "The show must go on. Come on, Dan, let's find a drink."

"I'll join you in a sarsaparilla," Dan Gantry said.

They left the little theater with its handmade signs announcing Tennessee Williams' *The Night of the Iguana* as the next attraction. The Friendly Dragon was a quiet little bar around the corner where Dan and Val usually went after a rehearsal, sometimes with other members of the cast.

"You do make a fine failed priest," Dan said, when they

had found seats. "Tennessee Williams would be proud of you."

"I can feel what a failed priest feels," Val said. "That knowledge that you set high standards for yourself but weren't able to make it. Then you have to go through life with a contempt for yourself. You aren't strong enough to match your self-image."

"You're a good actor."

"Yes, pretty good," Val said. "Maybe I should have gone into the theater. Which is a greater contribution to the world—to cure a bellyache or give people a belly laugh? There's a moral problem for you, padre."

"I'm just a humble preacher, what do I know about moral problems? I know about organizational problems. I know about administrative problems. I know about the problems of church politics. But moral problems?"

"Who does know about them?" Val said. "The important ones are all ambiguous."

"What I know," Dan said in a kindly voice, "is that it took a lot of guts for you to come to rehearsal tonight, the funeral being only this morning. Nobody would have blamed you for skipping."

"I know that. But don't make a hero out of me. I came for myself. Why sit and cry? I feel better, I think less when I'm assuming my responsibilities. Did you know that I saw patients for a while this afternoon? Why not? It was good for them and good for me."

"The book is closed, why linger over it?"

"Exactly. A long book, but closed now forever. Well, drink up. Tomorrow is a working day. As I said earlier, coining a brilliant phrase, the show must go on."

"My turn to pay," Dan said, as Val Julian reached for his wallet. "And don't patronize me with that rich-doctor line. I know you are disgustingly overpaid, and I receive a contemptible pittance for laboring in the Lord's vineyard. But I can buy a friend a drink."

"Thanks, friend," Val said as he slid out of the booth. "I'll walk with you down to the church, or, more accurately, the hotel. I'll catch a cab there." He sauntered to the door and went out. Dan waited for change.

As Dan came out the door, he saw a man in a dark hat pulled low and a raincoat draped over his arm step up to Val, and heard him ask, "Dr. Valorous Julian?"

"Yes," Val answered. "Why?"

"Sorry about this, doctor," the man said. He extended his raincoat-covered arm, and there was a muffled "plop." Val said, "Oh!" and clutched his middle, crumpling to the sidewalk.

Dan dived for the man, who saw him too late. Dan slammed him into a parked car, wrenched the gun out of his hand, and clobbered him on the side of the head with the gun's butt. He collapsed, half-sitting, against the car.

Dan ran to Val Julian, knelt beside him. "Val? Val?" There was no answer. He felt for Val's pulse. There was a beat. He looked up at the small crowd that had gathered. "Somebody call the cops and an ambulance."

"I already done that, Dan." It was Herbie, the bartender from the Friendly Dragon. A police car screeched around the corner and slammed to a stop. Two uniformed cops were quickly kneeling by Dan and Val. One tore Val's shirt open, looked at the wound, then felt over his heart. "Pretty bad," he said dispassionately. "Who shot him?"

"That guy by the car."

"Him? He's out pretty good. What happened to him?"

"He stumbled," Dan said. "Where in hell is that ambulance?"

The ambulance, siren whining like some great beast in pain, slid in behind the police car. Two men in whites quickly pulled a stretcher out of the ambulance and knocked its collapsible wheeled legs into place. The one with a stethoscope listened briefly to Val's heartbeat, applied a bandage to the wound to stanch the blood. They got Val onto the stretcher.

"Take him to the Julian Hospital," Dan instructed. "He's Dr. Valorous Julian."

"It's the closest, anyway," the man with the stethoscope said. "You know him? Come along if you want."

"We'll follow," one of the cops said. "Got to get the story."

Inside the ambulance, Dan asked the man with the stethoscope, "How is he?"

"Bad," the man said. "Bad, but alive."

"Oh, Christ, Val," Dan wailed. "What's happening to your family?"

Nineteen

Clarence Higbee removed the silver cover from a large serving platter, releasing an aroma that stimulated Randollph's stomach to growl with anticipation. He slid one of the portions onto a warmed plate and spooned liquid over it. From another dish he ladeled up puffy brown balls of potatoes, then set the plate in front of Samantha Stack.

"What is this heavenly-smelling dish, Clarence?" she asked.

"Tournedos Pompadour, ma'am," Clarence said, continuing his serving.

"Tournedos are supposed to be beef," Sam said. "This looks like ham."

"You will find the beef beneath the ham," Clarence said.

"Are they hard to fix?"

"Quite simple, ma'am. Sauté the tenderloin slices quickly in butter and olive oil, place them on croutes, then add a little red wine to the pan and cook it a bit longer. Smear the tenderloin with tomato puree, top with slices of sautéed ham and a slice of truffle. The liquid I spooned on it is the pan juices. To my mind, a nice plain dish for late supper."

Sam tasted, chewed, and smiled an other-worldly smile. "Clarence, will you marry me? I could work and earn our living, and you could cook. It would be a perfect marriage."

Randollph wondered how Clarence would handle a Samantha Stack, but he saw that he need not have worried.

"Were I not a confirmed bachelor, ma'am, I'd be delighted," he said. He turned to Randollph. "I'd suggest a claret if you wish a wine, sir."

Randollph looked at his guests.

"Tea for me at this hour of the night," Sam said.

"Could I have a beer?" Casey asked.

"Of course, sir," Clarence said. "I hope you don't mind an import. I have not stocked any domestic brands. I find all of them somewhat flavorless."

"I'd always have imported if it didn't cost so much," Casey said.

Randollph said he'd join the lieutenant in a beer, and Clarence departed. They all ate hungrily for a few moments; then Randollph said, "I think I'd better tell you about an experience I had this afternoon, lieutenant. I was visited by a lady who, I suspect, is Laura Justus." He told the story, omitting only Ms. X's statement that she had his letters to Lisa Julian. It might be withholding evidence, it might be less than honest, might even be a venial sin—if you wanted to grade sins. But he wasn't going to prejudice his case with the girl he was going to persuade—if at all possible—to marry him.

"Well, I'll be damned," Sam said.

Casey, whose spirits had been visibly improved by the food, now looked glum again.

"If it weren't for that woman, I'd haul in Dr. Brandt," he said. "He's the only one with a strong motive and maximum opportunity. I'm almost sure he did it. We shook, ah, we questioned the loan shark this afternoon. Turns out he threatened the doctor, and Brandt begged for a little more time. Said he'd be coming into a lot of money before long. Now, where was he going to get a chunk of money except from the insurance policy on his wife?"

"You've asked him about it, I take it?"

"Sure. He says he just made it up to keep the shark off his back. That's what you'd figure him to say if he'd done it."

Randollph toyed with his beer bottle. "Löwenbräu," he read from the label, "since 1383. When I was in seminary we called this Martin Luther beer. As a good Catholic, you wouldn't know why, would you, lieutenant?"

"The study of the life of Luther was not encouraged in parochial school," Casey replied. "We were just taught that he was Satan's representative."

"A view which, I believe, has now been abandoned," Randollph said. "Luther was born a hundred years to the year after the Löwenbräu brewery was established. It makes good beer. Luther was fond of good beer. Therefore, we concluded, Luther must have been fond of Löwenbräu. Have you given up on the idea that Lisa was killed by a burglar?"

"Just about."

"What other possibilities have you eliminated?"

Casey poured more beer into his glass. "We thought Manny Friedman—he's the loan shark—might have had it done. But our, ah, interrogation pretty well convinced one of our most effective officers that he had nothing to do with it."

"What about the Hollywood people?"

"They're not eliminated, but we can't find a speck of evidence leading to any of them."

"And that leaves Dr. Brandt. And Laura Justus." Something flickered in Randollph's brain as he said the names, but went out before he could fan it to flame.

"Dr. Brandt for sure. Laura Justus I can't fit in. Brandt's right for it. 'Go for the guy with the overpowering motive' is a good rule to follow in homicide. It could be someone else, but he's likely to be it."

"Unless someone had an overpowering motive you haven't uncovered."

"Laura Justus?"

"Perhaps. If you think of this affair as a scene in a play, her recurring appearances are as yet unexplained. Couldn't you trace her, lieutenant, if you put ample resources behind the effort?"

Casey's frustration made him almost brusque. "It's possible. But we don't have a single lead to trace her by."

Sam Stack spoke up. "Didn't she tell you, C.P., that she was an avenging angel?"

"That's what she also told Brandt and Kitty Darrow," Casey said.

"Then she must be a friend of Lisa's," Sam said. "Couldn't you find her by that? And if she's an avenging angel like she claims, then she wouldn't have had anything to do with the killing."

"I've been thinking about that," Randollph said. "She was trying to find out if Lisa had ever told me anything about her past life—something unusual or out of the ordinary in some former relationship that might furnish a clue to the killer. She also asked substantially the same question of Brandt and Miss Darrow, didn't she, lieutenant?"

"Yes." Casey was interested now. "What's your point?"

"I'm not sure how valid it may be, but my point is that suppose Laura Justus, whoever she is, had a powerful motive for killing Lisa, a motive connected to Lisa's past. So she does kill her. Then, she wonders if Lisa may have confided her secret to someone else. To whom would she have confided it? Likely to her husband."

"And you, reverend. Why you?" Sam put the question with false innocence.

"Ah, I would guess that Laura Justus, if she was a close friend of Lisa's, would have known that at one time Lisa and I were good friends."

"Hah!" Sam said.

"And, since I am now a pastor—was briefly her pastor—well, the combination of long acquaintance and my role as a spiritual adviser might have induced her to confide in me. I expect it was this knowledge, or this assumption, that brought Laura Justus to the chapel." Again, that flicker in his brain. Again, it would not catch.

"You're saying that Laura Justus is the killer?" Casey asked.

"Lieutenant, I don't know anything about homicide investigation. As a professional historian, I know something about how people behave. This lady's behavior strikes me as being very peculiar."

"Keep talking. This is interesting."

"She poses as an avenging angel. She threatens to shoot Dr. Brandt, but when she is convinced that he doesn't know anything along the lines of her question, her gun jams, and she is not perturbed, but strolls nonchalantly away. She threatens me, but when satisfied that I do not have the answer she wants, she doesn't harm me."

"Which adds up to what?" Casey asked.

"That she was interested not in our knowledge but in our ignorance of facts that might point to someone—probably her—as killer."

"But what would her motive be?" Casey, right elbow propped on the table, chin in hand, pressed Randollph. "You have to have a motive that makes sense."

"Ah, that looks marvelous, Clarence," Randollph said.

"Gooseberry tart, sir. His grace, the bishop, told me that you are partial to gooseberries." Clarence carved the large pie into portions and transferred them to dessert plates. "I'll have coffee here in a moment, sir."

"No, lieutenant," Randollph said. "A motive has to make sense only to the person that holds it. What drives another person may be obscure to us, but plain to him. At least he knows that he is driven. As a theologian of sorts, I am never surprised by what appear to me as eccentric and bizarre motivations for human conduct. Original sin is manifested in every conceivable variety of behavior."

Casey unconsciously loosened the knot of his tie and unbuttoned his collar. "I was brought up to believe that Adam-and-Eve-and-snake story," Casey said. "And I'm a practicing Catholic. But I quit believing that old myth a long time ago. I'm surprised that a modern Protestant clergyman still holds to it." He sat back and smiled complacently, sure that he had bested Randollph at theological one-upmanship.

"You didn't abandon belief in the myth. You just quit taking it as a literal description," Randollph assured him. "Original sin is simply the fact that all of us treat our own concerns as more important in the scheme of things than an objective assessment would warrant. Of all people, a policeman has to believe that. You see it illustrated every day. G. K. Chesterton said that original sin is the only empirically demonstrable Christian doctrine."

"He was a Catholic." Casey was determined to salvage something from this debate.

"Truth isn't sectarian," Randollph said. "If I were you, I'd find Laura Justus."

"We'll have a go at it," Casey grumbled, "but we don't have enough men to do everything. I'm going to put everyone I can spare on Dr. Brandt. Comb his background, his associates, everything. Ten to one we find something."

"I'm not a gambling man, but I'd like a little piece of that bet," Randollph said.

"You would? Do you know something I don't?"

"No, of course not," Randollph said. "You've just come from talking with Brandt, and, I take it, it was an unsatisfactory interview—"

"Very unsatisfactory."

"He's not a prepossessing personality," Randollph observed. "He acts guilty. There is evidence against him. You have experience and skills in homicide detection, and I do not. Nonetheless, I'll wager he didn't do it."

"Oh, you will? Mind telling me why?"

"His character. His morals aren't exemplary, to be sure, but he's essentially weak. And his motive isn't that strong."

"He had plenty of motive!"

"Not for killing. He had alternative sources for money if he was desperate."

"Such as?"

"His father-in-law," Randollph said. "Unpleasant as it might have been for Brandt, he could have obtained a loan from Dr. Rex Julian by coming clean. Remember, his earning capacity had been greatly accelerated by the gift of a full partnership in the clinic. Certainly a solution less dangerous and distasteful than murder."

"Maybe he isn't smart enough to have figured that out." Casey did not give up easily.

"Dr. Brandt is avaricious, and the greedy are always canny about money," Randollph replied. "You may be sure that Brandt was aware of every possible source of money. He wouldn't have overlooked a rich father-in-law."

Casey pondered this. "Assuming you're right, which I'm not, then who've we got?"

"Annette Paris, perhaps, someone else from Lisa's past that you don't know about."

"Not enough evidence in that direction."

"Laura Justus."

"Mr. Gantry for you, sir." Clarence set a phone in front of Randollph and plugged it into the jack. "He says it's urgent."

"Excuse me," Randollph said. "Yes, Dan."

"Boss, Val Julian's been shot."

"What! How?" The change in Randollph's voice told Casey and Sam that something in the nature of a disaster was going on.

"We stopped by a bar for a drink, like we usually do after rehearsal. When he walked out the door ahead of me, a guy stepped up and shot him."

"Calm down, Dan," Randollph said. "Is he dead? Where is he?"

"At the hospital. They're operating. He's bad."

"The Julian Hospital?"

"Yes. The family's all here. I'll do what I can to be a pastor to them, but I'm pretty shook-up. He's one of my best friends. Also, I socked the guy that shot him. I'm still shaking. Maybe you ought to be here." It was a plea.

"I'll be there as soon as I can make it."

Randollph hung up. "Dr. Val Julian's been shot."

"Oh, my God!" Sam said.

"How very distressing!" Clarence Higbee stopped clearing the dessert plates. "If I may say so, sir, it has an Old Testament sound to it. Violent and brutal. Two members of a family done away with." He shook his head and began to clear the table. Casey, without asking, had immediately grabbed the phone.

"I'm going too," Sam announced, as if someone might try to stop her. "Val's my friend."

"I think you ought to come," Randollph said. "Your presence will be a comfort to me."

Sam was surprised. "What a lovely thing to say, C.P."
She leaned her head against his shoulder.

Casey put down the phone. "The creep that shot him's a
well-known local punk. He's pretty well busted up, but he's
singing. He got the contract through a fellow he met in a
bar. Doesn't know him. Thirty-five down. Thirty-five after
the job. Somebody had to be laying out ten, twelve grand
for this contract, counting the fee to the contact man.
Somebody wanted Val Julian dead pretty bad. Let's go."

They moved toward the door. "If you don't need me
anymore, sir, I'll be retiring as soon as I've cleaned up,"
Clarence Higbee said.

"Of course. By the way, what was it you said a moment
ago, Clarence?"

"I beg pardon, sir?"

"About the Old Testament."

"Oh. It just came to me, sir, that this bloody business
with the Julians sounds like those stories of vengeance and
brutality you come across in the Old Testament. Perhaps in
Kings or one of the Samuels."

The flicker in his brain caught fire this time, but the
flame was too weak to illuminate. "Do you have your Bible
handy?" Randollph asked Clarence.

"Of course, sir. It's the King James Version. The newer
translations have their merits, but I regard the King James
as the true Bible."

"May I borrow it?"

Clarence went to the kitchen and returned carrying a
worn black morocco-bound Bible with limp overhanging
edges.

When they were about to get in Casey's unmarked police
car, which Casey had left in a no-parking zone, Randollph
said, "I think I'll get in the back. If you'll be so good as to
leave the dome light on, lieutenant, I can do a little

research as we ride. And, lieutenant, get to the hospital as fast as you can. I'd like to talk to Val if he's still alive."

Sam Stack, sitting by Casey, turned and looked at Randollph. "We'll be quite a sight, driving through the Loop with a priest in the back seat reading the Bible by the dome light."

But Randollph was too intent on leafing through the Old Testament to hear her.

Twenty

Randollph had never been part of a deathwatch. He supposed that veteran pastors were accustomed to such scenes, if one ever could become accustomed to them. He wished that Freddie had briefed him on what to say to a family waiting for the surgeon, knowing that his face would tell them if it was life and hope, or death and the end. He wondered how many times this room, just down the hall from the operating theaters, had looked on this sad drama.

Mrs. Rex Julian, her blond head on the old doctor's shoulder, was sobbing noisily, the retching sounds punctured by wails of "Oh, my baby! Oh, my poor baby!" Dr. Rex Julian patted her occasionally, his face, as usual, grave and impassive. Dr. Kermit Julian, apparently summoned from an evening of lounging before the television or reading about the latest hot-shop operation in one of his medical journals, wore rumpled tan flannels and a pullover sweater. His dark good looks were frozen in a glum stare that he was directing at the tips of his tatty loafers. Dan Gantry, sleeve of his old tweed jacket torn and a bandage on his face, sat beside Sam Stack. No one spoke.

Randollph said, "Excuse me, I need to make a phone call." The family appeared not to hear. Lieutenant Casey was in the hall talking to two uniformed policemen and writing in a pocket-size notebook.

Randollph found a pay phone down the hall and dialed the bishop's apartment from memory. After six rings a sleepy voice answered, "Yes, hello."

"Freddie, Val Julian's been shot. I'm calling from the Julian Hospital. He's on the operating table now, and the family's all here. Thought you ought to know. Thought you might like to be here."

"I'll be there as fast as I can get into my trousers, C.P."

The bishop, Randollph reflected as he hung up the phone, had the reactions of a professional pastor practiced in his calling. No startled gasps. No exclamations of surprise. No stammered questions about how did it happen or who did it. Grasping, without consciously thinking it through, that an emergency existed which required or would be benefited by his presence, Freddie had reduced his response to the necessary essentials—getting into his britches and getting out there.

Randollph was reluctant to return to that funereal room and sit. The only legitimate excuse he could think of for absenting himself was to go to the bathroom, even though nature was not pressing him. He wandered down the hall until he found a door marked "Men." Inside, it was clean as a laboratory. He put Clarence Higbee's Bible on top of a paper-towel dispenser and washed his hands. He took out a pocket comb and touched up his hair, which did not need it, thinking regretfully that the gray specks were more numerous than they ought to be.

He retrieved Clarence's Bible and opened it to a place he had marked. He read again the story of love and hate. Was this ancient story a rough parallel to the bloody Julian business? Or was the similarity apparent only to an imagination fevered by abundant exposure to mankind's boring repetition of vices, follies, and irrational excesses of the spirit? The penalty for being a historian, he knew, was a tendency to see historical precedents where there might not be any.

He closed the Bible and left the rest room. When he came within sight of the waiting room, he saw that not far from it Lieutenant Casey was talking to Dan Gantry.

"I came out just as this creep said, 'Sorry about this, doctor,' " Dan was saying to Casey. "Then I heard this noise, sounded like a cough, and Val grabbed his guts. The creep hadn't expected me, he started to walk away, and I just went for him. I should have gone right to Val, but I didn't even think, I just went for the creep." Dan, Randollph could see, was still worked up. When he came down, he'd likely come down hard.

"You knocked him around pretty good," Casey said dryly.

"Did I? Soon as he folded up, I realized it was Val that mattered. I forgot about the creep and went to Val."

Casey turned to Randollph. "What was all that business about the Bible just as we were leaving your place? I see you're still carrying it."

"Why, lieutenant," Randollph said, "I'm surprised that you find a Protestant pastor carrying a Bible in any way out of the ordinary. Wouldn't you expect your pastor to have a breviary with him at all times?"

"The Catholic clergy is drilled in the holy habits of the devotional life," Casey replied with a grin, glad for a moment of banter to relieve the tension of the evening. "Now, if you were a disciple of the Reverend Dr. Billy

Graham, I would not be surprised. *They* carry Bibles. But you aren't that kind of Protestant. Therefore, I am surprised."

"I've nothing against holy habits, lieutenant, unless they become a meaningless routine, or are exhibited for the purpose of proclaiming one's piety. One leads to a sterile spirituality, the other to spiritual pride. No, I do not normally carry a Bible. It just came to me, when Clarence Higbee mentioned that this whole bloody business had a biblical sound to it, that the Scriptures might shed a little light on it."

"And do they?"

Randollph was about to answer when the bishop hurried up to them.

"Hello, Dan, lieutenant. Where is the family?" he asked.

"I'll show you," Randollph said, leading him toward the waiting room.

"How is Val?"

"Still alive, so far as we know. Not much more than that."

The bishop, as he had done before, went directly to Dr. Rex Julian and grasped his hand without speaking.

"It was good of you to come, bishop," the old doctor said. His grave expression softened around the eyes.

"Oh, my baby!" Mrs. Rex Julian wailed. The bishop apparently deemed it useless to speak to her, but patted her hand. He turned and shook hands with Dr. Kermit Julian, who did not take his eyes from his shoes. Dan and Casey came in, followed by Dr. Carl Brandt in shapeless green surgeon's pajamas, an operating-room mask dangling beneath his chin. Randollph was surprised to see that Dr. Brandt had a substantial belly, which good tailoring trimmed down but which cheap cotton drawers and blouse outlined unflatteringly. His surgeon's hat, like a squashed-down campaign cap, brought out his heavy, sensual features.

The people in the room waited. He shook his head. "I don't know," he said in a heavy voice. "It's touch and go. We've done everything we can. Now we wait."

"Is he conscious, doctor?" Randollph asked.

"Barely."

"Let me have a prayer with him."

Dr. Brandt considered the request. "I guess a prayer might help. Nothing else can now. I'll take you to him."

Randollph felt a fleeting guilt. The prayer was an excuse to talk to him. But the Almighty, he was certain, would absolve him of this clerical duplicity, as much as it was to a worthy end.

Dr. Brandt took him to the intensive-care unit. "I'll wait outside here," he said. "Don't be long."

Valorous Julian was hooked up with clear plastic tubes feeding him blood plasma, oxygen, and heaven knew what else. Electronic instruments monitored his vital functions with subdued beeps. Dr. Valorous Julian, to Randollph's inexpert eyes, did not look long for this world.

"Val," he said.

Val opened his eyes, "Hello, Con," he said in a whisper. "Do you administer last rites?"

"Val," Randollph asked, "do you know Laura Justus?"

Val closed his eyes. "Yes, I know her."

"Tell me about her. Just the essentials."

In whispered, pain-punctuated sentences, Val told him.

"I think I'd like a prayer, padre," Val said at the end of his brief recital.

Randollph remembered that he still had the bishop's prayerbook in his pocket. But he judged that this was no time for standard prayers, no matter how elegantly composed.

"Let us pray," he said. "O God, from whose love and care no earthly thing can finally separate us . . ."

When Randollph returned to the waiting room, Mrs. Rex Julian was still wailing, "Oh, my baby! Oh, my baby!" But she quieted down when she saw Randollph.

"He's alive." Randollph answered their unasked question. "I talked with him."

Randollph sat down. There was no more that he could tell them about Valorous Julian's chances in this mortal life. Silence.

Finally the bishop said, "Lieutenant Casey, I understand you have the man who shot Valorous in custody?"

"Yes, we do. But he's just a hired gun. We don't know yet who hired him, or why."

Dr. Kermit Julian looked at his father, his stepmother— whose wails had abated to a sobbing—and at Randollph.

"How long do you think you can live with it, doctor?" Randollph asked him.

Dr. Kermit's stony expression did not change. He stared at Randollph for what seemed a very long time. Then, with a sigh of resignation, he said, "I never thought that I could live with it." He turned to Casey. "You will want to arrest me. I hired that gunman to shoot my brother."

With an inarticulate animal scream Mrs. Rex Julian lunged at Kermit, flailing and clawing. It was all that Dan, Casey, and Randollph could do to tear her away from him. Dr. Brandt disappeared briefly, returning with a hypodermic syringe, and quickly injected it in the struggling woman. Orderlies appeared, strapped her to a cart, and wheeled her away. Dr. Rex Julian looked at Kermit, then followed his wife. He wanted to hear no more.

When they had gone, Casey asked, almost gently, "Why, doctor?"

"Because he killed my sister," Dr. Kermit Julian said.
Sam's mouth dropped open. Dan Gantry looked stunned.

"But why? Why would he do that?" Casey was trying to
hide his surprise.

"Because he had, they had ..." Dr. Kermit Julian's flat,
emotionless voice stopped, then began again. "They were,
had been, years ago they had an ..." He didn't go on.

"Try 'illicit relationship,' doctor," Randollph said.

Dr. Kermit Julian seemed grateful for the help. "I knew
about it. I saw them one time. They didn't know I knew. I
watched Val for years, and I could tell it had done
something to him. I don't think he ever got over it. He
never tried to form a lasting attachment to a woman. He
was warped. I guessed right away he had killed Lisa, and I
accused him of it. He admitted it, but said there wasn't
anything I could do about it. But there was something I
could do. I couldn't turn him in to the police. But he had
to be punished. I did what I had to do."

After the police officers had taken away the unprotesting
Dr. Kermit Julian, Casey said, "All right, doctor, how did
you know?" The question wasn't belligerent, but it was
brusque.

"I didn't know, I just made what you'd have every right
to call a wild guess," Randollph answered.

"My God," Dan was saying, mostly to himself, "my God,
I can't believe it. Val. I can't believe it."

"I do not have the privilege of wild guesses," Casey said.
"I have to present a credible explanation for a homicide.
I've got to account for Laura Justus, for example. You
don't."

"Oh, Val was Laura Justus, lieutenant."

"What!"

"Dan," Randollph said, "you told me that Val did an

excellent impression of his sister at the bachelor party. Was he especially good at female impersonation?"

"He was a good actor, boss. Good at any part he played. He had the ability to get inside almost any character. He didn't play the person, he was the person. Come to think of it, he's done the female bit several times. He could just become female."

"Did you figure that out?" Casey asked Randollph, without bothering to hide his skepticism.

"No. I thought Laura Justus might be Miss Darrow." He looked at Dr. Brandt, who, he guessed, was trying to conceal his elation at being off the hook. "I even thought she might be Mrs. Rex Julian."

"Why Mrs. Julian?"

"She was single-minded about the welfare of her son. If you wipe out the other Julians, then Val would have been sole inheritor of the Julian medical empire. Farfetched and sordid. But not unreasonable, lieutenant. Throughout history, mothers have done atrocious things for the benefit of their children."

"Let me get this straight," Casey said. "Val Julian registers at the hotel as Laura Justus the day before the wedding. Then he slips away from the reception, goes to his room, changes to Laura Justus. Then he phones the bridal suite pretending to be from the hospital and lures Dr. Brandt away. Brandt isn't exactly Jack Armstrong, the all-American boy—sorry, doctor—but he is very conscientious about his work. Then Laura Justus gets Lisa to let him in, and kills her. The he—she—goes back to his room and changes back to Val Julian and sneaks into another reception and pretends to be sleeping off a drunk. That's what happened?"

"I expect so," Randollph said. "Although it would be my guess that he didn't phone Dr. Brandt. He probably expected to kill the doctor, too. If you wanted to look hard enough, you might find that one of Dr. Brandt's friends made that call as a joke. They'd be afraid to admit it, of course, for fear of getting involved in a murder."

"Doesn't matter now," Casey said. "And Laura Justus doesn't check out of the hotel, because she wants us to go chasing after a nonexistent woman. Right?"

"I hadn't figured that out, lieutenant," Randollph lied. "I'm sure that's the explanation, though."

Casey looked a little more comfortable. "And she, he—dammit, this is confusing—Laura Justus nails you and Dr. Brandt because she, because Val's afraid Lisa might have told one or both of you about their, their ..."

" 'Incestuous relationship.' " Randollph supplied the phrase Casey was groping for.

"Yes, whatever." Casey hurried over the ugly fact. "Val Julian's not a killer by nature, and doesn't want to bloody up the landscape more than necessary. But he's prepared to knock you off, and Dr. Brandt too, if he thinks you know about it. He trusts his brother to keep his mouth shut to protect the family, but he can't trust you two guys."

"Oh, Jesus," Dan said, "What a mess!"

"If you had known about the relationship, you'd have figured it out in a minute," Randollph assured an increasingly self-confident Casey.

"Well, you made a lucky guess." Casey thought a minute, realized he was ungraciously pandering to his own ego. "No. You made a smart guess. I wish I had made it."

"Your professional education did not include Bible study, lieutenant. Mine did."

"I don't get it, Randollph. What's the Bible got to do with it?" It was a puzzled and stricken-looking Sam Stack asking.

Randollph picked up Clarence Higbee's Bible from the

end table where he had laid it, and opened it. "When
Clarence remarked that the Julian killings sounded like a
story out of the Old Testament, my memory was prodded. I
seemed to recall a story with the general character of the
Julian tragedy. Had I been that disciple of Dr. Billy
Graham you mentioned earlier, lieutenant, I could no
doubt have located the passage immediately. They more or
less memorize the Bible. But I didn't learn my Scriptures
that way."

Casey grunted. "That's why you were reading in the back
seat, huh?"

"I was searching. I didn't have a concordance handy."

"What's a concordance?" Sam asked.

"A book that lists every word in the Bible alphabetically,
followed by the exact chapter and verse where that word
can be found. Easy way to look up a verse or a passage
whose exact location has slipped your mind."

"What did you turn up, C.P.?" the bishop asked. "I've
heard the Scriptures quoted for strange and even dubious
purposes, but never as a clue in a homicide investigation."

"I turned up the thirteenth chapter of Second Samuel.
The story of Amnon, Tamar, and Absalom."

"Ah, yes," the bishop said. "I should have thought of it
myself."

Randollph read to them. " 'And it came to pass after this,
that Absalom the son of David had a fair sister, whose name
was Tamar; and Amnon the son of David loved her. And
Amnon was so vexed . . .' " Randollph stopped and put his
finger on his place in the Bible. "The Revised Standard
Version used the word 'tormented' instead of 'vexed.'
" '. . . that he fell sick for his sister Tamar . . .' " Randollph
paused. "I'll skip some of this," he said. "Amnon is so
obsessed with his sister, actually his half sister, that he tricks
her into coming to his tent. When she catches on to what

he has in mind, she begs him not to do it. But he has abandoned all reason, and, as the story tells it, 'being stronger than she, forced her, and lay with her.' "

"I love the delicate way the Bible talks about sex," Sam said. "Why doesn't it just say he raped her?"

"My Hebrew is awfully rusty," Randollph answered. "Maybe it doesn't even have a word for 'rape.' "

"Every language has a word for 'rape,' " Sam said, "because rape is standard male procedure in every country on earth. And incest. Why doesn't the Bible call it incest?"

"Because it wasn't considered incest back then," Randollph told her. "By the law of Israel at that time, a marriage between a half-brother and sister was perfectly legal. But to get on with it, when Amnon had finished copulating with her—"

"Copulating! That's a nicey-nicey word," Sam interrupted. "Why don't you just say when he'd finished—"

"Ahem!" Randollph said, looking at the bishop. "As I was saying, Amnon's passion for his half-sister turned to loathing. The verse I remembered, and the one which tells us the motive, lieutenant, is this: 'Then Amnon hated her exceedingly; so that the hatred wherewith he hated her was greater than the love wherewith he had loved her.' "

"The Bible is a dirty old book," Sam said.

"It is," Randollph agreed, "if by 'dirty' you mean it has quite a lot of sexual material in it. A modern novelist who used the theme of Tamar and Amnon would bring packs of pious, self-appointed censors to the attack."

"You mean that's why Val killed his sister—his half-sister? He hated her because, well, because of what they did? That's a motive?" Casey looked blank.

"Get a psychiatrist to explain the intricacies of Val's emotional state. I'm not qualified to do it," Randollph said. "I can only make guesses."

"Make some."

"I'd doubt that Val-Lisa is an exact parallel to Amnon-Tamar. Knowing Lisa, I'd guess that she cooperated fully." Randollph avoided looking at Sam. "She might even have been the aggressor. I'd guess that it was Val, unlike Amnon, who lost his virginity in the encounter. What it did to him internally, I do not know. Dr. Kermit says it warped him. Maybe, unlike Amnon, he never got over his love. Anyway, when Lisa decided to get married, it triggered a hate reaction. Perhaps he thought of the marriage as a final rejection. All the old feelings he had kept buried came surging up. It's incredible to us, but what he did made sense to him. He was driven. He had to do it. He couldn't help himself. The hate with which he hated her was greater than the love with which he had loved her. Can you think of a stronger motive for murder than consuming hatred, lieutenant?"

"No," Casey admitted, "that's what causes most of the dreary Saturday-night killings I have to handle. A little booze, and the hatred comes out. Then bang, somebody's dead. Usually a wife or a husband or brother or father. Not too different from this. I've had plenty of experience with incest, too. Only, it's always among the, well, what we think of as the lower classes. You know what I mean. You don't expect that kind of behavior in the high-rent districts."

"What you think of as the better classes are more adept at concealing their moral irregularities," Randollph said. "Original sin again. Money and status do not exempt us from it. They just motivate us to be clever at masking it."

"Boss," Dan asked, "I know I'm showing my ignorance, but I can't remember what happened to Amnon. Did he get away with it?"

"No," Randollph said. "His brother—half-brother—Absalom, found out what had happened. By the mores of the time, Tamar—no longer a virgin—could not expect to marry. There was no place for her in society. Amnon didn't kill her, but he might as well have. So Absalom considered it his duty to avenge the wrong done his sister. He has a sort of party where Amnon gets drunk, then some of Absalom's servants kill him."

Casey shook his head. "All out of the Bible."

"Val knows something about the Bible," Randollph said. "When I asked her—him—in the chapel if her name was Laura Justus, he said, 'My name is legion.' "

"I don't get it," Casey said.

"A reference to the Gadarene demoniac in the Gospel of Mark. When Jesus asked him his name, he—or the evil spirits in him—answered, 'My name is legion.' "

"Meaning what?"

"Meaning that Val knew he was mentally warped, that what he was doing was insane. I recognized the quote, of course, but I didn't understand it at the time."

"Weird." Casey shook his head. "Weird as hell."

"There was one other thing that niggled at my mind," Randollph said. "And probably at yours, too, lieutenant," he added hastily.

"What was that?"

"The name Laura Justus. It had a familiar sound to it, but I couldn't place it. Then, after I found the Bible passage, it came to me that the name Justus is a kind of symbolic name, something a twisted mind would think up, perhaps to reassure himself that what he was doing was right, and it is a sort of alias for 'Lisa Julian.' "

Casey was tempted to say, yes, he'd had the same feeling, but he resisted. "It never crossed my mind," he said.

"Let's go home," Sam said.

Randollph was grateful for the glass that separated the

front and back seats of the cab. Though installed to protect the driver from the predatory plans of killers and robbers, it afforded the passengers some privacy. At least the hackey wouldn't be listening in on what he intended to say.

Sam put her red head on his shoulder. "Oh, God, but I'm tired," she said.

"I know." He spoke gently. "This is the worst day, and the worst hour, and the least romantic situation possible for me to say this. Simply, I love you as much as I think it is possible for a man to love a woman. I want to spend the rest of my life with you. I am asking you to marry me."

He felt her stiffen in his arms. Then she began to sob quietly.

"I'm sorry if I upset you," he said. She continued to sob.

The streets, he noticed glumly, were as quiet as Chicago's streets ever were. North Michigan Avenue was nearly deserted, a scattering of pedestrians making for home after a late night, and light traffic keeping it alive. A bright full moon smiled coldly on the sparse human comings and goings which marked the lateness of the hour, knowing that soon the city would shake itself awake once more.

Sam stopped her sobbing. "You didn't upset me. In the midst of all this killing and ugliness, you say to me a beautiful, beautiful thing. It's like saying that life isn't all nastiness and hate—that it can be lovely and good, at least some of the time. Oh, Randollph"—she buried her face on his chest—"I love you too. I can't explain it. I can't understand it. We're wrong for each other. I'm an agnostic, and you're a preacher. What would a congregation say—"

"They'd say—"

"No, let me finish. What would they say if you announced that you were marrying an agnostic? And I love my career. I don't think I can give it up, even for you. I hope you can understand that. It's not that I love you less . . .'"

She began to sob again. "I'm a one-time loser, and that's left some scars that aren't all healed. I'm so mixed up."

"I'm not pressing you, my love," Randollph said. "Take time to sort it all out. But I'd be less than honest if I didn't tell you that ultimately, I'll not take no for an answer. I can be very persuasive when I put my mind to it. *Amor vincit omnia.*"

The cab stopped in front of Sam's apartment house. "What's that mean, *Amor vincit omnia?*" she asked him.

"That's Latin for 'Love conquers all,' " he told her.

She swabbed her eyes with a Kleenex. "Randollph, dear friend," she said, "why don't you come up, and we'll talk about it? I'm not as tired as I thought I was."

THIS BOOK BELONGS TO:

A WORLD FULL OF ANIMAL STORIES

WRITTEN BY **ANGELA McALLISTER**

ILLUSTRATED BY **AITCH**

Frances Lincoln
Children's Books

CONTENTS

EUROPE

AUSTRALIA AND OCEANIA

APPENDIX

FOR VIOLET

ABOUT THE AUTHOR

Angela McAllister is the author of more than 80 books for children of all ages. Her books have been adapted for the stage, translated into more than 20 languages, and have won many awards.

ABOUT THE ILLUSTRATOR

Originally hailing from Romania, Aitch's tactile, folky illustrations are inspired by her love of travel and nature. With mediums as diverse as textiles and watercolor, her dreamy characters hide among bold blooms and retain a strong sense of her Romanian heritage.

ACKNOWLEDGMENTS

With thanks to Luke and Eleanor Farmer, Clare Faull, and Sally Brown for their story suggestions and Sandra Leonard for sharing tales from her Mexican childhood—A.M.

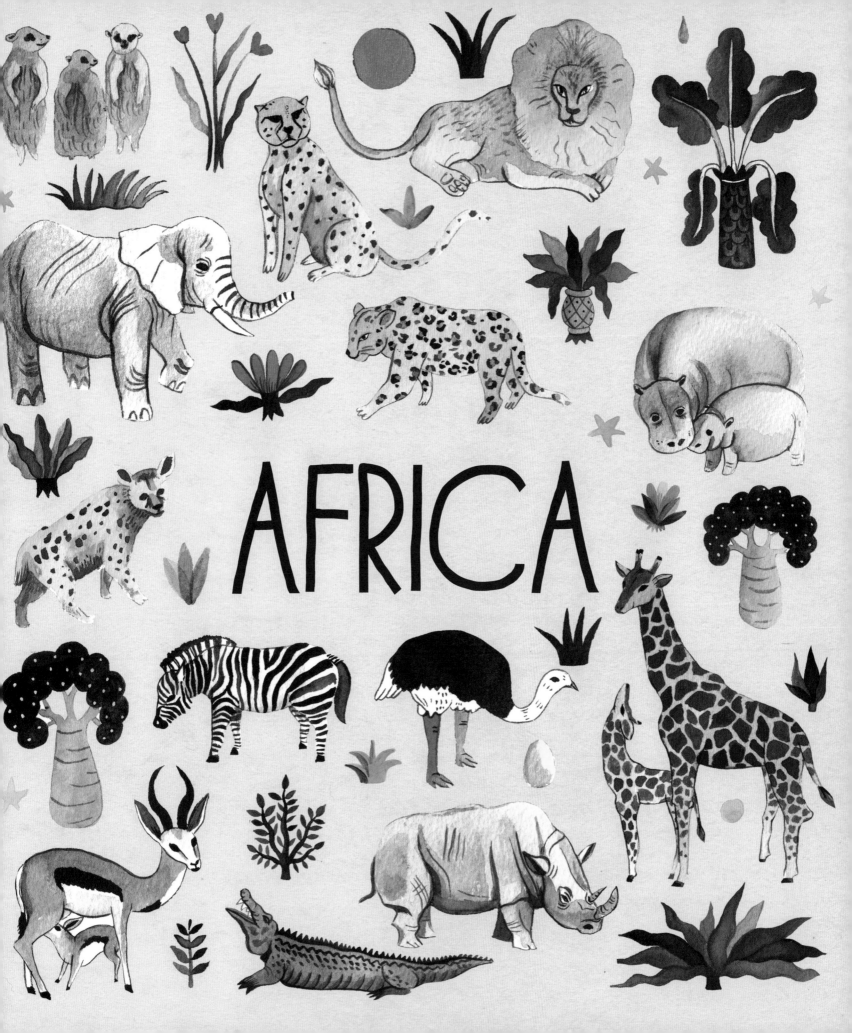

AFRICA

AFRICA
A STORY
FROM KENYA

THE TEN LITTLE OSTRICHES

Ostrich was very proud of her ten new chicks. All day she preened them and fussed over them, and told them how perfect they were. "You may be little fluff balls now," she said, "but remember, you are fine ostriches and when you grow up you'll have beautiful feathers and run as fast as the wind."

One morning, Ostrich went to find food for the chicks. She wasn't gone long, but when she returned they had disappeared. Ostrich searched among the bushes, calling for her lost chicks, but they were nowhere to be found. Then, to her horror, she saw Lion's paw prints beside those of their tiny feet.

"Oh no," she cried. "My poor little ones!" Ostrich followed the tracks to Lion's den. There, she saw her ten chicks nestled in Lion's arms.

Ostrich stepped forward bravely. "Give me back my chicks!" she demanded.

Lion stared at her and smiled. "What can you mean?" she purred softly. "All I have are my own cubs." And she nuzzled the ten fluffy chicks with her whiskery nose.

Ostrich was amazed at Lion's words. "Those aren't your cubs," she said indignantly. "They're ostriches—and they're mine!"

"I think you'll find that you're mistaken," growled Lion. "Anyone can see they are ten perfect lion cubs. If you don't believe me, fetch the other animals and ask them."

Ostrich flapped her wings helplessly. "I can't rescue those poor chicks on my own," she thought, so she hurried away to fetch the other animals. She found Zebra and Antelope, Wildebeest, Giraffe, and Baboon, who all listened to her story and agreed to meet her at Lion's den later that day. Then Mongoose came along. When she heard about Ostrich's problem Mongoose thought for a while. "I think I can help you," she said, "but first there is something you must do."

"Of course," said Ostrich. "I'll do anything to get my poor little chicks back."

"Near Lion's den there's a huge anthill," said Mongoose. "You must dig a hole under it, with an entrance at the front and an exit at the back, and then wait for the other animals to arrive."

Ostrich found the anthill and did exactly as Mongoose instructed. The other animals soon arrived and stood before Lion's den.

"There," said Ostrich, "look at those little chicks with their beautiful beaks and long necks. Tell Lion who they belong to."

The animals stared at the ten fluffy chicks and then they looked at Lion. Slowly, Lion stood up. She stretched her claws and yawned, baring her sharp white teeth.

Zebra shuffled his hooves uneasily. "Well, um…in my opinion…it's plain to see that they're lion cubs," he said.

"Yes, no mistake," stuttered Antelope. "Definitely not ostriches."

"Lion cubs, without doubt," mumbled Wildebeest. Giraffe and Baboon nodded in agreement.

Ostrich couldn't believe her ears. Then Mongoose jumped up. "What nonsense!" she cried. "Have you ever seen a mother with hair and a baby with feathers?"

Lion fixed her eyes on Mongoose and snarled angrily, but Mongoose only stepped a little closer. "We all know those are chicks, not cubs, and they belong to Ostrich," she said. "Lion is a thief!" With that, Mongoose spun around and scooted toward the anthill.

Lion roared with fury and leapt after her, but Mongoose dived into the hole Ostrich had made just in time. At once, Ostrich rushed into the den and gathered up her ten little chicks. However, Lion didn't twitch a whisker. She stood looking into the anthill and didn't notice Mongoose run straight out of the back exit.

Quietly, all the animals crept away. Ostrich led her ten little chicks home and they never tired of hearing the story of that day when Lion was left staring into an empty hole.

AFRICA
A ZULU STORY

WHY THE CHEETAH'S CHEEKS ARE STAINED WITH TEARS

One morning, a lazy hunter sat under a tree, watching a herd of springbok graze nearby. He couldn't be bothered to hunt that day, but before long, he noticed a cheetah approach the herd.

The hunter watched the cheetah creep through the grass, her eyes fixed on a young springbok who'd strayed away from the rest of the herd. Suddenly, she sprang forward, and ran so fast that her paws hardly touched the ground. Before the springbok could escape, she was upon it.

The cheetah took her prize to a patch of shade where her three hungry cubs were waiting.

"If only I had someone to hunt like that for me," thought the hunter. This gave him an idea. He knew that cheetahs never attacked men, so he decided to steal a cub and train it.

The hunter waited until the mother cheetah went off for a drink at the waterhole and then took his chance. He crept up to the patch of shade where she'd left her cubs and looked down at them. "Which one shall I choose?" he asked himself. Unable to decide which cub to take, he stole all three.

When the cheetah returned and found her cubs gone, she cried in despair. All night she cried and all the following day, until her tears made dark stains down her cheeks.

An old man who knew the ways of the animals came to ask what was wrong. When he heard what had happened, he went at once to tell the elders of the village.

"This hunter is not just a thief," said the elders angrily. "He has broken the traditions of our tribe and dishonored us—a hunter must use only his own strength and skill." So they banished him from the village.

The old man gathered up the stolen cubs and returned them to their mother. But, since then, her tearstains appear on every cheetah's face, as a reminder that hunters should respect traditional ways.

AFRICA
A STORY FROM EAST AFRICA

WHY HIPPO LIVES IN WATER

Tortoise was very happy moving slowly. He didn't want to swing like Monkey or run like Cheetah. He enjoyed having a good look at the world as he plodded steadily here and there, taking his time.

However, there was one problem with being slow. Tortoise couldn't easily escape from danger. Whenever he took a walk, he had to keep an eye out for trouble—and the worst trouble for Tortoise was Hippo, who lived nearby.

Hippo had enormous, heavy feet and he also had seven wives. Together that made thirty-two enormous, heavy feet, which were very dangerous whenever they came tramping toward Tortoise.

So far, Tortoise had managed to avoid being stamped on by Hippo and his wives, although he'd had a few near misses, but he feared that his luck wouldn't last forever.

There seemed to be nothing Tortoise could do about this, until one day Hippo gave a big feast for everyone. Tortoise arrived last so that he didn't get stepped on. When Hippo looked at all the delicious food that his seven wives had prepared he felt mighty hungry.

As everyone was about to sit down to eat he said, "Friends, you have come to eat at my table, but none of you know my name."

The guests looked at each other in surprise—it was true. None of them knew Hippo's name.

"Well," said Hippo, "if you cannot tell me my name, then you cannot eat at my table!"

The guests shook their heads sadly and turned to go.

But just as greedy Hippo sat down to eat, Tortoise spoke up. "What will you do if one of us tells you your name?" he asked.

Hippo smiled to himself, knowing that only his wives knew his name.

"We shall have another feast in seven days' time," he said. "If anyone can tell me

my name then, I will do whatever they ask!" And he tucked into his enormous meal, pleased with how clever he was.

Tortoise made his way slowly home, thinking up a plan.

The next day, Hippo and his wives walked down to the river, as they loved the water and bathed every morning. Tortoise usually kept out of the way, but this particular morning he hid in the bushes and watched them walk past.

When they were all in the water, Tortoise crept into the middle of the path and dug a hole. Then he hid in the bushes again.

Hippo finished his bath and started off home, with his wives trailing behind. Tortoise waited until the last two wives stepped out of the river and then he half buried himself in the hole, with his shell sticking out.

When the two wives came along, one of them knocked her foot against Tortoise's shell. "Oh, Istantim, my husband," she cried, "I have hurt my foot!"

Tortoise didn't wait for Hippo to return. He crept slowly away, grinning to himself.

A few days later, everyone gathered for Hippo's second feast. Once more, Hippo asked if anybody knew his name.

"I do," said Tortoise. The guests made way for him to step forward. "Your name is Istantim!" he announced to everyone.

Everyone cheered. "Now you must keep your promise, Hippo," they said.

Hippo had to agree. "What would you like me to do, Tortoise?" he asked.

Tortoise smiled. "I'd like you and your wives to live in the river, then I can walk on the land without danger," he said.

So, after the feast, Hippo did just that and he has lived happily in the river ever since.

AFRICA
A STORY
FROM GHANA

ANANSE AND THE PYTHON

There was once a village in Ashanti with a big problem—an enormous python had come to live in the riverbank nearby. The python had a huge appetite, which he satisfied by eating the village goats and sheep.

The people of the village were afraid of the enormous python and worried that they would soon go hungry themselves, but nobody could think of a way to get rid of him, so they called on the Sky God for help.

When the Sky God heard about their problem he shook his head. "I cannot judge what to do," he said, "for the python is also one of my creatures."

"Then who can help us?" asked the villagers.

"Go and see Ananse," said the Sky God. "He's always boasting about how wise he is and I'm tired of hearing it. If he can prove his wisdom by getting rid of the python then I will reward him, but if he fails I will punish him for his bragging."

The villagers thanked the Sky God and went to Ananse's house.

Ananse was very pleased to hear that the Sky God had sent them. "I am, indeed, extremely wise," he said. "Whatever your problem, I will solve it." So the villagers told him about the enormous python.

"That is a terrible problem, my friends," said Ananse with a frown, "but not difficult for someone as wise as me. Tell me, how long is this python?"

"Longer than your house, Ananse," said one of the villagers.

"Longer than your house and the yard," said another.

"As long as your house and the yard and the house next door!" said another, and everyone nodded in agreement.

Ananse smiled to himself, and then he made a solemn promise. "I, Kwaku Ananse, will use

my great wisdom to save you from the enormous python. But first I will need three things—a dish of mashed yam, a bowl of palm oil, and a basket of eggs."

The villagers agreed to bring Ananse what he asked for, but as they walked away they worried that his wisdom might not be enough to save him from the huge appetite of the enormous python.

The next morning, Ananse went into the forest and chopped down a tall, straight tree. He tied it up with creepers and called his family to help him tug it down to the riverbank. There, he found the villagers waiting with a dish of mashed yam, a bowl of palm oil, and a basket of eggs.

"Now hurry away," whispered Ananse urgently. "I need silence for my great wisdom to work." The villagers said a sad farewell to Ananse, fearing that they might never see him again, and left him alone.

As soon as they were gone, Ananse sat down beside the python's hole and started up a conversation with himself.

"This is a rare creature," he said. "I've heard he is the biggest, most beautiful python in the world."

The python inched a little closer to the entrance of his hole to listen.

"That's a lie," scoffed Ananse in a deep, gruff voice. "He's nothing special. Why, he couldn't even swallow a piglet!"

"It's not true," continued Ananse as himself. "He's an enormous fellow. He could swallow a whole herd of goats if he wanted to. The villagers should be proud to have him as a neighbor and bring him gifts of food, like me."

"Who would want a python as a friend?" the gruff voice said scornfully. "He's just a common old snake in the mud."

Then the python heard a thump and a scuffle and the sound of feet running away.

"Good riddance!" exclaimed Ananse. "If only the python knew how I had defended his honor. I'd like to give him this gift of mashed yam and palm oil and eggs."

At this offer of his favorite food the python slithered out of his hole, right at Ananse's feet. The sight of the python's powerful body and greedy eyes filled Ananse with dread, but he gathered all his courage and pretended not to be afraid.

"Good day, friend," said Ananse. "I've brought you a gift."

The python coiled himself around the dish and the bowl and the basket and devoured every morsel inside.

"Delicious!" he hissed. "Thank you for defending me."

"That's nothing," said Ananse. "Anyone can see you must be the biggest, most beautiful python in the world."

"In the whole world?" said the python.

"Most definitely," insisted Ananse. "In fact, I brought along this tree to prove to

everyone that it's the truth. If you wish, I can measure you with it?"

"How is it done?" asked the python.

"Just lie alongside and I'll take a measurement," explained Ananse. "When the villagers see proof of your enormous size they will all honor you with delicious food, just as I have done."

The python, feeling well fed and pleased with himself, slid his enormous body alongside the tree trunk. "It's about time I got the admiration I deserve," he murmured to himself.

"Now, I need to tie you to the tree, to make sure you are stretched out to your full length," said Ananse. "Then we shall see exactly how magnificent you are." And he tied the python to the tree, from head to tail, counting aloud as he went.

It wasn't until Ananse pulled the last knot tight that the python realized he was caught. All he could do was hiss angrily at being tricked.

"You may be magnificent," laughed Ananse, "but you're not welcome here!" And he shouted for the villagers, who came running. To their amazement, instead of finding Ananse inside the python, they found him sitting on top of it!

With great relief, they carried the python far away from the village, so that he wouldn't bother them again.

"You have earned your reward, Ananse," said the Sky God, reluctantly. "I shall make sure that the python does not return, and you shall have a pot of wisdom."

Then, in his frustration, he flung the pot of wisdom down so hard that it nearly split Ananse in two, giving him a narrow waist for evermore.

AFRICA
A STORY FROM NIGERIA

THE ANTS AND THE TREASURE

In a village in Africa there lived a poor man who was very kind to animals and birds. He grew a little food, which he shared with his parrot, and every morning he sprinkled some crumbs outside for the ants.

The ants were grateful and showed their thanks by not eating anything in the poor man's vegetable patch.

On the other side of the village lived a miser who'd collected a large pile of gold coins by tricking people out of their money. He kept his hoard of treasure in a hut, which he guarded day and night.

The miser was selfish and cruel. He threw stones at any animals or birds who came near his hut and crushed ants beneath his feet.

The ants tried to think of a way to punish the cruel miser.

"Isn't it a pity that the man who is our friend is so poor and the man who is our enemy is so rich?" said their king. This gave the ants an idea.

They dug a tunnel between the miser's hut and the poor man's house. Then they carried some gold coins along the tunnel and left them by the poor man's bed.

The poor man was amazed when he woke up and found a heap of gold glittering on the floor. "This must be a gift from the gods," he thought happily and he put the coins under his bed.

Meanwhile, the miser was alarmed to discover that some of his treasure was missing. He couldn't understand how anyone could have entered the hut while he'd been keeping watch.

That night the ants carried more gold coins along the tunnel to the poor man's house. As there was no more room under the bed the poor man covered the pile of coins with a cloth.

The miser was angry to discover that more of his treasure was gone, but still he had no idea what had happened.

On the third night the ants carried all the remaining coins to the poor man's house. As before, he thanked the gods and covered the coins with the cloth.

The miser shouted with rage when he found the hut was empty. His neighbors came to see what was wrong.

"There must be magic at work," they said when they heard what had happened. But when the miser searched the hut he found the tunnel.

"Aha!" he cried. "If we find the other end of this tunnel we'll have the thief!"

Everyone in the village joined in the search. Before long the other end of the tunnel was found in the poor man's house, along with the gold coins beneath the cloth.

"I'm not a thief," protested the poor man. "I thought this treasure was a gift from the gods. How could I crawl through a tiny tunnel like that?"

"You must have made yourself small with magic!" said the miser.

The villagers locked the poor man in a hut. "We'll decide your punishment tomorrow," they said.

The ants were upset that their plan had caused such trouble. The king called for all his people to help rescue their friend.

Thousands and thousands of ants arrived and, while the villagers slept, they ate the whole hut—roof, walls, and door.

In the morning, the villagers looked at the remains of the hut and shook their heads. "The gods must have decided this punishment," they said. "Ants have eaten the hut and the prisoner!"

The ants smiled to themselves. Only they knew that their friend had escaped from the hut, fetched his parrot and the gold still beneath his bed, and walked away from the village to start a new life.

AFRICA
A STORY
FROM WEST AFRICA

THE LEOPARD AND THE RAM

Ram wanted a good place to build himself a new house. Then, one day as he was exploring the forest, he came to a clearing that seemed the perfect spot. "Here is a light, dry place, with plenty of wood to build my house," said Ram to himself. "I shall fetch my tools and begin work right away."

While Ram went home to fetch his tools, Leopard arrived at the clearing and had exactly the same idea. "This is the perfect place to build a new house," he said to himself and he started to gather the wood he needed.

When Ram returned, he was surprised to see a great pile of wood had been gathered for his house. "There must be a kind spirit in this forest," he thought and he got to work.

The following evening, when Leopard arrived, he was astonished to find that his house was already begun. "It must be the work of a good spirit," he thought, and he continued where the work had left off.

They carried on this way, with Ram building in the day and Leopard working at night, never seeing each other, until the house was finished. Then they both arrived to move in. At first, Ram and Leopard were astonished to learn the truth about their fine house, but after a friendly discussion they decided to live in it together.

All went well. Ram and Leopard both had sons who played happily together while their parents went hunting.

After a while, Leopard noticed that Ram caught just as much game as he did, even though he had no claws or sharp teeth. He was curious to know how it was done, so he asked his son to find out from the young ram.

The next day, while their parents were away, the little leopard asked the young ram how his father hunted.

"I'll show you how he does it if you show me how your father hunts," said the young ram, and the little leopard agreed. They fetched two large pieces of plantain stem and went into the woods.

First, the little leopard propped up his piece of plantain. Fixing his eye upon it, he moved from left to right, bowing and peeping, just like his father did. Then he sprang forward and pounced on it.

"Bravo!" cried his friend.

"Your turn," said the little leopard. The young ram put his piece of plantain in position and then backed away from it.

When he was ready, he took aim, charged and tore the plantain to shreds. "That's how it's done!" he said.

That evening, the little leopard told his father what he'd learned. "Beware," he said, "if you ever see Ram go backward, then you know he's about to charge."

The leopard thanked his son for the information and good advice.

A few days later it rained, making the floor of the house very slippery. Leopard invited Ram to share a meal with him, as usual, but as Ram came through the door he slid backward on the wet floor.

Remembering what his son had told him about Ram's hunting technique, Leopard feared that Ram was about to charge at him. "Run!" he cried and they all fled together, out of the house, across the clearing, and away into the woods.

Ram and his son called them back, but Leopard refused to return, and from that day on, all leopards have lived in the forest, while rams have remained at home.

AFRICA
FROM
EAST AFRICA

WHY THE WARTHOG IS UGLY

Warthog was once a handsome beast who was very proud of his fine looks. He loved to admire himself and often boasted about his beauty to the other animals of the savanna. He was so vain and rude that nobody liked him at all.

Warthog had made his home in an abandoned aardvark hole, which he'd enlarged to make a comfy den. It was also a safe place to hide whenever his rude remarks got him into trouble.

One morning, Warthog went out to look for some breakfast. He didn't notice Porcupine, who'd been awake all night and was searching for somewhere to sleep.

As soon as Warthog was out of sight, Porcupine slipped into Warthog's den and scuttled down to his cozy bed for a nap.

Meanwhile, Warthog enjoyed a good meal, followed by a drink at the waterhole and a long wallow in the mud. Then along came Lion. Warthog was feeling so pleased with himself that he couldn't resist telling Lion how scruffy his mane looked, compared to his own fine bristles.

"I'll teach you not to be rude to me," roared Lion angrily and leapt for the hog.

Warthog realized he was in trouble. He clambered out of the water as fast as he could and ran toward home with Lion at his heels.

As Warthog came in sight of his den, he breathed a sigh of relief. He shot inside, thinking he was safe. Unaware that there was a visitor inside, he crashed straight into Porcupine and got a face-full of sharp quills.

Out he came again, howling with pain.

"Let that be a lesson to you," said Lion as he walked away.

It took Warthog a long time to remove Porcupine's quills. None of the other animals would help because he'd been rude to them all. To his dismay, his swollen face was left covered in ugly warts and bumps.

From that day, Warthog lost his handsomeness—and always entered his den backward!

ASIA

THE ELEPHANT AND THE BLIND MEN

There was once a wise man who traveled the world on a fine elephant. One evening, while looking for somewhere to stay for the night, he came upon a house that was owned by six brothers.

The wise man knocked on the door and asked the brothers if they would be kind enough to provide him with a bed and somewhere for his elephant to sleep for the night.

The brothers looked puzzled. "What is an elephant?" they asked.

"You've never seen one?" exclaimed the wise man. "Then prepare to be amazed!"

But the sun had already slipped below the horizon and there was no moon that night, so the wise man said to the brothers, "It's dark now. Let us sleep tonight and then you shall see how magnificent an elephant is in the morning."

The brothers smiled. "We are all blind," they told the wise man. "The darkness is nothing to us. Come, lead us to this magnificent thing that you call an elephant immediately, as we are eager to know all about it!"

Then one of the brothers fetched a lantern, which they kept for guests, and the wise man led them outside to where his elephant was standing, nibbling the leaves of a tree. The wise man stroked the gentle elephant's head.

"Here, I have brought six new friends to admire you," he said.

The six blind brothers gathered around the elephant. The first one stepped forward and put out his hand. He touched the elephant's leg. "Aha, it's like the pillar of a building," he said.

The second brother took hold of the elephant's tail. "No," he said, "it's like a thick rope."

The third brother reached out and felt the elephant's trunk. "Not at all," he remarked. "It resembles a thick branch with rough bark."

The fourth brother brushed his hand against the elephant's ear. "What are you all talking about?" he said, crossly. "I say it feels like a leather apron."

The fifth brother bumped into the elephant's belly. "You're all talking complete nonsense!" he insisted. "I can tell you that an elephant is obviously like a large tent!"

The sixth brother reached up and grasped the elephant's tusk. "No, I say you're all wrong. It's like a curved pipe."

The blind brothers began to argue fiercely among themselves. Each one was sure that he understood exactly what an elephant was like.

"How can it be like a tent when it swings like a rope?" said one brother.

"It can't be like an apron when it's hard like a pipe!" said another.

"I'm the eldest and I say it's like a pillar, not a rough branch!" said a third.

The wise man sat in the lantern light and smiled quietly to himself.

After a little while, he interrupted their quarrel. "Friends," he said, "there is no need to fight among yourselves. You are each right in what you have discovered. But you are all wrong to think that what you know is the whole truth.

"An elephant is made up of many parts. If you want to discover how magnificent he really is, I suggest you listen to what each of your brothers has learned and has to say on the matter!"

Then the six brothers felt ashamed of their outburst and apologized to each other.

"Forgive us," said the eldest brother. "We may not yet understand the magnificence of the elephant, but we all recognize the words of a wise man."

ASIA

ASIA

A STORY

FROM JAPAN

THE WHITE BUTTERFLY

Old Takahama lived in a little house beside the cemetery of the temple of Sozanji.

He was always kind to his neighbors, who were very fond of him, although they thought it strange that Takahama had never married, or even looked for a wife.

One summer's day, old Takahama felt unwell. He sent for his brother's widow.

The widow came and brought her son who loved his uncle dearly.

"I know I have not long to live," sighed old Takahama.

"Then we shall take care of you," promised the widow.

The following day, as Takahama was sleeping, a white butterfly flew into his room and settled on the pillow, beside his head.

The boy gently drove the white butterfly away, but moments later it returned. The same thing happened again and again, until the boy finally chased the white butterfly out into the garden.

He followed the beautiful creature into the cemetery, where she fluttered around an old tomb and then disappeared. The boy read the name inscribed there: "Akiko."

Although the tomb was over fifty years old, someone had cleared the moss away and laid white roses before it.

The boy returned to the house, to find that his uncle had just died. He told his mother what he'd seen at the cemetery and, to his surprise, she smiled.

"When your uncle was young, he loved a beautiful girl named Akiko," she explained.

"Sadly, Akiko died before their wedding day. Takahama vowed he would never marry anyone else and built this house by the cemetery so that he could always pray at her grave.

"Every day, in sun, rain, or snow, he swept her tomb and left flowers for Akiko." Then the boy saw that his uncle was peacefully smiling too; for the white butterfly was Akiko and they were together at last.

ASIA
A STORY FROM TIBET

THE COUNTRY OF THE MICE

Once, there was a country ruled over by a good king, in which there lived a great number of mice. The mice usually had plenty to eat, as they collected grain that was left lying in the fields after the farmers had harvested their crops. But one year, the harvest was bad and they couldn't gather enough grain to fill their stores for the winter. So one of the mice put on his finest clothes and went to see the king to ask for his help.

When the king heard that a mouse wished to see him he was very amused and ordered that he be shown into the throne room. It was the custom for a visitor to give the king a silk scarf, so the mouse solemnly presented him with a little silk thread.

"Thank you, Brother Mouse," said the king. "How can I help you?"

"Your Majesty," said the mouse, "the harvest has been poor this year, so the mice don't have enough food for the winter. If you lend us some grain, I promise that we will repay you at the next harvest."

"How much do you need?" asked the king.

"One of your big barns should be enough," replied the mouse.

"But how will you carry it all?"

"Leave it to us," said the mouse. "If you give us the grain, we will carry it away."

The king admired the little mouse's boldness, so he ordered his guards to open the doors of a big barn full of barley.

That night, the mouse summoned all the mice in the country. Hundreds and thousands came and each one took away as many grains as he could carry; in his mouth, on his back, and curled up in his tail.

In the morning, the king was very impressed to hear that not a single grain of barley was left in the barn.

ASIA

Thanks to his kindness, the mice had plenty to eat all winter. Next harvest, they repaid the loan by filling the king's barn with grain, just as the mouse had promised. "I see they are trustworthy as well as clever," said the king to himself.

A few months later, the ruler of the neighboring country declared war on the country of the mice. He brought his powerful army down to the river, which was the border between the two countries, and prepared to invade.

Once more, the mouse went to the palace. He found the king looking very gloomy. "Your Majesty," said the mouse, "last time I came here you did my people a great favor. Now I have come to offer you our help to defeat your enemy."

Although his troubles were heavy, the king smiled. He lifted the little mouse onto his hand. "Thank you, Brother Mouse," he said. "But how can you help? Our neighbor's army is ten times greater than ours."

"Last time you doubted that we could carry away a barn full of grain, or repay your loan," said the mouse. "But we did both. If you trust us again then I promise we will get rid of this invading army."

The king had learned to trust the mice and so he agreed. "What do you need for this task?" he asked.

"A hundred thousand cakes of dried yak dung," said the mouse, "to be laid along the riverbank." The king was puzzled by this request, but ordered it to be done at once.

The following evening, all the mice of the country gathered at the riverbank. They put the cakes of yak dung in the water and climbed on board. Then they pushed off from the riverbank and sailed to the other side.

The enemy's soldiers were all asleep, some in their tents and some outside, with their weapons beside them. Silently, the mice scattered throughout the camp. Each one

ASIA

began to nibble whatever he could find; some nibbled the strings of the soldiers' bows or the slings of their muskets, some the fuses, others bit their clothes and pigtails, some chewed the tents and sacks of food, tearing everything to shreds. Then, without a sound, they sailed back across the river, leaving every man still fast asleep.

The next morning, when the enemy soldiers awoke, they were alarmed to find their clothes in tatters, their pigtails cut off, their tents destroyed, and their weapons ruined. In great confusion, the men started to accuse each other and a huge argument began.

At that moment, the king of the country of the mice ordered one of his men to blow a bugle. The enemy thought it was under attack! The soldiers were too disorganized to defend themselves, so they turned and fled in a panic, without a shot being fired.

The king thanked the mice. "The whole country is grateful for your bravery," he said. "What can I do to repay you?"

"We mice have to face two dangers," said the mouse. "Many of our burrows are near the river and when the water overflows it floods our nests. If you build a dam along the bank then we will be safe." The king agreed to do so. "And what is the second danger?" he asked.

"Cats, Your Majesty!" said the mouse.

"Of course!" The king laughed. "From this day forward, I forbid anyone in my kingdom to keep a cat." And so the mice returned to their homes, to live without any fear of danger.

Then the king sent a herald across the river with a message for the ruler of that country. "Today you have been defeated by my mice alone," he said. "But if you try to invade again, I will send my dogs; and if they don't succeed, I shall send the wild beasts of my country."

When the king's enemy heard these words he shuddered with fear. "If the mice of that country are so fearsome, then we must sign a treaty of peace at once," he said. And that is exactly what they did.

ASIA

A STORY FROM INDIA

THE FARMER AND THE MULE

One morning, a farmer heard a strange noise coming from his well. He peered over the edge and saw, to his dismay, that his old mule had fallen inside.

The farmer felt sorry for the mule, who was stamping and braying in distress, but he didn't know what to do about it.

He went next door to ask for his neighbor's help.

"Well, we can't reach him," said the neighbor. "You'd better put him out of his misery."

The farmer sadly agreed. "This dry well is no use anyway," he said. "We should fill it with earth and bury the poor old mule."

So they fetched their shovels and began to throw earth into the well.

When the first shovel of earth hit the mule's back he kicked his hooves angrily. With the second shovel of earth, he realized that he was not going to be rescued and began to panic.

Then he heard the cockerel crow in the yard.

The mule calmed himself. "I'm not just going to stand here and be buried at the bottom of this well," he thought, and so he shook the earth off his back, stamped it down, and stood on top of the pile.

"Shake it off and step up!" he told himself.

Although he was in a tight spot, afraid and bruised from his fall, the old mule started shaking off the earth heaped upon him and stepping onto the pile.

"Don't give up, shake it off, and step up!" he repeated to himself. Slowly, little by little, he began to rise…

The farmer and his neighbor worked long and hard trying to fill the well that day, but they dropped their shovels and danced with joy when the stubborn old mule stepped right out in front of their very eyes!

ASIA
A STORY FROM INDIA

THE LION AND THE CLEVER JACKALS

Deep in the jungle, there lived a fierce lion. Every morning, he would stand at the entrance of his den and roar a terrible roar that echoed through the jungle. When the other animals heard this terrifying sound they would run around in alarm, and then the lion would leap out and pounce on them.

He was so powerful that nobody ever escaped his mighty claws.

This went on for a long, long time until, at last, there were no living creatures left in the jungle, except two little jackals.

The little jackals had no rest. They had to keep on the move and use all their cleverness to avoid being ambushed by the lion.

"I'm sure he will catch us soon," sighed the youngest jackal.

"Don't be afraid," said his sister. "I'll take care of you. Just keep close to me."

Meanwhile, the lion grew very hungry and very mad.

At last, the youngest jackal felt he could run no more. "I'm so tired," he said. "If only there was another way to save ourselves."

His sister felt sorry for him. "I have an idea," she said. "Follow me just a little further." And, to the youngest jackal's astonishment, his sister walked right up to the lion's den. "Be brave," she whispered to her brother, "and all will be well."

When the lion saw the jackals approaching he shook his mane and roared. "Come and be eaten!" he said. "I've had no dinner for three days and you've made me run all over the jungle after you."

The youngest jackal shook with terror, but his sister took a step forward. "Oh, Mighty Lion," she said, "we would have come to be eaten sooner, but there is a much bigger lion in this jungle who has been chasing us away."

ASIA

"What do you mean?" growled the lion. "There is no other lion in this jungle but me!"

"We have seen him with our own eyes," said the jackal. "His face is like a flaming fire, his roar is like thunder, and he has the strength of ten lions."

"Impossible!" said the lion angrily. "There is no beast mightier than me! Take me to him. I will show him who is the strongest."

The jackal beckoned to her brother and they set off through the jungle with the lion following.

When they came to a large well, the jackal stopped. She pointed at the water, pretending that she was too afraid to look into it herself. "There," she said, "that is where the great lion lives."

The lion stared down into the well and thought he saw another lion glaring up at him. He growled and shook his mane.

To his annoyance, the other lion did exactly the same back!

"See how fierce and powerful he is," said the jackal. "Surely no one can defeat him?"

"How dare you say such a thing? This imposter is nothing compared to me!" snarled the lion, and his reflection snarled back at him.

He opened his jaws and bared his teeth, and the other lion did exactly the same. At this, the lion flew into a rage.

"This is my jungle!" he roared and he leapt at his reflection, plunging with a loud splash into the cold, deep water of the well.

The little jackals cheered and danced with glee.

"Get me out!" spluttered the lion, trying to grasp the steep sides with his paws.

"You'll pay for this with your scrawny bones!" growled the lion.

But the two jackals scampered away, happy that the jungle was safe at last.

A STORY FROM JAPAN

URASHIMA AND THE TURTLE

Many years ago, on an island in Japan, there lived an old fisherman and his son, Urashima. The old fisherman had taught his son all the skills of the sea and Urashima loved nothing better than to spend the day in his boat, rocking on the great green waves.

One day, when he was out fishing, Urashima felt something heavy on the end of his line. He tugged the catch out of the water and, to his surprise, a young turtle dropped into his boat. Urashima unhooked her gently from the fishing line. "Don't be afraid," he said. "I've heard that a turtle can live for a thousand years. I will set you free to enjoy your long life." Urashima lifted the turtle over the edge of the boat, released her into the sea and she disappeared under the waves.

The following day, while Urashima was out fishing, the turtle reappeared beside his boat. To his astonishment, she spoke.

"I have come to thank you for saving my life, Urashima," she said. "Would you like to see the palace of the Dragon king?" Urashima had heard many tales about the Dragon king's palace under the sea.

"Yes," he answered excitedly, "but how can I travel beneath the waves?"

"Sit on my back," said the turtle, "and your wish will come true." Before his eyes she grew, until she was big enough for him to sit comfortably on her shell. Then the turtle dived beneath the waves and Urashima found himself riding through the ocean, marveling at the curious creatures of the sea.

The turtle swam on. Urashima was so enchanted by everything he saw that he had no idea how long they traveled. At last, they came to a garden of pink coral, where the trees glittered with jewels. The turtle stopped before a shimmering gate of golden seaweed and told Urashima that there they must say goodbye. "The Dragon Princess, Otohime, is waiting to greet you," she said.

ASIA

Wide-eyed, Urashima stepped through the golden gate and found himself in front of a gleaming palace made of shells and pearls. There to greet him was a beautiful girl, with skin as white as blossom, hair as black as night, and eyes as bright as flecks of sunlight on the waves.

"Welcome, Urashima," she said. "I am the Dragon Princess, Otohime."

Urashima was so overcome that he couldn't speak. He followed the princess into the palace, where her attendants clothed him in robes of silk. "The turtle you set free was my handmaiden," said Otohime. "She told me about your kind heart, so I wished to meet you. Will you stay and keep me company for a while?"

Urashima gazed at Otohime. He forgot about his boat. He forgot about his old father at home. "Yes," he said. "I will stay with you."

Then Urashima and Otohime shared a banquet of delicious food and were entertained by fine fish musicians. Afterward, she showed him the most precious treasures in the palace.

From that day forward, Urashima and Otohime were always together. They traveled far and wide throughout her father's watery kingdom exploring the fabulous seabed and, before long, their hearts were full of love for each other. The Dragon king gave his blessing for their wedding and all the creatures of the ocean came to celebrate their joyful marriage.

Urashima was so happy, he didn't count the days and months that passed. But one afternoon, a dark shape glided far above his head, like a rain cloud crossing the sky.

"Don't be alarmed," said Otohime, "it's only a fishing boat passing overhead."

At these words, Urashima suddenly remembered his own boat and his old father, waiting for him at home.

ASIA

"What is wrong?" asked Otohime.

"I must go home and tell my father all that has happened," said Urashima. "He will be worried about me."

The princess was dismayed. She tried to persuade Urashima not to go. "If you leave me you will never come back!" she cried and her eyes filled with tears. But Urashima told her that he loved her dearly and would not be away for long.

"When I return we shall be together forever," he promised.

Otohime dried her eyes and fetched a little silver casket. "Take this," she told Urashima. "It will bring you home to me. But whatever happens, never open the box." Then she called the turtle to carry Urashima back to the shore.

Urashima walked up the beach grinning to himself as he thought of the good news he had to tell his father. But when he reached the place where his house should have been, he found nothing but a pile of mossy stones.

"What happened?" he cried aloud. "Father? Father?"

A man in strange clothes walked up the path. "Can I help you?" he asked.

"Where is the house that stood here?" asked Urashima.

"There hasn't been a house here for centuries," said the man. "Nobody wants to live here because of the sad story of the fisherman whose son sailed away one day and never returned."

"What happened to the old man?" asked Urashima in disbelief.

"He died three hundred years ago," said the stranger.

Urashima rushed into the village. The houses were different, but the graveyard hadn't changed. There, to his dismay, he found his father's tomb and the terrible proof of the stranger's words.

Urashima was overwhelmed with grief. "I must return to Otohime," he sighed. But when he went back to the beach, the turtle was nowhere to be seen. Urashima paced up and down the shore, calling out to his wife, but no one appeared. Then he remembered the silver casket. "Otohime promised this would bring me home," he thought desperately.

Completely forgetting the princess's warning, Urashima opened the casket. Inside was nothing but a wisp of white smoke. Suddenly, his fingers began to grow thin. His arms felt weak and his breath was short. "I'm growing old!" he gasped and Urashima knew that he would never return to the palace under the sea.

With a deep sigh, Urashima sat and gazed out across the waves. He thought of his beautiful wife and his father, waiting for him somewhere, until the silver casket fell softly from his withered hands.

34

ASIA
A STORY FROM CHINA

THE NODDING TIGER

A long time ago, in a village outside the walls of a great city in China, there lived a young woodcutter named T'ang and his old mother. They were very poor, but T'ang would walk up the mountain each day and cut firewood, which he sold at the market. In this way, he earned enough money to buy all the things his mother needed.

One morning, T'ang took his ax and went up the mountain as usual, but by late in the day he hadn't returned. "He should be home by now," fretted Widow T'ang, "or else he will miss the market." As night fell she was sure that some terrible fate had befallen him.

"My poor T'ang!" she cried. "My good, kind son!" She took up her stick and hobbled to her neighbor's house to beg him to look for the missing boy.

The neighbor fetched a lantern and set off along the mountain path. Halfway up, he found a little pile of torn clothing spattered with blood and the woodcutter's ax lying beside it. With a heavy heart he returned to tell Widow T'ang the terrible truth—that her son had been carried off by a tiger.

Widow T'ang wept with grief. "He was my only son," she cried. "Who will take care of me now?" She was so distressed that nobody could comfort her.

However, the next day, to her neighbor's surprise, she set off down the road to the city. "Poor woman," he thought, "she has no one to support her now."

When she arrived at the city, Widow T'ang went to the courthouse. She sat on the steps and began to wail and cry. The Mandarin heard the old woman and called for her to be brought into the court. "What troubles you?" he asked.

Widow T'ang dried her eyes and told the Mandarin what had happened to her son. "I am old and poor, with no one to look after me now," she said. "I ask for justice. The tiger must be punished for his crime."

The Mandarin looked at her in astonishment. "How can a tiger be brought to justice?" he exclaimed. "You ask the impossible!" At these words, Widow T'ang started wailing and howling even louder than before.

"All right, all right," said the Mandarin. "Go home and it will be done."

But the old woman knew he was just trying to get rid of her. "I won't go until I see you give the order," she said. The Mandarin, who was not unkind, took pity on the poor widow. He asked for a volunteer to arrest the tiger, but nobody came forward. However, at the back of the room, one of his assistants, a lazy man named Li-neng, was fast asleep. Just at that moment a sneeze woke him up and he jumped to his feet.

"Thank you, Li-neng," said the Mandarin, thinking he had volunteered. "You shall arrest the tiger and bring him to justice."

Widow T'ang was satisfied with this and went home. But Li-neng looked at the Mandarin in horror. Arrest a tiger? It couldn't be done!

The other assistants explained to Li-neng what had happened while he was asleep. "It must be a joke," he thought. "The Mandarin just wanted to get rid of that old woman." So the following day he reported that the tiger couldn't be found.

The Mandarin was not happy. "I gave Widow T'ang my word," he said. "You shall lose a week's pay if you don't arrest the tiger."

Li-neng saw he had no choice but to gather some hunters and go up into the mountain. They searched the hills and caves but without any success. Once more, Li-neng reported that the tiger couldn't be found.

ASIA

ASIA

"Then you shall lose a month's pay," said the Mandarin and he sent him off to try again. When Li-neng returned without a tiger for the third time the Mandarin was very mad and told him he would be banished from the city unless he brought the tiger to court.

Li-neng was miserable. "Why don't you run away?" suggested the other assistants, but Li-neng shook his head.

"I can't leave my family," he said. Feeling hopeless, he went to the mountain temple to pray. "What can I do?" he sighed. "I've been given an impossible task and a terrible punishment."

Just then he heard rustling nearby. Looking up he saw a huge tiger standing at the temple gate. Li-neng was too unhappy even to feel afraid. "So," he said, "you have come to put me out of my misery!" He told the tiger about the old woman who depended on her only son, how he had lost his pay because he hadn't arrested the tiger, and how he was going to be banished from his home and family. "So you might as well eat me," he said. "I have nothing to live for."

While he spoke, the tiger listened closely. Then, to Li-neng's amazement, he padded slowly toward him, picked up a rope in his mouth, and hung his head. Li-neng slipped the rope around the tiger's neck and led him down the mountain.

When Li-neng brought the tiger into the courtroom everyone was filled with wonder. Widow T'ang heard the news and came at once. The tiger sat calmly in front of the Mandarin, like a huge cat.

"Tiger," said the Mandarin, "did you eat the woodcutter, T'ang?"

The tiger nodded his head.

"Justice!" cried Widow T'ang. "Give him the punishment he deserves!"

"Tiger," said the Mandarin, "this helpless old woman loved her son and has no one else to depend on. Do you promise to take the place of this woman's son and support her from now on?"

The tiger nodded his head.

"Very well, then, justice is done," said the Mandarin and he ordered the tiger to be freed. Then the tiger walked out of the courtroom and went back to the mountain.

The old woman was very angry. "Whoever heard of a tiger taking the place of a son?" she cried, but there was nothing more to be done and she returned home, brokenhearted.

The next morning, she found a deer on her doorstep. Her tiger-son had begun to keep his promise. She took it to the market and sold it for lots of money. A week later, the tiger came to her door with some birds for her to sell. Widow T'ang saw that the Mandarin had acted wisely and was grateful.

The tiger grew attached to the old woman and often purred at her door so that she would pet him. When, at last, Widow T'ang died, the faithful tiger lay on her grave and mourned her, before vanishing into the mountains, never to be seen again.

ASIA
A STORY FROM TIBET

THE LEGEND OF THE PANDA

Some say that, long, long ago, the pandas that lived in the mountains of Tibet were as white as snow. One day, a panda cub wandered away from its parents and got a thorn stuck in its paw.

Four shepherdesses who were watching over their flock of sheep saw the cub cradling its paw and befriended it.

One of them gently removed the thorn and, to their delight, the cub stayed with them, eating bamboo shoots and playing happily with the lambs.

Suddenly, a leopard leapt out of the bushes to attack the panda cub.

The shepherdesses threw themselves in front of the frightened cub and grabbed sticks to beat the leopard away.

While they fought the leopard, the little cub ran home to safety. The leopard was angry at being denied his prey and so he killed the brave shepherdesses instead.

When the other pandas heard what had happened, they were deeply saddened by the news. They smeared their arms with black ashes, which was the local custom, and went to the funeral of the four shepherdesses.

That day, the pandas cried with sorrow. As they wiped the tears away, their eyes were stained with ash. The guests at the funeral wept so loudly that the pandas covered their ears, turning them black too. When the pandas comforted each other with a hug, their bodies were blackened from front to back. In honor of the brave shepherdesses, they made a vow never to wash the ash from their fur.

Then the earth shook and a great mountain rose out of the grave into the sky. The four shepherdesses were transformed into four peaks as a reminder of the sacrifice they made for the little cub, and pandas have found safety in the mountain's arms ever since.

ASIA
A STORY FROM JAPAN

HOW THE JELLYFISH LOST HIS BONES

In the beginning, Jellyfish had a round shell, as white as the moon, and four legs so that he could walk along the seabed.

Sadly, he lost his fine white shell and his four strong legs by being foolish, and this is what happened.

The Kingdom of the Sea was governed by the Dragon King. One day his wife, the queen, fell ill. The Dragon King sent for the fish doctor, who examined the queen and gave her a dose of medicine. But the medicine didn't make the queen feel any better, so he gave her a pill, and when that didn't work, he tried a soothing ointment. However, despite all his remedies the queen only felt worse.

"Isn't there anything else you can do, Doctor?" asked the Dragon King.

"There is one thing that might cure the queen," said the fish doctor, "but it can't be found under the sea."

"What is it?" demanded the Dragon King impatiently.

"They say eating the liver of a monkey can sometimes cure an illness like this."

"Then we must try it right away," insisted the Dragon King. "Where can we find one?"

"Monkey Island is not far from here," said the fish doctor. "But how could any of your subjects go ashore and catch a monkey?"

The queen sighed and gave a little cough. "Send Jellyfish," she said weakly.

"Of course, my dear," exclaimed the Dragon King. "Jellyfish can walk on land. Somebody go and fetch him at once!"

Jellyfish was brought to the palace and instructed to swim to Monkey Island and catch a monkey. "We need its liver to make the queen well again," explained the fish doctor.

"How will I get the monkey to come with me?" asked Jellyfish.

"Tell him about the wonders of our kingdom under the sea," said the Dragon King, "and invite him to join us for a banquet

40

at the palace. He will not be able to resist such an offer."

Jellyfish promised to do what the king asked, feeling very proud to have been chosen for this important task, and he set off right away.

When Jellyfish reached Monkey Island he walked ashore and soon found a monkey, sitting in the branches of a persimmon tree.

"Good day, Monkey," he said. "This is a fine island."

"Yes," agreed Monkey. "It's the best place in the world."

"Oh, no," said Jellyfish. "I'm afraid you're mistaken there. The best place in the world is the kingdom of the Dragon King. Why, it's more beautiful than anything you could ever dream of."

"Is that so?" said Monkey.

"Yes," said Jellyfish. "In fact, I've been sent to invite you to a banquet at the palace, if you would like to see it."

"How would I get there?" asked Monkey.

"By taking a ride on my shell," said Jellyfish. "It isn't far."

Monkey liked the idea of a banquet, so he agreed. He slipped down from the persimmon tree and followed Jellyfish to the shore. There, he climbed onto Jellyfish's round white shell and they set off together across the sea.

After a while, Jellyfish laughed at how clever he'd been.

"What makes you laugh?" asked Monkey.

"I've tricked you, Monkey," he said.

ASIA

ASIA

"The Dragon King wants your liver for the queen to eat so she will recover from her illness," chuckled Jellyfish.

"Oh dear," sighed the monkey. "I wish you'd told me this before we left the island."

"Why would I do that?" asked Jellyfish.

"Well," said Monkey, "you see, my liver is rather heavy, so I take it out and hang it on the persimmon tree every morning. I was so excited to see your wonderful land that I'm afraid I left it behind."

Jellyfish, who didn't know anything about monkeys or livers, wasn't sure what to do.

"Don't worry," said the monkey, "I'm sure the Dragon King won't mind and the queen will be fine without it. Let's get along to the banquet."

"No, no," said Jellyfish, "I can't bring you to the banquet without it. We'll have to go back." And with that, he turned around and swam back to Monkey Island.

As soon as they reached the island, Monkey scampered back up into his persimmon tree.

"Have you got your liver now?" called out Jellyfish.

"Yes!" laughed the monkey. "It's safe inside me and that's where it's going to stay!" At that moment the jellyfish knew that he'd been tricked.

There was nothing he could do but return to the palace and explain to the king what had happened.

When the Dragon King found out that Jellyfish had failed to bring the cure for the queen, he ordered his guards to remove Jellyfish's beautiful white shell and pull all the bones out of his legs as a punishment.

And so, the jellyfish never walked on the seabed or the shore again.

However, when the queen heard the story of how Monkey had tricked Jellyfish, she laughed so much that she felt much better.

NORTH
AMERICA

NORTH AMERICA
A BLACKFOOT STORY

NORTH AMERICA

BUFFALO AND EAGLE WING

A long time ago, there were only tall, straight trees and bushes, with enough space between them so that a man could walk without a path, and the land was smooth under his feet, without any stones.

A great buffalo wandered across the land. He had a spirit power, which enabled him to change things from one form to another and he gained his power by always drinking from a certain pool.

Buffalo often traveled across a high mountain. One day, he said to the mountain, "Would you like to be changed into something else?"

"I would like to be something that nobody climbed over," said the mountain.

Buffalo used his spirit power to change the mountain into a very large stone. "Now you are hard so that no one can break you," he said, "and smooth so that you cannot be climbed. And I give you the power to change into anything else, as long as you don't break yourself."

On the other side of the mountains lived men who hunted animals. Buffalo decided to visit them and try to persuade them to change their ways.

Buffalo crossed the mountains to the other side. He came to a lodge, where he was greeted by an old woman and her grandson, who made him welcome.

"I have the power to change you into anything you choose," said Buffalo. "What would you like to be?"

"I want only to be with my grandson," said the old woman. "Wherever he goes, I wish to be."

"Then come home with me," said Buffalo. "We will teach the boy to be a swift runner and wherever he goes, you shall be."

So the grandmother and the boy followed Buffalo over the mountains to the other side.

The other buffaloes promised to teach the boy to run swiftly, if he agreed to teach his people

44

not to hunt them when he got older..

Then Buffalo drank from the pool and used his spirit power to change the grandmother into Wind so that wherever the boy went, she would be.

The boy stayed with the buffaloes until he was a man. Then the buffaloes reminded him of his promise and he returned to live with his people.

As he was such a swift runner he soon became the leader of the hunters and he was given the name Eagle Wing.

One day, the chief asked Eagle Wing to lead the other hunters over the mountains and bring back the meat and hide of the buffaloes for the tribe.

"If you do this for our people you will become chief one day," he said.

Eagle Wing was ambitious and wanted to be chief of his people, so, forgetting his promise, he agreed.

He led the hunters over the mountains, but ran so swiftly that he was soon far ahead. When he reached the land of the buffaloes he hunted them without mercy.

The great Buffalo was away roaming the valleys when this happened. On his journey home, he was struck with thirst and, as he was too far from his special pool, he drank from another. When he saw what Eagle Wing had done he was very angry. He tried to turn the hunters into grass, but because he had drunk from another pool his spirit power was gone.

Buffalo went to the stone that was once a mountain. "Help me punish the hunter for what he has done," he asked.

Then Stone bent and tangled the straight trees and bushes so that men could never again find an easy path, and broke himself into many pieces so that men hurt their feet on the scattered stones. This punishment Eagle Wing brought upon his people, for not keeping his promise to the buffalo.

NORTH AMERICA

NORTH AMERICA
A KARUK STORY

PRAIRIE WOLF

In the beginning, the Karuk people lived who on the shores of the Klamath River had everything they needed—except fire. Nights were long and cold in their country, but the only fire in the world was guarded by two old sisters who lived beside the mouth of the river.

The Karuk tried to persuade the old sisters to share their fire and some tried to steal it, but without success.

At last, they decided to ask cunning Prairie Wolf for help.

The Karuk traveled to the desert to find Prairie Wolf. They presented him with fine buffalo steaks, for they knew he was always hungry, and offered him friendship in return for his help.

Cunning Prairie Wolf saw that helping the Karuk would be an easier way to fill his belly than hunting all day, so he agreed to fetch the fire.

That night, Prairie Wolf made a plan. The next morning, he asked Frog to wait near the Karuk's camp and Squirrel, Bat, Bear, and Cougar to wait further along the track.

Lastly, he instructed one of the Karuk to hide close to the hut where the old sisters lived.

Then Prairie Wolf hung his head and scratched at the door of the hut. One of the sisters opened the door. Behind her, Prairie Wolf saw the bright fire blazing. Pretending to be weary and cold, he staggered inside and dropped to the floor with a shiver.

The old sisters weren't afraid of Prairie Wolf.

"Come near the fire," they said, so Prairie Wolf settled himself near the fire. Then, when they weren't looking, he edged a little closer and a little closer.

As soon as he was within a paw's reach of the flames, he barked a signal to the Karuk warrior who was hiding in the bushes nearby.

When the man heard the signal he began to hurl stones at the hut.

The angry sisters hurried outside to see who had dared to cause them trouble.

At once, Prairie Wolf seized a burning stick from the fire, and rushed out of the hut and down the track.

The old sisters saw the flame dance away through the trees and realized they'd been tricked. They chased after Prairie Wolf, shrieking with fury.

Prairie Wolf ran like the wind, but the old sisters followed at such a pace that they were soon close behind.

As they stretched out their bony hands to grasp his tail, Prairie Wolf flung the burning stick to Cougar, who caught it and ran on.

Cougar leapt along the track until he saw Bear ahead of him and handed him the burning stick.

Bear then carried the burning stick on until Bat swooped down to take her turn.

Bat tried to lose the old sisters in the wood, but still they followed. When she could fly no longer, Bat dropped the stick for Squirrel, who scampered along the track to where Frog was waiting. By this time, the stick was almost burned away.

At last, Frog reached a lake close to the Karuk village. He swallowed the stump of fire stick and dived into the water.

When the two old sisters reached the water's edge they could only stand and shake their bony fists, for neither of them had ever learned to swim.

On the other side of the lake, the Karuk were waiting with kindling for the fire. Frog climbed out of the water and spat the last few sparks at the kindling, which blazed into life.

At last, the Karuk could roast their meat and sleep warmly. They rewarded Prairie Wolf with fine food and friendship so that he never needed to hunt again.

However, it wasn't long before the Karuk asked Prairie Wolf to help them once more.

The two old sisters had the key to a great dam, which was keeping all the salmon from swimming upstream. "Will you open the dam for us, Prairie Wolf, and let the shining salmon swim free?" they asked.

NORTH AMERICA

Prairie Wolf agreed to try to help, but decided to wait until his winter coat had changed color.

When spring came, the two sisters didn't recognize the well-fed Prairie Wolf who knocked on their door. They welcomed him and let him rest in their hut.

The next morning, one of the sisters took the key of the dam from the cupboard so that she could fetch a salmon for breakfast. Prairie Wolf stood up, stretched, and followed her idly outside.

Once the sister had set off along the path, he ran ahead and flung himself between her feet so that she tripped and let the key fly out of her hand.

Prairie Wolf seized the key, hurried to the dam, and unlocked it.

Then the shining salmon escaped into the river in such numbers that the water seemed alive with fish. They swam away upstream, where the Karuk were waiting.

From that day forward, the Karuk caught all the salmon they wanted.

They were thankful and showed Prairie Wolf great honor.

However, Prairie Wolf grew very proud of his adventures and wasn't satisfied with their friendship.

He became so pleased with himself that he wanted to dance with the stars.

Night after night he howled at the sky, until a blue star took pity on him.

She called down to him and told him to stand on the high cliff, and there she reached down to him with her hand.

Prairie Wolf took the star's hand and together they danced through the night sky. But as she lifted him higher he began to grow cold.

Still he danced on, going higher and higher, and getting colder and colder, until his paws were numb. Suddenly, he slipped from the star's hand…

With a howl, proud, cunning Prairie Wolf fell down into the great chasm between the sky and the earth at the edge of the world and he was never seen again.

NORTH AMERICA

NORTH AMERICA
A STORY FROM CANADA

THE MERMAID OF THE MAGDALENES

NORTH AMERICA

Far off the coast of Canada are a group of lonely, rugged islands called the Magdalenes. Many fishermen used to sail there and risk the wild waves and rocks to catch tiny sardines, which they packed into boxes and sold onshore. The traders who bought them became wealthy by selling the sardines all around the world.

There was nothing the sardines could do to escape the fishing nets and their numbers grew smaller and smaller. In despair, they went to Lobster, who was the most powerful creature in the undersea kingdom, and asked for his help.

Lobster called a meeting of all the creatures of the sea, who came from the rock pools and the open water and the deep, dark ocean bed.

"The sardines are in danger," he told them. "Men are catching so many of them that soon they will all be gone."

"What can we do to help?" asked the skate.

"We must punish anyone who eats or fishes for a sardine," said Lobster. The creatures of the sea agreed. They all took an oath to punish anyone who ate or fished for their tiny cousins.

A short while later, a ship packed with boxes of sardines was wrecked on the rocks of the Magdalene Islands. The wild waves smashed up the wreckage and flung it onto the shore.

That evening, when the water was calm, a young girl whose father was a trader took a walk along the beach. To her delight she found a box of sardines. The young girl loved the taste of the little fish more than anything and so she decided to eat them. However, try as she might, she couldn't open the box. With a sigh, she sat on a rock and sang to herself.

"*I love sardines when they're boiled with beans*
And mixed with the sands of the sea."

Nearby, the skate heard her singing and swam up close to the shore. When he heard the words of her song he remembered his oath to the sardines, but he was too shy to punish the girl, so he swam away.

Beyond the rocks, a merman also heard the song. He wanted a wife from the land to live with him in the sea, so he dressed in a suit of seaweed and hurried to the shore.

When he heard the words of the song he, too, remembered the oath he had made to the sardines. But with one glance, the merman had fallen in love with the young girl and couldn't bear to punish her, so he, too, swam away.

The moon came up and the girl grew hungry. She knocked the box against a rock, hoping to break it open, without success. Unknown to her, she woke Lobster, who had been fast asleep under the rock. When the girl began to sing again he listened to her words.

"I love sardines when they're boiled with beans
And mixed with the sands of the sea."

Lobster came out of his hiding place. "Let me help you open that box," he said gently.

The young girl thanked him and knelt down at the water's edge. But as soon as she held the box out to him, Lobster grasped her hand with his strong claw and swam away with her far out to sea.

Nobody knew what happened to the young trader's daughter, but some say she married a merman. She often sings, trying to lure islanders onto the rocks to keep her company. On those nights, the fishermen stay ashore, leaving the tiny sardines to swim safe from harm.

NORTH AMERICA

NORTH AMERICA
A NATIVE AMERICAN INDIAN STORY

WHY THE SWALLOW'S TAIL IS FORKED

In the beginning, the Great Spirit made all the animals content but, before long, he was disappointed to hear them complaining to each other, so he asked them to come to his lodge. The first to arrive were the creatures that could fly, then the creatures that walked, and lastly the creatures that slithered and crawled.

"I have heard you complaining to each other," said the Great Spirit. "Tell me your troubles and I will do what I can to help."

Bear stood up. "I don't like to hunt for so long for my food," he said.

Then Bluebird spoke. "I don't like building a nest."

"I don't like living in a tree," said Squirrel and, one by one, all the animals came forward with their complaints. The last one to speak was Man.

"And what troubles you?" asked the Great Spirit.

"Snake likes to feast on my blood," said Man. "Can you give him some other food?"

"Why should I do that?" asked the Great Spirit.

"Because I am the first of all the creatures you made," said Man.

"That is true," agreed the Great Spirit. "You are the first, but I am father to them all. Snake has a right to his food. But maybe there is something I can do." The Great Spirit gazed upon all his creatures. "Mosquito," he said, "you travel far and wide. Fly among my creatures and find out who has the best blood for the snake. We shall all meet again to hear your judgement in a year and a day."

The animals went away to their homes in the rivers and the mountains, the forests and the prairies, to wait for the mosquito to do what the Great Spirit had commanded. For a year and a day, he traveled around the world tasting every creature to find out whose blood would be best for Snake.

NORTH AMERICA

When it was time to gather once more at the lodge of the Great Spirit, all the animals came from the rivers and the mountains, the forests, and the prairies. On the way, Mosquito looked up and saw Swallow.

"Good day," he said.

"Good day," said Swallow. "Have you discovered whose blood is best for Snake?"

"Oh yes," said Mosquito, "I have tasted every animal's blood and there is no doubt that it is the blood of Man."

Swallow was Man's friend, but she knew that Mosquito didn't like him.

"How can I prevent Mosquito from delivering his judgement?" she wondered. Then she had an idea.

She asked, once again, whose blood was best for Snake. This time, when Mosquito opened his mouth to answer, she pecked out his tiny tongue.

"Ksss-ksss-ksss!" buzzed Mosquito angrily and he flew away to the lodge of the Great Spirit.

When all the animals were gathered together once more, the Great Spirit turned to Mosquito and asked whose blood was best for Snake, but Mosquito could only buzz. "Ksss-ksss-ksss!"

Everyone was puzzled.

"Great Father," said Swallow, "Mosquito is shy and cannot answer you. When I met him on his way here, he told me that Frog's blood was best for Snake. Isn't that so, friend Mosquito?"

Mosquito darted about in a temper, but all he could say was "Ksss-ksss-ksss!"

"So, Snake shall eat Frog's blood," said the Great Spirit, "and Man will no longer be troubled by Snake."

Then Snake was angry with Swallow, for he didn't like the taste of Frog's blood.

As Swallow flew past, he seized her by the tail and tore a little piece away.

That is the reason why the swallow's tail is forked and why Man always thinks of her as a friend.

NORTH AMERICA
A STORY
FROM CANADA

RABBIT AND
THE MOON MAN

It was midwinter. Deep snow lay everywhere and Rabbit and his grandmother were hungry.

Rabbit had set traps around the forest to catch something to eat, but for several days his traps had been empty. When he went to inspect them, he found plenty of animal and bird tracks in the snow, but nothing for him to take home for dinner.

"I think somebody is stealing from my traps," said Rabbit.

"Then you must go out earlier and get to them before the thief," said his grandmother. But no matter how early Rabbit went out, he always returned empty-handed.

He would tiptoe silently, moving like a shadow from tree to tree as he approached his traps, in the hope of catching the culprit. But no matter what he tried, the thief would always evade him.

Then, one morning, after a fresh fall of snow, Rabbit noticed an unusual footprint beside one of his traps; it was long and thin and as light and delicate as a moonbeam.

That night, Rabbit made a snare from a strong bowstring and laid it beside the trap. Then, holding the other end of the bowstring, he hid from sight behind a clump of trees and waited.

"At last I shall see who has been stealing my dinner," he thought to himself. "When the thief comes along and steps into the snare, I shall pull it tight and tie him to a tree!"

Rabbit sat silently watching the snow sparkle in the moonlight as he waited for the thief to arrive. Suddenly, the Moon disappeared and only the stars were left to light the night sky.

Rabbit felt nervous in the dark. Suddenly, he heard the sound of someone moving through the trees. A white light appeared, dazzling Rabbit's eyes. It moved slowly toward the trap and stopped exactly where Rabbit had laid his snare.

"Now I've got you!" cried Rabbit.

He pulled the bowstring tight and quickly tied the other end to a tree. There was the sound of a struggle, but the white light stayed fixed to the spot.

Rabbit was afraid of the dazzling light, but he bravely crept closer to take a look at the man of the long-foot.

However, staring into the brightness made his eyes sore, so Rabbit bathed them in a nearby stream.

But that didn't help, and only made him mad. He threw snowballs at the light to try to put it out, but the snowballs just melted away. Then he took fistfuls of mud from the stream and hurled them at the shining light.

"Ouch!" cried a voice. "You've splattered my face with mud! Come and untie me at once. I am the Man in the Moon and I must get away before sunrise."

Rabbit was frightened. He ran home to tell his grandmother. "Oh dear," she cried, "you must untie him or there will be trouble!"

Rabbit returned to the Man in the Moon but kept his distance. "I will free you," he said, "if you promise never to come to earth and steal from my traps again."

"I swear by my light," promised the Man in the Moon. Then Rabbit shut his eyes and crept forward, feeling his way.

His lip quivered at the great heat of the Moon and his shoulders were scorched, but just as the first light of dawn glowed through the trees, Rabbit edged close enough to gnaw through the bowstring with his teeth and release his prisoner.

The Moon jumped into the sky at once and has kept his promise to stay there ever since.

Sometimes he goes away to try to wash off the marks of the mud Rabbit threw at him, and then the sky is dark. But on a moonlit night, you can still clearly see from the splats on his face, that he never succeeds.

Sadly, since their encounter with the Man in the Moon, rabbits have never been quite the same either.

To this day, they have never managed to soothe their pink eyelids, which are still sore from staring into the bright light. Their lips still quiver from the fear of approaching such a scorching heat, and their shoulders remain a burnt yellow, even when they are wearing their white winter coats.

NORTH AMERICA

NORTH AMERICA
AN IROQUOIS STORY

WHY THE BEAR HAS A STUMPY TAIL

One winter's day, Bear met Fox, who was carrying a string of fish. Bear gazed at the fish with hungry eyes.

"That's a good dinner you've got there," he said. "How did you catch so many?"

"It's easy if you know the secret," said sly Fox. "Someone with a fine tail like you could catch himself plenty of fish."

Bear licked his lips at the thought of it. "What's the secret?" he asked.

Fox looked over his shoulder to check that no one else was listening, as if he was going to share a big secret.

Then he whispered to Bear, "Go out onto the frozen lake and cut a hole in the ice. Then stick your tail through the hole into the water and wait for the fish to bite." Bear listened carefully.

"The fish won't be able to resist your fine, fat tail," said Fox. "It may hurt a little when they bite, but be patient—the longer you can wait, the more tasty fish you'll catch.

"When you think you've got enough, just pull your tail out with a quick, strong tug," continued Fox with a smile.

Bear thanked Fox and hurried down to the lake, eager to catch himself a good dinner. He licked his lips hungrily at the thought of all the fish he would catch.

He cut a hole in the ice and sat with his tail dangling in the water. The cold soon made his tail hurt. "Aha!" he thought. "The fish are starting to bite!" All afternoon he sat, imagining the delicious fish he was catching. At last, he couldn't wait any longer.

But when Bear tried to stand up he couldn't move. "These fish are heavy," he thought with a smile. Then he remembered that Fox told him to pull his tail out with a quick, strong tug.

Bear tugged hard and up he stood—but not one fish came out of the ice hole, and not much tail either, for it was stuck fast in the frozen lake!

Since that day, bears have always had stumpy tails and have never trusted a fox.

NORTH AMERICA
AN INUIT STORY

THE BLIND BOY AND THE LOON

Long ago, in a land of snow and ice, a woman lived with her daughter and son in an igloo. The boy was skilled at hunting with a bow and harpoon and always returned from a hunting trip with plenty of game on his sled. This he gave to his mother, who cleaned and skinned the animals and prepared the meat. Thanks to the boy's love of hunting, the storage platforms around their igloo were always well packed with food and the family were never hungry.

The girl was grateful for everything her brother caught, but their mother was lazy and complained about all the tasks she had to do. "Your brother causes me work, work, work without rest," she moaned. As time went by, the woman began to hate her son's hunting trips.

One day, while he was sleeping, she cut a small piece of blubber and rubbed it onto his eyes. As she did so, she wished that he would become blind.

When the boy woke the next morning, his eyesight was gone.

The boy's sister comforted him, but being blind meant he was no longer able to hunt and could do nothing but sit on his bed all day. Then his mother scorned him for his uselessness. When their food ran out, she trapped foxes and squirrels to eat, but only gave the boy scraps in his bowl and dirty water to drink.

The family lived this way for many months until, one winter's day, a huge polar bear came to the igloo and began beating at the thin ice window. The boy felt blindly for his bow, took aim, and shot an arrow toward the bear, killing it at once.

"Fool!" cried his mother. "You just frightened it away." But soon the boy smelled bear meat cooking and knew that she had lied. His mother kept the good meat and handed him a bowl of old fox stew. The boy said nothing, but as soon as his mother went out to fetch water, his sister gave him her own supper.

Four years passed. The woman treated her son no better than a dog and it was only thanks

57

to his sister's kindness that he kept strong.

Then, one night, while his mother and sister slept, the blind boy heard the haunting cry of a loon. Knowing that the bird would be on the lake, he crawled out of the igloo on his hands and knees and followed the bird's voice down to the water's edge. There he sat and imagined the moonlit view.

To his surprise, the loon spoke. "Your mother made you blind while you slept," she said. "Let me carry you down into the water of the lake, for it will wash away your blindness."

"How can that be?" asked the boy in wonder.

"Trust me," said the loon. "Lie on my back and take a deep breath. When you can hold your breath no longer, lay your head against my neck."

The boy was sure that the loon was too small to carry him, but as he reached out to climb onto her back he felt her grow as large as a kayak. He took a deep breath and she dived into the water of the lake.

Down, down, down she dived and the boy held tight as the cold water streamed across his face. When he could hold his breath no longer, the boy laid his head against her neck, and she returned to the surface.

"Now, what can you see?" asked the loon.

The boy blinked and stared. "A pale light," he said.

"Then we must dive again," said the loon.

When they came up for the second time she asked the boy what he could see.

"Everything!" he said in amazement. "I can even see the tiniest rocks on the far mountain!"

"That is too much," said the loon, and she took him down into the water of the lake once again. When the boy emerged the third time, his eyesight was restored to its normal strength.

NORTH AMERICA

NORTH
AMERICA

"How can I thank you for your kindness?" he asked the loon.

"Just put some fish in the lake for me now and then," said the loon. "I need nothing else."

When the boy went home he was horrified to see that the skins his mother had made him sleep on were covered in lice and his bowl and cup were filthy, but he said nothing. He waited until his mother woke up and asked her for a drink. Moaning as usual, she filled his cup with dirty water and handed it to him.

"Throw that away and give me the fresh water you drink yourself!" said the boy.

His sister gasped with joy. "You can see!" she cried. His mother pretended to be pleased but there was anger in her eyes.

It took many days for the boy to regain his strength after sitting in the igloo for so long, but as soon as spring came and the ice melted, he was eager to go hunting once more. "Come with me, Mother," he said, "and we shall catch a whale."

His mother was very fond of whale meat, so she followed her son down to the shore and they took his old whale boat out to sea. They soon saw many small whales, but the boy paddled on until a big whale swam close to the boat.

Working quickly, he took aim and threw his harpoon so that it caught fast in the whale's back, and then he slung the other end of the harpoon line around his mother's wrist and pulled it tight. With a scream she tried to free herself, but the whale tugged her over the side of the boat and away through the water.

Some said the woman became a narwhal when she disappeared beneath the waves that day. Some say they can still hear her cruel voice on the icy wind.

NORTH AMERICA
A NATIVE AMERICAN INDIAN STORY

THE FIRST WOODPECKER

In times past, the Great Spirit would come down from the sky and walk among his people on earth, in the form of an old man.

Once, as he walked through the forest, he came across a woman sitting outside her wigwam. "I have fasted for many days," he said. "Will you give me some food?"

"Come into my wigwam," said the woman. "If you wait, I will make you a cake."

"I will wait," said the Great Spirit.

Then the woman made a very small cake and put it to bake on the fire. When it was cooked she was surprised, for it seemed larger than before. "I'm not going to give an old man a good cake like that," she thought. She put it away for herself and asked him to wait while she made another one.

"I will wait," said the Great Spirit.

To her astonishment, when the second cake was baked it was larger than the first. "This is fine enough for a feast," she thought.

"That cake was not good enough," she told the Great Spirit. "If you wait a little longer I will make another one."

"I will wait," said the Great Spirit.

Then the woman made another cake. This time she made it much smaller than the others, but when it was cooked it was the biggest of all, as the Great Spirit had worked his power upon the cake.

"This will feed me for many days," she thought. So she hid the cake under a blanket and told her guest that she had nothing for him after all. "Go and find yourself food in the forest," she said. "There are plenty of insects to eat in the bark of the trees."

The Great Spirit was angry. He stood up and threw back his cloak. "A woman should be kind and good-hearted, but you are selfish and cruel," he said. "Therefore, you shall live in the forest from now on and find insects to eat in the bark of the trees."

Then the Great Spirit stamped his foot and the woman began to shrink. Feathers grew all over her body, her arms became wings, and she became the first woodpecker.

THE BADGER AND THE BEAR

Old Father Badger was a great hunter. He had many children who were always well fed and their underground home on the edge of the forest had a good store of meat, which Mother Badger sliced and dried and packed into painted bags.

One day, Father Badger stayed at home to make new arrows and his children gathered around to watch and learn. Suddenly, they heard a noise outside the door. A huge shaggy bear pushed open the door flap and peered inside, sniffing the scent of food. The young badgers were frightened of the stranger's gruff voice and long claws, but their father invited him inside.

"You look hungry, friend," said Father Badger. "Will you share our meal?"

"Yes, I'm starving," said the bear. "Give me meat to eat, my friend." And he sat down by the door with crossed shins.

Mother Badger cooked up her best venison and gave the bear all he could eat and when he was full he smacked his lips with satisfaction and returned to the forest.

After that, the bear came most days to be fed, always sitting by the door with crossed shins. Mother Badger put a fur rug in his place so that their guest was comfortable.

As weeks passed, the bear grew strong with Mother Badger's good cooking. One day he arrived with a wicked gleam in his eye. Instead of sitting in his usual place he stood tall on the rug.

"Welcome, friend," said Father Badger. "Will you share our meal?"

The bear raised his paw. "See how strong I am now?" he said with a menacing smile. At the sight of his sharp teeth the little badgers hid behind their mother in fear.

"I have no home, no bags of dried meat, or arrows," said the bear. "You must give me yours!"

"We have shared our food and friendship," said Father Badger. "Please don't take our home!"

But the bear stepped forward and growled fiercely. Mother Badger gathered her children and hurried them out of the house.

"This is my home now!" roared the bear. "Be gone or I'll throw you out." Father Badger took one last look at his home, his bags of dried meat, and his arrows, and hurried out of the door.

The Badger family fled into the forest.

"Don't worry, my children," said Father Badger, "I will build us somewhere to sleep tonight." When they came to a clearing, he built a small hut out of bent willows and covered it with dry grass and twigs. But, without his arrows, Father Badger couldn't hunt for food. The sound of his children crying with hunger hurt him like a poisoned arrow wound.

"I shall go begging for food," he told to his wife the next morning. Then he disguised himself in a long robe and went back to their old home.

The bear had fetched his cubs to join him and sat outside, slicing meat to dry while they played in the sunshine.

"I am starving, friend," said Father Badger. "Will you give me meat to eat?"

The bear snarled angrily. "Be gone," he growled, shaking his paw, "or I'll kick you out!"

With a heavy heart Father Badger turned to go, but he tripped over a big root and fell to the ground. All the bear cubs laughed except the youngest, who was not unkind because he was used to being laughed at himself. The youngest bear cub followed Father Badger back to his willow hut. When he saw the little badgers crying with hunger he felt sorry for them, so that evening, he slipped away from home and left a small piece of meat outside the badgers' hut.

NORTH AMERICA

The next day, Father Badger went back to the bear and begged for food again, but the bear just roared angrily and pushed him to the ground. However, beside the place where Father Badger fell, there was a leaf red with blood that had dripped from a piece of buffalo meat, so he waited until the bear turned away, hid it under his robe, and took it back to his family.

Father Badger showed the buffalo blood to his wife. "I shall pray to the Great Spirit to bless this," he said. First he built a small lodge, where he performed a sacred ceremony; sprinkling water upon hot stones to purify himself and the buffalo blood. Then he asked the Great Spirit for a blessing. After sitting in silence for a while, Father Badger stepped out of the lodge. To his surprise, a fine young brave carrying a magic arrow followed him.

"My son!" exclaimed Father Badger, admiring the brave's buckskin trousers and long fringed quiver. "You have sprung from the blood of the buffalo to answer my prayer."

"Yes, Father," said the young brave. "I am here to help you."

Then Father Badger told the young brave how his kindness to the bear had been repaid with cruelty. "My children are starving and, without arrows, I can only beg the bear for food."

"Then tomorrow I shall go with you," said the young brave.

The next day, as the bear was taking some slices of meat off the drying poles, he saw Father Badger come out of the forest. Before he could raise his paws in anger, the young brave stepped forward, carrying his magic arrow. Bear had heard about the coming of a man with a magic arrow long ago and was afraid. "Friend," he said, "take my knife and cut yourself some meat."

"This is my father's knife," said the young brave. "You must return all that belongs to him."

Bear cowered with fear. He dropped to his feet, called his cubs and ran away to the forest.

"Now justice has been done," said the young brave and the grateful badgers thanked him warmly and returned to their home.

NORTH AMERICA

HOW THE KING OF THE BIRDS WAS CHOSEN

NORTH AMERICA

There was a time, long ago, when the birds of the Mayan land often quarreled with one another. Their noisy arguments disturbed the Great Spirit, who wanted peace among his creatures, so he called a meeting in the forest and told the birds to choose themselves a king, to settle their disputes.

Many birds wanted to be king. The cardinal bird strutted before the others, displaying his brilliant red feathers. "Look at my beautiful crest," he boasted. "It looks just like a crown. I should be king!"

But the mockingbird laughed at him. "A king must have a fine voice so that his subjects pay attention to him," he said and he performed a beautiful melody. "Everyone listens to me when I sing, so I should be king."

"No, no, no," gobbled the wild turkey. "What use is a pretty voice? A king must be powerful so that he can protect his subjects. I'm the biggest, strongest bird of us all, so it should be me who becomes your king."

One bird after another put himself forward and showed off his talents, but none seemed to have all the right qualities. Nobody could agree on who would make the best king.

Meanwhile, Quetzal watched from the back of the crowd. He was clever and ambitious, but he knew that his drab feathers wouldn't impress the others. He slipped away and went to find his friend Roadrunner, who was busy with his job as a messenger of the roads.

"Roadrunner, my friend," said Quetzal, "there is no one to rival the beauty of your handsome feathers, but I know you are too humble to put yourself forward as king of the Birds. However, I am very suitable for the job, with my superior intelligence and great wisdom, but I lack a magnificent coat to wear when I present myself before the other birds."

Shy Roadrunner fluttered his emerald-green wings and swished his long, shimmering tail.

Quetzal hopped a little closer. "Sadly, I cannot lend you my brilliant mind," he said, "but you could lend me your feathers awhile, just to impress the other birds."

Roadrunner wasn't keen to part with his stunning feathers, but Quetzal worked hard to persuade him of his good intentions and friendship. "When I am king I will repay you with great riches and honors," he promised. At last Roadrunner agreed that Quetzal would make a good king and should be given a chance. As soon as he did so, the feathers began to disappear from his body and grow upon Quetzal.

Proud Quetzal admired his new jewel-like coat and elegant tail. Raising his golden beak with a royal air, he went to present himself before the other birds. "You all know that I am clever and wise," said Quetzal, "but a king must also be magnificent and there is no other bird in the forest as magnificent as me!" Then all the birds agreed that Quetzal was the most impressive and the Great Spirit was pleased and declared that he should be their king.

But once he was crowned, Quetzal was kept busy settling quarrels and keeping the peace among his fellow birds and he forgot about returning the feathers he had borrowed.

Some of the birds noticed that Roadrunner had not been seen since the day of the king-making and organized a search for him. They soon found him hiding, cold and hungry, without a feather on his body. When they heard what had happened, each bird gave Roadrunner some feathers of their own. Today, Roadrunner still wears a strange suit of many different feathers and calls "Puhuy?" which means "Where is he?"

NORTH AMERICA

NORTH AMERICA
A STORY FROM MEXICO

THE BEAR PRINCE

Once upon a time there was a poor woodcutter who had three daughters.

One day, while he was working in the forest, a huge bear appeared and grabbed the ax from his hands.

"How dare you chop down the trees in my forest," roared the bear. "I have a mind to chop you down instead!"

The woodcutter fell to his knees, trembling. "Please forgive me," he said. "I only take wood to sell so that I can buy food for my three daughters. If you chop me down they will starve."

The bear looked at the ax thoughtfully. "I will spare your life if one of your daughters will be my wife," he said. "Then you may take all the wood you need."

The woodcutter was horrified at this request, but to refuse would leave all his daughters to starve, so reluctantly he agreed to the bear's demand.

The bear returned the ax and the woodcutter hurried home. When he explained what had happened, his two eldest daughters turned pale. "Marry a bear? Never!" they cried. "We would rather starve, Father!"

But the youngest daughter, Ninfa, saw the despair in her father's eyes.

"I will keep your promise, Father," she said.

So, the following day, with a heavy heart, the woodcutter fetched the priest and took Ninfa into the woods to marry the bear.

Once they were married, the bear led Ninfa to his cave. He brought her a chest of beautiful clothes and left her until sunset. When it was dark he returned and chanted: *"Bear so hairy, Bear so alarming, change into a prince, handsome and charming."*

In an instant, the bear became a handsome prince. "Don't be afraid, Ninfa," he said. "I've been cursed by a witch to live like a bear and only return to my true form at night. You have shown such bravery.

67

Can you keep my secret?"

Ninfa promised to keep her husband's secret. The next morning, at sunrise, the prince said:

"Prince so handsome, prince so charming, change into a bear, so hairy and alarming."

And he became the bear once more.

Ninfa was happy with her Bear Prince, but as time passed she missed her family and asked if she could visit them. The Bear Prince agreed and reminded her not to reveal his secret.

Ninfa's father greeted her with great joy, but her sisters saw the beautiful clothes and were jealous. They taunted her for marrying a bear. "What a waste of fine silk when nobody will see you but a hairy brute!" they said. At first, Ninfa took no notice, but they kept repeating their unkind words until she lost her temper and told them the prince's secret.

Her sisters were amazed. "You must break the curse!" they told Ninfa. "Wait until the prince is asleep, then tie a scarf around his mouth so that he cannot say the magic words. You'll save him from being a bear forever."

When Ninfa returned to the Bear Prince she did just as her sisters had told her. "He will surely be pleased," she thought.

The prince woke at sunrise to find that he couldn't repeat the magic words and so the curse was ended, but to Ninfa's dismay her husband looked brokenhearted.

NORTH AMERICA

"You forgot your promise," he said sadly. "To undo the spell we had to live as man and wife for a year and a day. Now I must leave and you must search for me until you find the Castle of Faith." And with those words he vanished.

Ninfa felt desperately unhappy, for she had grown to love the prince. But she knew that her tears wouldn't unite them again, so she set off to find the Castle of Faith.

Ninfa hadn't traveled far when she met a wizard and asked him the way to the Castle of Faith. The wizard hadn't heard of it, but he told her to walk on to his father's house and ask there.

"Take this nut," the wizard said. "If you are ever in trouble, break it open."

The young girl thanked him and continued on to the house of the wizard's father, where she asked him the same question, but he knew nothing about the Castle of Faith. "Go to my brother's house and ask him," he said and he gave her another nut. "If you ever find yourself in trouble, break this open."

The third wizard didn't know where to find the Castle of Faith either, but he suggested that she ask the Moon. Like his brother, he gave Ninfa a nut and told her to break it open if she were ever in trouble.

Ninfa thanked the wizard and walked on to the house of the Moon. It was night by the time she reached it. The Moon was so cold she made Ninfa shiver. "I cannot help

you," she said, "but the Sun may know how to find the Castle of Faith."

Although she was weary, Ninfa went on, still believing she could find the prince. When she came to the Sun's house it was so hot that she had to hide behind the fence. "I know the castle you seek," said the Sun, "but I cannot go out after dark. I will call for my friend the Wind to take you there."

To Ninfa's delight, the Wind came and swept her up in his arms. With hope in her heart she flew across the land until he set her gently down beside a castle, where a fiesta was taking place. "Good luck!" whistled the Wind and he rushed away.

Ninfa crept quietly into the ballroom, but what she saw made her heart turn to stone. There sat the prince with a new bride, eating a wedding feast. She didn't know that the bride was a witch who had blinded the prince with magic and tricked him into the

marriage. Suddenly the witch saw Ninfa. She screamed at the servants to throw her out, which caught the prince's attention.

The prince recognized Ninfa at once, but before he could speak, the witch's servants were upon her.

Ninfa remembered the nuts she'd been given by the wizards. She broke one and instantly became a little rat.

When the witch saw this she turned into a cat and chased her. Ninfa sprang onto the prince's plate and broke the second nut, which turned her into a grain of rice. She hid herself among the other grains on his plate, but the witch turned into a chicken and began to peck at the rice.

Then Ninfa broke the third nut, turned into a coyote, and ate the chicken whole. At last she returned to her true form and was reunited with the prince, and from that moment they were never parted again.

NORTH AMERICA

COYOTE AND THE TURTLE

In a deep, cool river, where alligators lazed all day, there lived an inquisitive young turtle. She loved to swim from one bank to the other and explore the rocks and stones on the riverbed, but no matter what she found, she was always curious to see more.

One day, Turtle decided to explore the world beyond the river, so she crawled out of the water and took a walk into the desert. Turtle wandered among the spiky cactus plants, discovering snakes and scorpions and spiders and many other creatures she'd never seen before. She walked on and on, amazed at the wonders around her, not paying attention to how far she was straying from home.

The sun rose high over the desert and Turtle soon began to feel very hot. She longed for a drink and the feeling of cool water on her face. However, when she turned to go home she saw that the river was now far away.

"I'm so tired and thirsty, I'll never be able to walk that far," she sighed with dismay. So she crawled into the shade of a cactus plant. Looking out at the strange desert world, Turtle suddenly felt so far away from home that she began to cry.

She didn't notice Coyote nearby. "That's a lovely song the Turtle is singing," thought Coyote. "I'll ask her to teach it to me."

He trotted up to Turtle, crouched in the shadow of the cactus plant, and asked her to teach him her song.

"I'm not singing, señor. I'm crying," sobbed Turtle.

Coyote thought he was being made a fool of. "I heard you with my own ears," he insisted. "If you don't teach me your song I'll eat you up right here for lunch!"

Turtle looked at Coyote's pink tongue and his sharp, pointed teeth and knew she must be clever to outwit him. She dried her tears. "I wouldn't be a good lunch for you," she said. "My shell is very hard and impossible to swallow."

Coyote looked at her shell and realized she was right. "Then I shall throw you out into the hot sunshine," he said.

"Oh, the hot sun doesn't bother me," said Turtle. "I've got very thick skin."

"So why are you hiding in the shade?" asked Coyote suspiciously.

"I'm not hiding, señor," said Turtle. "I'm just listening to the cactus tell a sad story. That's why I was crying." Coyote stared at Turtle in disbelief, but he couldn't resist bending forward to hear for himself if it was true.

"Come closer," whispered Turtle. "The voice of the cactus is very quiet." Coyote bent closer and closer and…pricked his nose on a cactus spine!

"Ouch!" he yelled angrily. "I shall throw you on the rocks, instead!"

"The rocks don't bother me," said Turtle. "I can pull my head and feet right inside my shell and just bounce away."

Coyote was determined to punish Turtle. "In that case," he said, "I shall throw you into the deep, cold river!"

Then Turtle pretended to be very afraid. "Oh, no, señor," she cried in a trembling voice, "please, not the river—I shall surely drown!"

"That will serve you right for making a fool of me," snapped Coyote, and he took Turtle in his mouth and flung her high over the cactus plants, over the snakes and scorpions and spiders, into the river with a splash.

Turtle plunged into the deep, cool water with delight. When she'd had a good, long drink she swam up to the surface. "Thank you for me home, señor!" she called happily and then Coyote realized just how cleverly he'd been tricked!

NORTH AMERICA

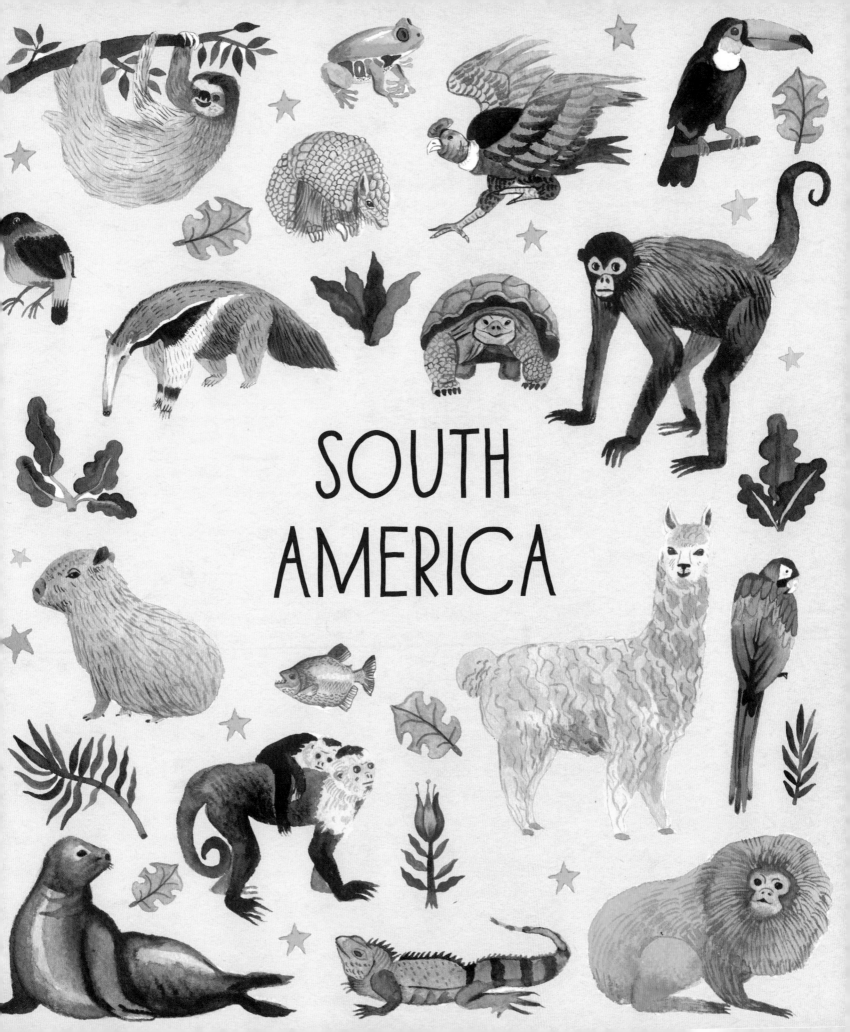

SOUTH
AMERICA

SOUTH AMERICA
A STORY FROM PERU

THE LITTLE FROG OF THE STREAM

SOUTH
AMERICA

There was once a frog who lived by a mountain stream. She could never bear to look at her reflection in the water, because she was born without the beautiful bright speckles that all her brothers and sisters had.

On a rocky ledge, high above the stream, lived a great condor. He had made himself a fine house there, with soft vicuña skins on the floor and a large feather bed.

One day, the condor noticed a young shepherdess tending to a herd of llamas in the meadow below. The shepherdess was called Collyur, which means "Morning Star."

"Now I have a fine house, I should have somebody to look after it," thought the condor. So, he flew down to the meadow, snatched Collyur up into the air, and carried her home.

Collyur had no choice but to work hard for the condor, cleaning his house and preparing his meals. From the rocky ledge she could see her own home in the village

far below, but she knew she could never escape the condor's sharp eyes.

Only the frog saw Collyur gazing sadly across the mountains. She wished that she could help the poor shepherdess.

One morning, Collyur asked the condor if she could go down to the stream to wash her clothes.

"No," said the condor. "You must stay here and cook for me."

"But the food is already cooked," said Collyur, "and all my duties are done."

The condor eyed her suspiciously. "How do I know you won't escape?" he asked.

Collyur thought fast. "You'll hear me beating the clothes on a rock to wash them," she said, "so you'll know where I am."

The condor reluctantly agreed to let Collyur go. "But don't be tempted to run away," he warned. "I shall be listening."

Collyur thanked the condor. She wrapped herself in a vicuña skin and made her clothes into a little bundle. Then she climbed down from the rocky ledge and made her way to the stream. There, she washed her clothes and beat them on a rock, crying bitterly.

The little frog hopped up beside her. "Why are you so sad?" she asked.

Collyur dried her tears and gazed at the frog's kind face. "The condor captured me and I cannot escape," she sighed.

"Maybe I can help you," said the frog. "I have the power to change my form for a few moments. If I take on your appearance and beat those clothes on the rock, then you will have a chance to escape."

"Oh, thank you!" cried Collyur and she kissed the little frog on the forehead. As soon as Collyur put down the clothes, the frog took on her appearance and began beating them against the rock.

The condor finished eating his dinner, unaware that his housekeeper was running away down the mountain. "Where is that girl?" he grumbled. "Her clothes must be clean by now!" But when he stepped out onto the ledge to call her, the shepherdess appeared to plunge into the water and vanish right before his eyes!

The angry condor swooped down to the stream, but Collyur was nowhere to be found. Only the frog and the fishes knew what had happened.

When the frog went home to her brothers and sisters, they all stared at her in amazement. "Look at your reflection!" they cried. For Collyur's kiss on the frog's head had become a sparkling jewel, as beautiful as the morning star.

Then the fishes told the story of the frog's kindness, and from that day she was always proud to see her reflection in the mountain stream.

SOUTH
AMERICA

SOUTH AMERICA
A STORY FROM BOLIVIA

THE SONG OF THE ARMADILLO

SOUTH AMERICA

Armadillo loved music more than anything else in the world. The sound of birds singing in the rainforest filled his heart with happiness and the rhythm of buzzing insects made his tiny feet want to dance.

When it rained, Armadillo loved to listen to the booming chorus of the frogs as they splashed in the forest pools. "I wish I could sing like you," he sighed.

But the frogs just laughed. "Don't be silly," they said. "Everyone knows that armadillos can't sing!"

Up in the trees, crickets were always chirruping a lively tune. "Can you teach me how to sing like you?" asked Armadillo.

But the crickets just giggled. "Don't be silly," they said. "Everyone knows armadillos can't sing!"

So Armadillo wandered through the forest, listening to the howling, squawking, twittering, drumming, warbling music of his fellow creatures, wishing with all his heart that he could make music of his own.

One day, Armadillo came upon a man with a cage of canaries, resting by the side of the road. The canaries were singing with the sweetest voices Armadillo had ever heard. He crept up beside them to listen.

"Please teach me how to sing," he pleaded. "I love music more than anything else in the world—all I want is to be able to make music of my own."

The canaries flitted about the cage in amusement. "What a ridiculous wish!" they twittered. "Who ever heard of an armadillo making music?"

But the man overheard their conversation. "Don't listen to those silly birds, my friend," he said. "I understand your wish. I am a musician myself."

"Can you help me?" asked Armadillo.

The man studied the armadillo carefully. "Yes, I think I could help you to make beautiful music one day," he said, "but not yet. If you come to me when you are very, very old,

I promise I shall help you make music that will fill people's hearts with happiness. Until then, you must enjoy the music of others. Can you be content with that?"

"Oh yes," said Armadillo gratefully. "If I know I will make music one day then I can be happy." So he thanked the musician and returned to the songs of the rain forest.

Armadillo lived a long, happy life, but when he knew he was near the end of his days he went to find the musician, who greeted him like an old friend.

"Do you remember your promise?" asked Armadillo, gazing in wonder at all the instruments in the musician's house.

"Of course," said the musician. "Spend your last days here with me and I shall look after you. Then, when you die, I shall make a wonderful instrument from your shell,

which will play music that will fill many hearts with happiness."

Armadillo was overjoyed to think that his wish was finally going to come true. He spent his last happy days with the musician, who played and sang to him, until he finally fell into a deep sleep and died.

Then the musician made a charango from the armadillo's shell and strung it with ten strings. When it was finished, the charango made bright, beautiful music, full of life and the musician traveled throughout the land, playing in memory of his friend Armadillo.

When the frogs and crickets and canaries heard the sweet notes of the charango they listened in wonder. "At last Armadillo has a voice," they said. "Who would have guessed he would make the most beautiful music in the world!"

SOUTH AMERICA

SOUTH AMERICA
A STORY FROM ARGENTINA

THE TWO VISCACHAS

Two young viscachas lived together on the rocky slopes of the Andes Mountains. They were best friends and loved to play all day, chasing each other among the boulders and jumping from ledge to ledge.

The two friends shared everything, especially any delicious patch of moss or lichen, which was their favorite food. At night, when the air grew cold and a chilly wind blew through the mountains, they would find shelter in a crevice and huddle together to share their warmth as best they could.

One morning, the two viscachas noticed something red caught on a thorny bush. They scampered closer to take a look.

"It doesn't smell like anything to eat!" said one of them sadly.

His friend tugged at the bundle of red stuff. "It's a scrap of blanket," she said. "Maybe it was thrown away, or blown here by the wind." As she pulled it free from the thorns, the little scrap of red cloth ripped in two. The viscachas took a piece each.

"This is a real treasure!" said the first viscacha. "But what a pity it isn't the right size to cover me."

"This piece won't cover me, either," said his friend. "If only they were still joined together, we'd have a big enough blanket to keep us both warm at night."

As they sat, wondering what to do with their newfound treasure, Señor Fox came along. He eyed the two viscachas with a crafty smile.

"Hello, amigos," he said. "What have you got there?"

"We found a treasure!" said the two viscachas. "It's a torn blanket. If only we could find a way to sew the pieces back together it would keep us both warm at night."

"Well, it's your lucky day!" said Señor Fox. "As it happens, I have a needle and thread.

I'd be happy to lend them to you, if you'll let me share your warm blanket on a cold night."

The two viscachas agreed that they must be very lucky and thanked Señor Fox for his offer, so he went to fetch a needle and thread from his den. When he returned, one of the viscachas sewed the two pieces of red blanket together. Señor Fox watched and waited. When the job was done, he took his needle, wished them both a good morning, and went on his way.

The two viscachas laid their precious blanket on a rock and went off to play.

That evening, as the sun set, a chilly wind blew across the mountains. The two friends shivered in the cold night air, but they smiled to each other. "Tonight we'll have our warm blanket to sleep under," they said and they hurried back to where they had left it.

But when they go there, sitting beside the red blanket was Señor Fox. "Good evening, amigos," he said. "I hope you remember your promise to share this warm blanket with me?"

"Yes, Señor," said the two viscachas, beginning to shudder with cold.

"Good," said Señor Fox. "It was my thread that stitched up the middle of the blanket so that part belongs to me." And he pulled the blanket right over himself so that the two viscachas had to lie on either side, with hardly any blanket to cover them at all.

That night Señor Fox enjoyed a good, warm sleep, but the little shivering viscachas didn't sleep at all.

In the morning they crept away and left their treasure behind.

"It's better to trust a friend than make a bargain with Señor Fox!" they agreed.

SOUTH AMERICA

SOUTH AMERICA
A STORY FROM BRAZIL

THE PARTY IN THE SKY

Toad didn't always look the way he does now, with lumps and bumps all over his body. There was a time when Toad had smooth skin and considered himself very handsome. In those days, all he thought about was going to parties and having a good time. Whenever Toad heard that a party was being planned, no matter how far away, he got himself invited.

One day, Toad overheard a pair of flamingos talking about a party that was going to be held in the sky. "That sounds fun," said Toad. "Will you ask if I can go too?" The flamingos agreed and a few days later, an invitation arrived for Toad.

His friend Armadillo saw the invitation and was puzzled. "How will you get to a party in the sky?" she asked.

Toad smiled. "I'll find a way," he said.

The next day, Toad went to visit Buzzard, who lived nearby, and found him playing his violin. Buzzard seldom had any visitors, so he was surprised to see Toad.

"Good day, Buzzard," said Toad. "Are you going to the party in the sky?"

"Yes," said Buzzard. "All the birds are invited."

"Well, I'm invited too," said Toad. "Maybe we can go together?"

Buzzard was pleased that Toad wanted his company. "All right," he said. "What time shall we leave?"

"Come to my house at four o'clock," said Toad, "and bring your violin – everyone loves music at a party!"

On the day of the party, Buzzard arrived at Toad's house, carrying his violin case. However, Toad said that he wasn't quite ready. "Leave your violin outside by the door and come in for a moment," he said.

Buzzard put down his violin and followed Toad inside. But while Buzzard waited for him get ready, Toad climbed out of the back window, hopped around to the front door, and hid himself inside the violin case.

Buzzard waited and waited. He called out to Toad but there was no reply. Eventually he gave up. He fetched his violin, grumbling that Toad was most unreliable, and flew off to the party in the sky.

When he arrived at the party, Buzzard laid down his violin and went to find something to eat. Out hopped Toad, laughing at his trick!

Soon, Toad was having lots of fun. Buzzard was astonished to find him singing and dancing. "How did you get here?" he asked.

Toad just chuckled. "I'll tell you one day!" he said.

Toad had a wonderful time, but Buzzard didn't enjoy the party. Nobody wanted to hear him play, or dance with him, so he went home early, forgetting about the violin.

At the end of the party, weary Toad climbed into the violin case and waited to be carried home. But nothing happened. He began to get worried. "I wish I'd never come so far away from home!" he whimpered.

Then Falcon noticed the violin case. "That belongs to Buzzard," he said. "I'll take it to him."

At last, Toad felt himself carried through the sky. But Falcon was also weary after all the dancing. "This violin is heavier than it looks," he puffed. "Why should I bother with it? Buzzard is no friend of mine." So he let the violin drop and down to earth it fell.

Toad peered out in alarm, calling for the stones below to get out of the way. But they had deaf ears and the violin crashed to the ground and splintered into a hundred pieces.

Buzzard never knew what happened to his violin, but Toad is still covered in bumps and bruises and doesn't go to many parties.

SOUTH AMERICA

SOUTH AMERICA
A STORY FROM BRAZIL

HOW THE BEETLES GOT THEIR GORGEOUS COATS

One morning a big rat scampered out of his hole and sat in the sunshine to clean his whiskers. He noticed a little beetle, scuttling along the top of a wall.

"Hey, Beetle," he said, "how can you move so slowly? You'll never get anywhere in the world creeping along like that!"

The little beetle didn't say a word. She just kept crawling forward on her tiny feet.

"I bet you wish you could run like this," cried the rat and he darted off at great speed to the end of the wall and back again. Meanwhile, the beetle had hardly moved at all.

The rat shook the dust off his tail. "That's how to get somewhere," he chuckled. "What a pity you'll never know how it feels to move fast like me."

"You certainly can run fast, Rat," said the beetle, but she'd been taught that it wasn't polite to boast and so she didn't mention the things that she could do well.

Nearby, on the branch of a mango tree sat a green-and-gold parrot. She'd been listening to the exchange between the rat and the beetle with interest. "Why don't you challenge the beetle to a race?" she said to the rat. "I'll offer the winner a bright new coat made by my neighbor, the tailor bird."

The rat glanced at his dull-colored fur. "I've always thought I'd look rather fine in a blue coat with tiger stripes," he said.

"For me it would be something shiny," said the beetle.

The rat exploded with laughter. "You'd never have a chance of winning against me!"

The beetle looked offended. "Well, you won't win either unless we have a race," she replied.

The rat grinned. "All right," he said. "Let's race!"

And so it was agreed. The parrot flew to a palm tree at the top of the cliff, which was to be the finishing line. When she gave a loud squawk the race began.

The rat scooted off as fast as he could, along the cliff path. Halfway, he realized that he didn't need to hurry, so he slowed down a little to catch his breath. "Why tire myself out?" he thought. "That beetle will still be scuttling along at sunset. It's hardly worth racing her at all." But then he thought of the fancy new coat he would win, so he took off again at top speed, eager to claim his prize.

However, when he reached the palm tree at the top of the cliff, the rat couldn't believe his eyes. There was the little beetle, sitting beside the green-and-gold parrot.

"How did you get here so fast?" he gasped in disbelief.

The beetle drew out the tiny wings from her sides. "Nobody mentioned any rules about running," she said, "so I flew instead."

The rat stared in astonishment. "I didn't know you could fly!"

"Never judge by looks alone," said the parrot. "You don't know when you may find hidden wings."

Then the parrot asked the beetle what colors she wanted for her new coat. The beetle looked around at the green-and-gold palm trees and the green-and-gold mangos.

"I choose green and gold," she said. So, the tailor bird made the beetle a shiny new green coat with flecks of golden light in it, and the foolish rat was left to wear his dull old coat of gray.

SOUTH AMERICA

EUROPE

EUROPE
A STORY FROM DENMARK

THE NIGHTINGALE

EUROPE

There once was an emperor of China who loved to surround himself with beautiful things. Visitors came from near and far to admire his magnificent palace and gaze at the flowers in his garden.

At the far end of the emperor's garden was a wood that went down to the sea. There, the water was so deep that ships could sail close to the shore and pass beneath the overhanging branches, and in those branches lived a nightingale.

The nightingale delighted everyone who heard her sing. Fishermen stopped to listen to her song and travelers sailing by the wood agreed that the nightingale was more precious than anything else the emperor possessed. It so happened that one of those travelers was a writer who described the nightingale in a book, and one day that book was given to the emperor.

The emperor was astonished to read that a nightingale was more precious than anything else in his palace or his garden.

"Bring me this bird," he said. "I wish to hear her sing."

The emperor's men couldn't find a nightingale in the palace or the garden, but at last they found a kitchen maid who had often seen the nightingale when she walked home through the wood. She was sent to ask the little bird to sing for the emperor.

"My song would sound better among the trees," said the nightingale when she heard the emperor's request, but she graciously agreed to come to the palace.

A perch was made for the nightingale and the whole court gathered to hear the little bird sing for the emperor. The nightingale sang so sweetly that she touched the hearts of everyone who heard her and brought tears of joy to the emperor's eyes.

The emperor was delighted and offered the nightingale rich rewards. The nightingale thanked him, and explained that she was already rewarded if her song had brought tears to the eyes of an emperor.

Then the emperor had a golden cage made for the nightingale so that he could hear her sing every day. The nightingale was allowed to fly into the garden, but only with a silk cord fastened to her foot so that she should not fly far. Soon, everyone in the palace was talking about the wonderful bird and, before long, everyone in the city had heard about her beautiful song.

One day, a parcel arrived for the emperor. Inside was a mechanical bird, studded with diamonds and rubies and sapphires. When the emperor turned a little silver key, the glittering bird began to sing a tune. "This is a wonder!" marveled the emperor. "The two birds must sing together."

The nightingale was brought to sing with the mechanical bird. However, their voices did not sound beautiful together.

"The mechanical bird is superior," said the emperor's clockmaker. "She will always keep perfect time and never need to rest her voice and she is so much prettier to look at than the dull little nightingale."

So the mechanical bird was put on the perch and sang her song all day for everyone in the palace.

That evening, the emperor asked to hear the real nightingale sing once more, but she couldn't be found. Everyone had been so dazzled by the mechanical bird that they hadn't noticed her fly back to the wood.

"You have the better bird here," the clockmaker assured the emperor. "True, the real nightingale's tune was ever-changing, but the mechanical bird is reliable; its tiny cogs and wheels will always give you the same song."

Then the emperor had the jeweled bird placed on a silk cushion in an honored position by his bed and, although it only sang one tune, that tune pleased him. Eventually he learned the notes and could sing along.

All was well for a year; the mechanical bird sang from morning to night without needing to rest her voice and everyone in the city loved her tune. Then, one day, there was a sudden "bang" and she fell silent.

EUROPE

The emperor sent for the clockmaker, who fixed the bird, but explained that some of her parts were almost worn out. "From now on she should only sing once a year," he said, "otherwise she will stop altogether."

Five years passed and the emperor became very ill. With heavy hearts, his doctors reported that he did not have long to live. The palace began busy preparations for his successor, but they covered the floors of all the rooms with cloth so that not a step would disturb the emperor's peace.

Meanwhile, the emperor lay in his room, feeling a great weight upon his heart. When he opened his eyes he saw that Death was sitting on his chest, surrounded by the scowling faces of the emperor's bad deeds and the smiling faces of his good deeds. They all began whispering to him about the things he had done in his life.

The emperor became very distressed. He wished that he could drown out their voices with music, but there was no one to play. He pleaded with the mechanical bird to sing her tune, but without a hand to wind her key she couldn't sing a note.

The emperor stared into the hollow eyes of Death. Suddenly, he heard a sweet familiar song; it was the nightingale singing at his open window. She had heard of the emperor's illness and had come to comfort him. At the sound of her pure voice, the ghostly faces began to grow pale.

The nightingale sang about the quiet churchyard where white roses bloom and Death felt a longing for his garden and retreated, like a shadow, from the room. Then the emperor felt his strength return.

"Precious bird," he said. "You have sung away Death. How can I reward you?"

"Let me come and go freely," said the nightingale. "I shall sing to you about everything that is good and bad beyond the palace so that you may rule with wisdom."

The emperor gladly agreed and lived many happy years, ruling his people wisely.

EUROPE

EUROPE
A STORY FROM NORWAY

THE THREE BILLY GOATS GRUFF

EUROPE

Three Billy Goats Gruff were climbing over the mountainside one morning, looking for breakfast, when they spied a meadow of green, green grass.

Big Billy Goat Gruff stopped to smell the delicious grass on the breeze. Middle-sized Billy Goat Gruff stopped to lick his hungry lips, but Little Billy Goat Gruff started up the mountain path as fast as his legs could carry him.

To get to the meadow of green, green grass, Little Billy Goat Gruff had to cross a deep river and the only way to reach the other side was over a rickety wooden bridge. However, under the bridge lived a great ugly troll, with eyes as big as saucers and a nose as long as a rolling pin.

Little Billy Goat Gruff set off, trip, trap, trip, trap, over the rickety bridge. Halfway across he heard a terrible roar.

"Who dares to go trip, trap, trip, trap, over my bridge?" demanded the troll.

Little Billy Goat Gruff trembled.

"It is only I, Little Billy Goat Gruff," he answered, "on my way to eat the green, green grass in the meadow."

"A goat, eh?" chuckled the troll. "Then I'm coming to gobble you up!"

"Oh no!" cried Little Billy Goat Gruff. "There's no meat on me, I'm only skin and bone. Wait for my brother who's coming along after me—he's much fatter than I am."

The troll thought for a moment, and then he said, "All right, be off with you." Little Billy Goat Gruff hurried over the bridge and away up the path to the meadow of green, green grass.

A few minutes later, Middle-sized Billy Goat Gruff arrived and started to cross, trip, trap, trip, trap, over the rickety bridge.

"Who's that going trip, trap, trip, trap, over my bridge?" demanded the troll.

Middle-sized Billy Goat Gruff trembled.

"It is only I, Middle-sized Billy Goat Gruff," he answered.

"Then I'm coming to gobble you up!"

boomed the troll.

"Oh no," cried Middle-sized Billy Goat Gruff, "please don't eat me. If you do, you won't have room for my big brother, who's coming along. He's much fatter than me."

The troll thought for a moment, and then he said, "All right, be off with you." And Middle-sized Billy Goat Gruff hurried over the bridge and away up the path to the meadow of green, green grass.

A few minutes later, Big Billy Goat Gruff arrived and started to cross, trip, trap, trip, trap, over the rickety bridge.

"Who's that going trip, trap, trip, trap, over my bridge?" demanded the troll.

Big Billy Goat Gruff stopped and snorted impatiently at the delay to his journey.

"It is I, Big Billy Goat Gruff!" he answered.

"Then I'm coming to gobble you up!" said the troll.

"You may have frightened my brothers, but you don't frighten me!" said Big Billy Goat Gruff and he stamped his hooves and lowered his horns. When the great ugly troll climbed onto the bridge, Big Billy Goat Gruff charged and tossed him high into the air. Up, up, up went the troll, then down, down, down, into the deep, cold river with a splash!

Big Billy Goat Gruff continued on his way, trip, trap, trip, trap, over the rickety bridge, to join his brothers for a delicious breakfast in the meadow of green, green grass.

EUROPE

EUROPE
A STORY FROM WALES

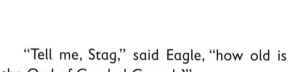

THE OWL OF COWLYD COOMB

The Eagle of the Alder Wood had lived for many tens of years and was very old and lonely.

His wife had died long ago and his children had flown away to raise families of their own.

"I need a new wife to keep me company," Eagle thought to himself. But he didn't want the bother of raising any more children, for he was too old and tired to feed a squabbling brood again.

"If I find a new wife she must be really old like me so that she will be happy just sitting quietly at my side."

A few days later, Eagle heard about an old owl who lived alone in a place called Cowlyd Coomb.

"Maybe she needs a companion," he thought to himself. But was she old enough to be his wife?

The eagle knew it would be impolite to ask the owl her age, so he went to see his friend, the Stag of Ferny-Side Brae.

"Tell me, Stag," said Eagle, "how old is the Owl of Cowlyd Coomb?"

Stag was sitting beside a tree stump. "For hundreds of years I watched this tree grow from a little acorn into the tallest, broadest oak tree in the wood," he said. "Then, for hundreds of years, I watched it die. I can tell you that when that little acorn fell from the branch, the Owl of Cowlyd Coomb was already old. But if you want to know more, ask the Salmon of Glynllifon. She is much older than me."

The eagle thanked the stag and went to find the salmon.

"Tell me, Salmon," said Eagle, "how old is the Owl of Cowlyd Coomb?"

Salmon flapped her tail thoughtfully. "I have lived a year for every scale on my body," she said, "and for every egg in my belly. But when I was just a small fry, the Owl of Cowlyd Coomb was already old. If you want to know more, ask the Ouzel of Cilgwri. He is much older than me."

The eagle thanked the salmon and went to find the ouzel.

"Tell me, Ouzel," he asked, "how old is the Owl of Cowlyd Coomb?"

The ouzel was perched on a rock.

"See that stone at your feet, no bigger than a nut?" he said. "Well, once it was a boulder so huge that it would have needed a hundred oxen to move it. The reason it wore away is because I have wiped my beak on it every day of my long, long life. But when I was a chick in the nest, the Owl of Cowlyd Coomb was already old."

"If you want to know more, you must ask the Toad of Cors Fochno. He is the only one older than me," he continued.

The eagle thanked the ouzel and went to find the toad.

"Tell me, toad," he asked, "how old is the Owl of Cowlyd Coomb?"

Toad gazed up at the distant hills. "On this bog there once stood a hill, as high as those you see with their heads in the clouds, but I have slowly, slowly eaten it up, taking only tiny mouthfuls of dust every day. I can assure you that when I was just a tadpole, the Owl of Cowlyd Coomb was already very, very old."

Then the eagle was sure that the owl was old enough to be a suitable wife, so he went to Cowlyd Coomb and asked her to marry him.

The ancient owl had been feeling lonely too, so she agreed. And there was never a happier, quieter wedding than that of the Eagle and the Owl of Cowlyd Coomb!

EUROPE

EUROPE
A STORY FROM SCOTLAND

KING OF THE CATS

In a lonely house in the mountains lived two brothers, Duncan and Frazer, with an old housekeeper and her cat.

One autumn afternoon, Frazer went off for a walk alone. When he wasn't home by sunset, Duncan began to worry. At suppertime Frazer still hadn't appeared, but all Duncan could do was watch and wait.

At last Frazer returned, exhausted and unable to speak. The brothers silently ate their supper and then sat before the fire, with the cat curled up on the rug.

Frazer stared into the flames, a haunted look in his eyes.

"Tell me now, what kept you out so late?" asked Duncan.

Frazer shivered, even though the fire was ablaze. "I've had a strange adventure, brother," he said. "On my way home a thick fog came down and I lost my way. I wandered blindly in the gloom until I saw a light ahead. It seemed to shine from within a great oak tree…"

Frazer paused.

"Go on," said Duncan and the cat opened an eye as if he was listening.

"I climbed up into the branches," said Frazer, "and there below me, inside the hollow trunk of the tree, I saw a candlelit church, where a funeral was taking place…"

"Go on," urged Duncan and the cat opened his other eye.

"Well, you won't believe it," said Frazer, "but the black coffin and candles were carried by cats!"

Duncan stared in disbelief and the cat jumped to its feet.

"On the coffin was a golden crown…" said Frazer, but he got no further, for the old housekeeper's cat let out a shriek.

"Old Peter's dead!" he cried. "I'm king of the Cats!" And he rushed up the chimney and was never seen again.

EUROPE

EUROPE
A STORY FROM NORWAY

DAPPLEGRIM

Once there was a man and his wife who had twelve sons. The youngest son, Lars, wanted to seek his fortune, so he said goodbye to his family and traveled until he came to a king's palace, where he found work in the stables.

After a year, Lars returned home, only to discover that his parents had died and all their belongings had been divided up between his brothers.

"What shall be my inheritance?" asked Lars. His brothers hadn't shared out the twelve mares grazing on the hill, so Lars took those for his own. Each mare had a foal and a big dapple-gray one caught his eye. "You are a fine fellow," said Lars.

"Yes," said the dapple-gray, "but if you kill the other foals and let me feed from all the mares you shall see how big and handsome I can grow!" Lars was curious, so he did as the foal suggested and went back to work in the palace.

When he returned, the dapple-gray had grown fat and strong, with a bright, shiny coat and all the mares had foals once more.

"Let me feed from the mares for another year," said the dapple-gray, "and you shall see how much bigger and more handsome I can grow!" So Lars did the same again.

Another year passed and the dapple-gray grew so tall that Lars couldn't reach to touch its neck and so bright that its coat glistened. Once more it asked to feed from all the mares, so Lars agreed.

The following year, the dapple-gray was so huge that it had to lie down for Lars to get on its back and its coat shone like a mirror. "Now we must go to the palace," said Dapplegrim, for that was his name.

They caused quite a commotion when they rode up to the palace, where the king was standing on the steps. "Only a noble man would ride such a magnificent horse," remarked the king and he offered Lars a position at court.

It so happened that, while Lars had been

away, the king's daughter had been carried off into the mountains by a troll. When some of the courtiers saw Lars being favored by the king they became jealous. They told the king that they'd heard Lars boasting he could rescue the princess.

The king sent for Lars at once and insisted that he should rescue the princess or be punished. Lars knew it was useless to protest, although he was certain that he'd been given an impossible task. However, Dapplegrim assured him it could be done. "Have four strong horseshoes made for me and I will help you," he said.

When Dapplegrim had his shoes, they journeyed for several days to the mountain of the troll. The mountainside was steep and smooth as glass. At first, Dapplegrim slipped down, with a sound like thunder, but he tried and tried again. At last he sprang up the rock and into the troll's cave.

Before the troll could reach for his club, Lars swept the princess up behind him and escaped with her down the mountain.

During the long journey home, the princess and Lars fell in love. At the palace, the king greeted his daughter with joy. He was grateful to Lars, but when he heard that the princess and her brave rescuer wished to marry he turned to his courtiers for advice.

"That boy is not good enough for the princess," they muttered jealously, so the king set Lars another task.

The palace was overshadowed by a huge hill that prevented the sun from shining in.

"If you can bring sunshine into the palace you shall marry my daughter," said the king.

Lars felt his heart sink. "I'll do my best," he promised and he went to tell Dapplegrim about the task.

"Have four new horseshoes made for me," said Dapplegrim, "and I will help you." When the shoes were made, Lars rode Dapplegrim to the top of the hill. Then the huge horse stamped his heavy feet and flattened it. Sunshine flooded into the palace.

"Now you must agree to let us marry, Father," said the princess, but once more the

EUROPE

king listened to his courtiers, who advised him to set Lars another task.

"If you wish to marry my daughter," said the king, "you must find her a horse as magnificent as yours to ride to the wedding."

Lars was sure that there could be no other horse like Dapplegrim. "There is one," said Dapplegrim, "but he lives underground and will not be easy to catch." Then he told Lars to fetch 12 barrels of corn, 12 barrels of meat, a barrel of tar, and 12 ox hides studded with spikes.

Lars gathered everything and set off on Dapplegrim, but they had not gone far when all the wild birds of the forest flew out to stop them. Dapplegrim told Lars to spill the corn from the barrels and the birds flew down to eat.

A little farther on, all the wild beasts of the forests came out to stop them, but Lars threw them the meat from the barrels and they were able to escape.

On they went, until they came to a wild heath. There, Dapplegrim stopped and neighed loudly. He was answered from beneath the ground. Quickly, he told Lars to cover him with the ox hides and pour the tar from the barrel.

Out of the earth galloped a magnificent horse, breathing flames from its nostrils. At once the tar caught fire and the two horses began to fight. "If the flames rise, I have won," cried Dapplegrim, "if they sink, I have failed." The fight was fierce, but Dapplegrim was so well protected that he couldn't be harmed. Lars watched the flames rise until the strange horse finally gave up the fight and Lars slipped a bridle around his neck.

The two horses were identical. When the king saw that Lars had done everything he'd asked, while his courtiers had done nothing but complain, he dismissed them all. Lars and the Princess were wed at last and they both lived happily ever after.

EUROPE

EUROPE
A STORY FROM SCOTLAND

THE EAGLE AND THE WREN

The birds of the mountains and the sea, the forests and the moorland, gathered one day to choose themselves a queen. But although they talked for many hours, they found it impossible to agree; some wanted Eagle to be their queen and others wanted Wren.

"Why not decide with a test?" suggested Wren. "Whichever one of us can fly the highest shall be queen."

The other birds thought this was a strange suggestion from the little Wren, but as they were all tired of arguing they agreed.

So the two birds took flight. Wren fluttered straight up on her tiny wings while Eagle stretched out her fine long feathers and soared in great circles. When Wren had risen as high as she could go, she dropped down lightly onto Eagle's back.

Eagle flew higher and higher, until the other birds watching below could only see a small speck among the mountain peaks. At last, she could rise no more, so she glided gracefully down to the ground.

"Eagle flew the highest!" said the birds. "She shall be our queen."

To everyone's surprise, a tiny head peeped out of the feathers on Eagle's back.

"No, it should be me!" chirped Wren. "I hid here until Eagle could rise no more and then I flapped my wings and flew a moment higher."

Wren's words caused much twittering and warbling and clucking and hooting, but this time everyone did agree.

"You didn't reach the mountain peaks yourself, Wren," said Owl. "Eagle flew the highest and she did so carrying you on her back." Then all the birds cheered for Eagle, their new queen.

Wren crept away but she learned wisdom that day, for she never flew far from the earth again or tried to be what she was not.

EUROPE

EUROPE
A STORY FROM IRELAND

SAINT DOMNOC AND THE BEES

Domnoc was descended from the royal family of O'Neil in Ireland, but he decided to leave his native country to become a monk.

He sailed to Wales, where he found a place at the monastery of David. David taught Domnoc and took him into his care, and when he wasn't studying or praying, Domnoc helped with the work at the monastery. Rather than cook or clean, Domnoc chose to work in the garden and was given responsibility for the bees, which the monks kept so that they had honey to give to the poor.

Domnoc loved the gentle, busy bees. He learned their habits and looked after their beehives. Before long, he noticed which flowers the bees loved best and planted them around the garden. As Domnoc went about his work, weeding the flowerbeds or tending the vegetables, he talked to the bees, who buzzed about him as if to keep him company.

The monastery bees were so well looked after that they made plenty of honey for the poor and Domnoc thanked God for his tiny friends.

After several years of study, Domnoc was ready to return home to Ireland as a monk. He was sad to be leaving his wise teacher, David, and all his friends at the monastery, and also sorry to have to say goodbye to his little companions, the bees. When he went down to the beehives for the last time, they gathered around him, as if they knew he was going away.

"Keep doing God's work, my friends," said Domnoc, and he left to board his ship, waiting in the harbor.

Domnoc boarded the ship, but before the crew could set sail they heard a strange humming sound. Out of the sky flew a great swarm of bees that came to rest upon the sail.

Domnoc knew at once that they had come from the monastery. "Go home, my friends," he told them. "You have important work to do, making honey for the poor." But the bees would not leave Domnoc, so he had to lead them back to the monastery himself.

Domnoc explained to David what had happened, and when the bees were in their hives once more, he returned to the ship and set sail across the Irish Sea. However, the crew soon noticed a hazy black cloud following the ship.

"The bees are coming!" they cried in alarm. Despite the lively wind, the bees struggled on until they reached the ship and settled on the sail once more.

"They've come so far on their tiny wings; they'll never be able to fly home," said Domnoc. "We must sail back to Wales."

Reluctantly, the crew turned around, and when they reached the shore, Domnoc led the bees back to the monastery again.

David watched Domnoc settling the bees back into their hives. "These bees wish to be with you, Domnoc," he said. "Take a basket with you on the ship this time. If they follow you again you must accept them with my blessing."

Domnoc thanked his teacher and took a basket back to the ship.

Sure enough, the bees followed Domnoc for the third time. When they reached the ship they were so weak and tired that they came to rest on the deck. "Don't be afraid," Domnoc told the crew and he gently gathered the bees into the basket, where they stayed for the rest of the voyage.

Home at last in Ireland, Domnoc set up a new church and planted a garden full of flowers. There, he taught others to live gentle, busy lives, providing for the poor, just like the bees.

EUROPE

EUROPE
AN ENGLISH STORY

THE THREE LITTLE PIGS

Once upon a time, there were three little pigs, called Snuffle, Spot, and Curly. Snuffle liked to eat all day, Spot loved a long nap, but their sister Curly was always busy with clever ideas.

As the little pigs grew bigger, their house became quite a squeeze. So, one day, they decided it was time to build houses of their own.

The three little pigs set out together.

Before long, Snuffle stopped by the wood to eat some blackberries. When he was full, he looked around for something to build his house with. "There are plenty of sticks here," he thought, so he built himself a house of sticks.

Farther down the lane, Spot found a pile of straw and stopped for a nap. When he woke up, he looked around for something to build his house with. "Straw is comfy," he thought, so he built himself a house of straw.

Meanwhile, Curly walked on until she found a pile of bricks. "These are perfect for strong walls," she thought, so she built herself a house of bricks.

The next day, a big, bad wolf tramped out of the wood.

He saw the stick house and smelled a little pig inside.

"Little pig, little pig, let me come in," he said in a tiny voice.

But Snuffle spotted the wolf's tail through the window.

"No!" he cried. "I won't let you in. Not by the hair on my chinny-chin-chin!"

"Then I'll huff and I'll puff and I'll blow your house down!" bellowed the wolf and he took a deep breath and blew…

Snuffle ran out of the back door and down the lane as fast as his little legs could carry him. He came to Spot's house.

EUROPE

"Help," he shouted, "the wolf is coming!" Spot opened the door and let him in.

Before Snuffle could catch his breath, along came the big, bad wolf.

He saw the straw house and smelled the little pigs inside.

"Little pigs, little pigs, let me come in," said the wolf.

"No!" cried Spot. "We won't let you in. Not by the hair on our chinny-chin-chins!"

"Then I'll huff and I'll puff and I'll blow your house down!" bellowed the wolf and he took a deep breath and blew...

Snuffle and Spot ran out of the back door and down the lane as fast as their little legs could carry them, until they came to Curly's house.

"Help," they shouted, "the wolf is coming!" Curly opened the door and they hurried inside.

Before Snuffle and Spot could catch their breath, along came the big, bad wolf.

He saw the brick house and smelled the little pigs inside.

"Little pigs, little pigs, let me come in!" said the wolf.

"No!" cried Curly. "We won't let you in. Not by the hair on our chinny-chin-chins!"

"Then I'll huff and I'll puff and I'll blow your house down!" bellowed the wolf and he took a deep breath and blew...

But nothing happened! The wolf huffed and puffed until his face was red, but he couldn't blow down a house of bricks.

"Hurray, we're safe!" cried the three little pigs.

However, a moment later, they heard footsteps on the roof. Curly thought fast and put a pan of water to boil on the stove.

The three little pigs held their breath as the big, bad wolf began to lower himself down the chimney...

A tail appeared and then...SPLASH! He fell into the boiling water! The big, bad wolf let out a mighty howl. Up he jumped, out he ran, and he was never seen again.

And the three little pigs lived together happily ever after.

EUROPE

EUROPE
A STORY FROM FINLAND

MIGHTY MIKKO

Once there was an old woodsman who had come to the end of his days. He called his son, Mikko, to his bedside.

"You are a good, kind young man, Mikko," he said. "I have nothing to leave you except this humble cottage and the three snares I've used for many years to catch animals in the forest. When I am dead, go into the forest and inspect the snares. If you find a wild creature trapped there, bring it home alive."

The old woodsman died shortly afterward and Mikko followed his father's advice. Sure enough, he found a little red fox trapped in one of the snares. Mikko gently freed the fox and carried it home, where he bandaged its bruised foot and gave it food from his own dish. When its foot was healed, the fox stayed with Mikko and they became friends.

One day the fox noticed that Mikko was lonely. "You need a wife to keep you company," he said.

Mikko smiled sadly. "I have nothing to offer a wife. Who would want to live in this humble cottage?"

"You are a good, kind young man," said the fox, "and handsome too, although you have no mirror to see it! The princess at the palace couldn't ask for more."

"You're making fun of me!" Mikko laughed. "It's true, I am lonely and they say the princess is loved by everyone who meets her, but she would never look at a poor boy like me."

"We shall see," said the fox and he went off to visit the king.

When he was shown into the throne room, the fox made a gracious bow. "I bring greetings from my master," he said. "He asks if Your Highness would lend him a barrel."

"That's an odd request!" exclaimed the king. "Who is your master and why does he want it?"

The fox put on an air of great importance.

"You must have heard of my master, the Mighty Mikko?" he said.

The king frowned. He had never heard the name, but he didn't want to appear ill informed. "Oh yes, Mighty Mikko." He nodded knowingly. "And why does he want to borrow a barrel?"

"My master wants to send a small gift to his bootmaker," said the fox. "He promises to return the barrel tomorrow." The king was curious and so he agreed.

On his way home, the fox stopped at the market, where he hunted beneath the stalls for all the coins that had been dropped that day.

The next morning, he pushed the coins into the cracks in the barrel and returned it to the king. The king noticed the glinting coins at once. "This fellow, Mighty Mikko, must be very wealthy if he gives a barrel of coins to his bootmaker," he thought, so he asked the fox if his master would visit the palace.

The fox shook his head. "That's impossible, I'm afraid," he said. "My master wishes to marry and has been invited by several foreign kings to meet their daughters. Tomorrow he sets off on his journey."

When the king heard this he thought of his own daughter, who was loved by everyone who met her, but had never fallen in love herself. "Ask your master to come here first," he said. "We will make him very welcome."

The fox sighed and stepped close to whisper in the king's ear, as if he didn't want the servants to hear. "I'm afraid your palace isn't big enough to entertain my master and all the men he travels with," he said.

The king was astounded. "Mighty Mikko must be truly noble to have such a huge company of men," he thought. "If only he would agree to come here, he might be a perfect husband for the princess."

The fox pretended to leave, but as he reached the door of the throne room he hesitated. "I'm sure my master would like to return your kindness for lending him the barrel," he said.

EUROPE

"Sometimes he travels around the land in disguise, dressed as a humble woodsman…"

"Then bid him come as a woodsman," said the king eagerly. "When he is here I will give him my finest clothes to wear."

Hiding a smile, the fox thanked the king and trotted home to Mikko.

Mikko was amazed to hear about the king's invitation. The following day, he went with the fox to the palace, where he was given a great welcome by the king and dressed in the finest clothes.

As the fox had predicted, Mikko's handsome face and good, kind nature soon won the heart of the princess and, like everyone who met her, he fell in love too. Nobody was happier than the king himself, and before long Mikko and the princess were married with his blessing.

All went well, until the king asked to visit Mikko's castle, to see where his daughter would make her new home.

Mikko was worried that his new happiness would quickly come to an end. "Leave everything to me," said the fox. "A day's ride from here is a beautiful castle, inhabited by a wicked old dragon named the Worm. Travel there with the king and ask anyone you see along the way to tell you who their master is." Mikko didn't like the sound of the Worm but he trusted his

faithful friend and so he agreed.

The fox set off ahead of the others, toward the castle of the Worm. On the way he met ten farmers plowing the Worm's fields. "A great king is coming to kill your master," he told them. "If you want to save yourselves, tell him that your master is Mighty Mikko." The farmers thanked him and he continued on his way.

A little farther on, the fox met 20 shepherds tending the Worm's sheep and he told them the same thing.

On he went to the castle, where the old Worm was counting his gold. The fox pretended to be afraid and told the Worm that he was running from the battle that was about to begin. "What battle?" asked the Worm in alarm.

"A great king is coming to kill you," said the fox, "and he brings a thousand men!"

The Worm knew that his fighting days were over. "I'll reward you with gold if you help me to hide," he said hurriedly. "Lock me in the gardener's shed; the king will never find me there."

The fox obliged and locked the wicked old Worm in the shed—and then he burned it to the ground!

Meanwhile, the royal party met the farmers and the shepherds, who all told the king that their master was Mighty Mikko.

When they reached the castle, the fox was there to welcome Mikko and his bride to their magnificent new home.

EUROPE

EUROPE
A STORY FROM FRANCE

THE SPECKLED HEN

O ne day, a speckled hen was scratching around for worms when she noticed something lumpy, half-buried in the ground. As she scraped away at it, the miller came along the road. "Silly bird," he scoffed. "What a waste of time scratching in the ground like that!"

"Not at all," said the speckled hen and with one tug of her beak she pulled out a purse, which fell open, spilling ten gold coins on the ground at her feet. "That was time well spent!" she said.

The miller eyed the gold coins. "What a bit of luck. Ten gold coins is just what I need. Lend them to me and I'll return them in eight days." The speckled hen was a kind bird. "Very well," she said and she gave the coins to the miller.

Eight days passed but there was no sign of the miller. The speckled hen realized that her coins would not be returned. "I shall go to the miller's house and get those ten gold coins back myself," she said.

Along the way, she met a ladder by the side of the road.

"Where are you going, Speckled Hen?" asked the ladder.

"I'm going to see the miller, who owes me ten gold coins. Will you come with me?"

"Yes!" said the ladder.

"Very well, get inside of me," said the speckled hen and the ladder jumped down her throat.

A little farther on, she came to a river.

"Where are you going, Speckled Hen?" asked the river.

"I'm going to see the miller, who owes me ten gold coins. Will you come with me?"

"Yes!" said the river.

"Very well, get inside of me," said the speckled hen and the river jumped down her throat.

The speckled hen walked on, into the wood. There she met a wolf.

"Where are you going, Speckled Hen?" asked the wolf.

"I'm going to see the miller, who owes me ten gold coins. Will you come with me?"

"Yes!" said the wolf.

"Very well, get inside of me," said the speckled hen and the wolf jumped down her throat.

The speckled hen walked on until she came to the miller's house. She marched straight inside and asked the miller for her ten gold coins.

The miller just laughed. "I knew you were a silly bird!" And he seized the speckled hen, carried her outside and threw her into the well.

The speckled hen thought fast. "Ladder, ladder, come out of me!" she cried. At once the ladder jumped out of her throat and the speckled hen climbed out of the well.

She marched back to the house and asked again for her ten gold coins.

The miller was angry when he saw that the speckled hen had escaped. He grabbed her with both hands and threw her into his oven.

The speckled hen thought fast. "River, river, come out of me!" she cried. At once, the river jumped out of her throat. It put out the oven fire and burst open the door, and the speckled hen bobbed out.

"I won't be made a fool of!" shouted the miller and he snatched up the speckled hen, took her out to the stable, and threw her among the oxen's heavy feet.

The speckled hen thought fast.

"Wolf, wolf, come out of me!" she cried. At once, the wolf jumped out of her throat. He chased the oxen out of the stable and then he chased the miller over the hill and far away.

The speckled hen soon found her ten gold coins under the miller's bed.

"That was time well spent," she said happily and off she went home.

EUROPE

EUROPE
A SPANISH STORY

THE WHITE PARROT

Mariquita lived with her father and her brother, in a beautiful house with a pretty courtyard full of flowers. One morning, Mariquita was watering the flowers and singing happily to herself, when she noticed an old woman at the gate.

"Is your father home?" asked the old woman.

"No," answered Mariquita.

"Is your brother home?"

Mariquita shook her head. The old woman peered through the gate. "What a charming courtyard," she said.

"Would you like to see it?" asked Mariquita proudly. She opened the gate and welcomed her in.

The old woman admired Mariquita's beautiful flowers. "Very pretty," she said, "but what you need is a fountain of silver water."

"How wonderful!" sighed Mariquita. "Where can I find such a thing?"

"I will tell you the place," said the old woman. "If you fill a jug from the fountain there and put it in your courtyard, it will become a fountain of silver water."

When Mariquita's father and brother returned, she told them about the fountain and wouldn't stop asking for one until her brother agreed to go in search of it.

He took a jug and set off. Far from home he met an old man.

"Who hates you so much to send you here?" asked the old man.

The boy explained that he was searching for a fountain of silver water.

"That's a dangerous task," said the old man, "but you may succeed. The fountain is guarded by a great lion. Take care! If his eyes are closed, he can see you, but if his eyes are open, then he is fast asleep."

The boy thanked the old man and walked on until he found the fountain. There, lying beside it, was a great lion. He waited until the lion's eyes were open, filled the jug, and hurried home.

Mariquita stood the jug in the courtyard and it became a beautiful fountain of silver water, just as the old woman had promised. It was the loveliest thing she'd ever seen!

The next day, when her father and brother were out, the old woman passed by again. Mariquita showed her the fountain.

"That's a great improvement," said the old woman, "but you really need a tree with leaves of silver and nuts of gold."

At once, Mariquita had to have one.

When her brother returned he saw there would be no peace until he agreed to go in search of it.

Once more, he met the old man and asked for help.

"Take that horse grazing by the path," said the old man, "it will carry you into the forest where there is a tree guarded by a deadly serpent. Wait until the serpent hides his head in his coils to sleep and then break off a branch. If you plant it, the branch will grow into a tree with leaves of silver and nuts of gold."

The boy did exactly as the old man told him and took a branch home to his sister.

Sure enough, when Mariquita planted the branch in the courtyard, it grew into a beautiful tree with leaves of silver and nuts of gold.

Mariquita was delighted. "Now our courtyard is the prettiest in town," she said.

A few days later, the old woman returned.

"That is a fine tree," said the old woman. "All you need now is a white parrot."

"A white parrot?" Mariquita gasped. "Oh yes, I must have one." For the third time, she pleaded with her brother until he promised to fetch it for her.

The boy set off, not knowing where to look for a white parrot, until he met the old man again.

"This is your most dangerous task,"

EUROPE

warned the old man. "Follow the path until you come to a beautiful garden. There, you will see a white parrot. Wait until it settles on a branch and puts its head under its wing to sleep, and then you may take it. But beware—if you touch the white parrot before it's asleep you will be turned to stone!"

The boy walked on until he found the beautiful garden. Swooping through the trees was a dazzling white parrot. The boy gazed in amazement. As soon as the parrot settled on a branch and began to tuck its head under its wing the boy reached out for it. But, alas, he was too impatient. As his fingers touched the parrot he was turned to stone!

At home, Mariquita waited anxiously for her brother. When he didn't return, she realized how foolish she'd been to send him away.

"I shouldn't have listened to that old woman," she cried. "I'd rather have my brother home than a courtyard full of white parrots!"

So, she set off to find him. Along the path, she met the old man.

"Your brother faced many dangers for you," he said, "but if you are brave you may save him." He told Mariquita what to do.

Mariquita soon found the beautiful garden. There, to her horror, she saw her brother turned to stone. The white parrot flew out of the trees and perched on his hand. Mariquita remembered the old man's warning. She waited patiently until she was sure it was asleep, and then she reached out… as her fingers touched the white parrot her brother came to life!

Mariquita hugged him tight. "I shall never be discontent again!" she promised and they set off for home for a happy reunion with their father.

EUROPE

THE UGLY DUCKLING

One summer, Mother Duck had six fluffy yellow ducklings, but when the last egg in the nest cracked open, out tumbled an odd gray duckling with a long neck.

The other birds in the farmyard laughed at him. "You're an ugly duckling!" they said. "You don't belong here."

Mother Duck told them not to be unkind, but while she was looking after the rest of her brood the other birds pecked at the gray duckling and made his life miserable.

One day, he ran under the hedge to hide, disturbing a flock of sparrows. "I must be ugly," he thought. "Even the sparrows fly away from me because they're afraid!" The ugly duckling felt so unhappy that he decided to run away.

Blinking back his tears, he waddled off across the fields and meadows until he came to a marsh, where he met a family of wild ducks.

"What an ugly duckling!" exclaimed the wild ducks. "You don't belong in our family."

The ugly duckling crept away into the reeds. "It seems I don't belong anywhere," he sighed.

The next day, he left the marsh and walked on until he came to a lake. None of the birds there made him welcome, so the ugly duckling was left to find a home among the water weeds alone.

Autumn came and the weather grew colder. One day, a pair of beautiful swans flew out over the lake. As the ugly duckling stared at their dazzling white feathers and elegant necks, a feeling of happiness flooded through him.

"I wish I could be as beautiful as those birds and fly with them on huge white wings," he sighed. But the swans soon disappeared beyond the woods and he was left alone once more on the gray, windy lake.

Autumn turned to winter. The lake froze and the ugly duckling shivered among the frosty reeds, with nobody to help him find

EUROPE

food and shelter from the icy north wind.

Just when he began to lose hope that winter would ever end, the lake began to melt and the ugly duckling felt the warmth of the sun on his back. Spring had arrived. He preened his feathers and stretched his wings. To his surprise, they had grown strong over the winter. The ugly duckling ran, raised his wings, and swooped up into the air. "I'm flying!" he cried excitedly, although there was nobody to hear.

He flew once around the lake and then onward, to explore what lay beyond. Down below he soon saw a sparkling river and there, to his delight, were the beautiful white birds he had admired in the autumn, gliding through the water with their heads held proud. The ugly duckling landed on the riverbank and watched them shyly, but the swans had seen him.

"Come, swim with us," they called.

The ugly duckling looked around, thinking they had spoken to somebody else, but there was no other bird nearby.

"Who, me?" he said. "I don't belong here. I'm just an ugly duckling."

"Come into the water," said the swans.

The ugly duckling stepped timidly into the water and the swans glided over to greet him. "Look at your reflection," they said.

He looked at his reflection. A beautiful white bird stared back at him, with a fine curving neck and dazzling white wings.

"What has happened to me?" said the ugly duckling in astonishment.

His companions smiled. "You were never an ugly duckling," they said. "You were a cygnet and now you have become a swan."

The beautiful swan was no longer ashamed. "I am a swan!" he cried. Great happiness flooded through him. At last he knew where he belonged.

EUROPE

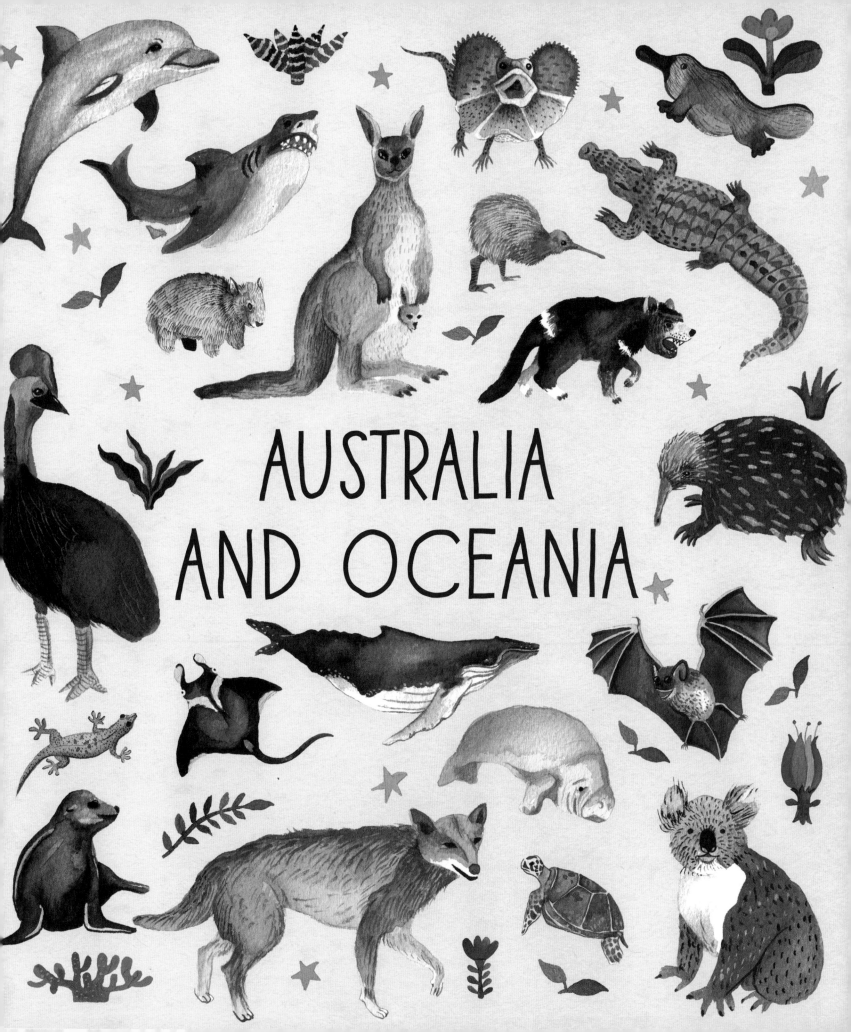

AUSTRALIA AND OCEANIA

AUSTRALIA & OCEANIA
A STORY FROM AUSTRALIA

HOW THE KANGAROO GOT HER POUCH

Kangaroo was watching her little joey play one day when an old wombat appeared, wandering blindly through the grass.

"I'm so weak," he moaned. "I'm so thirsty and hungry. I haven't a friend in the world."

Kangaroo felt sorry for the old wombat. "I'll be your friend," she said. "I'll lead you down to the creek to drink and find you some tasty grass."

She told the blind old wombat to take hold of her tail and warned her joey to stay close, as her arms were too small to carry him. Then Kangaroo led the wombat slowly down to the creek.

The joey followed, but he was full of curiosity and forgot to stay close to his mother. While the wombat enjoyed a long drink and some tasty grass, Kangaroo looked around for her joey but he was nowhere to be seen.

At that moment she spotted a hunter nearby. Kangaroo realized that the wombat was in danger.

She stamped her feet to attract the hunter's attention and then bounded off into the bush to lead him away from the defenseless wombat.

The hunter followed Kangaroo for a great distance until at last, exhausted, he gave up the hunt.

Kangaroo returned to the creek, relieved to find her joey asleep under a gum tree. But the wombat had vanished. To her surprise, the Sky Spirits appeared.

"Our Sky Father came here as a wombat to find out which creature had the kindest heart," they explained. "You alone cared for him, so he has sent you this present." And they gave Kangaroo an apron made of eucalyptus bark. When Kangaroo tied it around her waist it became a pouch to carry her joey!

Such was the Sky Father's pleasure, that every kangaroo mother has had the same pouch as a gift ever since.

AUSTRALIA & OCEANIA
A STORY FROM HAWAII

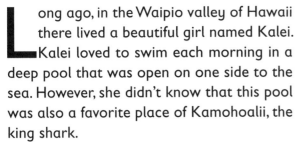

NANAUE, THE SHARK BOY

Long ago, in the Waipio valley of Hawaii there lived a beautiful girl named Kalei. Kalei loved to swim each morning in a deep pool that was open on one side to the sea. However, she didn't know that this pool was also a favorite place of Kamohoalii, the king shark.

One day, as Kamohoalii swam toward the pool he noticed Kalei diving from the rocks into the water. He held back to watch, admiring her beauty and skill as she gracefully entered the water without a splash. Wishing not to frighten her, he turned away, but he came back the following morning to watch Kalei swim again, hiding at the shadowy edge of the pool so she wouldn't see him.

Day after day Kamohoalii came to gaze at Kalei and before long he fell in love with her and wanted her to be his wife.

As he possessed the power of a god, Kamohoalii transformed himself into a handsome young man and waited for Kalei on the beach. When she approached, he raised a gigantic wave to crash upon the shore. Kalei ran from the terrifying wave but, just as it threatened to sweep her out to sea, Kamohoalii ran forward and rescued her. Kalei was grateful to the handsome stranger and from that moment they became friends. Every morning they walked and swam together and, before long, she too had fallen in love and they were married.

Kalei and her husband lived happily together by the sea until, one day, she told him she was expecting a child. Then Kamohoalii knew it was time to tell her about his true nature. Kalei was afraid when she heard that her husband was the powerful god, King Shark, but her love for him was strong.

"If I stay here our family will be in danger," he told her, "so I must return to my people. I will always love and protect you and I will make a safe place for our child to play at the bottom of the pool."

When the day of the birth was close, Kamohoalii gave Kalei a feather cape for the child to wear and warned her never to let him eat meat or it would bring tragedy on the village. Then they said their sad goodbyes and Kalei watched her husband walk into the sea and disappear under the waves.

A short while later, their son was born and she called him Nanaue. He was a healthy normal boy, but on his back, between his shoulder blades, was the mouth of a shark. Then Kalei knew why her husband had given her the cloak.

Kalei kept her son's extraordinary birthmark a secret from everyone in the village. Nanaue grew up always wearing the cloak to cover his back, except when he swam in the pool by the sea, where Kalei often saw Kamohoalii in the shadows, watching over them both.

While he was a child, Nanaue never ate meat with his mother, but one day his grandfather told Nanaue that he had reached the age when it was traditional to eat with the other men of the village. Kalei couldn't protest without revealing her son's secret, so Nanaue began to eat his meals with the other men. There, his grandfather fed him plenty of meat to make him strong and he soon became famous for his big appetite.

"Eat up quickly," the older men would say to each other, "here comes Nanaue, as ravenous as a shark!"

Meanwhile, people often wondered why Nanaue never removed his cape and never took part in village games, preferring to work alone on his mother's vegetable patch. Sometimes the other boys met Nanaue as they walked down to the sea and asked him to join them, but he always refused and warned them to be careful.

Then Nanaue's grandfather died and strange things began to happen. People swimming in the sea came home with shark bites. Some of those who met Nanaue on their way to the beach never returned.

King Shark had always forbidden his people to harm the villagers, but now they became afraid of the water.

One day, Umi, the king of Hawaii, sent an order for every man in Waipio to work for ten days on his plantation. All the men of the valley went to work for the king, except Nanaue, who was afraid his secret would be discovered. But when King Umi heard about Nanaue he sent for him and put him to work.

AUSTRALIA
AND OCEANIA

Although the work was hard and the sun burned down, Nanaue kept the feather cape over his back.

The other young men teased him. "Isn't it hot enough for you, Nanaue?" they cried and one of them boldly tugged at the cape, which slipped off Nanaue's shoulders, revealing the shark mouth on his back. Everyone stared in horror.

"He's a child of King Shark!" they cried. "That's why our people have been disappearing!"

Nanaue ran off through the plantation and the men chased after him. He ran on through the valley with the strength and stamina of the shark people, until he reached the deep pool, where he dived into the water before anyone could catch him.

When the men got to the pool they threw rocks into the water, but Nanaue was safe in the place that his father had made for him, and when they gave up and left, he took the form of a shark and swam out to sea.

Then the villagers brought Kalei before the king. "She must be punished for bringing tragedy to our valley," they said.

But wise King Umi listened to Kalei's story. He heard how Nanaue's father had tried to protect them by forbidding his son from eating meat and he shook his head. "I see this tragedy was the grandfather's fault," he said. "Kalei should not be punished for the love of her husband and child."

So Kalei was left to live peacefully by the sea, where she often saw a pair of sharks swim together and remembered Nanaue and his loving father, Kamohoalii.

AUSTRALIA
AND OCEANIA

AUSTRALIA & OCEANIA
A STORY FROM NEW ZEALAND

PAIKEA AND RUATAPU

Long ago in Hawaiki, the ancestral homeland of the Māori people, there lived a chief named Uenuku, who had many wives. Over time, his wives gave him seventy-one sons. Seventy of these sons had mothers of noble birth and the eldest of these was Kahutia-te-rangi. However, the youngest son, Ruatapu, was the child of a slave wife Uenuku had taken captive after a battle.

One day Uenuku decided to have a magnificent canoe built for his sons, beautifully carved and painted red. When the canoe was finished, he called his sons together.

"Here is my gift," he said. "But before you take up your paddles I will comb your hair with the sacred comb of our people, and tie it in the traditional way, so that everyone shall know of your noble birth."

Uenuku's sons thanked their father and knelt before him, one by one, to have their hair combed. Last in line was Ruatapu.

When he saw Ruatapu, Uenuku laid the comb down. "This is not for you," he said.

"But I'm your son, too, just like the others," said Ruatapu, feeling the eyes of his brothers upon him.

"Your mother is a slave wife," said his father. "You are not a son of noble birth, Ruatapu. You may take your place in the canoe but you have no right to be honored with the sacred comb."

Ruatapu felt ashamed at being rejected by his father in front of his older brothers. Burning with anger, he ran away to hide.

That night Ruatapu planned his revenge. While everyone was asleep, he crept down to the water's edge, drilled a hole in the bottom of the canoe, and plugged it with wood chips.

The next day a ceremony was held to launch the canoe. Ruatapu took his place and paddled out to sea with his brothers. But as soon as they were beyond sight of land, he knocked the

wood chips out of the hole with his heel. At once, the canoe began to fill with water.

Uenuku's sons searched frantically for the bailer to scoop out the water, not knowing that Ruatapu had thrown it out of the canoe.

Ruatapu took advantage of the confusion. He pushed his brothers into the sea and beat them with his paddle. Every one of them was drowned, except Kahutia-te-rangi, who kept out of his reach.

"You will not drown me, Ruatapu," cried Kahutia-te-rangi. "Porpoise and whale are my ancestors. I am descended from Tangaroa, the god of the sea!" Then he called out to Tangaroa to save him.

Suddenly the water darkened and the sea heaved. A pod of whales surfaced, shooting spume and spray into the air. Kahutia-te-rangi climbed onto the back of a whale, his wet skin glistening in the sun, and it carried him away.

Ruatapu was furious to see his brother escape. "Rise up, waves," he chanted. "Follow the whale rider and drown him like the others." Then five towering waves arose and rolled across the sea after Kahutia-te-rangi.

Kahutia-te-rangi rode the whale with such strength and skill that it seemed as if they had become one. However, instead of heading for Hawaiki, they traveled to a new land.

When they reached the shore, Kahutia-te-rangi slipped off the whale's back and stepped onto the beach. Just as he did so, Ruatapu's waves came crashing onto the sand. But instead of drowning him, they rolled over and rushed back across the sea, to drown Ruatapu himself.

From that day, Kahutia-te-rangi took the name Paikea, which means "whale." In time, he became the father of two tribes, and the land of the whale rider is now known as New Zealand.

AUSTRALIA
AND OCEANIA

AUSTRALIA & OCEANIA
A STORY FROM AUSTRALIA

EMU AND THE BRUSH TURKEY

Long ago, in Dreamtime, Emu had the strongest wings and could fly far across the plains. Brush Turkey, whose flight was clumsy and weak, was jealous of Emu's wings.

One day, Brush Turkey thought of a way to trick Emu. She sat in the grass, with her own wings tucked out of sight. When Emu flew down to peck for worms, Brush Turkey sighed loudly. "What a pity you have to carry those heavy wings around, Emu," she said.

"Anyone can fly—clever birds walk these days."

Emu looked puzzled. "But I've seen you fly," she said.

"Not anymore," said Brush Turkey.

Emu walked away. "My wings are certainly heavy," she thought. "Maybe Brush Turkey is right." So she clipped her wings to make herself lighter.

The next day, when Brush Turkey saw Emu she spread her wings and flew up into a tree. "Now I have the strongest wings!" she boasted, and Emu realized that she'd been tricked.

A few days later, Emu hid ten of her chicks under a bush and took just two of them for a walk past Brush Turkey's nest.

"How foolish to feed twelve chicks," she said loudly. "With only two to feed mine will grow much bigger and stronger."

"But you have lots of chicks," said Brush Turkey.

"Not anymore," replied Emu.

Brush Turkey looked at her hungry brood. "Maybe Emu is right," she thought, so she chased ten of her chicks away.

Next day, Emu returned with all her little ones together. "A clever bird knows that her strength is not in her wings, Brush Turkey," she said, "but in the family around her!"

And that is why emus cannot fly and brush turkeys lay only two eggs.

AUSTRALIA & OCEANIA
A STORY FROM PAPUA NEW GUINEA

HOW THE FLYING FISH LIVED IN A TREE

In the old days, all the land was dry. The sea was held like an enormous raindrop in the branches of a gigantic tree, but nobody knew it was there.

In a village nearby, lived an old woman called Kemiana, who relied on her husband to take care of her. One day, as usual, her husband went out hunting, but didn't catch anything to eat. He was about to return home empty-handed when he realized that his dog was missing. The old man retraced his steps and found his dog under a tree, eating something wet and shiny.

"You seem to be enjoying that strange food," he said. "Maybe it will be good for Kemiana." He didn't know that his dog was eating a flying fish that had fallen out of a hole in the sea.

The man brought some flying fish home and cooked them for Kemiana, who ate them gratefully and then fell into a deep sleep.

The next morning she didn't wake up and her husband grew worried that the flying fish had made her ill. He called in his neighbors. "I gave my wife a strange food and now I fear that she will never wake up," he said anxiously.

The neighbors gathered around Kemiana's bed and began to weep because they thought that she was dying. But suddenly she opened her eyes and smiled. "I have never slept so well, husband," she said. "Bring me more of that wonderful food."

News of the new food soon spread around the local villages. Everyone wanted to try it. However, the waves of the sea only washed a few flying fish out of the hole each day and there was not enough to feed everyone, so the men of the two local tribes decided to cut the gigantic tree down.

First, the men of the Aurana tribe chopped at the tree, while the men of the Lavarata tribe prepared food. But when the Aurana men rested and sat down to eat, the Lavarata men tricked them and kept on chopping until the tree came crashing down.

Then the great bubble of the sea burst with a terrific roar, spilling out a torrent of foamy water, alive with fins and tails and tentacles, which spread across the low land to become the ocean. All the Aurana men were washed away in the flood, doomed to become seafolk forever.

Many fish rushed into the sea that day, but the flying fish stayed behind in the swamp. It wasn't long before the village women discovered that they could catch them easily there. They stopped working on their vegetable gardens and spent their days at the swamp filling their baskets with flying fish instead.

When the men saw their vegetables choked with weeds they weren't happy. "How can we encourage our wives to give up fishing and tend to the garden?" they sighed.

An old man came forward.

"I will send the fish away into the ocean," he said, "but you must promise only to catch them there in season and share them fairly among you."

The men agreed to the old man's wishes and followed him down to the swamp, where he called out to the flying fish. "It is time for you to leave this place, fish that fly. Rise up and return to your home in the great blue belly of the sea."

Then he threw a handful of broken coral over the fish and, with a flash of silver, the flying fish shot out of the swamp and soared away on their shimmering wings into the ocean.

Thanks to Kemiana's husband, there was good food to be caught in the sea and plenty for everyone to share.

AUSTRALIA
AND OCEANIA

SOURCES

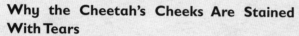

The Ten Little Ostriches
The Masai: Their Language and Folklore by A. C. Hollis. Pub. The Clarendon Press 1905

Why the Cheetah's Cheeks Are Stained With Tears
When Hippo Was Hairy by Nick Greaves. Pub. Struik 1988

Why Hippo Lives in Water
Folk Stories from Southern Nigeria by Elphinstone Dayrell. Pub. Longmans, Green & Co 1910

Ananse and the Python
Tales of an Ashanti Father by Peggy Appiah. Pub. Andre Deutsch 1967

The Ants and the Treasure
Yoruba Legends by M. I. Ogumefu. Pub. The Sheldon Press 1929

The Leopard and the Ram
West African Folk Tales collected by W. H. Barker and Cecilia Sinclair. Pub. C.M.S.

Why the Warthog Is Ugly – Traditional

The Elephant and the Blind Men – Traditional

The White Butterfly
Myths and Legends of Japan by F. Hadland Davis. Pub. George G. Harrap & Co. 1912

The Country of the Mice
Folk Tales of Tibet Collected and translated by Capt. W. F. OConnor. Pub. Hurst and Blackett Ltd 1907

The Farmer and the Mule – Traditional

The Lion and the Clever Jackals: *Old Deccan Days or Hindoo Fairy Legends* Collected by Mary Frere. Pub. John Murray 1898

Urashima and the Turtle
Green Willow and Other Japanese Fairy Tales by J. Grace. Pub. Macmillan & Co 1910

The Nodding Tiger
A Chinese Wonder Book by Norman Hinsdale Pitman. Pub. Dutton and Co. 1919

The Legend of the Panda – Traditional

How the Jellyfish Lost His Bones
Japanese Fairy Tales by Yei Theodora Ozaki. Pub. Grosset & Dunlap 1908

Buffalo and Eagle Wing – Traditional

Prairie Wolf
American Indian Fairy Tales by Margaret Compton. Pub. Dodd, Mead and Co. 1907

The Mermaid of the Magdalenes
Canadian Wonder Tales by Cyrus MacMillan. Pub. John Lane, The Bodley Head. 1920

Why the Swallow's Tail Is Forked
The Book of Nature Myths by Florence Holbrook. Pub. Houghton, Mifflin & Co. 1902

Rabbit and the Moon Man
Canadian Wonder Tales by Cyrus MacMillan. Pub. John Lane, The Bodley Head. 1920

Why the Bear Has a Stumpy Tail
The Book of Nature Myths by Florence Holbrook. Pub. Houghton Mifflin & Co. 1902

The Blind Boy and the Loon
A Treasury of Eskimo Tales by Clara K. Bayliss. Pub. Thomas Y. Crowell & Co 1922

The First Woodpecker – Traditional

The Badger and the Bear *Old Indian Legends* by Zitkala-Sa. Pub. Ginn and Co. 1901

How the King of the Birds Was Chosen – Traditional

The Bear Prince – Traditional

Coyote and the Turtle
Fairy Tales of Mexico by Barbara Ker Wilson. Pub. Cassell & Dutton 1960

The Little Frog of the Stream
Latin American Tales by Genevieve Barlow. Pub. Rand, McNally & Co 1966

The Song of the Armadillo – Traditional

The Two Viscachas
The King of the Mountains by M. A. Jagendorf and R. S. Boggs. Pub. The Vanguard Press 1960

The Party in the Sky
Fairy Tales from Brazil by Elsie Spicer Eells. Pub. Dodd, Mead & Co. 1917

How the Beetles Got Their Gorgeous Coats
Fairy Tales from Brazil by Elsie Spicer Eells. Pub. Dodd, Mead & Co. 1917

The Nightingale
New Fairy Tales by Hans Christian Andersen. Pub. C.A. Reitzel 1843

The Three Billy Goats Gruff
East O the Sun, West O the Moon retold by Gudrun Thorne Thomsen. Pub. Row, Peterson & Co. 1912

The Owl of Cowlyd Coomb
Wild Wales by George Borrow. Pub. John Murray 1906

King of the Cats
Fairy Gold—A Book of Old English Fairy Tales chosen by Ernest Rhys. Pub. J. M. Dent & Co. 1913

Dapplegrim *The Red Fairy Book* by Andrew Lang. Pub. Longmans, Green and Co. 1890

The Eagle and the Wren
Scottish Fairy and Folk Tales. Selected by Sir George Douglas Bart. Pub. A. L. Burt and Co 1892

Saint Domnoc and the Bees
The Lives of the British Saints Vol. 2 by Baring-Gould and Fisher. Pub. The Honourable Society of Cymmrodorion 1908

The Three Little Pigs
The Green Fairy Book by Andrew Lang. Pub. Longmans, Green and Co. 1892

Mighty Mikko
Mighty Mikko Finnish Folk and Fairy Tales by Parker Fillmore. Pub. Harcourt, Brace & Co. 1922

The Speckled Hen – Traditional

The White Parrot
Tales of Enchantment from Spain Retold by Elsie Spicer Eells. Pub. Harcourt, Brace and Co. No date.

The Ugly Duckling
The Orange Fairy Book by Andrew Lang. Pub. Longmans, Green and Co. 1906

How the Kangaroo Got Her Pouch – Traditional

Nanaue, The Shark Boy *Hawaiian Folk Tales* Compiled by Thos. G. Thrum. Pub. A. C. McClurg & Co 1912

Paikea and Ruatapu
Te Ao Hou—The Māori Magazine No. 40 Pub. The Dept. of Māori Affairs 1962

Emu and the Brush Turkey
Folk Tales of the World—Australia by Rene Beckley. Pub. E. J. Arnold & Sons Ltd. 1965

How the Flying Fish Lived in a Tree
Papuan Fairy Tales by Annie Ker. Pub. Macmillan & Co 1910

Quarto is the authority on a wide range of topics.
Quarto educates, entertains and enriches the lives of
our readers—enthusiasts and lovers of hands-on living.
www.quartoknows.com

First published in the U.S.A. in 2017 by Frances Lincoln Children's Books,
an imprint of The Quarto Group,
142 W 36th Street, 4th Floor, New York, NY 10018, U.S.A. QuartoKnows.com
Visit our blogs at QuartoKids.com

Important: there are age restrictions for most blogging and social media sites and in many countries
parental consent is also required. Always ask permission from your parents. Website information is
correct at time of going to press. However, the publishers cannot accept liability for any information or
links found on any Internet sites, including third-party websites.

A World Full of Animal Stories © Frances Lincoln Ltd 2017
Text copyright © Angela McAllister 2017
Illustrations copyright © Aitch 2017
The right of Angela McAllister and Aitch to be identified as the author and illustrator
of this work, respectively, has been asserted by them both in accordance with the Copyright,
Designs and Patents Act, 1988 (United Kingdom).

A catalogue record for this book is available from the Library of Congress.

ISBN 978-1-78603-045-0

Illustrated in pencil and watercolour

Designed by Karissa Santos
Edited by Rebecca Fry
Published by Jenny Broom

Manufactured in Shenzhen, China, RD122018
5 7 9 8 6 4